IN 1937, F. SCOTT FITZGERALD was a troubled, uncertain man whose literary success was long behind him. In poor health, with his wife consigned to a mental asylum and his finances in ruin, he struggled to make a new start as a screenwriter in Hollywood.

The last three years of Fitzgerald's life, often obscured by the legend of his earlier Jazz Age glamour, are the focus of Stewart O'Nan's heartfelt new novel. With flashbacks to key moments from Fitzgerald's past, the story follows him as he arrives on the MGM lot, falls in love with brassy gossip columnist Sheilah Graham, begins work on *The Last Tycoon*, and tries to maintain a semblance of family life with the absent Zelda and their daughter, Scottie.

Fitzgerald's circle and the Golden Age of Hollywood are brought vividly to life, with friends including Dorothy Parker, Ernest Hemingway and Humphrey Bogart depicted with great wit and sensitivity. Written with striking grace and subtlety, this wise and intimate portrait of a man trying his best to hold together a world that's flying apart, if not gone already, is a modern masterpiece.

— • —

County Council Library

2277887

F/2277887

WEST
OF
SUNSET

FICTION

The Odds

Emily, Alone

Songs for the Missing

Last Night at the Lobster

The Good Wife

The Night Country

Wish You Were Here

Everyday People

A Prayer for the Dying

A World Away

The Speed Queen

The Names of the Dead

Snow Angels

In the Walled City

NONFICTION

Faithful (with Stephen King)

The Circus Fire

The Vietnam Reader (editor)

On Writers and Writing by John Gardner (editor)

SCREENPLAY

Poe

WEST
— OF —
SUNSET

STEWART O'NAN

ALLEN&UNWIN

ACKNOWLEDGMENTS

My deepest thanks to Joan Bayley Weamer for sharing her memories of working on the MGM lot in the 1930s, and to Holly Watson for connecting us.

Abject thanks, as always, to my faithful early readers (and listeners): Manette Ansay, Paul Cody, Lamar Herrin, Stephen King, Michael Koryta, Dennis Lehane, Trudy O'Nan, Lowry Pei, Alice Pentz, Mason Radkoff, Susan Straight, Luis and Cindy Urrea, and Sung J. Woo.

And lastly, grateful thanks, again, to David Gernert and to Paul Slovak for believing.

First published in the United States by Viking Penguin,
a member of Penguin Group (USA) LLC, 2015.

First published in Great Britain in 2015 by Allen & Unwin

First published in Australia in 2015 by Allen & Unwin

Copyright © Stewart O'Nan, 2015

The moral right of Stuart O'Nan to be identified as the author of this work has been asserted by her in accordance with the Copyright, Designs and Patents Act of 1988.

All rights reserved. No part of this book may be reproduced or transmitted in any form or by any means, electronic or mechanical, including photocopying, recording or by any information storage and retrieval system, without prior permission in writing from the publisher.

This book is a work of fiction based on real events.

Allen & Unwin
c/o Atlantic Books
Ormond House
26–27 Boswell Street
London WC1N 3JZ

Phone: 020 7269 1610
Fax: 020 7430 0916
Email: UK@allenandunwin.com
Web: www.allenandunwin.co.uk

A CIP catalogue record for this book is available from the British Library.

The names of some individuals who appear in this book have
been changed to protect their privacy.

Hardback ISBN 978 1 92526 609 2
Trade paperback ISBN 978 1 92526 678 8
E-Book ISBN 978 1 92526 659 7

Set in Palatino
Designed by Spring Hoteling

Printed in Italy by Grafica Veneta
10 9 8 7 6 5 4 3 2 1

Once again
to
Trudy

There are no second acts in American lives.

—F. Scott Fitzgerald

. . . .

Nothing was impossible—
everything was just beginning.

—F. Scott Fitzgerald

WEST

— OF —

SUNSET

CHIMNEY ROCK

That spring he holed up in the Smokies, in a tired resort hotel by the asylum so he could be closer to her. A bout of pneumonia over Christmas had provoked a flare-up of his TB, and he was still recovering. The mountain air was supposed to help. Days he wrote in his bathrobe, drinking Coca-Cola to keep himself going, holding off on the gin till nightfall—a small point of pride—sipping on the dark verandah as couples strolled among the fireflies rising from the golf course. Outside of town, Highland Hospital crowned the ridgeline, a spired Gothic palace in the clouds worthy of a bewitched princess. He couldn't afford it, as he couldn't afford the other private clinics they'd tried, but he pleaded poverty and hashed out a discount with the trustees, begging the money from his agent—an onerous form of credit, borrowing against stories he'd yet to imagine.

He had no choice. At Pratt they left her too much alone. She'd strangled herself with a ripped pillowcase, nearly succeeding, the livid band across her windpipe a reminder. One night while she was strapped to her bed, the Archangel Michael appeared, glowing, and told her the world would end unless she could move the seven nations to repent. She took to wearing white and memorizing the Bible. In her paintings the faceless damned writhed in fire.

At Highland her new doctor believed in diet and exercise. No cigarettes, no sweets. Every day the patients hiked a prescribed distance, sturdy nurses spurring them on like coaches. She lost weight, her skin tented over her cheekbones, her nose a blade, recalling that awful year in Paris she whittled her body down trying to remake herself for the ballet. Yet not manic, not frenzied like then, her knees bruised black, feet cracked from practice. After her insulin treatments she was calm, subdued by sheer lack of energy. Instead of sinners she painted flowers, big blowzy blooms just as corrupt. She could sleep now, she said, a mercy he envied. Her cursive returned, neat lines running like waves down the page instead of the bunched, slanted hand he'd come to dread.

Oh Goofo, every day I think of the warm skin of the sea and how I ruined our eyes for each other. You were angry and shut me in when I wanted the sun. Maybe I was never meant to be a salamander, just this thing they wrap in sheets and feed when the bell rings. I'm sorry I cost you all those cities all those perfect boulevards with their lights burning down around us in the night.

They spoke mostly by letter. Though he could see the hospital from the steps of the town library, he rarely saw her, which made her changes more striking. Dr. Carroll limited their visits, doling them out, like any privilege, by a strict reward system. Weekends they might be allowed a few unscheduled hours together, strolling the grounds, even leaving the mountain for lunch at a diner or in a quiet corner of the hotel restaurant, tooling back up the winding, rhododendron-lined drive in his roadster to the long sunset view at the top, but the week was reserved for the hard work of recovering herself. The patients woke before dawn, like farmers. At nine they played tennis, at eleven they painted. The idea was to keep her regimented, which he understood, having disciplined himself to write though otherwise his life had lost any semblance of order.

At forty, by a series of setbacks he ascribed to bad luck, he'd become a transient. With Scottie off at her boarding school, he no

longer had to keep a house, a relief, since it meant one less expend-
iture, except now they had no home to go back to, their most cher-
ished possessions given up to musty storage. He'd pared down
where he could, and still there was no way he could pay both the
hospital and Scottie's tuition, but—out of misplaced honor or plain
delusion—he refused to skimp on his responsibilities. It would be
too easy. Every month Zelda's mother petitioned him to let her
come home to Montgomery. She wasn't ready, if she'd ever be. His
hope was that Dr. Carroll would help her get well so he could go
to Hollywood and make enough to cover his debts and maybe buy
himself time to write the novel he owed Max.

There was interest at Metro, the promise of a thousand a week,
but so far Ober couldn't get them to commit. He had to be honest
with Scott, the studio had concerns about his drinking—his own
fault for publishing those mea culpas in *Esquire*. All March he pestered Ober for word, assuring him he hadn't touched a drop, when
his bottom drawer was heavy with empties.

With Zelda everything was a test. For their anniversary they
were allowed to take a day trip to Chimney Rock. He was to be
both husband and chaperone, charged with cataloging her con-
duct, speech and intake—observations he registered automatically yet resented sharing, as if, after so long in captivity, they had
a shred of privacy left. It was a balmy Saturday, the dogwoods
frilled with pink, the visitors' lot busy with gussied-up loved ones
toting picnic baskets. Dr. Carroll himself delivered her to the front
desk, handing her over to Scott like a doting father.

In her twenties, baby faced and petite, she'd seemed girlish.
She'd been an athlete and a dancer, a notorious flirt, her stamina
and fearlessness irresistible. Now, just shy of thirty-seven, she was
pinched and haggard, cronelike, her smile ruined by a broken
tooth. Some well-meaning soul had fixed her hair for the occasion,
gathering the unruly honey-blonde mop back into a knitted black
snood which sat catlike on one shoulder—a style he'd seen on
shopgirls and waitresses but one she would never choose, especially since it made her face even sharper, hawkish. The carmine
sundress was an old favorite, though it had faded from hard

washing and hung on her, robelike, the yoke of her collarbone hol-
lowed, a sheer scarf knotted like a choker to conceal her throat.
When he leaned down to greet her, she turned her face into his,
her lips grazing his cheek.

"Thank you," she said, pulling away, as if he'd done her a
favor.

"Happy anniversary."

"Oh, Dodo. Happy anniversary." It always surprised him to
hear her soft Dixie lilt coming from this wizened stranger, as if,
hiding somewhere inside, his fresh, wild Zelda still existed.

The doctor congratulated them. "How many years is it?"

"Seventeen" she said, looking to Scott to check her math.

"Seventeen years," he confirmed, nodding, uncertain if this
fact was happy. The number was as illusory as their marriage. As
his wife she'd now been hospitalized as long as not, and in fretful
moments the question of whether she'd been mad all along and he
attracted to that madness unsettled him.

"Enjoy yourselves," the doctor said.

"We will," she said, and took Scott's hand, squeezing it as they
walked through the vaulted lobby and into the bright day, relinquishing it only when he opened the car door and helped her in
like a footman.

On her seat rested a present he'd bought at the hotel gift shop.

"Dodo, really, you needn't have."

As he closed the door, he palmed the knob, silently locking it.

"It's nothing—a token."

"And here I didn't get you anything." She didn't wait, shuck-
ing the paper to reveal a shallow candy box. "If this is what I think
it is . . . You devil. You know I can't resist peanut brittle."

"*Pecan* brittle."

"It's lovely, darling, but I don't think it's allowed."

"I promise not to tell."

"You'll have to help me then."

"To dispose of the evidence."

"Precisely."

How quickly they were conspirators, as if it were their natural state. Together, in another age, they'd been famous for their fashionable trespasses, the stuff of magazine covers and scandal sheets, and perhaps because his fall had been less spectacular, and far less punitive, at times like these a nostalgic guilt pricked him, as if, impossible as it was, he should have saved her.

Leaving the grounds, he had the sensation that they'd escaped. Though he knew it was exactly the wrong attitude to adopt, once they were outside the gates he liked to pretend they were any other couple off on a jaunt. A similar denial applied to his driving. At Princeton he'd been witness to a deadly wreck, and more than once, careering late at night over the darkened roads of Long Island or the Riviera, in the hands of stimulated friends, he'd been frightened for his life, with the result that, drunk or sober, he was cautious to a fault, going so slowly that he posed a hazard to others. Now, instead of guarding their new anonymity, he succeeded in attracting the wrath of everyone stuck behind them.

Another driver held up both hands as he passed, as if to ask what he was doing.

"Get off the road, you old fart!" a young twerp shouted.

Scott waved them on.

Beside him, squinting like a sailor, her scarf luffing in the breeze, Zelda sat with one elbow propped atop the door, pointing out the rushing streams and burgeoning pear trees. He broke his concentration on the road to murmur appreciation and steal a glance at the knob, still locked. Once, on a bluff above Cap Ferrat, she'd opened the door as they traversed a curve and stepped out onto the running board before he could stop the car. She laughed like a child playing a naughty trick. She was just angry over a remark he'd made to Sara and Gerald about Marion Davies, or so he thought. To his shame, looking back, he couldn't pinpoint when she'd lost control of herself, or how long it had taken him to notice. Now he watched her closely, knowing from terrible experience that at any second she might lunge across and grab the wheel.

She reclined and closed her eyes, basking. On her neck, peeking from beneath the thrashing scarf, was a freshly healed scratch the color of raspberry jam. When she caught him looking at her, she stuck out her tongue playfully, then made a point of shifting her body to watch him.

Down in town they had to wait for the sole traffic light.

"You look tired," she said.

"I am."

"You're not drinking."

"I'm not sleeping," he said.

"Come spend a week with me. It'll do you wonders."

"Someone in this family has to work."

"Don't be a dodo, Dodo. Mama can help."

"Let's let Mama worry about Mama."

They turned north, leaving Tryon, climbing into the mountains again, the air in the green hollows cool and damp. They saw a sharecropper with a lop-eared mule plowing a hillside, and a skirmish line of wild turkeys, and a groundhog that scurried away as they approached, each diversion making it easier and more of an occasion to be together, as if, in the future, they might remember the day as a happy interlude.

Not wanting to set her off to no purpose, he'd postponed telling her about Hollywood. As with anything delicate, it was a matter of timing. Cowardly or hopeful, he figured it would be safer once she was home. Today was another step toward that goal, and while he remained vigilant for the slightest sign, so far he was pleased.

Equally tricky was the question of when to broach the possibility of Scottie coming down after exams. The last time they'd been together, in Virginia Beach, Zelda hadn't been right and Scottie was annoyed and short with her, leading to a blowup on the boardwalk he foolishly tried to referee. Since then he'd had to prod Scottie to write her, both apologizing for the circumstances and trying to instill in her a sense of duty he himself had never felt toward his own mother. That they should reconcile had become a preoccupation, though how he might effect that was a mystery. So much of his life now was making arrangements, and he'd never been any good at it.

They crested the summit and coasted over the far side. The road was switchbacked, stepping down the mountain, hairpin turns giving on sheer drops. Far below, neatly splitting the valley, lay the thin blue puddle of Lake Lure. They poked along, Zelda soaking in the view. A circus of hawks banked and tilted above the rocky outcrops. He was occupied with keeping the car between the lines and was surprised to find a red park tour bus looming behind them, surging closer and closer till it filled the mirror. The driver swiped his arm sideways across the windshield as if shooing a pesky fly.

Zelda twisted in her seat. "I think he wants you to pull over."

"There's no room."

He sped up slightly, convinced of his right to the road. He wouldn't be bullied into doing something stupid. He hunched over the wheel, concentrating, afraid to look back. He was going too fast to slip into the scenic turnoffs, and as the bus hounded them down the curves, brakes juddering, he wondered why, if the passengers were sightseers, they were in such a blasted hurry.

At the base of the mountain the road straightened out, regaining its shoulder. The bus flashed its lights. Still he didn't yield.

"There," she prompted, pointing to a rustic country store ahead. "Please, darling."

He braked and veered into the unpaved lot, sliding sideways, raising a cloud of dust that settled around them as the bus roared past, horn blaring.

He shook the back of his open hand at it, a curse they'd learned in Rome. "Ought to have his license taken away."

Her laughter shocked him—raucous, head tipped back with delight. The gesture seemed false and histrionic, a typical symptom.

"What?"

"Remember in Westport? You used to say that all the time. Everyone should have their license taken away. And then what happened?"

He'd had his revoked for running their Marmon into a pond on a lark with Ring. Ring, who was as dead as his mother. Those days seemed to belong to another age, another person he'd been—heedless, charmed.

"Thank you for reminding me."

"I'm sorry, Dodo. You're so easy to tease."

"Too easy."

"Ohhh, don't be cross."

He wasn't, not with her. It was humbling how quickly anger turned him into an idiot, and he resolved, as always, not to let his frustrations get the better of him—a pledge that seemed even more timely when, after apologizing, he swung the car past the open door of the log cabin and realized it was a bar, the neon darkness inside inviting. Back on the road, neither mentioned it.

At Chimney Rock the sun had brought out the throngs. Along one edge of the lot sat four tour buses parked nose to tail, making it impossible for him to single out the culprit. He found a shady spot on the far side, head-in against a split-rail fence, as if he might hide the car. She waited for him to come around, letting him unlock the door and help her dismount.

Among the dungareed, overalled tourists swarming the walkways they were strangely formal, dressed for the theater or the philharmonic, yet when they cleared the cherry trees and the great stone column rose into the sky above them, piled precariously as children's blocks, they stopped and shielded their eyes like everyone else. The rock stood alone, a chase of staircases stitching the cliff face behind it. High up, at the very top, outlined black against the wispy clouds, a narrow catwalk spanned the final gap. The profusion of tiny people clambering over the scaffolding reminded him of an ant farm. The idea of joining that mass dismayed him, and protectively he thought of lunch.

She was already heading for the stairs.

"Aren't you hungry?"

"Come on," she taunted, and before he could argue, she was off, cutting through the other gawkers and taking the first flight at a gallop, her snood bouncing behind like a tail.

He followed, trying to keep her in sight, but the doctor's regimen had worked. He wasn't entirely well either. He spent too much time at his desk, smoked too much, drank too much, and by the second turning he'd lost her. He knew she wouldn't stop: it was a game. The higher he climbed, already winded, the more he reassured himself that she was just being the old, playful Zelda. He was sweating, and shed his jacket, stripped off his tie. Once, in Macy's, around Christmastime, Scottie had gotten away from him; now he felt the same helpless panic. He kept on, using the banister to haul himself up, resting on the landings, peering skyward, hoping to find her laughing at him from the catwalk. His fear, remote yet real, was that when he reached the top she wouldn't be there, a crowd gathered where she'd climbed the rail and swan dived.

Once across the catwalk, he saw her immediately, her red dress a flag. She stood at the far end of the rock, bellied up to the rail, looking out over the valley with everyone else. When he slid in beside her, she covered his hand with hers. Now that he'd stopped, he was pouring sweat, drops gathering in his eyebrows.

"You're getting old, Dodo."

"You always were faster than me."

"You should really take better care of yourself. I suppose that's partly my fault. I'm supposed to take care of you, aren't I? I'm afraid I've been a grave disappointment in that category."

"I can take care of myself."

"Not hardly."

"We're supposed to take care of each other," he said.

"I don't want you to have to take care of me. I just want to go home."

"I know."

"I've been good, haven't I?"

"You have."

"I try so hard and then things go wrong and I can't stop them. I wish I could."

"I know you do."

"You do?" she asked.

"Of course. I'm the king of things going wrong."

"And I'm your queen."

"You are," he said, because, though the throne had sat empty for many years, and the castle, like the kingdom, long since fallen, she was. Despite all they'd squandered, he would never dispute that they were made for each other.

On their way back to the catwalk they came across a group of schoolchildren kneeling over sheets of paper, making charcoal rubbings. The rock was embossed with fossils—trilobites and skeletal fish—evidence that all of this had once been underwater.

"They're beautiful!" she cooed, a judgment he automatically resisted as sentimental. As she went from child to child like a teacher, praising each, he thought he should be more sympathetic. Wasn't every world, ultimately, a lost world, every memento a treasure? As a writer he might believe that aesthetically, but here, in real life, he didn't feel it. What was gone was gone.

The descent seemed longer, and then in the racketing cafeteria they had to wait. The special was goulash with noodles. He made the comment that the food wasn't much better than the hospital's, expecting her to argue. She said nothing, kept chewing vacantly as if she hadn't heard. He leaned over his plate and waved his fork to get her attention. Even then it took an effort to rouse herself from the spell.

"I'm sorry, darling," she said. "I'm just tired."

He was so used to watching for signs. He understood. He was tired too.

Back at the car, the sun had moved. The pecan brittle had melted into a gluey mess taking the shape of the box.

"You can wait till it hardens," he offered, "then break it again."

"I shouldn't be eating it anyway."

Once more it felt like they were escaping, leaving the throngs and the crammed lot behind. They passed the log cabin with its growing rows of cars outside and climbed the switchbacked road up the mountain at their own pace, stopping at the top to appreciate the view and the rarefied quiet, sharing an illicit cigarette. Far below in the trough of the valley, Lake Lure sparkled, sunstruck.

A few stray clouds draped black shadows over the slopes, remind-ing him of Switzerland.

"Remember our chalet in Gstaad?"

"The one where Scottie split her chin open."

He'd been thinking of the antler chandelier and the great, sooty fireplace and the eider duvet on their bed, but now he could picture the polished hardwood staircase, and Scottie trying to climb it in her Doctor Denton's, the missed step and the solid knock of bone shocking them like an alarm. Strange, how the past was both open and closed to them, but she'd remembered. So often she couldn't.

"I was thinking," he said. "What do you think about Scottie coming down for a bit before she goes to camp?"

She dipped her head and drew a line in the dust with the tip of her shoe. "She doesn't want to see me."

"Of course she does. I think this is a good opportunity. She might not be able to for a while."

"You're not making her."

"She wants to see you—if you think you're up to it. I think you are."

"I would like to see her."

"I figured."

"I wish I could tell you I'll be good for her."

"I understand," he said, and looked at her to seal the pact. She could be so reasonable. For an instant he thought of kissing her cheek, but—today, especially—feared she might misinterpret it. They gazed out over the silent vista again, and then, after she'd taken a last drag of the cigarette and dropped it in the dust for him to crush out, turned and headed back to the car.

As they coasted down the far side, he said, "I wonder if groundhogs like pecan brittle."

"Southern ones do. I can't speak for you Yankees."

"I believe they prefer peanut brittle."

"Oh, Dodo, it's been such a nice day. I don't want to go back."

"I know."

"Seventeen years," she mused. "It doesn't seem that long."

"No," he said, though he could disagree.

At the same time, he could feel the day waning, and their moments alone together. Visiting was always hard, but these field trips were a torture, even more so when they went well. In the end, he was charged with returning her to her cloister. There was something of a surrender to it that chafed his honor, as if he should be fighting for her. All the way through the hot, flat town and up the long, winding hill, instead of relief, he felt he was conspiring in his own defeat, a traitor to them both.

He checked her in at the front desk. The doctor was busy with other visitors, and a chipper nurse took her from him, asking if they had a nice time.

"Very nice," Scott said.

"It's our anniversary," Zelda said.

"I know," the nurse said. "Happy anniversary."

"Thank you. Happy anniversary, Dodo."

"Happy anniversary," he said, chastely embracing her, then letting go.

"Poor Dodo. Don't look like that. I'll see you next weekend. I'll be good, I promise."

"I'll talk to Scottie."

"Do, please. Till then, my love." She blew him a kiss and let the nurse lead her away through the doors toward the women's wing, leaving him alone again.

Outside, he maundered to the car, sapped of purpose. Her pecan brittle sat in the backseat, evidence of his meager effort. Later, on the darkened verandah, it would serve as his dinner.

Monday, when he met with the doctor, he reported that she'd been fine. They'd gotten along. Her memory was sharp, her speech clear, her thoughts coherent. He didn't mention the cigarette or the pecan brittle, or her manic gallop up the stairs, or her blank face as she chewed her goulash. The doctor seemed pleased, and agreed that seeing Scottie would be good for her, but then, after Scott had successfully lobbied Scottie, Zelda attacked her tennis partner with her racket, breaking the woman's nose, and was moved to the locked ward. Scottie went off to camp as planned, and when Ober called and said Metro wanted him to come to New York for an interview, he took the first train from Asheville. For two full days he was completely, wrackingly sober, and passed. Six months at a thousand a week. He wanted to tell Zelda face-to-face, but she was in isolation. The doctor forbade him from seeing her, an affront and a reprieve. He waited till the last minute—in fact, after he'd packed up and left town—composing the letter in the Roosevelt Hotel in New Orleans, across from Union Station.

Dearest Heart, he wrote. *Please forgive me. I have to leave for now to pursue our fortunes. I wish there were any other way. Keep working and try to be good, and I will where I am.*

The next day, on Metro's ticket, he took the Argonaut west.

THE IRON LUNG

The train took three days, with stops in El Paso, Tucson and Yuma. He'd sworn off even beer, and the ceaseless drumming and swaying infiltrated him like a sickness. He wrote Scottie and Ober and Max, read and smoked and slept. At breakfast Palm Springs shimmered like a mirage. After the salt wastes of the desert the mountains were a welcome respite, the crawling ascent up the grade, then the headlong rush through the dusty ranches and orange groves and garden suburbs with their Okie motor courts and endless rows of stucco bungalows. As they breached the city limits, an eastbound freight blew past, clattering, rocking the car, and then they were racing along the dense, peopled streets of L.A., the horn calling a warning at every crossing. He was searching the skyline for the ivory trophy of city hall when, abruptly, as if they'd lost power, they slowed and coasted into the switchyard, clanking past the stilled freights and shuttling donkey engines and into the dark shed of the station, slipping by amber caution lights and soot-caked pillars, until, with a final, grinding squeal, they lurched to a stop.

He'd come here twice before, as two very different men. The

first time, he'd entered the city triumphant, the golden wunder-
kind and his flapper bride, signing autographs and mugging with
Zelda for the cameras as they detrained. The last, after the Crash,
she was recovering in Montgomery, and he got off at Pasadena to
avoid the reporters. Now as he stepped down onto the platform
there was no one to greet him. He gathered his bags, flagged a cab
and disappeared into traffic.

As if to quarantine him, the studio was putting him up in
Santa Monica, the last stop on the car line, at the Miramar, a grand
seaside mansion that had outlived its silver magnate builder. The
new management had chopped the place into apartments, and the
hallways were dank and empty, the only hint of life the clashing
of the elevator grate. Out of habit he tipped the bellman too much,
then locked the door and put his few things away, a task that, once
done, was somehow discouraging. He'd come so far to be in this
room. From the curved turret window he watched the blue Pacific
roll in foaming beneath the pier. It was Wednesday and the beach
was teeming, a riot of striped umbrellas. The unrelenting sunlight
burning down on the bathers and the gaudy palms flanking the
boulevard and the tawny mountains sloping to meet the sea made
him think of Cannes and those vagabond years that now seemed
a fever dream.

That afternoon, to get his bearings, he took the streetcar to
Hollywood, an interminable journey that left him sweating and
thirsty. The other riders were mainly Mexicans in shirtsleeves and
dungarees, and he felt foolish in his suit. In his absence the city
had proliferated, its sensible trellis of streets overgrown with a
tangle of new parkways and boulevards. Along Wilshire, fringed
with pennants and tinsel, the asphalt car lots ran for miles, the
polished fenders and windshields glinting in the sun. With the
proceeds from the roadster, he bought a used Ford coupe, a sturdy
if unlovely steed, and promptly got lost.

For dinner, he ventured out among the torpid, sunburned
crowds dragging home their beach gear, and thought of Scottie,
the lazy days at Saint-Tropez. He headed south down Ocean
Boulevard along the palisades, crossing the top of the ramp that

descended like a slide to the pier. He passed a bottle shop playing a ball game on the radio, then, after some unremarkable sole, passed it on the way back.

He'd forgotten how long the sun lingered over the Pacific, how, once it was down, night fell like a painted backdrop. Out on the pier, the lights of the Ferris wheel turned merrily. From his open window he could hear tiny shrieks, and the piping of a calliope. Farther out, beyond the yacht harbor and its protective jetty, on the bay proper, the gambling ship *Rex* sat at anchor, its empty masts strung with Japanese lanterns, beckoning the swells and high rollers. One night, on a bet, he'd jumped over the side in his evening clothes. As he surfaced, still breathless from the shock of the water, he saw Zelda in her white silk launch herself off the top rail like a gossamer angel. She didn't jump like he did. She dove.

"I win," she said, treading water. "What was the bet?"

He no longer remembered—as if it made any difference. She would always go him one better, or so he'd thought. Now, a decade later, he still couldn't believe she'd cracked, though soon enough her older brother Anthony provided brutal confirmation that they shared the Sayre legacy. Exiled to an asylum in Mobile, he'd flung himself from a high window rather than rot in a hospital. For all their self-made aspirations, their lives were circumscribed by family. The Greeks knew: you couldn't outrun blood. It might be, he thought, that you couldn't outrun anything, yet here he was.

Dearest Heart, he wrote, in his bathrobe. *I have arrived at last at the blessed end of the continent, well and rested and ready to do battle with Goldwyn and Mayer and whatever third head of Cerberus guards the gates.*

Like a new schoolboy dreading his first day, he was afraid of being late, waking to the strange room at three-thirty, and four-fifteen, and again at five, to birds shrieking in the trees. He packed his briefcase with fresh legal pads and pencils and set out early, arriving well before the prescribed time. The facade of the studio was an imposing colonnade of Corinthian pillars, and, like everything there, a monumental fake, made of lath and plaster. They had his pass waiting at the gate, or one for a Mr. Francis Fitzgerald. His last time on the lot he'd been a guest of the real boy wonder, Irving Thalberg, chauffeured around in his Rolls like a prized pet. Now that Thalberg was dead, and Metro's best intentions with him, Francis Fitzgerald had to find his own parking spot.

He left the Ford behind the paint shop and walked back up Main between the numbered, warehouselike soundstages, slipping into the flow of gaffers and grips and extras dressed for a Western. At the corner of Fifth Avenue, a flock of impossibly tall hula dancers in mock-coconut bras gabbed and snapped their gum while they waited for a prop man rolling a golden sarcophagus to cross, then went on, their grass skirts rustling, shedding fronds. Was there anything more heartbreaking than starlets, their sisterly camaraderie, their shared dream so nakedly on display? A veteran, he was better at concealing his ambition and fear. He'd been worried, uncertain of the wisdom of his return, but the goofy business of production soothed the song-and-dance man in him. Here was a game company and a waiting stage, all they needed was a decent book, a few catchy tunes. He had to believe he was still capable of that.

The old Writers' Building, a stucco block the color of chopped liver, had been replaced by a poured concrete mausoleum the size of a high school named, unjustly, after Thalberg. The lobby was as cool as a theater. In a nod to honesty, the roster by the elevator didn't list a single writer, only the producers on the fourth floor.

Eddie Knopf, who'd interviewed him in New York, had an office on the third, his name in gilt on the frosted-glass door. It was a leap from the story department bullpen, where he'd had a desk in a roomful of junior editors. That he was Scott's lone champion there, a holdout from the old days, Ober had made clear, and while Scott was grateful, the change in their stations puzzled him as if it were a mistake.

Scott smoothed his hair with a hand, knocked and stood back like a salesman.

"Come!"

He opened the door and poked his head in as if he might be told to leave.

"Scott!" Eddie said, getting up and bounding across the room, his hand extended. He had only the one. The other he'd lost to a grenade in the Argonne, his sleeve folded under and safety-pinned to cover the stump. He was a big, bluff man, and, jacketless, in shirtsleeves and suspenders, seemed even burlier. He had a dab of a mustache, aping Gable's, and a hand-painted tie, maroon with a white iris. "Great to see you, you look great. Come, sit. You're early. Like the new digs—swanky, huh? You'll see, everyone has their own window." His desk was layered with scripts, one of which he was fixing in blue pencil. He was having coffee and a donut, and offered Scott the same.

"I had breakfast at the hotel, thanks."

"When'd you get in? Everything all right? How you liking the Miramar? Great crab salad, if you haven't had it. You've got good timing. We're supposed to be getting new pages by the weekend."

"Oh?" Scott said, because he'd assumed the script was finished. *A Yank at Oxford*, the picture was called. They'd brought him in, with his eye for campus life, to punch up the dialogue. It didn't matter that he was forty, or that he'd never graduated.

"Monday or Tuesday at the latest—Wednesday at the very latest. Don't worry, you'll have more than enough time, a pro like you. I'm actually thinking of you for another project we're just getting started. Tell me what you think. These three soldiers, they come back from the war to their little town in Bavaria, and each of them has to find his way home, or figure out what home is now. There's a girl that two of them are in love with, only one of them comes back a cripple. Great role for Tracy."

Scott didn't volunteer that he'd never been to war and, unlike Eddie, was neither German nor crippled. He hadn't planned on being pitched his first day back, which only showed how long he'd been gone, and how much he'd forgotten. He knew the novel, had considered it pat and maudlin when it was published a year ago. As Eddie spun out the story line, he smiled and nodded at the right places, chiming in with prescient questions so as not to seem too ingratiating, with the result that, as happened so often now, he felt utterly false, and, though it was his own doing, used. Even as he wondered if he'd ever possessed Eddie's venal enthusiasm, he reminded himself that, just for sitting there listening to him, he was being paid. He thought the idea should buoy him more.

Though he had nothing to work on, there was an office waiting for him. As Eddie led him down the hall, they passed the gilt-edged names of several old friends. Aldous Huxley was here, and Anita Loos, and Dottie Parker with her husband Alan Campbell—or not, since their offices were dark and the only typing he heard issued from an anonymous transom.

"That's Oppy," Eddie said with a dismissive wave, as if the scrivener never left his cell.

His own office had no name and a view across Culver Boulevard of a billboard in a vacant lot touting a coming subdivision artfully christened Edendale, and, in its shadow, as if in rebuttal, a string of flaking stucco bungalows and a corner drugstore, outside of which a wooden Indian chained to a downspout stood like a sentinel. On the desk sat an impressive new Royal, which, though he didn't use a typewriter, he appreciated as a piece of machine design. Beside the desk stood a bookshelf, half full, and around the walls, as in a gallery, hung framed stills of Metro's moneymakers. Garbo and Lon Chaney, neither known for their sparkling repartee, were both well-represented, as were Buster Keaton and John Gilbert, outmoded now, casualties of the talkies. In one corner a gooseneck lamp and end table attended a thronelike leather easy chair.

"What'd I tell you?"

"It's plush," Scott admitted, as the air-conditioning kicked in with a shudder. The vent on the wall exhaled a long, low bass note like the sigh of a leviathan.

"It does that. Coffee and donuts are in the lounge, supply closet's at the end of the hall. Anything you need, feel free. Settle in. I'll come grab you for lunch."

"Thanks, Eddie." Out of obligation as much as politeness, Scott shook his hand again. "I can't tell you how much I appreciate this."

"You don't have to. Just write something great."

"I'll try."

"You will," Eddie said, pointing at him.

Left alone, he pawed through the desk and then the bookshelf, where he was surprised to find, among the latest masterpieces by Kathleen Norris and Edna Ferber, a coffee-stained copy of *Nostromo*. The chair was comfortable, but Conrad was too weighty an undertaking so early, and he soon gave up and stood at the window, watching traffic on the shadowless boulevard below, listening to the asthmatic vent wheeze. Down the block, across from a come-on for Oxydol, trolleys dropped off and picked up overalled workers by the side gate. Otherwise there wasn't much action. From time to time cars parked in front of the drugstore, disgorging patrons who returned with their mysterious purchases, then went on their way. In St. Paul, as a boy, he used to spy on his neighbors from the third-floor gable. Now, regulating each breath like a sniper, he felt the same inner stillness. Between the bungalows, a postman tramped across the lawn. Scott watched their mailboxes like baited traps, and was rewarded when an old Japanese man in bare feet and an undershirt came out on his porch, then stood at the top of his stairs, calling through the megaphone of his hands "*Eeee*-to, *Eeeeee*-to." Not long after he'd gone inside, a gray cat emerged from the weedy jungle behind the billboard and sauntered up the walk, at the last moment pausing to look back, stockstill, as if it was being followed.

A knock at the door startled him, as if he'd been caught. He sat down at the desk and fumbled for a pencil. "Yes?"

It was Dottie Parker, with Alan in tow. He rose to greet them.

"Scott, darling. Sorry to barge in—Eddie said you were here. Welcome to the Iron Lung."

"Thank you," he said, stooping to receive her kiss. She looked tired, lined around the eyes and a little thicker, almost matronly, not the dark pixie he'd known those incoherent years in New York. Once or twice, drunkenly, they'd ended up in bed, though now, perhaps mercifully, he could barely recall the details. They remained friends, partly because he admired her wit and courage, and partly because they never spoke of it.

"Good to see you again," Alan said. His grip was supposed to be manly but came off as a butch imitation. He had the lean build and generous features of a leading man. It was a curious sort of Boston marriage. They both preferred younger men, and fought like mongooses, yet were inseparable.

"Eddie says you were here at eight," Dottie said. "You know you can't do that."

"You'll make the rest of us look positively slothful," Alan finished.

"And you're not."

"Only milkmen do their best work before ten."

"He speaks from experience," Dottie said. "Where do they have you staying?"

"The Miramar."

"No," Alan said, scandalized.

"Yes."

"You don't want to be there," Dottie said. "It's not near anything."

"It's near the beach."

"The beach is for people who can't read," Alan said.

"The beach is for people who can't afford a pool," Dottie said. "We have a pool where we are, and it's cheaper than the Miramar."

"I like that."

"Who comes all the way to Hollywood to live in Santa Monica? You really shouldn't be out there by yourself. We'll talk at lunch. We just wanted to say hi. You know Ernest's going to be in town tomorrow."

God, no. "I didn't."

"We're having a little fund-raiser for Spain at Freddie March's. Ernest's going to show his film, but that's no reason not to come."

" 'To grow the harvest,' " Alan intoned gravely, " 'the farmers of the village need rain.' "

"It's ghastly, but it gets the big fish to write big checks."

"It sounds like they need more than checks over there."

"I wish Hollywood made airplanes," Dottie said. "They barely make movies, which is what we have to go do."

F/2277887

LIBRARY

"Back to the salt mines." Alan waved playfully. "Glad you're back."

Scott resumed his vigil at the window. The cat was gone. A Cord roadster with a bottle blonde in the passenger seat idled outside the drugstore. The paradise of Edendale beckoned. The vent soughed.

It was like Dottie to adopt him, but why of all people did it have to be Ernest visiting, and why had his initial reaction been alarm? He was the one who should be angry, after that crack about him and the rich in Ernest's story—a shrill, predictable story at that. They all were now. The precise quietude that excited Scott in his early work had given way to broader, more blatant gestures. His last novel might have been written by Steinbeck or any of those New Masses copycats, and yet, because it outsold *Tender Is the Night*, he was the one who told Max that Scott had betrayed his gift. It was this judgment, partly true yet wholly unfair, coming from Ernest, which kept Scott from wanting to see him.

He was reading *Nostromo* when the noon siren blew, summoning the lot to lunch. Doors opened and the hall filled with voices as if class had let out. After the quiet, the noise was intimidating. He waited for Eddie to come get him, thinking he'd been too much by himself lately.

Eddie had with him a squat, balding man in a pumpkin-colored muumuu of a sport shirt—Oppy: George Oppenheimer. He was an old pro, Eddie said. Been around since before *Ben-Hur*. Scott didn't remember him.

"Welcome aboard, pal." Oppenheimer wore a ruby pinkie ring like a Brooklyn bookie. His grip was soft and moist, and as they walked the half-block to the commissary he dabbed at his forehead with a rumpled handkerchief. While Scott was tempted to ask what project had him bashing away at his machine at eight in the morning, he obeyed the professional courtesy of letting the writer volunteer that information. As he'd hoped, Oppenheimer didn't make him confess he'd left a sick wife and budding daughter to doctor *A Yank at Oxford*.

The commissary wasn't new, the exterior had just been remodeled. Unlike the rest of the world, Metro had done well this last decade, and, like any triumphant regime, hadn't been able to resist the temptation to decorate itself. So many buildings had been redone in sleek Streamline Moderne, the lot looked like a harbor full of ships at anchor.

The first familiar face he saw in the Lion's Den was Joan Crawford's, on her way out with a box lunch. From habit he played the doorman for her, earning a smile and a nod. Once she would have known his as well, but that had been fifteen years ago, in the silent era, and she passed without a word.

While the interior of the commissary had changed to a deco chrome-and-pale-green-Formica scheme, the layout was the same, and the smell—the salty steam of chicken broth and dishwater. Dottie and Alan had saved them space at the writers' table, against the far wall, a perfect spot to watch the producers at the main table in the center of the room. Sleeves rolled to his elbows, the molelike L.B. Mayer was holding forth on some matter of import to a group that included George Cukor, but Scott was more interested in gimlet-eyed Myrna Loy, in the powdered wig and heavy pancake makeup of a courtesan, picking the hard-boiled egg out of her chopped salad.

"How's Louie Pasteur treating you, Oppy?" Dottie asked.

"The guy's a pain in the keister. Go ahead, laugh, it'll be your turn next. You try and sell an old French fart as your lead."

"Oppy's our resident romantic," Alan said. "When your producer asks, 'Where's the love interest?' Here he is."

"Boy meets germ, boy loses germ," Dottie said.

Dottie and Alan were working on *Sweethearts* for Jeanette MacDonald and Nelson Eddy, cast as a beloved song-and-dance team who hate each other offstage.

"How's it coming?" Eddie asked.

"Very well, thanks," Alan said.

"It's absolute shit," Dottie said. "You'll love it."

Having nothing to add, with a view of the whole room, Scott lost himself in stargazing. Right beside Ronald Colman, Spencer Tracy was tucking into a triple-decker club; next to him, her famous lips pursed, Katharine Hepburn blew on a spoonful of tomato soup.

Mayer and Cukor were showily spinning an hourglass-shaped cage of dice to see who'd pay. It was much like Cottage, his dining club at Princeton: while the place was open to all, the best tables were tacitly reserved for the chosen. The rest of them were extras.

Since he'd been on the wagon he relied on sweets to give him a midday boost. He decided on the ham salad sandwich and was mulling ordering the tapioca when a portly Fu Manchu in a red silk cape and kimono, long black braids and stiff lacquered mustache pulled out the chair opposite him.

"Would you look what the Depression dragged in," Fu Manchu said, extending a hand.

Scott gathered his napkin and stood, then realized with dismay that it wasn't an actor under that getup but Dottie's old Algonquin partner Bob Benchley. Years back, Scott had taken him and all the Round Table to task in the *New York World* for not producing anything serious. Now he'd become a kind of minor celebrity, starring in his own zany short subjects.

"How's business?" Scott asked.

"Grand, just grand. Actually, Hem and I are having lunch tomorrow. He wanted me to see if you'd like to come along."

"I don't know that I can get away." He looked to Eddie.

"It's fine. We won't have pages for you till Monday anyway."

"Perfect," Benchley said. "Come by my place around noon."

They were all staying at The Garden of Allah in Hollywood, right on Sunset. Everyone was there—Sid Perelman and Don Stewart and Ogden Nash. Dottie knew of at least two villas that were open.

"She gets a finder's fee," Alan said, so deadpan that Scott wasn't sure it was a joke.

When the waitress came to Benchley, without consulting a menu he ordered the sea bass meunière with mashed potatoes and corn, and the tapioca. Scott had just the sandwich, which was dry, and watched as Fu Manchu gobbled everything down.

"I wish I could stay," Benchley announced, dabbing at his mustache and pushing back his chair, "but I have a dynasty to maintain."

"The Dong Dynasty," Alan said, because it was rumored to be prodigious.

"That rises and falls," Dottie said.

"So I've heard."

"Personally I've never heard it," Benchley said. "But if it starts speaking, Alan, you'll be the first to know."

Back in his office, reading Conrad, Scott was unsure whether Ernest wanting to see him was good or not, and yet he was flattered that he'd asked after him. He liked to think he had a sensitivity to and unselfish reverence for talent—or was it just a weakness for success? All his life he'd been attracted to the great, hoping, through the most diligent exertion of his sensibility, he might earn his place among them. It was harder to believe now, and yet, if he could still count Ernest as a friend and rival, perhaps he wasn't the failure he accused himself of being. He'd never had any doubts about Ernest's powers, only his misapplication of them, a judgment he trusted was reciprocal.

Despite the air-conditioning, *Nostromo* was putting him to sleep. He needed a Coke and snuck out the side gate and across Culver to the drugstore. Waves of heat played over the trolley tracks and the road, making him think of summer in Montgomery, the shuttered houses and deep shadows beneath the trees. In the evenings he buttoned up his dress grays like the other young lieutenants and set off for the country club, where the local belles chose among them, dancing so close beneath the colored lanterns that their perfume clung to him through the next morning's inspection, a giddy memento. To always be favored so, that had been his dream as a young man. Walking the weedy block in the heat, knowing that on the third—or even fourth—floor of the Iron Lung someone was watching to see if he would come out of the drugstore with a bottle, he wondered when he'd stopped seeing life as a romantic proposition.

As if in answer, the same gray cat from before vaulted onto the windowsill of his house and, tail twitching, watched Scott pass.

"Hello, Mr. Ito. Yes, I agree, it's too hot."

The store sold Gordon's, his brand. The price they were asking seemed high, as did his Coke and the Hershey bar he couldn't resist. Everything was inflated because of the location, right by the gate. He paid, declining a bag, and walked back across the street and the train tracks, the Coke bottle in his hand visible proof of his virtue.

The sugar gave him the lift he needed to get through the afternoon. Left alone in the cold room, he managed to sketch out the story of a reserve halfback who fumbles to lose the big game and becomes a campus outcast. He knew it was slight, a pat magazine piece, but it felt good to work, and when the siren blew at six he had four solid pages. Even more satisfying was the knowledge that today he'd made two hundred dollars.

He bade Eddie and Dottie and Alan and Oppy good night on the steps of the Iron Lung and turned up Main Street, against the tide of technicians and day players streaming for the gate. The studio was emptying out, like a city evacuating. The deeper he ventured into the lot, the fewer people he saw, until, taking a left on Fifth and passing beneath the water tower, he was alone. Above the door of Stage 11, a caged red light wheeled, warning away any intruder who might disturb the creation of the dream. The director was BEVINS, according to the slate, but exactly what production was a mystery, and though it was likely the shallowest of melodramas, starring actors he'd just witnessed chowing down meatloaf and chicken divan, he had to admit that from the outside the process still possessed a glamour and excitement he'd found nowhere else save Broadway. It was more than the simple collision of money and beauty, those commonest of ingredients. His late, lamented patron Thalberg knew what the robust L.B. Mayer never would. Gross as moving pictures were, in the best of them, as in the best writing, undeniably, there was life. Twice he'd journeyed west and failed to capture anything approaching that spirit. Now, standing outside the closed set, he resolved that instead of exile, he would accept his time here as a challenge.

His car was waiting, stifling inside. When he turned the key, nothing happened. He had gas, that wasn't the problem. He pulled out the choke, deliberately depressed the clutch to the floor. Nothing. He tried again, quickly this time, as if he might surprise the engine—in vain. He'd only owned the blasted thing a day. He thought of the salesman on Wilshire, saw him smile, sizing him up, an eastern rube in a wool suit. He rubbed his face with both hands as if he were washing, got out, slammed the door and, already sweating, started walking back to the main gate.

THE GARDEN OF ALLAH

As soon as he pulled in he realized he'd been there before, at a mad party, the last time he'd been out here. The place was a Moorish variation on an L.A. staple, the square block of courtyard apartments. The swimming pool behind the main house was shaped like the Black Sea, an homage to Yalta, birthplace of the former owner, a kohl-eyed co-star of Valentino, fallen now, reduced to playing a lodger in her own home. True to its name, the landscaping aspired to an oasis, with nodding date palms, spindly eucalyptus and rampant bougainvillea attracting hummingbirds and butterflies and hiding the Garden from the outside world. Grouped around the pool like tourist cabins were Mission-style villas, white stucco with terra-cotta roofs. He remembered Tallulah Bankhead standing naked and sleek as a hood ornament at the end of the diving board, finishing her martini and regally handing the glass to her second before executing a perfect gainer, so like Zelda that even as he clapped, he mourned her. He couldn't recall if Benchley had been there, or Dottie. Possibly. There were years like phantoms, like fog. Often he wondered if certain memories of his had really taken place.

Benchley, in a coat and tie, was lounging by the pool with Humphrey Bogart and a jet-haired woman in a white one-piece who turned out not to be his wife—Mayo Methot, an actress Scott had never heard of. In his swim trunks Bogart looked like a muscled puppet, his head too large for his body. He hopped up to shake Scott's hand, taking it animatedly and turning his maniacal bad-guy smirk on him.

"Well, well, Scott Fitzgerald. You don't remember me, do you?"

"Of course—*The Petrified Forest*," Scott said, noting that, though it was still technically morning, his breath carried the medicinal perfume of juniper. On the table between their chaises sat two highball glasses, an ice bucket and a crystal ashtray heaped with cigarette butts.

"The Cocoanut Grove?" Bogart prodded. "In the cloakroom?"

Scott could see the palm trees and Gus Arnheim's band playing on stage, the ceiling winking with false stars. Long ago they'd stayed at the Ambassador and danced there every night. This had been during Prohibition, and after a few weeks they'd been asked to leave. It had been Zelda's idea to take all the furniture in their room and make a big pile in the middle, crowning it with the unpaid bill.

"Sorry," Scott said.

"You gave me this." He turned his head and pointed to a white scar at the corner of his mouth no larger than a grain of rice.

"Supposedly," Benchley said, "you were of the mind that someone had gone through your coat pockets."

"I apologize. I'm sure I wasn't in my right mind."

"That's all right, neither was I. As I recall, I got you pretty good too. Plus I've gotten a lot of mileage out of the story. For a while it was my one claim to fame."

"It still is," his girlfriend said broadly, obviously smashed. "I swear to God, he tells everybody we meet. 'F. Scott Fitzgerald split my lip.'"

"The thing is," Bogart said, "before that I'd never read any of your stuff."

"Just tell him and get it over with," she said. "He thinks you're the greatest writer in the history of the world, blah-blah-blah."

"I didn't say that!" he scolded her, then, theatrically, turned back to them, smiling again. "When Bench told me you were coming over, I just had to meet you and tell you how much I like your work, that's all."

"Thank you," Scott said. "I did enjoy you in *The Petrified Forest.*"

"That's kind of you to say, but really, I think *The Great Gatsby* is a masterpiece. 'And so we all beat on, boats against the current, borne ceaselessly back into the past.' That's the stuff, brother."

He'd confused a few words and mucked up the rhythm, but, more flattered than embarrassed, Scott didn't correct him. Bogart offered him a drink, then when Benchley said they had to run, promised to buy him one sometime.

"He's between engagements," Benchley explained on their way into the hills. He had an absurdly large Packard, bought with movie money, and was driving faster than Scott liked. The drop on his right was dizzying. On the horizon, across the hot plain of L.A., the sea was a dark blue line. He thought he could see Catalina. "She's permanently between engagements. When they're engaged with each other, it can get pretty loud. She has a gun. Sometimes we get to hear it. But good neighbors, salt of the earth."

"Where's his wife?"

"On Broadway. She'll never leave New York. She's older, met him when he was just breaking in. I don't think she minds. They're actually a very charming couple, which might be the problem."

"He likes a challenge."

"Don't we all," Benchley said.

If the slip was inadvertent, he didn't apologize, and in a larger sense it was true. What man wanted a woman without fire, and vice-versa?

"By the way," Benchley said. "Oppy?"

"Yes."

"Never lend him money. He drops it on the nags."

"Okay. Thanks."

"And don't bounce anything off him. He'll steal it. That's how he's hung around so long."

"Got it."

Ernest was staying with friends, was all Benchley would say, as if sworn to secrecy. It was typical, Scott thought, the needless intrigue. For years, to the delight of Condé Nast readers, Ernest had traveled the globe indulging his self-dramatizing streak, trying on swashbuckling costumes, while Scott stayed home, hoping to patch things together, a labor for which he discovered he had little talent. At one time they'd been equals, and happy to be, but the last few letters he'd received from Ernest had been dismissive, if not outright combative, and rather than reply in kind, he'd appealed to Max, thinking he might broker a peace between them. It hadn't happened, and as Benchley's pompous car climbed the curves, he felt a queasy mix of dread and self-righteousness, like a wronged party before a duel. If he was flattered by the invitation, he was also leery of an ambush.

They reached the top of Laurel Canyon and wound west on Mulholland, following the ridgeline several miles until Benchley turned down an unmarked, dusty spur lined with boulders. It dropped sharply, shadowed by tall pines, their sweet fragrance reaching in the windows. As they went, the air grew cooler, tinged with a clammy hint of ocean. After a last blind curve the road leveled off. They rocked along, passing rutted drives that disappeared into the forest. There were no signs, no mailboxes, no gates. They might have been deep in the Smokies except for the distant line of sea winking through the trees.

Knowing Ernest, he expected a gloomy stone hunting lodge decorated with heroic taxidermy, but the house below the end of the road was a glass box set into the hillside, overlooking the ocean. He imagined how much trouble bringing in everything to build it must have been, and pictured it at night, lit like an aquarium against the blackness. It was at once splendid and foolhardy, entirely incongruous, a home only someone in pictures would imagine. He and Benchley had to descend a flight of stairs steep as a slide to reach the door, and by then their host was waiting— Marlene Dietrich, in a plain white blouse and black skirt, like any hausfrau.

He was so used to her face from the screen that he was shocked to see the lines about her mouth. In real life, her famous bedroom eyes drooped, giving her the look of someone drugged or on the verge of passing out. He knew it was unfair—his own oft-photographed profile had long ago softened, his skin ceded the bloom of youth—yet he was disillusioned, as if all this time she'd been fooling him.

"I should warn you." *Vahn* you. "He's not well. The doctor says he needs rest. He says he doesn't. So."

They each declined her offer of a drink, though instantly, in retrospect, the novelty of being served by her appealed to Scott. She led them to the equivalent of a living room with an endless view, where Ernest, in striped briefs and a ribbed undershirt, balanced on a single crutch, his right shin swathed in a wasps' nest of gray bandages. He was heavier than Scott remembered, and hadn't shaved in a while, or washed his hair, it appeared, which was flat on one side as if he'd just woken up. She announced them brusquely and retreated to an unseen corner of the box.

"*Mi hermano,*" Ernest said, throwing an arm wide, and Scott crossed to him. Instead of a handshake, Ernest embraced him, kissing one cheek and then the other. His breath was foul—not with drink, but rotten, as if he had an abscessed tooth. "You look well."

"I'd say the same but I'd be lying."

Ernest subsided into his chair, swinging his leg onto a hassock. "What did she tell you?"

"You're supposed to be resting."

"Lousy Krauts—all they do is give orders. It's just a blood clot. They operated on it over there and didn't get it all."

"Red badge of courage?" Benchley asked.

"Our hotel was being shelled and I tried to hide under a desk. Bumped my head too." He pulled back his greasy bangs to show a yellow-and-grape egg. "And that's how I won the war."

"I hope you at least had room service," Benchley said.

"No food, no water and no ammunition. Otherwise things were ducky."

"Which is why you're here," Scott said.

"I'd rather be there. The whole thing's been bitched since New York. The cops shut us down in Boston. They didn't even let us into Chicago. You'd think it wouldn't be a hard sell, with the Krauts involved."

"The country's not in the mood to buy a used war," Benchley said. "Another one, I should say."

"First off," Scott said, "they don't have the money."

"They're going to have to buy it sometime, and the price is just going up."

"I agree," Scott said. "But they're not going to buy it from the Reds."

"We will," Benchley said. "New York and Hollywood."

"Might as well be the Reds to the rest of the country," Scott said.

"I know," Ernest said. "And no one wants to back the wrong horse."

"Is it the wrong horse?"

"It's the right horse," Ernest said. "Just the wrong time."

"I don't see how being anti-Fascist can be premature," Benchley said.

"It's tough," Ernest said. "All we can do is hope we lose well enough so people will be ready the next time."

Scott looked to Benchley to see if he'd heard him correctly. Benchley sat with his arms crossed, biting his lip.

"It'll all be over by spring, no matter what we do. Then it'll be someone else's turn."

"Austria," Scott said.

"Very good," Ernest said.

"Thank you."

"Which is why I wanted to talk with you. I hear you're going to be working on *Three Comrades* for Metro."

Scott didn't know why, but how he'd heard so quickly frightened him. It wasn't out of the question that Ernest knew Eddie Knopf, or that Eddie had run it by some of the other producers. Maybe all of Hollywood knew, via rumor, and naturally he, the unwitting subject, heard it last.

"Nothing's settled yet."

"If you do," Ernest said, "do me a favor and remember Spain."

"I will."

"You know the first movie Hitler banned?"

All Quiet on the Western Front," Scott said, making the connection plain.

"They'll do everything they can to stop this one, or gut it," Ernest said. "There's an attaché from the German consulate named Reinecke who screens everything before it goes to the foreign distributors. He's basically their censor for Europe."

"Don't the studios have final say?" Even as Scott said it, he realized how naive he sounded. Like any leaders who ruled through and solely for money, when threatened, the studio heads were geniuses at appeasement.

"Thalberg had final cut on everything," Benchley reminded him.

"You know how to get things past an editor," Ernest said. "That's your strength, making heavy things seem light—not like me. I couldn't write a *Saturday Evening Post* story to save my life."

You've never had to, Scott thought.

"Just be aware," Ernest said, "that certain people are going to be very interested in what you're doing."

"That's good to know," he said, though, knowing how powerless he was, he felt he'd been given an impossible assignment.

They ate on a terrace noisy with birdsong, commanding a broad view of the sea. Dietrich served them cold trout and salad and went back into the house, from time to time peering out of the kitchen window like a servant. Scott had ice water rather than the Mosel.

"On the wagon—good for you," Ernest said, toasting him. "I'll be joining you in a few months if it's any comfort."

"It's not," Scott said cheerily, toasting him back.

As they were saying good-bye at the bottom of the stairs, while Benchley was gushing at Dietrich about the lunch, Ernest discreetly asked after Zelda.

Scott shrugged. "No better, no worse."

"I'm sorry."

"Thank you." He didn't ask after Hadley, or the new Mrs. Hemingway, just returned his embrace and said he'd see him to-night. Afraid of seeming familiar, he reached to take Dietrich's hand. She drew him to her like an old friend. She smelled of lilacs, and the silk of her hair against his skin made him shiver. In the car he wanted to ask Benchley if that had happened to him, but didn't.

He was glad to have seen Ernest, because that night they barely had time to say hello. Fredric March's place in Beverly Hills was a timbered mock Tudor mansion complete with formal gardens and classical statuary. There, nibbling hors d'oeuvres and sipping cocktails passed by Filipino servants, they honored the brave Spanish peasants by talking shop and writing checks. For Holly-wood it was an oddly homely bunch. The only star he ran into besides their host was Gary Cooper, who stood a foot taller than anyone in the room. The rest were older—balding, bespectacled gnomes: writers and directors and composers, most of them Jews, recent émigrés from the continent. In a last-ditch act of self-interest, half a millennium after the Inquisition, the refugees were taking up a collection to save their persecutors.

Ernest, sans Dietrich, was slicked-up in a buttercream linen suit that might have come from Metro's wardrobe department. He limped over to the mantel and held forth on Franco and Catalonia and the defense of Madrid while a projectionist erected a screen. To his credit, he told the party the same tale of his war wound he'd told Scott and Benchley, including bumping his head.

"I think we're ready," he said, and signaled someone in back to kill the lights.

The film, as Dottie prophesized, was stultifying, all long shots and portentous voiceover. Ernest had written the script, and the repetition of key words, instead of being powerful, was lulling. Via an insistent montage, the Republic's hopes were linked to the farmers' harvest, so that in the end the rain darkening the dry soil and rushing muddy through the ditches was accompanied by heroic and, to his ears, vaguely Soviet crescendos. It was ridicu-lously simple, and even more frustrating after what Ernest had told them at lunch. Was the cause somehow nobler, being lost?

Emotionally, yes, conceded the southerner in him; practically, reminded the northern boy, no. He hoped this wasn't what Ernest expected him to do with *Three Comrades*, because he was incapable of it.

"Wasn't that something?" Dottie asked the gathering as the lights came up, and they applauded once more. As president of the Anti-Nazi League, it was her job to pitch them, and she did, nakedly, calling on them to do what was right. "I don't have to tell you what's at stake."

When it came time to pledge, he wrote a check for a hundred dollars—a pittance compared to what others were giving, but more than he could afford, so that he felt at once righteous and extravagant and doubly guilty. It was a great weakness of his, being unable to resist even the least gesture.

The evening was wrapping up, the waiters collecting the empty glasses. Already there were cars idling out front. He made to congratulate Ernest, but he was mobbed by admirers. Dottie and Alan were throwing a party for him back at the Garden. Scott figured he'd see him there.

As a matter of courtesy, he sought out Fredric March to thank him.

"Thank *you*, sir," March said heartily, clearly unaware of who he was, a fact Scott dwelt upon, cruising the neon gauntlet of Sunset. L.A. had never been his city, and as the glowing late-night coffee shops and drive-ins slid by on both sides, he thought he understood why. For all its tropical beauty there was something charmless and hard about it, a vulgarity as decidedly American as the picture industry which thrived on the constant waves of transplants eager for work, offering them nothing more substantial than sunshine. It was a city of strangers, but, unlike New York, the dream L.A. sold, like any Shangri-La, was one not of surpassing achievement but unlimited ease, a state attainable by only the very rich and the dead. Half beach, half desert, the place was never meant to be habitable. The heat was unrelenting. On the streets there was a weariness that seemed even more pronounced at night, visible through the yellow windows of burger joints and drugstores about to close, leaving their few customers nowhere to go. Inconceivably, he was one of that rootless tribe now, doomed to wander the boulevards, and again he marveled at his own fall, and at his capacity for appreciating it.

After dark, the Garden of Allah was the oasis it claimed to be, alive with racketing jazz and flickering with torchlight. A console radio blared from a balcony, and the patio had become a manic dance floor, the chaises tossed in a pile. Bogart and Mayo were in the shallow end of the Black Sea, sitting on carved armchairs that obviously belonged to someone's villa.

Bogart saluted Scott. "Jump in, old sport."

"We're playing boozical chairs," Mayo said.

He was tempted, but just returned the salute and went to find Dottie.

Instead, Sid Perelman, who he knew from Westport, found him. Sid was at Metro too, writing gags for the Marx Brothers.

"I'm telling you, it's a nightmare. The funny one doesn't talk and the others won't shut up."

"What about Zeppo?"

"He's the funny one."

Don Stewart, from St. Paul, called his name as he wobbled past on a bicycle with a blonde in a sarong and a sombrero on the handlebars. Behind him came Benchley with a sloshing punchbowl loaded with sangria and quartered oranges, a ladle jutting obscenely from his pocket.

"How was the picture?" Sid asked.

"In focus, sadly," Benchley said, not stopping.

"Have you seen it?" Scott asked Sid.

"I've had the pleasure not to. Do the Spanish win?"

"I don't think there is a winner."

"Not my kind of picture. I like a winner. That's why I'm so depressed when I go to the track."

"Leave 'em laughing," Scott said.

"And if you can't, just leave them. That's very important. You don't want them following you home."

Dottie caught Sid by the elbow. "Your wife is looking for you."

"What's the good news?"

"She's either very drunk or very pregnant."

"Either way," he said, "save me some punch."

"I see you found your way," Dottie said.

"I've been here before. Were you here when Tallulah Bankhead was here?"

"That Tallulah Bankhead?" She pointed to the woman herself, preening by a tile fountain with a highball as a pack of ingenues paid court. "She's actually at the Chateau Marmont. The walls are thicker there. She's like the clap—you think you've gotten rid of her but she keeps coming back."

"Like me," Scott said.

"I was trying to be polite." The orchestra on the radio struck up a slow tango. She took his hand. "Dance with me."

As one of two boys at Miss Van Arnum's School of Dance, he'd been taught to never refuse a lady. She was small, and light in his arms. They'd danced before, in New York, at all-night parties that topped the next morning's gossip columns. They'd been young then, trouble. He remembered her upturned face, her chin tipped slightly away to reveal a fetching length of neck. Despite her solidarity with the peasants, she was wearing diamond studs, and, as if she'd been hiding them, he was surprised to find she had tiny, perfect ears. He flung her out and reeled her back in. She spurned him, averting her face, making him circle her, strutting like a bullfighter. They moved well together, graduates of the same classes meant to raise their station. It had worked, partly. So many of his fondest moments had taken place on a crowded floor. Around them, the flames and other couples whirled, the palms and lit windows, Bogart and Mayo thrashing in the pool, trying to splash them. She pressed herself against his chest, lingered a beat, then retreated, only to return again in a swoon of clarinets, the tortured lover. She wasn't Ginevra or Zelda but any girl on any starry night in thrall to the music, and he wanted the song to go on and on. In the end, she went to her knees, clutching his leg in devotion. He helped her to her feet as the announcer broke in with a plug for Lux soap, drawing taunts from the crowd.

"Another?" he asked. "If Alan doesn't mind."

"Alan doesn't mind."

"I'm next," Mayo called from the edge of the pool.

"Trying to steal my gal, eh?" Bogart said, grabbing her and waltzing her toward the deep end.

The pianist struck a sentimental chord, the horns swelled, and, as if directed, he and Dottie faced each other like partners. This tune was slower, a torch song. He bent his head to hers and she sang in his ear. *Mean to me, why must you be mean to me?*

Not halfway through, Alan cut in on him with news. Ernest wasn't feeling up to snuff and had begged off.

"That damn Lenny," Dottie said.

"He's probably tired," Alan offered.

"He wasn't in the best shape when I saw him," Scott seconded, but she wouldn't be placated. She stormed off, only to reappear on the near balcony. She turned the radio down and called for quiet.

"I'm afraid our guest of honor can't make it."

Booo, the crowd let out.

"He's too busy having his cock sucked."

They laughed and cheered.

"By definition, a party is stronger than any one member. Don't let one cocksucker ruin it for everybody." She raised a glass. "Viva la Republica!"

"Viva la Republica!" Bogart crowed.

"Viva la Republica!" they bayed, and the music leapt, louder now.

He danced with Dottie again, and Mayo, getting his front wet, and a skinny blonde with an overbite named Anne from Dayton, Ohio, and a willowy, high-cheeked Tatyana who watched her husband dancing with another woman the entire time. When the broadcast was over and the station signed off, Don Stewart dragged his massive Capehart to the door of his villa and they danced to records. Several couples stripped to their underwear and joined Bogart and Mayo in the pool, precipitating a round of chicken fights. To cool off, he had a single gimlet, on ice, with lime, and lay on a chaise, gazing up through the palms at the stars. The moon was a thin white sickle, and he thought of that last summer in

Antibes, before the Crash, when Zelda was still his and everything was possible.

As he was slipping into his usual reverie, he noticed a dark figure standing on the balcony of the main house, watching them, her pale face flickering in the torchlight—Alla, the Garden's namesake, her black mane and widow's weeds lending her an operatic madness. She seemed to be looking directly at him, and, emboldened by the gin, he gave a little wave.

She raised an open hand, like the pope, then lowered it again. When he tapped Don Stewart to look, she was gone.

"It was probably her housekeeper, not Alla. I've lived here three years and I've never seen her."

"I met her once," Alan said, "at Jean Harlow's funeral. Even then she had a veil on so you couldn't really see her. She's more of an indoor person." He mimed sliding a needle into the crook of his arm.

Driving out the foggy boulevard to Santa Monica, Scott took his seeing her as a sign, as if she recognized he belonged there. The Miramar was spectral, a ghost ship, the hallways desolate, his room humid. He emptied his jacket, setting his checkbook on the desk, and the lost hundred dollars stung him like an ulcer. The day was gone and he'd gotten nothing done. But Ernest had been warm, and Dottie and Alan, Bogart and Mayo, Don Stewart, Sid. After so long alone, it would be a relief to live with people who knew him.

There were actually four villas available. Saturday he toured them all, choosing the least expensive, the top half of a duplex with a view of the main house and the pool. He signed the lease and received his keys.

"Welcome to the Garden of Alan," Dottie said.

Later he would see it as fate. If he'd stayed at the Miramar he wouldn't have been sitting in Benchley's living room the night of Bastille Day when the English girl walked in. At first he thought it was an awful joke. While she was a lighter blonde, and her hair was waved, she might have been Zelda's twin.

For twenty years, all around the world, in triumph and sorrow, he had sought and found those same eyes, kissed those lips. He knew her face better than his own, had recalled that younger, fresher version of her so many times that he almost laughed at the uncanniness of the impression. Now he understood why a changeling was so frightening. It was like running into someone raised from the dead. She even scratched absently behind one ear like her, peering around the crowded room. She glanced his way, plainly saw him yet pretended not to take him in, betraying an indulgent slip of a smile, and continued to survey the party, deadpan—another reason he suspected it was a trick. She had to be an actress, made up to play a part.

Recovered, he saw that her imitation wasn't perfect. Turning to her escort, an older continental type with a ridiculous frigate bird of a Windsor, she was clearly taller, and full-figured, not girlish at all but plush, womanly. As he marveled at the resemblance, she was eclipsed by his downstairs neighbor, fat Eddie Mayer, steering her and her friend outside, where Bogart was preparing to set off fireworks to "La Marseillaise." Scott hesitated, afraid the punch line would be laying for him on the patio. There were no limits to Benchley's humor, or Sid's, or Dottie's for that matter. The crueler the gag, the bigger the laugh, and so he waited, listening to the whistling shrieks, the echoing booms and appreciative *ooos*, letting the delay deflate whatever humiliation they'd arranged for him. He expected an audience, but when the music switched back to jazz and he strolled outside, the air stank of sulfur, everyone was dancing again, and she was gone.

SECRETS OF THE STARS

S he was no Cinderella. Everyone in town knew exactly who she was. Her name was Sheilah Graham, and she wasn't an actress but, of all things, a gossip columnist—reason enough to steer clear. She was also, Eddie Mayer reported, engaged to the old gent who'd accompanied her, the Marquis of Donegall.

The news was a blow yet also a relief, since Scott wasn't supposed to be thinking of her. It was his first full week on the job. As promised, the new pages for *A Yank at Oxford* were in, and awful, and he spent his days casting her as the female lead. At lunch he dropped by the newsstand on the lot and stood there reading her column—absolute trash, except for her picture, which he resisted tearing out and slipping in his pocket. He was a fool. She was too young for him anyway.

He remembered her trying to ignore him, and her slip of a smile. She had miraculous teeth for a Brit, and he wondered if she'd come from money.

He thought he was being discreet, casually asking after her around the Garden, gathering tidbits. No one commented on the resemblance—not Don or Dottie, both of whom knew Zelda well—until he understood that only he could see it.

"You mean the gold digger with the bazooms?" Mayo said.

"Give a fella a break," Bogie said. "Can't you see he's gaga for her?"

"Married men. Pff."

"You like 'em well enough."

"They're good for two things."

"What's that?" Bogie asked.

"I'll tell you when I remember."

Zelda's birthday was coming up, a helpful distraction. Saturday he was getting paid. He wanted to bring Scottie out for a visit before she headed off to school in the fall. Now he saw a chance to fly back with her in September and visit Zelda. He busied himself making arrangements, filling in his calendar, as if that might settle his future, but late at night, lying awake in his bungalow while the music rioted outside, he whispered her name like a magic word.

He'd always been given to fascinations. Even before Ginevra, back in Buffalo, he'd made himself a slave to half the class at Miss Van Arnum's. They'd moved again, and, being new, he found everything new himself. At balls and parties, because he was fair and practiced at flattery, his dance card was always full. With his brilliantined hair and courtly manners, he was seen by the more athletic boys as prissy and standoffish, hardly a threat. On the gridiron they'd ride him down hard and dig a knee in as they stood up. His revenge was getting the top girl. A breathless exchange of letters, a fleeting kiss—for him that was the extent of romance. At that age any attempt to become a public couple crumbled under the pressure of rumors and friends, the sexes being kingdoms unto themselves, rife with intrigue, and a week later he discovered a new Juliet. When they moved back to St. Paul he was in eighth grade and the girls were bursting, and the same torturous whirl obtained, only sweeter and more painful. Nothing changed until he met Ginevra, and then he realized that all that time he'd been a child. He thought he'd known what it meant to be lonely.

Like those old crushes, Sheilah Graham was a phantom. He tried to empty his mind of her, but *A Yank at Oxford* was a romance between an American soldier and an English girl, and all day he was writing love scenes. He'd seen her face for only a moment, yet already she occupied vast tracts of his imagination. He had plans for them, landscapes and sunsets and declarations. Standing at his office window, watching the browned yards for Mr. Ito Hirohito, he scourged himself for building this dreamy kingdom. But wasn't she, being a palimpsest, a measure of how much he missed Zelda?

Like all men preoccupied with the truth, he was a wretched liar, his smallest evasion nagging at him. This one was great, and complicated. Though he knew it, because he loved her, because he hated what had happened to them, he couldn't admit Zelda wasn't coming back, so at the same time he held her return as a matter of faith, the fatalist in him understood that any protestations concerning the girl were empty, a traitorous balm. He was as callow now as the boy he'd been, stranded in a new place and trying to find some comfort.

At least he was at the Garden. His friends didn't let him wallow in solitude. Bogart and Mayo knocked on his door like neighbors checking up on a shut-in, coaxing him out into the torchlight to swim and play ping-pong. The game that summer was charades, which Benchley hated, but which Scott took to like the drama club impresario he'd been. He and Dottie shared a stunning clairvoyance and weren't allowed to be on the same team. Loosened by a gimlet or two, laughing at Sid's Delancey Street impersonation of Lon Chaney, he tipped back his chair and gazed up at the stars and was glad he was there.

Dottie spent more time organizing for her various causes than writing, and after his hundred dollars to save Spain, made sure to invite him to every fund-raiser. The Screenwriters' Guild was one he supported out of self-interest if not always principle. They were having their annual dinner dance at the Ambassador, she said, in the Cocoanut Grove. All the best people, et cetera. Did he have a tux?

It was old, the lapels cut wide in the style of 1925, and barely fit. At one point he might have worn it to the Cocoanut Grove, maybe when he'd split Bogie's lip.

"I don't recall what you were wearing," Bogie said. "Just that you were a mean son of a bitch."

"Now look at me."

"Now look at you. You're a mean, *old* son of a bitch."

He drove, and so was late. Making for the front doors, he heard his car stall out on the valet and kept going.

Walking into the Cocoanut Grove with the orchestra trilling a swoony ballad was like traveling back in time. The lights were low, and above the dance floor massed with shuffling couples, the same fake palm trees salvaged from Valentino's *The Sheik* rose storklike, here and there a papier mâché monkey clinging to a trunk. On the backdrop behind the band the full moon illuminated a white plume of a waterfall, and from the dusk-blue vault of the ceiling the stars shone down. Here, beneath this same make-believe sky, he'd swayed with Joan Crawford before she'd ever heard the name Joan Crawford. His fascination then had been Lois Moran, already a star at seventeen, a sweet, clever kid whose mother wisely traveled everywhere with her. The fascination was mutual, and Zelda had been jealous, flinging the platinum Cartier watch he'd bought her out of the train window as they left for New York, reclaiming him the only way she knew how. Now, stag, in his dusty old tux, he missed those strange, confusing days.

The dinner was formal, with a numbered seating chart laid out like a blueprint for the new arrivals. Dottie had bought a table for ten. Beside theirs was one sponsored by Gabe Brenner—a union boss Scott had met his last time out, working for Thalberg, and whose agitating on and off the lot had probably shortened his patron's life. The one on the other side was bankrolled by an old Gonk Round Table pal of Dottie's, Marc Connelly, who'd won a Pulitzer for a mawkish all-Negro musical based on the New Testament that might as well have been played in blackface. Scott stood at the top of the broad, carpeted ramp that led to the dance floor. Waltzing by, cheek to cheek in a dizzying clockwork like a Metro production number, spun a dozen writers making a hundred grand a year, celebrating their ascension to the proletariat.

When he found their table, it was empty. Everyone was off dancing, so he took a seat facing the action. He dearly wanted a drink, but knew people would be watching, and when the waiter swung by, asked for a Coke.

"There you are." Dottie was cutting through on some vital clerical mission with a sheaf of papers. "Can a lady ask a gentleman to dance?"

"Are there ladies here? I'm afraid I was misinformed."

"Don't go anywhere, mister."

She stalked off purposefully, leaving him to watch the other couples. He wondered where Alan was. The waltz ended, to a ripple of applause, and a bumpy rhumba started. The waiter came with his Coke. Scott tipped him, sipped and set the glass down again, swizzled the ice. He didn't like sitting by himself, and was scanning the crowd for Sid or Bench or Don when he saw her.

She was just leaving the floor, sweeping gaily along the fringe of the parquet in an ash-gray evening dress with a red velvet sash that accentuated her neck and the rosy glow in her cheeks. Perhaps it was her hair, pulled back tight as a cap, or her vermillion lipstick, but the resemblance had mostly faded, only her eyes still reminding him. She was alone, no crusty marquis in tow, and headed straight toward him. She was no phantom. For all his daydreaming, he'd forgotten how tall she was, how strong. He had to suppress an urge to rise and bow to her. She saw him but didn't look away this time, making him aware of his wedding band. Her engagement ring didn't look real, the stone was so big. She slowed just before she reached him. He was afraid, ridiculously, that she might turn and flee, or, worse, come up to him and ask him to please stop staring. Instead, as if she remembered their first meeting, she gave him that slip of a smile and turned in to sit at Marc Connelly's table, also empty, in his exact same attitude. For a long moment they sat side by side, two wallflowers watching the party.

When he turned to her, she turned to him in pantomime. It was an old Marx Brothers bit, an imaginary mirror between them.

She smiled, making him smile.

"I like you," he said, testing.

"I like *you*," she said, her accent making her sound slightly surprised.

With that settled, she turned back to the dance floor. He did too.

"Why don't we dance?" she asked, almost formally, like a scientist proposing an experiment.

"I'd love to, but I'm afraid I've promised the next one to a friend."

"She must be a very good friend."

"A promise is a promise."

"That's honorable."

"Or foolish," he said, "depending."

Dottie reappeared, empty-handed, and he excused himself and rose to intercept her. He took her hand and joined the other couples, set a course for the middle of the floor.

"I see you found a friend," Dottie said.

"Everyone's my friend tonight."

"There are friends and there are friends. Which is she?"

"A new friend."

"Don't forget your old ones," she said, holding him closer. "You know what they say: a friend in need . . ."

He'd known Dottie long enough to know when she wasn't joking, and felt sorry for her. Why was he surprised when other people were desperate?

"Alan needs you."

"Once a month, whether he needs it or not—like a cat getting a bath. He shuts his eyes and makes faces."

"We all do that."

"He makes me feel old and fat."

He shook his head. "It was a long time ago."

"Don't say that."

"It was."

"She's too young for you."

"You're probably right."

"She just wants your money."

"I don't have any money. I don't have much of anything right now."

"Okay," she said, "be a dope."

"I will," he said.

"You've always been a sucker for a pretty face—your own."

"Don't be jealous."

"I was born jealous, I can't help it."

"It's not like I've been lucky in love," he scoffed.

"You were lucky with me."

"I was," he said, since there was no graceful way to say it had been a mistake, though even now he thought of her tenderly. It was the past he was trying to leave behind.

The song wound down until they were barely swaying, then ended with a mournful flourish. The lights came up.

"Go ahead," she said, except as they were leaving the floor, the band set aside their instruments and filed offstage, and the president of the Guild stepped to the microphone.

"Please take your seats. We'll be starting the program momentarily."

" 'Momentarily'?" Scott asked.

"He's a lawyer," Dottie said.

There was confusion as the dance floor cleared and the room settled. Waiters shouldering trays hustled about the periphery. He was afraid the girl would be gone when he and Dottie reached their table, but she was waiting in the same seat, head bent, engaged in conversation with the elfin Anita Loos, who'd written for Griffith. On her far side sat Connelly himself, discussing something with his old pal John O'Hara and Sid's crazy brother-in-law Pep West, and Scott realized that for her this wasn't a night out. She was working.

He took his seat again. The way they were situated he had to lean back to see her. He waited, pointedly ignoring his neighbors, willing her to look up. When she did, he tried to apologize with a helpless shrug.

She shook her head pityingly as if he'd missed his chance.

He clasped his hands together in supplication, and she laughed, showing her perfect teeth, and he was hers. Her smile and how coyly she tucked her chin into her bare shoulder told him he could relax now. Just sitting there, trading glances during the president's prefatory remarks, they were different, separate, as if together they were keeping a secret from the rest of the world.

The speeches were interminable, futile. They all turned on management acknowledging the means of production, labor standing in solidarity and the workers demanding a fair wage. Spain and Germany were cited freely, as if their enemy wasn't Louie B. Mayer but Hitler, which made sense, since they were the same crowd that had written checks at Freddie March's. His neighbors ate their salads and sand dabs and consulted their programs hopefully.

He contented himself with glimpses of her, watching with curiosity as she gradually made her way around the table like a hostess. She focused her full attention on each guest, including the wives, listening intently, prompting them with a question, all the while playing with her silver bracelet, turning it about her wrist, flirting. She didn't take notes, though she had ample chances. What was she hoping to get out of them? He thought she was at a disadvantage, a spy with no cover, but she laughed and patted Belle O'Hara's arm and moved on. He was oddly proud of her, gracefully infiltrating a hostile camp. The wit it took—the nerve and patience. She was so new to him, he was moved to see in her every marvelous quality. He wouldn't have been surprised if she produced a bouquet of roses from her sleeve, or a trio of linked rings. And then, as the treasurer finished his report to grateful applause, she caught his eye and tapped a nail to her wristwatch. She gave him a little wave and stood with her silver clutch purse, and without a glance in his direction, made her way past him and through the tables to the rear of the club, leaving a wake of turned heads.

His instinct was to wait a safe interval and follow her, but was that what she wanted? She'd said goodnight, after a fashion. Maybe this was all part of the chase. Dessert was being served as they suffered yet another speech, the waiters reaching past them to set down plates. Across the table Dottie was watching him. He nodded for coffee, stirred in a spoonful of sugar, but after a few sips relented and excused himself as if he needed to use the restroom.

He'd given her enough time to leave, if that had been her intent. If not, she'd be waiting for him in the lobby.

He strode up the ramp and through the arch of crossed palms, the words of the speaker nattering at his back. Besides the shoeblack at his stand and the woman manning the cigar counter, the lobby was empty, its wall of phone booths dark. He crossed beneath the chandeliers to the main entrance, a valet anticipating him, holding the door open.

Again, no one. He scanned the parking lot for motion, then Wilshire. Above the red neon topping the crown of the Brown Derby, searchlights scissored against the dark sky.

"Car for you, sir?"

"Just getting some fresh air."

As a last resort he detoured down the hall to the restrooms, stopping at the cigarette machine for an alibi. In the mirror his mouth was grim, his bow tie cockeyed. Despite his excitement, he was disappointed. Too soon the night, which might have taken them anywhere, was over.

Dottie noted his return but didn't comment on it. He opened his new pack of Raleighs and lit one, wondering if the girl was purposely feeding this craving in him. Was she just a flirt? That she was engaged mystified him. Maybe this was a last fling, a final reckless gesture at his expense. There was still another speech to be endured, and more dancing, but it all seemed pointless. He wanted to go home and burrow under the covers in his tuxedo and sleep. Instead he drank his coffee, lukewarm now, and clawed at a corner of his sheet cake with his fork, already fretting over when he would see her again.

Felicitations on this most auspicious day, he wrote Zelda. *May your returns be multitudinous and joyful. I hope you enjoy the pastels. I remember how you loved the Redons glowing in that black room in the* back of the Louvre. If you need more, or anything for your art within reason, I've replenished your canteen, so please don't hesitate. All is well here, just settling to the task. Attended a compulsory function at the Cocoanut Grove the other night and thought of our evenings and mornings there. If I weren't so aware of time and our own ghosts floating about the halls I would say nothing has changed. The ocean on a calm day is still the color of your eyes. The hope now is that Scottie will see you and make a stop in Montgomery before heading out here, and I, Metro Goldwyn and Mayer all permitting, will return in September so you and I can take a few days together at the shore. Know that I think of you often and tenderly, and remain, in this bright, forsaken place, Your own Do-Do.

A YANK AT OXFORD

Mornings, by design, he woke at five. He loved the newness of the day, the hungover quiet of the Garden broken only by the plashing of fountains, birds twittering in the hedges. Over the years he'd watched Hollywood devour his friends from back East, sapping their nobler ambitions as it filled their pockets. The heat was as much to blame as the money, the whole city drowsy with a subtropical languor. After a shift in the Iron Lung, even he was tempted to loll around the pool and do nothing. Dottie and Benchley and Sid could afford to slough off, with their Guild cards and laundry lists of credits, but he still needed to sell stories to pay the bills.

His plan was to get up early and do his own work while he was fresh, except he hadn't honestly slept in years, a side effect of his Cokes and his smoking. The bed he and Zelda once shared languished in storage outside of Baltimore, likely full of mice by now. At night he relied on two Nembutals and a few teaspoons of chloral hydrate to soothe him. In the morning, standing before the medicine cabinet, he washed down an equally necessary pair of Benzedrine, and soon evened out again. He shaved and showered, whistling ditties of his own invention, put on his suit as if he were going to work, made himself a pot of coffee, hung up his jacket and sat down at the kitchen table to write.

For three hours he wrote badly, rushing things, frustratingly aware of the ugly clock above the sink, sometimes stalking out to his car in a rage because he'd had to leave in the middle of a scene, and yet every morning he managed to produce a couple of pages. They might be rickety, but he had the eye and the patience of a professional used to fixing worse. As with his Grandmother Mc-Quillan's black pudding, nothing was wasted. If a scene didn't play, he took the good lines and saved them in his notebook for later. The one thing he could trust in this world was his sensibility. If he had failed his talent, as Ernest held, it had not been through under-use, but, rather, as he thought some mornings, his heart galloping from too much coffee, the opposite. Like an athlete, he had trained himself, day after day, and trusted that when he came to the arena he would naturally perform. He'd been doing it since before the Armistice, even when Zelda fell apart, and now, alone, saw no end, no respite. He was terrified he would die, pencil in hand, leaving an unfinished sentence and Scottie a legacy of debt. These still mornings in the kitchen were a kind of penance meant to exorcise that fear. When he was working, it worked. It was when he stopped that the world returned, and his problems with it, which was the reason he worked in the first place. He was a writer—all he wanted from this world were the makings of another truer to his heart.

The story he was working on was a burlesque about a man who wakes up one morning to find a noose cinched tightly around his neck. The man realizes that the rope attached to the noose runs across the room and out the door of his apartment and down the stairs of his building, so he gets up and follows it in his pajamas. Outside, the man sees the rope goes to all the places he frequents—the newsstand, the grocery, the tavern—crossing and recrossing the street so cars and buses and trolleys run over yet never sever it. The rope wraps pythonlike around light poles and fire hydrants and mailboxes. So far that was all he had, but the possibilities were legion, and driving to work, he happily searched La Cienega for details to use.

His second week at Metro his car had been towed. Eddie Knopf had neglected to tell him parking was a privilege of the stars. Since then he'd found a dirt lot across the boulevard for fifteen cents which the day players used, entering the side gate each morning with the hopeful hordes. Unlike all of his hall mates except Oppy, who never seemed to leave, he was punctual. Eddie's door was closed, but as he walked past he liked to believe his diligence was being tallied toward some future reward. In his Frigidaire of an office he lifted a brace of Cokes out of his briefcase and set them next to the air vent, then sat down at his desk with pencil and paper to ply his trade, shivering like Bob Cratchit.

A Yank at Oxford was a patch job. A simple fish-out-of-water conceit with high-toned scenery, the original novel had been improved upon by a succession of writers responding to producers' notes, adding larger and larger climaxes to satisfy some crude concept of drama. It was all fistfights and mistaken identities, an insult to the most casual moviegoer, let alone the dons of Oxford. Beyond the problem of Robert Taylor trying to play twenty years younger, who would buy, for instance, that any student, no matter how drunk, would be fool enough to sucker punch the dean of students at a party, then accuse his rival and, merely because he was English, be believed? Or that our hero's girl, who knew he was innocent, would break off with him, only to return, cheering him to victory during the big finale of the track meet? It made no sense, yet because it was his first assignment, he threw himself at these absurd scenes, trying to find a hidden inner logic that might knit them together.

"You can't spin gold out of shit," Dottie said, leveling a scathing look at Alan, and though it wasn't lunchtime, Scott wondered if she was drunk.

"What did they ask for?" Alan asked.

Eddie had told him to punch up Robert Taylor's dialogue, make it tougher, snappier.

"Then do that," Alan said.

He did, slowly going through the whole script, pacing, playing Taylor's scenes to the boulevard and the pictures on the wall, and gradually it began to take shape. The story didn't need to be consistent, only the hero. Everyone and everything else existed merely to reveal his true character, which, at the end of the picture, after the obfuscating plot, proved to be that of the star himself.

"We need more of the girl," Eddie said during their first story conference. "Forget the set-up, forget him—it's a romance. That's gotta come first. We don't got that, we got bupkis."

Because he saw Sheilah as the girl, he thought it already worked. He studied the scenes between them coldly and discovered he was wrong. She was shy and bookish, a don's daughter despite her good looks. She had none of Sheilah's charm or elusiveness, none of her toughness. To remedy that, he made her a fencer, introducing her in a new scene. Now they met cute in the gym. Walking along, the hero snared an errant foil she'd struck from an opponent's hand. He noticed her raven hair fanning out behind her visor and waited, as she disarmed her opponent again, to catch a glimpse of her face. When he'd finished the scene, he was pleased. The delay would make the audience curious, as well as adding a hint of mystery. The payoff would be the actress's face, utterly fresh, since this was her U.S. debut. Like Sheilah she was a Brit, and irresistible in a dark way. He kept her headshot above his desk for inspiration—Vivien Leigh.

His own curiosity was about to be quelled. His downstairs neighbor Eddie Mayer knew Sheilah's agent, and through a complicated back-and-forth, arranged for the two of them to have dinner, with one condition: that Eddie play chaperone.

To Scott, it was a victory. She could have just said no.

He asked Bogie where they should go.

"You want to make yourself look good," Bogie said, "take her to the Clover Club. It's pricey, but the food's swell and the band's smooth, plus there's always some action in back."

"She's not that kind of girl," Mayo said.

"What's that supposed to mean?"

"She's a lady. She's going to be a duchess or something."

"Not if our boy has anything to say about it. Ain't that right, Fitz?"

"We're just having dinner."

"Sure," Bogie said. "You just want to make sure everything's gonna be hunky-dory, I know how it is. I been to dinner a few times myself."

Bogie offered him the use of his new pinstripe suit, and his car, a fat DeSoto, but he could see, with a writer's built-in pre-science, how that would eventually become a lie. Eddie said he could drive, but that too was somehow less than honest. As if the date were a test of his honor, Scott would drive his own car and wear his own clothes, and if they weren't good enough for her, so be it. He was prepared for her to say that the most they could be was friends. Knowing he shouldn't be seeing her in the first place, he'd already accepted defeat.

Her place was up in the hills above Sunset, a salmon-tinted villa overlooking the bowl of the city, golden with the day's end. They were early. Like the chaperone he was playing, Eddie accompanied him to the door, then let Scott ring the bell. Though the sun wasn't quite down, the outside light popped on. She'd been waiting for him. Standing there empty-handed, he wished he'd brought flowers, a possibility he'd initially vetoed and still considered too pushy. He thought he should be doing this by himself, not attended by a familiar. He should have begged off, held out for a better chance. He should have given up completely. Faced with the fulfillment of his most tenuous, ill-conceived desire, he was second-guessing everything, and then the door opened and she smiled and gave him her hand and her cheek to be kissed and she was just as thrilling and regal as he remembered.

"You found me."

"We did."

She wore a pearlescent silk blouse and dove gray skirt under a short black Oriental jacket, and in what might have been a concession to his height, flats. She still had her ring.

"Hello, Eddie," she said, as if amused by his presence.

"Evening," Eddie said, then tagged along after them to the car.

Scott opened the door for her and handed her up. The awkward formality of the situation appealed to the gallant in him, whose sense of etiquette harkened back to Miss Van Arnum's and the ice cream socials of Buffalo.

"Why, thank you, kind sir," she said, tucking in her skirt so he could close the door.

His manners were learned, hers innate. Her every look, her every gesture was meant to put him at ease. He intuited that she'd grown up around money.

"Is this your car?" she asked.

"It is."

"It has character."

"It has the indispensable quality of being paid for."

"I thought perhaps your Rolls was in the shop."

"So you've had one then," he said.

"I can't say I've had the pleasure." *Cahn't.*

"What do you have in your garage?"

"You'll laugh."

"I promise not to."

"A Ford."

"With character."

"I'm working on it."

They'd reached the foot of her street and were idling at the stop sign, waiting to take a left on Sunset. "You have to stick your nose out, otherwise you'll never get across. That's it. Go quickly. They'll stop."

As he pulled out, another car almost broadsided them, honking as it shot past. Scott refrained from giving him a Roman fig.

"Are you always such a cautious driver?" she asked when they were safe.

In back Eddie laughed, and Scott found him in the mirror. "Around here you have to be."

"It's true," she said. "The drivers here are a menace."

Widely known to be mob-owned, the Clover Club was only a couple of blocks down Sunset, a prisonlike edifice built into the hillside. Save a strip of windows on the third floor, the front was blank to keep the police from raiding the place too easily. A ramp of a driveway circled around back, where two bouncers in suits guarded a canopied entrance. The cars in the lot reflected the club's clientele, gangsters and show people. The first open spot he saw was next to a forest-green Rolls. He pulled in beside it to keep the joke going.

"Not in the shop," she noted.

"Not my color."

"Nor mine."

She waited for him to come around and let her out. He offered his hand, and again she gave him hers, a wordless gesture intimate as a kiss, even with Eddie rolling his eyes behind her. She moved like a dancer, a loose-limbed precision that snapped the bouncers to attention. He wouldn't have been surprised if she'd spent a season with the ballet, perhaps as a teen, before she'd bloomed. Zelda had never had the height or the upright carriage. He could see it in Sheilah, and remembered his own boyhood poise lessons, balancing the city directory on his head as he tightroped across the parlor.

"Evenin', Miss Graham," one of the torpedoes said, holding the door for her.

"Good evening, Billy," she nodded. "Tommy."

He'd forgotten, this was her world. He was the greenhorn.

At the bar they ran into Bogart and Mayo. "Well, well, what a surprise." Bogie broke into a smile and rose, offering his stool to Sheilah. "You kids have time for a drink? I've been telling Mayo what a swell writer you are—not you, Eddie, I mean Fitz here. Better'n Hemingway, and I mean that. What'll you all have?"

While the banter was improvised, Scott asking for a Coke was scripted, as was making Eddie's rye a double. Sheilah sipped her sherry, pinching the stem of her glass as if she were at charm school. As always, they talked shop. Rumor was, Metro was bringing in Mervyn LeRoy for *The Wizard of Oz*. Sheilah knew that Bogie had worked with him on Broadway.

"Smart cookie. Knows his way around a big number."

"Scott says you're gonna be a duchess," Mayo said wetly. "Wha'zat like?"

Above her permanent smirk, her eyes swam, unfocused, and he flashed on a frightening thought. He could not recall ever seeing her sober.

"A marchioness," Sheilah said. "It's intimidating for a lifelong commoner like myself."

"A marionette? Doesn't sound that fun to me."

"Easy, Sluggy," Bogie said.

"What? 'm asking a question. You're no Prince Charming yourself."

"And that," Bogie said, taking her arm, "is our cue. You kids have fun now."

"That was interesting," Sheilah said upstairs as they waited for a table.

"She's always like that," Eddie said.

"I mean Bogart. He must like you."

"He's an old friend," Scott said.

"Doing you a favor."

He saw that he would lose more by not admitting it. "Yes."

She laughed. "Better than Hemingway. That is truly desperate."

"I didn't tell him to say that."

"He's a great reader," Eddie said.

"It was the timing I found suspect. *Are* you better than Hemingway?"

"I'm a better dancer."

He would have a chance to prove it. Their table was in a dim corner opposite the bandstand. Candlelit, with a fresh lily in a crystal vase, it would have been romantic if they were alone. After they ordered, he led her out onto the dance floor, leaving Eddie to nurse his rye. They fit nicely. She was just his height, and when she leaned in he could smell the perfume of her skin, a warm mix of lavender and vanilla. It was an old song, a lively two-step, once a bright novelty. *I'm making hay in the moonlight, right in my baby's arms. A little harvest or two is just bound to come through.* Her palm resting lightly on his shoulder, she followed his lead, gliding, perfectly upright, all the time meeting his eyes. The ease with which she matched him demolished his boast.

"I could tell you were a dancer," he said.

"How so?"

"The way you carry yourself."

"How's that?"

"Dramatically." He threw his shoulders back.

"I don't know if I should be flattered or insulted. You look rather like a chicken."

"Proudly," he amended. "For a lifelong commoner."

"Please don't."

"What?"

"Don't joke about that. I can't bear it."

It was their first dance, yet he wanted to ask her flat out if she loved this marquis. He was holding the hand with the ridiculous ring, and he imagined kneeling at the end of the tune and sliding it off her finger. Like the fool he was, married and penniless, he was ready to declare himself.

"I don't mean to make fun," he said. "You make me nervous, and I don't know—"

"Let's not talk," she said. "Let's just dance. You said you were better than Hemingway."

"I am."

"Shh," she said.

They danced a foxtrot and a rhumba and a tango, their shared silence a challenge and then, once he surrendered to it, a closeness—as if, again, there were an unspoken bond or secret between them. They moved together, absorbed, borne along on the orchestra's sinuous rhythm. Between songs he noticed their waiter had arrived with their dinner. So did she, but the new song that swelled up was a sad ballad, and as a lonely oboe purled she laid her cheek against his shoulder and held him close and he didn't dare say a word.

"Our food's getting cold," she said when the music ended.

"Eddie can have it."

"We shouldn't leave him alone. It's not polite."

"I didn't invite him."

"You didn't invite me either—he did."

"I know," he relented. "Next time, can it be just the two of us?"

"Next time."

"Dinner, Tuesday?"

He was being abject, asking too much too soon. He still wasn't sure what she was doing here. In contrast, his own motives seemed obvious, and tawdry.

"You can't tell anyone," she said.

"I won't."

"Don't look so pleased with yourself."

"Why not?"

"You have no idea what you're getting yourself into."

"I could say the same thing."

"But why would you?" she said.

"How old are you?"

"How old are you?"

"Forty."

"Twenty-seven." If it was a lie, it wasn't a big one. Thirty was still young. You couldn't see it around her eyes.

They returned to the table, where Eddie was finishing his steak. By prior agreement, Scott was paying for everything, and the number of empty glasses dismayed him. Now that he was happy, he could be unhappy again.

The food, as Bogie said, was swell, though neither of them ate much. They ordered coffee and dessert and danced again, fretting about Eddie as if he were a child bored by the grown-ups' conversation, and though Scott wanted the night to go on and on, they decided out of fairness to leave after a last slow song. He closed his eyes and moved with her, thinking how it all might be a dream, like his recurring one of walking through a thawing St. Paul finding piles of silver coins on the sidewalks. He might wake up and find himself in bed, bereft, but no, he was holding her, she was humming in his ear. The promise of Tuesday made the poignancy of their last dance even sweeter, and when the song finished he clapped for the band with gratitude.

Outside, the night was warm and scented with eucalyptus. The Rolls was gone, and he thought of its owner, a producer returned to his dark mansion, still haunted by the vision of the lovely English girl at the club. She would be the image of his dead wife, a star of the silent age lost to some wasting disease. Fast as a reflex, the notion carried him to a world he half knew, a future patched together from the past, peopled by shades, constructed of unwritten scenes like empty rooms. Later he would remember the feeling as much as the idea, the urge to both leave and discover himself again in this man who had everything yet nothing—the opposite of him, now, thanks to her.

They climbed into the hills above Sunset, his lights sweeping across windows and hedges. In the dark he didn't recognize anything, and she had to direct him, pointing out her mailbox. After a half-dozen doubles, Eddie's effectiveness as a chaperone was limited. They left him dozing in the backseat and walked toward the yellow light.

He waited while she dug in her clutch purse for her keys. She opened the door and stepped inside before turning to him. As he took her hands he felt the ring, as he was sure she felt his.

"Can I tell you a secret?" he said.

"Yes."

"I like you better than Hemingway."

"Can I tell you a secret?" she said. "I like you better than Hemingway too."

"He won't like that."

"Too bad. Eddie was sweet to come."

"He was," he said, drawing closer, hoping for a kiss, wondering, acutely, what his producer would be feeling at this moment.

She held him off. "Tuesday."

"Tuesday," he agreed, because his man would be patient and unsure too, and waved as she closed the door.

He played chauffeur to Eddie, then valet back at the Garden, helping him to his bungalow and putting him to bed. Bogie and

Mayo's lights were on, and Benchley was in the middle of some commotion by the pool. Rather than break the spell, he climbed the stairs to his place and locked the door behind him. Even with the pills, he couldn't sleep, and for a while he sat in front of the picture window, watching the balcony of the main house, imagining his hero, like Alla, looking out over the lights of the city, dreaming of his girl, as if this last, fey love might redeem the irretrievable past.

The next morning he got up at five and wrote.

THE SWEETEST
PIE IN HISTORY

T hough as a family they'd never lived anywhere for more
than a few years, and then unhappily, one of his deepest regrets was that Scottie no longer had a home. Since she'd been
away at school, the Obers' in Scarsdale served as a base for holiday
breaks, her summers split between camp and visiting her mother
at the clinic, her grandmother Sayre in Montgomery and him,
wherever he might be.

He'd never gotten along with the southern branch of the family, and Zelda's illness only widened that rift. Her father had been
a judge, and making plans with her mother was like trying to seat
a jury. For every proposed schedule, she had a list of objections, as
if her calendar were full of anything more pressing than her
weekly bridge club. Scottie also disliked Montgomery, with its stifling heat and antebellum pretensions, so that often he felt neither
of them actually desired this visit, but, out of loyalty to Zelda and
some ideal of family, he persevered, a diplomat hashing out a
peace treaty, the conditions of which were that Scottie would
spend two weeks there, followed by a month in Hollywood.

He didn't have room in his bungalow, so he arranged for her to stay at the Beverly Hills Hotel with old Broadway friends Helen Hayes and Charlie MacArthur, who'd known her since she was a toddler. The plan had been for her to arrive Sunday via the Argonaut, but the telegram the Western Union courier mistakenly delivered to the main house so that it sat there for two days before Don Stewart found it changed all that. Because her grandmother Sayre had fallen and broken her wrist, now Scottie would be arriving late Tuesday morning. By his calculations, she was already on the train.

When he called Sheilah to cancel their date, she thought he was ducking her.

"I'd like to meet her," she said. "Why can't the three of us have dinner?"

The reasons seemed large and obvious to him, but he could feel the edge of complaint in her voice, and though he knew he would dread every second of it, he called the Trocadero and changed their reservation. Instead of a quiet table in back, he asked for one with a view.

Tuesday he took off work to meet Scottie's train at the station. It was late, and as he waited, one of a slowly accumulating crowd, he pictured his empty office and the hot boulevard outside. He was rewriting *A Yank at Oxford* again, with no end in sight. Eddie said he loved what he'd done with the girl, but wanted him to bring the rivalry story line forward, since the last third turned on that. Scott wanted to say if that was the case, the movie wouldn't be any good. When he tried making the girl the Brit's to begin with, the jealousy played too shrill. Maybe if she was his sister, though that was just as old hat. He was so used to coming up with solutions that to have nothing panicked him, and the harder he worked on it, the more hopeless it seemed. To get a credit, he had to make the script his, not just polish the dialogue. So far all he'd really added was the fencing scene.

The station presented no answers, and the rest of his day was dedicated to Scottie. As ungenerous as the thought was, it was a bad time for her to visit, with everything unsettled. Once he was more established he'd be better able to entertain her, though he'd fallen back on the same flimsy excuse in Tryon and Asheville and all his other interim stops. Since Zelda had been away, he'd done his best to give Scottie something resembling a regular life, even when it meant insulating her from his own itinerant existence. His success only deepened the contradiction. Even as he sacrificed to pay for her boarding school, he held himself as a cautionary figure, the father as absent drudge, a role he'd learned from his own father, a bankrupt and drunkard rescued and then forever reminded of it by his mother's side of the family. He recalled playing ball with his friends in the backyard of the townhouse they rented in St. Paul, and his father, having come home stinking from the bars, taking the bat from another boy's hands and flailing wildly at Scott's pitches, whiffing again and again until he wished he would stop. "Come on, try that one more time," his father taunted, laughing, and Scott, no older than ten, had been tempted to whip the ball at his face. He promised himself he would not be that kind of father to Scottie, and yet at times he was afraid he had been. At nine she'd gone back to Gstaad with him, skiing away the blinding white days, nights writing to her mother in the clinic while he tippled gin. After her bedtime story, he drank with angry purpose, and woke to broken glass and skinned knuckles. They'd been thrown out of their old chalet, and then the hotel, finally landing in a pension frequented by college students and prostitutes. It was the end of the season, and she wanted to leave. "Where do you think we should go?" he asked, because the lease had run out on their Montparnasse walk-up, and Zelda still wasn't well. The decision to come home was the beginning of their wandering.

As if they could sense the engine approaching, a squad of redcaps rolled their clattering baggage carts up the platform. Above, pigeons roosting in the beams flapped and circled the rotunda, the rails sang like a knife sharpener's wheel and the station filled with noise. Pullman after Pullman shrieked by, losing speed. He searched the windows as they passed, bristling with the smiling faces and frantic hands of arrivals, impatient after the long haul. The train slowed so porters could hop off and walk alongside, greeting the redcaps like old friends. He was afraid he'd missed her, but no, there she was, in the very last car, framed by the window. It was closed, and unlike most of the passengers she was seated and facing straight ahead, her chin tipped down, solemnly concentrating, and he saw with a doubletake that she was reading.

She was not beautiful, a fact that saddened him, since it was his fault. She had her mother's strawberry hair and slight build but his features, the moony Irish eyes and sharp nose and dimpled chin growing more prominent now that her baby fat was melting away. In five or six years, if she was careful, she might be handsome, but at fifteen she was still unfinished, a chubby-cheeked girl with freckles, an indiscriminate love of animals, and, like himself at that age, an ear for absurd lyrics. He gazed on her fondly, wishing, as always, that he could shield her from life's unhappiness, including his own. He had done a poor job of it so far. Just then she looked up and smiled at him, and once more he resolved to be a better father.

She leapt on him from the steps, squeezing him like a child. "Daddy."

"How's my Pie?"

"Tired."

The book was Aeschylus, *The Persians*.

"I hope that isn't for my benefit."

"Summer reading. We have to do one each of the Greeks."

"Have you done Euripides?"

"*Medea*."

"I was going to suggest *Orestes*. It's fascinating how he uses the chorus to anticipate the action."

"Too late."

"You should read it anyway. I think mine's in storage."

"Rats," she said, snapping her fingers.

He didn't broach the more awkward topics until they were in the car, starting with Montgomery. Mrs. Sayre had tried to step over the dog, who she thought was sleeping. Sensing her, the dog raised its head, catching her toe, and down she went, taking a candy dish with her. It was her right wrist. She had a cast and a sling and sat in her rocker ordering Aunt Sara around. Scottie tried to help but didn't know how to do anything right. She hated that every time her grandmother scolded her, she called her "young lady."

"How was your mother? Glad to see you, I imagine."

"Oh, you know. She was good the first day. We rode bikes and played badminton and she was fine. She asked how camp was. The second day she was okay. After that it was hard."

"I'm sorry. Thank you for seeing her."

"Do you know anyone named Reynolds?"

"I don't think so."

"We were on the lawn having a picnic and she stopped talking for a long time the way she does. Then out of nowhere she starting talking about Reynolds and all these things he supposedly told her. Stuff about the planets and the solar system and music coming from another universe." She shook her head, gritting her teeth and popping her eyes in comic alarm.

"I'm sure it doesn't mean anything, it's just one of her delusions."

"It was actually kind of interesting. She said Reynolds lives inside the sun and travels on rays of light. I was thinking of writing a story about him."

"It's probably better you didn't. Did you tell Dr. Carroll?"

"I did."

"Good. They need to know if they're going to help her."

"She didn't seem any better."

"Did she seem worse?"

"She seemed the same," she said.

"Does she seem well enough to go home?"

He didn't ask this rhetorically. In all the world she was the only person he trusted to tell him the truth about Zelda.

"No," she said, and though he gave her room to qualify her answer, watching the road, she left it at that.

Outside the entrance of the Beverly Hills, a great old Stutz landaulet sat like an emblem of bygone glamour. Elegance herself, Helen was waiting for them in the lobby. A slender, wide-eyed beauty, she headlined on Broadway and now for Paramount by projecting the innocence of the convent school novitiate she'd been. Scottie said she remembered her, but might have been star-struck.

"We used to call you Scottina," Helen said, taking her in hand like an aunt.

"We still do," Scott said.

She and Charlie had an extra room in their bungalow. To reach it, they had to walk past the pool, surrounded by a trucked-in beach of dazzling white sand, then through a jungle of banana trees. Like so much of the city, it was hokum, a kind of open set, yet he could see it enchanted Scottie. All he wanted was for her to be comfortable, and yet, after the last few years, he had to admit he would welcome it if she attributed at least some of that magic to him.

The plan was to let her get situated and maybe take a nap.

"We're having dinner with a friend of mine," he warned, as if that might prepare her, and then it was he who was surprised, a few hours later, when she called and said two boys she knew from Hotchkiss were in town. Could they join them for dinner?

"Why oh why are you such a pie?"

"Please, Daddy?"

"Of course," he said, already regretting it.

Sheilah was understanding over the phone, and at the Troc seemed not to mind this further intrusion. She'd dressed not for him but for Scottie, in a simple black sheath, seed pearls and silver sandals for dancing. No matter how demure her outfit, she couldn't disguise her figure, the equal of the stars who were her daily company, and the boys, rather than vying for Scottie's attention, naturally doted on her.

Fitch and Neddy. Ostensibly he'd met the two before, and recently, in Baltimore, at the dance he'd thrown for Scottie before Christmas, but he'd been tight that night and had no recollection of them. Tall, blond and bronzed from a summer crewing an uncle's yacht out of Catalina, they seemed interchangeable to him—brash and garrulous in a familiar Episcopalian way, regaling them with overlapping tales of seasick Angelenos. They were both from Chicago, and he imagined the homes they'd come from, the Gold Coast mansions with terraced gardens sweeping down to the lake in earnest midwestern imitation of Newport, the gleaming cat-boats and runabouts waiting at the dock paid for by the charnel products of feedlots and slaughterhouses. From Hotchkiss they would process to one of the lesser Ivies, Cornell or Dartmouth or Brown, and from there back into the family business of adding and subtracting, incurious as cash registers, all the while main-taining that sportsman's idle optimism, depending, of course, on how old and well-insulated their money was. He knew several classmates from Princeton who used to summer at White Bear Lake and Harbor Springs who'd had to sell their cottages after the Crash, but these two were far from any decision harder than which of his girls they should ask to dance.

The orchestra struck up "Lovely to Look At."

"Miss Graham?" they both offered as Scottie looked on.

Neddy deferred to Fitch.

"Miss Graham, may I have the honor?"

"I'm afraid my first dance is spoken for," she said, taking Scott's hand.

For a moment both boys were mum, trumped, and then, be-latedly, as if just remembering she'd invited them, Neddy asked Scottie.

"Don't fight over me now."

"Be nice," Scott admonished, earning him a dirty look which he parried, unwilling to play the oblivious father.

"I feel badly," Sheilah said when they were dancing.

"Don't. She's a big girl."

"She's just a baby."

"A very charming baby," he said, because across the floor Neddy was laughing at something she'd said. As Sheilah watched, Scottie peered over his shoulder and gave them a mocking, false smile.

"I don't know why she's acting like this," Scott said.

"I don't think she likes me."

"Why do you say that?"

"I don't know, it's just the feeling I get."

"A little jealousy's healthy, but there's no excuse for being rude."

"I don't want her to be jealous."

"You can't help the way you look, which is divine, by the way."

"I mean jealous of me being with you."

"Are you with me then?" She was still wearing her obscene bauble of a ring.

"I'm not against you."

He pulled her close. "Now you are."

Lovely to look at, heaven to touch . . .

"Why do you confuse me so?"

"Me? You're the one engaged to a duke."

"You're the one married to a wife."

"Yet here we are."

"Here we are," she said.

In the milling crowd Scottie and Neddy had found them. As if this were the Nassau prom, Neddy half bowed, asking permission to cut in. A gentleman, Scott couldn't refuse, handing Sheilah off and taking Scottie from him. The new couples spun away in different orbits.

"She's taller than him," Scottie said, amused.

"Is he the one you like, or is that Fitch?"

"I don't like either of them that way, they're just fun. I can see you like her."

The accusation was delivered so casually that he was almost proud.

"Miss Graham is very likeable."

"Apparently."

"What I like most about her is that her real talents aren't the apparent ones. She's worked very hard to become a success in a tough business, and she's done it on her own."

"I think I've heard this speech before."

"Then you understand why I admire her."

"An admirer," she noted.

"I admire ambition in any young person."

"Plus she has an accent."

"A very charming one, it's true."

"I wish she wasn't so pretty. Is that awful of me?"

"Pie," he sympathized, patting her back. It was as much of an answer as he could offer her, and as much as she wanted, because they left that topic as if they were finished with it, moving on to the awkward murals of Parisian landmarks that marred the walls. In wildly varying scales, the Arc de Triomphe and Eiffel Tower and Notre Dame were crammed onto panels that ran unbroken around the room, unsubtle as a folder of postcards. Scottie was properly horrified. Having been to the real Trocadero made the place seem what it was—an overpriced supper club with starlets for hatcheck girls.

"Remember the first time you ate escargots?"

"You told me they caught them right there in the Tuileries."

"From then on you always looked for them in the flower beds."

The song ended and another began. *Why should I suffer? Why should I care?* Fitch cut in on Neddy, who gallantly circled back for Scottie. Their ungainly number guaranteed an odd man out, a role Scott hated playing, but as host he had no choice. Alone at the table with his Coke, he soaked in the long view across Hollywood and the darkened city, the dwindling rows of streetlights like the runways of an endless airport, then the black mass of the sea. Somewhere out there was the *Rex*, and the past, the night steadily moving west, dragging the stars and tomorrow along behind it. In the hospital it was midnight, Zelda asleep, if there was any mercy. He imagined his producer, insomniac, coming in on a night flight from back East, floating over the vast emptiness of the desert, clearing the last treacherous crown of mountains and seeing Glendale and all the carnival of lights, bright and lively as a marquee, knowing that somewhere below, the girl who might save him waited. Here was life again, after the loneliness of airports, the untethered hours aloft fixing others' scripts, parsing the meaningless dreams it was his genius to sell the sleeping country.

The band took five and the dancers returned.

"Are you taking notes?" Sheilah joked, sitting down beside him.

"Always," Scottie said. "Be careful what you say around him."

"I'll forget it if I don't write it down. Blast, now I've lost it."

"I'm sorry," Sheilah said.

"The other day you were telling me about a hermit who lives in the hills."

"He has a lean-to behind the sign. They say he did lights for Griffith."

"And went mad," Scottie guessed.

"That I don't know. I suppose."

"He lives there year round?" Scott asked.

"He's not much of a hermit. Everybody knows him. We could go see him if you like."

"No," he said, because the actuality was suddenly unappealing, the scene in which his producer visits him cheap, flatly emblematic. He wasn't writing the life of a saint.

Dinner wore on, each course followed by a turn about the floor. Scottie and the boys ordered dessert and coffee, adding another five dollars and twenty minutes to the evening. For no reason he was ill-humored, and then felt stingy when they thanked him for paying.

"It was all just lovely," Sheilah seconded, and what could he do but agree? After so long alone, he'd forgotten how it felt to be the man of the family.

The boys could have taken the streetcar but he gave them a ride, dropping them at Marina del Rey with a handshake and a promise to take them up on their offer of a cruise. When they were gone, from the backseat, Scottie said, "Thank you, Daddy."

"You're welcome, Miss Pie."

"Thank you, Sheilah."

"Please, there's no need to thank me, dear."

"I told Daddy I wished you weren't so pretty. Now I wish you weren't so nice."

"I think that's a compliment," Sheilah said.

"It is," Scott said, though, knowing Scottie, he could feel the needle of honesty in it.

The Stutz was still sitting outside the Beverly Hills, yet instead of a welcome fixture it now seemed a moribund ornament. He excused himself to Sheilah and escorted Scottie across the sands and through the jungle. Tomorrow she was going with Helen to the studio, where, as a surprise, they'd arranged for her to meet her idol, Fred Astaire—an elaborate gesture meant to impress her, he supposed, with the reach of his old fame. Why was he so prideful with her, when, more than anyone, she knew the depth of his failings? Or was that it, every overdone production designed to redeem him in her eyes? If so, tonight didn't fit.

Why do you confuse me? Sheilah had asked.

Because I'm confused myself, he could have answered. *Because I don't know what I'm doing anymore.*

He knocked on the door. "Did you have fun?"

"I did, thank you."

"Your friends seem like nice boys."

"They are."

"Sheilah likes you very much."

"I like her too," Scottie said, noncommittal, as Helen opened the door for them, and he felt let down, as if he had more to say to her, as if he might explain. At the same time, he wasn't sure he wanted to hear what she honestly thought of him running around with a woman closer to her age than his.

Charlie was there, looking hale. He was a drinker but had recently been through the cure, and greeted him with the exuberance of the newly rescued. He was over at Universal, adapting his last play, a task Scott imagined was like slowly poisoning your own child. He and Helen had been reading, their separate books set aside and waiting on matching armchairs flanking a cathedral Philco leaking Brahms. If Scott had to leave Scottie with anyone, they were a commendable choice, yet their restored happiness only cast his situation in starker relief, and though he would see her tomorrow and every day for the next month, leaving her recalled all the other times he'd abandoned her to the world, and walking back through the jungle and the pool and the lobby he

brooded on this, so that when he returned to Sheilah he was subdued, and rotten company, and aware of it.

"Thank you," he said. "You were wonderful with them."

"It was easy. She's very mature."

"She can be."

"I'll confess I was a little intimidated when she ordered."

"Her French is actually better than mine because she's had to
keep it up. She needs it if she wants to get into Vassar."

"You must be very proud of her."

He was, and soberly. For all their skirmishing over grades and
smoking and pocket money, he'd come to admire her character.
With Zelda gone, the two of them relied on each other that much
more, especially living at a distance, and if her absence had forced
Scottie to grow up prematurely, it also gave her a sense of responsibility and a grasp of the world he wished he'd had at her age.

"Why," Sheilah asked, "what were you like at her age?"

"A fool. Still am."

"I bet the girls all went for you."

"Which only made me act a bigger fool. I was a very selfish
child, though I suppose all children are. I haven't changed much,
really."

"That's not true. I think you're the most considerate man I've
ever met."

"Don't say that."

"Why not?"

"Because then I'll have to live up to it. I'm married and I drink,
and when I drink I have a terrible temper."

"Then you shouldn't drink."

"I agree, but I do, and I wouldn't want you to get the wrong
impression."

"See?" she said. "You're being considerate by telling me. You
didn't have to."

"Stick around and you'll find out soon enough."

"I just might."

"What about the marquis?"

"His mother doesn't like me."

"Who is she, Lady Somebody?"

"Lady Donegall. She thinks I'm a climber of the worst sort. That's why he went back to England, to convince her I'm worthy of the title."

"Without you?"

"She won't speak to me."

"That's awful," he said, inwardly exulting.

When they'd first made the date, he pictured asking her back to the Garden, maybe dancing with her in the living room of his bungalow. Now, buoyed by this news, he slowed for her street and turned up into the dark hills. This time she didn't have to tell him which light was hers.

Walking her to her door, he thought the night had not been the ordeal he dreaded, just awkward. All in all, besides a few cross moments, they'd acquitted themselves well. She was fearless, a natural diplomat. He was glad she'd asked to come. Tomorrow Scottie would have a good day at the studio, he'd get back to work, and everything would settle again.

They stopped before the stoop. A moth orbited the light, its wings beating madly.

"It's Tuesday," she said.

Lost in his thoughts, he didn't know what she meant, and was overwhelmed when she leaned in close and kissed him.

The heat of her mouth surprised him, as if it were a trick. She tasted of coffee and peppermint from the restaurant. He hesitated slightly, and she pulled back, laughing. He thought she might be making fun of him, but she opened the door, took his hand and led him inside, where it was dark. She dropped her keys on a table and kissed him again, pushing her full front against his, and then she was pulling him up a narrow flight of stairs and into her bedroom, the made bed lit by the glow of the city below, and she was relieving him of his jacket and unbuttoning his shirt, and though he wanted to stop her and ask whether this wasn't too sudden, too serious to blunder into, he tugged at the zipper of her dress and watched as she let it drop and stepped out of it, her body backlit, eclipsed.

"No," she said when he reached to undo her brassiere.

It was her one withholding. She kept it on while they made love, the stiff, padded fabric spectral against her skin, so that even as she was giving herself to him, he felt she was hiding something even dearer. As much as he wanted her, he didn't know her at all. He'd told her his secrets, which she absorbed like a spy, without relinquishing any of her own. He thought it should bother him more, but she was young and warm and lovely, and he was grateful and patient enough, rocking in the dark, to abide this mystery. To Zelda, the girlish Zelda he'd left behind, all he could say was *I'm sorry, I'm sorry, I'm sorry.*

THE GRAVEYARD OF
THE ATLANTIC

As he feared, he didn't get a screen credit for *A Yank at Oxford*. After a month of story conferences, with no warning, Eddie called him into his office and took him off the picture. The studio wasn't unhappy with his work, Eddie said, they just decided to give another writer a stab at it. *Who?* he wanted to ask, but there was no sense protesting. They were paying him, and, honestly, he'd done everything he could. He took down the head shot of Vivien Leigh, slipped it between the pages of his last draft and filed the script in his bottom drawer.

There was no privacy in the Iron Lung. By lunchtime everyone knew he'd been reassigned, the writers' table needling him with the brusque camaraderie of the locker room. His replacement was Julian Layton, a Brit whose farce *Quicker, Vicar!* had been the rage of the West End ten years ago. The consensus was that *Three Comrades* was a better set-up anyway.

"So," Alan said, "you've gone from writing for Robert Taylor as a wisecracking vet to Robert Taylor as a wisecracking vet."

"And *Spen-cer Tra-cy*," Benchley projected like a ring announcer, saluting Tracy at the next table.

"He's just showing off his range," Dottie said.

"It doesn't matter what you write for Mankiewicz," Oppy said. "He'll make it about the girl."

"And slap a happy ending on it," Dottie said.

"Leave 'em laughing about Hitler," Benchley said.

"Mank's like Jane Austen," Alan said. "It could be Hitler, Franco and Mussolini. By the end they're all getting married."

"He's a sucker for the old slow build to a kiss," Oppy said.

"You would know," Alan said.

"And a third act reversal," Dottie said. "I guarantee he'll ask for one in rewrites. He thinks he invented it."

"That and the close-up on the phone," Benchley said. "It can't just ring, we have to see it physically exists."

"Better'n Selznick with his memos," Oppy said.

"God yes," Dottie said. "Imagine being his secretary."

"Imagine being his wife," Benchley said. " 'It has come to my attention that we are spending far too much on wardrobe.' "

Scott laughed along with them, but still, he was disappointed. He wasn't used to having his work dismissed, the long days and weeks of fretful effort he'd devoted to it wasted, fruitless. He'd come west not just for the money but to redeem his previous failures here, the scripts he'd believed in rewritten by hacks or ditched entirely. After the last few years he knew he was lucky to have the chance, and to immediately fall short was disheartening. That the project wasn't his to begin with mitigated it somewhat, or so he told himself. What puzzled him most was that, until this morning, he thought he'd done a decent job.

His goal with *Three Comrades* was to keep it his and his alone. Ideally he'd dash off a draft, then build it up before turning it in to Mankiewicz, except he didn't have time. In two weeks he had to take Scottie back East.

Between her and Sheilah, he was scattered. He kept them separate, mostly. Every night he showed Scottie the town, taking her to the Brown Derby and Horseshoe Pier, dropping her at the Beverly Hills and going directly to Sheilah's, coming home late, only to wake to the birds chirping. This sweet espionage was exhausting, and made him feel craven and old. At his kitchen table, slugging back coffee, he blocked out his master scenes. On the lot he punched in early and had lunch delivered. Rather than leave behind something rough that Mankiewicz could hand off to another writer, he polished the first two acts, hoping their promise would be enough, and then, at the very last, submitted them with misgivings.

That night he said good-bye to Sheilah. Her balcony jutted above the treetops, giving on a starry vista. The two of them sat watching the lights and listening to the industrial thrum of the city. They were subdued, as if they'd been fighting, or were anticipating it. She knew the reason he and Scottie were going was to see Zelda, and that they would spend part of their time at Myrtle Beach as a family. To quell any speculation, he let her know he and Zelda would have separate beds, though just saying it felt like a betrayal, and he wished he were already gone.

"It's none of my business," she said.

"Of course it is."

"I told you I didn't want to do this."

"What?"

"This. I'm such an idiot. I told you you didn't know what you were getting yourself into. Now I'm in it."

What could he do but apologize.

Hours later, after they'd patched things up, as he was driving Sunset back to the Garden, he thought of the correct response. *I know,* he should have said. *I know, and I don't care.*

It was three when he got home, and he hadn't packed yet. He dozed, rolling and mumbling, then rose at six to pick up Scottie, skipping his usual pill. He figured he could sleep on the train.

Though he'd been there barely two months, leaving the city felt like a defeat. They were taking the Sunset Limited to El Paso, first class. As he'd hoped, the stateroom with its cleverly hidden amenities delighted Scottie, yet even as they lay across from each other on the drop-down bunks, comparing them to the army cots on the Argonaut, he dwelled on all he'd left undone. Outside, the orange groves and motor courts slid by, hot and sharp in the thin morning light. They climbed the pass at San Dimas, rushed down the other side, and were in the desert. "Next stop, Palm Springs. Palm Springs next." All he wanted was to drift off to the clicking of the trucks, but he thought Scottie should have some breakfast. They staggered to the diner where they were served Rocky Mountain trout and scrambled eggs by a porter with a walleye, staggered back, mildly seasick, pulled the shades and slept.

When he woke, it was still day. They were still rolling over the desert. In the shimmering distance a line of snow-capped peaks rose like an island. For miles there was nothing, cracked hardpan and washboard roads angling off into mesquite. As with the sea or sky, the vastness compelled him. He imagined being stranded out there, the train breaking down, a plane crashing in the mountains. His producer, returning from an important meeting in New York. It would be weeks before anyone would find the wreckage. Who, and what would they find? Money, obviously. A gun. His hero's talisman, a monogrammed pen—no, a briefcase. Across from him Scottie moaned in her sleep, and before he could stop himself he pictured her coming upon the debris field. Not just one girl, but a group of children from a nearby town, out exploring on horseback. Four of them, all very different. Because of the money, they wouldn't tell. How would their secret change them? That was his ending, the new future's loss of innocence. It fit with the producer abandoning his dream, and with Hollywood overall, maybe too neatly. How his man came to that low state was another question.

He had to raise the shade an inch to take notes. He was working on his fifth page when Scottie sat up, shielding her eyes.

"Where are we?"

"I have no idea."

"It's hot in here. Aren't you hot?"

He held up one hand and kept writing.

"Daddy."

"Yes, Pie, it's hot in here."

They stayed overnight in El Paso, then flew east the next day, stopping to refuel at Kansas City and Memphis before the final leg to Spartanburg. As they came in, he marked the great swaths of piney woods that hid black ponds and swamps. A plane could go down in a remote lake and never be found, though dramatically that might be unsatisfying. Someone had to find it. As with *Gatsby*, there had to be a witness the reader could believe.

Because it was supposed to be a vacation, he hired a roadster in Spartanburg much like the one he'd sold. They grabbed a quick dinner at a barbecue pit on the way to Tryon. Dusk was falling by the time they pulled up to the hotel. He wasn't surprised to find his old rooms were available, though at a higher price. He saw no improvements, but it was only for the night, and the shredded rattan bedroom set was somehow comforting. He and Scottie rocked on the verandah, watching the fireflies. He tried not to think of Sheilah.

"She won the tennis tournament," he offered.

"That's good, after what happened last time."

"You have to forget that. It's always like starting new with her."

"That's what makes it so hard."

"You never know, she might be delightful. It's only three days."

"Three days is a long time."

"We won't see her again until Christmas, so let's try to make it nice for her."

"I always try to be nice."

"I know you do, and I'm sorry she's not always nice back. You know she loves you."

"I know."

"The doctor says she's been doing well with the new treatment, so we'll see."

"We will," she said.

The next morning, after winding their way up the mountain, the change was clear from their very first glimpse of her. He didn't recognize the stout woman the nurse escorted toward them—her hair was darker, longer, her bangs bowl-straight—until he saw the gap left by her cracked tooth.

She was fat. When he'd left two months ago she'd been a scarecrow. Now she was doughy and bloated, double-chinned and thick-waisted, her face strikingly different, as if her role had been taken over by a pudgy understudy. He'd never seen her so big, even when she was pregnant. He smiled to cover his alarm, asking how she was as they embraced.

"I look awful, don't I?" she said, taking Scottie in her arms.

"How do you feel?" he asked.

"I feel fine, I just look like a pig. My eczema's better." She pulled down the collar of her blouse to show them the smooth skin of her chest.

"It's gone," he said. "That's wonderful."

"I've got tits again. That should make you happy."

It was the kind of scandalizing thing she used to say in mixed company, but with Scottie right there it seemed off. Worse, the breasts he pictured weren't hers.

"I'm happy you feel better," he said.

"My deepest apologies," she said to Scottie. "Apparently I'm not supposed to say 'tits.' Yours look nice, by the way."

"That's enough."

"Thank you," Scottie said.

"Everyone has them, you know," she told him. "It's not a secret."

"It's not news either."

"This is going to be fun," she said, linking arms with them like a chorus girl and pulling them toward the door. *"Allons-y!"*

"First I need to sign you out."

"I forget, I'm a prisoner of love."

He registered the insinuation, but let it pass, saving it for Dr. Carroll.

"What happened to your car?" she said in the lot.

"I told you, I sold it."

"Dodo." She pouted. "I liked that car."

"I know you did. That's why I hired this one."

"What a gentleman, always thinking of me. Remember the Delage whose roof wouldn't go up?"

"I do."

Scottie ceded the front seat, and they were off, cruising down the swooping drive, through the gates and out into the world, the three of them reunited. In town, he turned right at the stoplight, heading south over the mountains for the coast. He'd never taken this route before, and drove even more slowly, as if undecided. The gray haze lingering in the hills reminded him of their forays into the French countryside, the jaunts to the Bois, the day trips to Lyon for dejeuner at the Institute Gastronome. Zelda noted each passing attraction as if they might miss something, making Scottie continually look up from her book. A new foal, a trash fire, a garden lined with whirligigs. It was just past nine. By his calculations they'd make Myrtle Beach around five. He didn't think she could keep up the bubbling stream of discoveries. He feared that, following her usual pattern, after this initial outburst she'd run down and eventually shut off, withdrawing to her inner world from which there was no extracting her, but for now she was keenly interested in everything, including him.

"Are you eating? You look like you've lost weight."

"I'm actually gaining. I eat out too much, and I drive everywhere."

"You look tired."

"I've been working."

"I wish I could come out there and look after you."

Just the thought stopped him.

"I know you do," he said.

"I'll bake you pies and iron your handkerchiefs."

"I wasn't aware you ironed."

"I'm working in the laundry. I can do all kinds of useful things."

He couldn't imagine it, though he knew she was telling the truth. Her life now took place beyond him, among people he'd never meet—as did his. He was proud of her accomplishments, but to pretend they still knew each other was a fiction.

It was what they were there to do: pretend everything could be the way it was. They'd stayed at the hotel before, years ago, when Scottie was five or six. In their albums were snapshots of her, freckled and chubby, tin bucket and shovel in hand, standing beside a sandcastle with an architect's pride. Zelda had been well then, one of her last good summers, back when they still made plans.

Hours in the mountains, then down through Columbia and the low country with its paddies and long tobacco barns. He'd wanted to stop just the once, for lunch and gas both, but as they approached Charleston, the women needed a restroom, prompting a visit to a second filling station. On they pressed, through the humid city and north along the shore, where there was more for Zelda to point out. Scottie had taken off her shoes and curled up on the seat, though whether she was truly asleep was guesswork.

"Smell the sea air," Zelda said, sniffing, and he did.

At Georgetown a new steel bridge crossed the sound, the open deck making their tires whine. The tide must have been going out, because the near rail was lined with negroes fishing off the side.

"Look at the pelicans," Zelda said, imitating them.

The island was a pine barrens flat as a runway. Miles ahead their hotel rose from the white dunes. Like the Beverly Hills, the Beachcomber was a coral monstrosity, its whimsical scale meant to impress. After the Crash it had changed hands precipitously, moldering empty for several seasons, but when they turned in, the topiary appeared freshly barbered, the croquet lawn perfectly manicured. They pulled up to the front and a platoon of liveried valets in knee breeches swarmed the Ford.

Though it was the end of the season, the gateway of Labor Day nearly upon them, the porches overlooking the gardens were teeming with Charleston society, even the men dressed in white, sipping gin and tonics and nibbling canapés. Inside, at the foot of a sweeping staircase, a man in tails was playing a grand piano over a ground bass of conversation. There was a line at the concierge desk. Were they with the Cabbagestalk wedding? In another time they would have said yes, danced with the bride and groom and drunk champagne until they couldn't stand. Declining the invitation, he felt dull and responsible, fatherly. Beside him, Zelda had finally gone quiet, looking around open-mouthed, as if overwhelmed by the posh decor, while Scottie studied her book, and he remembered this trip was his doing, and that it was going about as well as he could expect.

He'd reserved a suite so they could be together, he and Zelda in the one bedroom, Scottie on the sleeper couch. The separate beds he'd promised Sheilah were a yard apart, at best a technicality.

As they unpacked, he noticed Zelda's clothes were wrapped like gifts in butcher paper.

"Hand-me-downs," she said. "I've outgrown all my own clothes."

"Who are they handed down from?"

"Donations. The lost and found. We get everything in the laundry. Don't worry, it's clean." With no attempt at modesty she pulled her shirt over her head and chose another.

Along with round, heavy breasts, she'd developed a mound of a belly, as if she were pregnant. The slender, long-limbed girl he married was gone. It was like she was another woman altogether.

The blouse she buttoned up—unironed, showing every fold—was a bright pistachio with a vestigial pocket over her left breast. It was a full size too big, and hung on her like a muumuu.

He looked away, too late.

"A gentleman doesn't stare," she said.

"Who said I was a gentleman?"

"You had aspirations once, if I recall."

"I gave those up. Too much work."

"I know what you mean."

He couldn't be sure if they were joking anymore. *All we have is work*, he could have said, but refrained. Now that they'd stopped moving he felt tired and letdown. Long ago the novelty of travel had worn off. Even before that last summer—'29, that cursed year—they'd run out of places to go, and reasons.

Scottie was lying on the couch with her book, and sighed when he tried to rally her for dinner.

"Don't be a sour Pie."

"Be a sweetie Pie," Zelda finished.

"And please put on something nice. We're going to be out in public."

She gave Zelda's shirt a quizzical look. "Yes, Daddy."

"Thank you."

She changed in their room and came back wearing a smart dress Helen had helped her pick out.

"Don't you look darling," Zelda said, plucking at Scottie's shoulders like a tailor.

"Daddy bought it for me in Hollywood."

"*Tres cher, n'est-ce pas?*" There was no reproach in her tone, though for months they'd been jousting over her canteen bill.

"*Oui.*"

"*Mais tres jolie aussi,*" Scottie said.

"*C'est vrai—comme toi, chou-chou.*" She kissed her on both cheeks, and while he was pleased, he had a sudden vision of Mrs. Sayre, her tottering walk and horsey rear.

He couldn't get used to her new size, or her wardrobe. As they descended the grand staircase, he imagined everyone in the lobby was staring at them, this mismatched family. At dinner he watched her for any sign of mania, but she ate at the same pace as both of them, and made polite conversation, laughing with Scottie when he got a spot of tartar sauce on his tie and reminding him of the oyster stew at the hotel on Capri. He remembered the hotel but not the stew. She skipped dessert, encouraging them to go ahead, then declining a bite of his trifle. He was so accustomed to diagnosing her, every slip a symptom, he didn't know how to stop.

After coffee they strolled the boardwalk beneath strings of naked bulbs, taking in the same flashing taffy parlors and midway games and dark rides that amused Sheilah in Ocean Park and Venice. He'd been gone three days now. He had an urge to cable her, send flowers, anything to let her know he hadn't forgotten, as if she might. Knowing it was wrong didn't change the feeling, only made the shadows stretching across the sand into the black water more sinister. In a thriller he would be the murderous husband, Zelda the helpless victim, the humid night a moody prologue. As much as he might protest, at heart it was true. To save himself he'd killed what once was best in him, and to his shame discovered he'd saved nothing.

"It's nice to be out at night," Zelda said, breathing deep and looking skyward. "It's a shame there's no moon."

He hadn't noticed, and sought it out, as if she were wrong. Scottie copied him.

"I'm on the top floor, so I always know where it is. That's how the ancients told time."

"Many moons," Scottie said.

"Blue moon, harvest moon, hunter's moon. Waxing and waning."

"So it should be a low tide," Scott said.

"The high tide will be lower and the low tide will be higher."

It sounded like prophecy. It wasn't something she would have known in their previous lives. Even if it was just a rote by-product of the hospital library, again her new abilities surprised him. One of his larger worries was her lack of a discernible future. Now he could picture her at home at her mother's, paging through books, rocking on the swing, working in the garden. It wasn't merely to assuage his guilt. He'd wanted her to be happy before he met Sheilah.

It was only the first day, as Scottie noted later, while Zelda was using the bathroom, but she seemed calmer, less frenetic.

"We'll see how she does tomorrow," he said. "Thank you for not commenting on her shirt."

"If she could stay like this it would be nice to see her."

He thought so too, though it was probably impossible.

He let her have the bathroom next, giving Zelda time to get settled, then when it was his turn, took his pills and brushed his teeth thoroughly.

"Good night, Pie."

"Good night, Daddy."

He could stall only so long.

In the bedroom Zelda was waiting for him. She hadn't turned out the light. She was in bed, her doughy shoulders poking from the covers. Even if there had been pajamas in the lost and found, she would never wear them. Her habit of shedding her clothes at parties, unlike his, wasn't a drunken stunt. She was at heart a naturist, happiest on the beach, open to the sun, free of any worldly constraints. It was her wildness that had attracted him, the desire to join her boldness to his own. He'd misread her—willfully, he suspected—as so often he'd misread himself. It wasn't her fault.

He turned out the lights to change into his pajamas and then stumbled against the dresser trying to get his leg in.

"Are you all right?"

"Just clumsy."

The sheets were clammy. He could tell he'd be hot later. In the dark he could make out the square of the open window, silvered from the glow of the boardwalk. Far off, softly, with the regularity of breath, the surf boomed. It had been months since they'd been alone like this. In Virginia Beach she'd been sick, lashing out at Scottie and him, then lapsing catatonic. Now she seemed fine. He didn't want to do anything to ruin it, and lay still as a mummy, hoping she'd go to sleep.

He thought of Sheilah in her brassiere, how different the two of them were, and what that meant. As well as he knew himself, he was helpless when it came to love—if that's what it was. His entire life he'd given himself wholly to only one woman. A romantic, he never imagined he could or would again.

He needed to tell Zelda, though he worried what the truth might do to her. What it would do for him was just as uncertain. For years now they'd pretended to a deathless bond, when long ago they'd stopped relying on each other for their daily happiness.

With a creaking of springs she sat up and pushed herself out of bed. She walked hunched over, her skin ghostly in the reflected light, taking baby steps, arms held in front of her, feeling her way like someone blindfolded. He was afraid she was coming for him, but when her knee discovered his bed, she circled the foot and groped her way to the window, where she stood in silhouette. They were on the fourth floor, the drop high enough to be fatal, yet he didn't move.

She sighed appreciatively, a wistful simper meant for him.

"What?"

"Remember the stars in Monte Carlo?"

"Of course."

"I used to wish on them. Every time we went there I wished we'd win a million dollars."

"What happened?"

"I was young and foolish. I should have wished for something else."

"You can still wish," he said. "We can still use a million dollars."

"Don't make fun."

"I'm not."

He sat up. She had her back to him, and the longer she stood there the surer he was that, if only to comfort her, he would go to her and take her by the shoulders, rest his chin on top of her head and gaze out over the sea so she wouldn't be alone.

"There," she said, turning from the window, her face shadowed.

"What did you wish for?"

"If I tell you it won't come true."

She crossed the room to him. Illogically, pettily, despite everything, he fixed on her new body. She came around the bed and he closed his eyes, as if that might erase his guilt, then, unable to resist, peeked. She'd stopped right beside him, brazen as an Amazon. Instead of getting into her bed, she knelt by his and laid her head on his chest. Out of reflex or common decency he stroked her hair, and lying there staring into the darkness, he thought it didn't matter that they were married, or that he loved some long-lost version of her. In his heart he knew it was wrong, and yet he couldn't push her away. He didn't know how he would explain it to Sheilah, but he would always be responsible for her.

"Okay," he said, patting her shoulder. "It's late."

"Just a little longer."

"Just a little."

He thought she must be uncomfortable, kneeling on the bare floor, but she didn't waver or complain. There was something terrible in her obeisance, a bloody tribute laid at his feet.

"Thank you, Dodo." She pushed herself off him and stood, lingered palely above him a second, almost posing, as if giving him a chance to reconsider, before getting into her own bed.

"Good night," she said.

"Good night."

Beyond the silver window, the waves broke and foamed, endlessly. If her wish was to go home, to be free again, he had the power to make it come true. If she wanted them to be together the way they had been, the time for that had passed. He didn't know what to wish for besides her peace of mind—a lie, since it depended on him. Why did every wish of his seem impossible? Whatever happiness he might find, her misery would always be his. As he gnawed on the problem with her breathing right beside him, he thought he'd never get to sleep, and then, as he was imagining the boardwalk going dark string by string, the touts and candy butchers locking their shutters against the fog, his pills drew him down into their murky undertow—a familiar surrender—and out of the world.

The next day she was fine, swimming like a fish and beating them at hearts. That night she came to him and he held her the same strange way, and then again their last night, ritually, as if this were now permitted them. It was harder to leave her when she was good-—as if condemning an innocent—and after putting Scottie on her plane he stopped in the airport bar and had a double gin. He remembered ordering a second, then nothing until Albuquerque. He was sprawled on someone's wet lawn, a sprinkler arcing over him. His money was gone and there was blood on his jacket, and when he called Sheilah, before he uttered a word, she told him she would not be spoken to like that and hung up.

THE RICH GIRL

He thought they would make up, but she stayed away. It was his fault. She didn't like him when he was drinking, and he was drinking with real purpose. *Three Comrades* wasn't his alone anymore. While he was gone, for no reason—as he'd promised he wouldn't—Mankiewicz had brought another writer on-board.

Scott knew him from New York: Ted Paramore, an ex-Broadway hack who'd snubbed him and Zelda at the Plaza when they were the city's reigning couple. To even things, he'd sent him up in *The Beautiful and Damned*, calling a sniveling character Fred Paramore. His understanding, at first, was that Paramore had been brought in to help tighten the structure and shore up any soft spots in the original script, which Mankiewicz said he liked on the whole, but soon it became clear that he was trying to take over.

Paramore had a dozen credits, most of them hijacked, and knew how to jigger a story conference. Instead of helping Scott make the script better, he questioned long-settled choices, down to the names of the three heroes, taken directly from the book. Mankiewicz listened to his suggestions as if Paramore were an equal—as if he'd written anything of consequence. Scott fought against the obvious but was overruled. He wasn't surprised. In all his dealings with Hollywood save one, the collaborative process was a case of the narrowest majority agreeing on the broadest effects to please the widest audience. The one exception, as he told anyone who'd listen, was Thalberg, and Thalberg was dead.

"The lucky bastard," Dottie said.

Line by line, scene by scene, Paramore was exacting his revenge, and Scott couldn't stop it. Each week came new instructions to dynamite his carefully turned work. Though they shared a hallway, outside of Mankiewicz's office they didn't speak. His secretary delivered his revisions to Paramore's, and vice-versa. Every knock on the door promised another assault. Occasionally, when Paramore had done more than his usual violence to his words, Scott thought of crossing the hall and beating the little weasel to his knees, and would have if he didn't need the paycheck.

"What do you think the rest of the world does?" Dottie said. "We don't all get to hobnob with countesses."

"He has a *German officer* say 'Consarn it.'"

"How do you say that in German?"

"Let's ask the countess," Alan said.

At the Garden he drank with Bogie and Mayo, doing dizzying backflips and punishing half-gainers, staying in the pool until the stars were out and his fingerprints shriveled. Like any bachelor, his fridge was empty, and Dottie and Alan had to prod him to eat. He ordered in sandwiches from Schwab's, washing down the salty pastrami with cold beer. Sitting in a camp chair in the shallow end, he watched the balcony of the main house for Alla but there was nothing, just the darkened windows.

Sheilah kept putting him off, saying she needed to see the marquis, leaving the reason unspecified. Scott saw it as punishment. While he was jealous, he was also angry with her. He'd told her he was an ugly drunk, and at the first sign of Mr. Hyde she disappeared.

That he'd warned her only meant he knew better.

"Knowing doesn't do anything."

"It has to do something," she said.

Lately they couldn't get beyond these impasses, her silence over the phone an indictment. Admitting he was wrong wasn't enough. She wanted promises she could hold against him when he trespassed again. He didn't tell her how many times he and Zelda had played this scene, at how many different pitches. His bats lasted for days then, expeditions through strange neighborhoods by freight elevators and fire escapes and back doors in alleys that opened at the magic word, the usual rules of time suspended in pursuit of rooftop sunrises and slow dances in the middle of bridges, ending only when he'd run out of money or friends, so that he would have to go home and face the damage, the needless waste. Once, inadvertently, he'd hurt her, slamming a door to cap an argument, not realizing she was chasing him. One side of her face ballooned, bruised black, and he vowed he would change. To his shame, he was still the same man, just older now, and tired.

I'm so glad we could all be together like old times, Zelda wrote. *The sea was warm and so were you and the Pie. I already miss the oysters and sandy sheets. The Beachcomber has aged gracefully, like a grandame wrapped in Irish lace. Dr. Carroll says Christmas is a possibility, but don't you think I might try to make a go of it at home? Mama's wrist is better and Sara can drive me if you think I'm ready. Here it's fall and every sunny road leads back to dusty summer and your tie waving like a flag on the boardwalk.*

He knew too well how quickly she could turn, especially after a good stretch, and expected word, any day, that she'd attacked someone, or hurt herself, or fallen into that faraway state he'd come to understand as her last hiding place. Retreating himself, he couldn't see her breaking free.

It was typical for him to be stirred up after a visit. In his dissipation he was almost grateful he didn't have to face Sheilah, except that he missed her. He sent her roses with poems begging forgiveness. They didn't move her, but, as he'd figured, she was too polite not to acknowledge them.

"Please stop," she said.

"Why?"

"Because I'm running out of vases."

"I'll buy you more."

"I don't want more. I want you to stop drinking."

"I've stopped."

"It's nine thirty in the morning."

"I haven't had a drink in two days." Which was true, if you counted today.

"I mean permanently."

"I'm trying," he lied.

She still wouldn't see him, so it was into this bitter limbo, one afternoon as he was stewing at his desk in the Iron Lung, that a wire arrived for him, not from Ober or Max or Dr. Carroll but Ginevra King.

She was in Santa Barbara, visiting her son Buddy at a clinic, and she'd heard Scott was working at MGM. Next week she had to come down to L.A. to take care of some business, and she wondered if they might get together.

His immediate reaction was that of a fugitive cornered by his pursuers. He hadn't spoken with Ginevra in twenty years, and hadn't expected to the rest of his life. He had loved her purely, with an undergraduate fervor, their romance mostly epistolary, his few visits to her family's place in Lake Forest heavily chaperoned. It was there that he first discovered the sequestered world of the privileged—the circuit of summer homes and northern resorts funded by the Chicago fathers and favored by the newly moneyed—to which, despite his shanty Irish cynicism, he aspired, and to which, by her side, he was admitted. After she'd thrown him over to marry the son of her father's partner, he still dreamed of her house, the French doors open to the stone terrace, the lawn sloping down to the dock and the glittering water, a lost idyll he would try to recreate again and again, never succeeding more than temporarily, though on the page he came close. At one time he would have been gratified to know she was thinking of him, but that was long ago. He thought, if not happy, he was reconciled to looking back at her role in his adolescent sadness with a wistfulness that time and the consolation of art had gradually sweetened to melancholy. That was the Ginevra he missed, the Ginevra of infinite possibility and perfect memory, not this Ginevra Mitchell, whose unfortunate son was heir to the spoils of the last century.

At the same time he was curious, and somewhat flattered. It was likely she'd read his work, perhaps even seen herself and him in his characters. She couldn't wound him any further, he figured, and he did want to see what she looked like and hear about her life—as if, by her beauty and special destiny, the hurtful past might be justified. Another, more immature part of him thought that perhaps she'd sought him out to finally apologize, to say she realized she'd made a mistake. Absurd as the idea was, wasn't her tracking him down a kind of admission? Why did she want to see him, if not to revive their friendship?

He told Sheilah, treating it like a joke on himself, the jilted beau.

"Am I supposed to be jealous?"

"She's married."

"So are you," she said.

"That's right, you're just engaged."

Her silence let him know he'd trespassed. Before he could apologize, she asked, "Do you think before you say these things, or do they just pop out of your mouth?"

There was no right answer.

"I hope you two have a lovely time," she said.

If she thought this would stop him, she was wrong. Now he was determined to make a success of it just to prove he was gallant, not awful.

The negotiations over the arrangements reminded him of Ginevra's elusiveness and her tendency to get her own way. He called her hotel and left a message, saying he'd received her wire. Two nights later she caught him at the Garden, her voice still low and thrilling. Just talking with her made him feel guilty, their planning illicit. She wanted him to come to a party Saturday at a friend's place in Santa Barbara. He was free that evening but it was too far up the coast and he wanted to see her alone, so he said he was busy. He proposed Sunday dinner at the Malibu Inn, halfway between them. She said she'd have to check her calendar, and the next night countered with lunch Monday at the Beverly Wilshire, since she had to meet with some people in town later that afternoon anyway. It was a compromise. If there was less pressure seeing each other in the daytime, without the sea and stars, there was still the romance of a grand hotel, but also, if things went badly, a built-in escape.

He would be sober for her. That weekend he abstained, prompting Bogie and Mayo to set his welcome mat on fire. In the morning, while they slept it off, he switched his for theirs, rang their doorbell and scurried away.

He also drove over to Bullock's Wilshire and splurged on two new shirts, wishing, as he pawed through the racks, that Sheilah were there to help him. He couldn't find a tie he liked, and then was dismayed, Monday morning, by his choices, finally settling on a striped number Zelda had picked out at Hermes on one of their first trips to Paris. Like many men in their forties, he tended to dress in the style of his youth as if it were the current fashion. His herringbone jacket had twice been patched at the elbows, the lining resewn, but as long as it fit him and was clean, he saw no reason to retire it. Likewise, the high-waisted slacks and white saddle shoes he wore to his lunch with Ginevra cried 1922 to the waiting valet and maitre d', as if he'd come directly from the set of a Harold Lloyd short—the snooty new beau who ends up walking home after being flattened by the lovebirds' flivver.

He was early, and was shown to a window table with a view across the boulevard of the wide, inviting fairways of a country club, which he thought fitting. The last time they'd seen each other had been at her parents' club, an end of summer cotillion, the luminous paper moons of Japanese lanterns floating in the live oaks. At her insistence they tore up their cards and danced the entire night together, fending off a whole stag line of highborn hopefuls pressing their right to cut in. Simple midwestern boys, they stood no chance against Ginevra's autocratic whims, an unhappy position he would assume back at Princeton a month later, when, with no explanation, she dropped him. She had been his and he hers, with flaming youth's boast that this would be so eternally, and then one day he was no longer wanted. He still had the letter, the last in a thick packet that had moved with him from St. Paul to Great Neck to Cannes and now resided, with most of his earthly possessions, in the locked garage outside of Baltimore. He wished he had it with him now, or one of the many responses he'd written but—out of pricked vanity as much as despair—never sent.

A waiter reached him. "Something to drink while you're waiting, sir?"

"Just water's fine."

Though he'd been there only a moment, he was alone in the huge room, and now, from his own trepidation over their meeting, he feared she wasn't coming. In that case, he thought, he would repair to the bar for the afternoon rather than go back to work and suffer more of Paramore's abuse. Across the boulevard, a twosome of women in knickers was teeing off, their drives reminding him of Zelda's fluid swing. When he turned away to check the entrance, the maitre d' was coming through the tables straight for him, with Ginevra hard behind.

He stood and stepped clear of his chair, attending their approach like a groom at the altar.

She was still striking—slim and long-limbed, gypsy-dark with shocking blue eyes set off by a sapphire brooch over her heart. Except for her hair being pulled back into a neat chignon that showed off her neck, she hadn't changed, making him aware of his own sallow flesh, as if marrying well had insulated her from the passage of time. It was only as she came closer that he saw the worry lines about her eyes, and the vain attempt to hide them with makeup.

She turned her smile on him, took his hand limply and kissed his cheek.

"I hope I didn't keep you waiting."

My whole life, he might have said. "Not at all."

The maitre d' gave them menus and left them alone.

"You look lovely as always," he said.

"Thank you."

"It's good to see you."

"It's good to see you too."

He asked after her parents, and she reciprocated. She was sorry to hear about his mother.

"How is Buddy?"

"He's well. I don't get to see him as often as I'd like, of course, but the place has done wonders for him."

When he'd known her, she'd been notorious among the Gold Coast set for not holding her tongue. Now, like Garbo, she had the reserve of a queen, making each word seem carefully chosen yet saying nothing. He hoped she would explain why she wanted to see him, but she took a pair of reading glasses from her purse and perused the menu. The prices were ridiculous for lunch.

"Have you eaten here?" she asked.

"Not in years."

"I wonder how the sole is."

What had they talked about when they were together? Themselves. Their plans. The next time they'd see each other. How they might find a way to be alone. Everything about her had seemed intriguing then, every moment brimming. Now they sat like strangers, or, worse, an old married couple.

Along with the sole, she ordered a glass of wine. He asked for a Coke.

"So," she said. "Tell me about Hollywood."

"It's actually rather dull. I go to work, I come home."

"I'm sure there's more to it than that."

He could have told her about playing cards with Gable, or meeting Dietrich, but chose the truth. "The money's good and the people are interesting."

"It sounds ideal."

"It is," he said, surprised to find that on the whole he agreed with himself. "How is dear old Chicago?"

"I'm actually at home right now. Bill and I have been—" She waved a hand in front of her face and shook her head. "It's all been a mess."

For a confession of that magnitude it was oddly glib, as if she were having trouble with the gardener. He could sense her gauging his reaction.

"Should I ask?"

"Oh, there's no scandal. We just can't seem to get along. It's been going on forever. It finally reached a point where we'd both had enough."

"I'm sorry." He waited, giving her the stage.

"It's going to be official next week. I wanted to tell Buddy in person, which was difficult but the right thing to do. I'm not sure how much he understands. I think it's going to be hard on him when he comes home for the holidays. He's so used to us being a single entity."

"Of course," he sympathized, without drawing on his own divided life, and then felt dishonest.

Was this why she'd come, to bring him news? Was he supposed to feel vindicated? Sorry for her? Because now it seemed doubly sad, an utter waste. Until Zelda, he'd never met anyone he thought more capable of happiness.

"You have children," she asked.

"One. A girl. A young lady, I should say."

"How old?"

"Too old. And wiser than her father, thank God."

"What's her name?"

As he related the barest details, he was aware that he was holding her off, as if in her misfortune he felt superior to her, when there was no reason. She was someone he'd known once, and then imperfectly, at a distance. Their courtship, in keeping with the mores of that select tribe, took place under the watchful eyes of her parents and the other club members. For all of their promises, he and Sheilah had been more intimate their first week together.

"And your wife?" she asked.

He faced the question rarely, if only because most people in his circle knew the answer. That she might be ignorant of his situation seemed unlikely, yet she'd asked casually, with no more than the requisite interest.

"Back East," he said. "Hollywood doesn't agree with her."

"Too hot."

"Too hot, too dry, too many earthquakes."

"How long are you out here?"

Again he found himself hedging, and was heartened to spy the waiter heading in their direction, shouldering a tray. He was suddenly hungry, and realized the only thing he'd eaten today was his pills.

Rather than lapse into silence, they felt compelled to keep the conversation going while they ate. What did she do? Besides taking care of her family, she volunteered at church and the YWCA. She was on the board of trustees at Buddy's school. She golfed and swam and rode. Traveled. At one time he'd aspired to that comfortable, orderly life, just as he'd dreamed of being with her. He'd had several chances but always his plans dissolved into chaos, and he wondered if constitutionally he was incapable of it.

Working at his sole with Ginevra sitting across from him and the bright world streaming by outside, he thought of Zelda and what she would be doing now. In the middle of the afternoon, like children, they had quiet time. She might be reading, or writing him a letter. He pictured her sitting in a wicker chair in the dayroom, the sun slanting through the Venetian blinds.

"You know we're all very proud of you back home," Ginevra said. "Not that I was surprised. You were always so clever with words. I remember your letters used to make me laugh. That's one reason I liked you."

"Not the only one, I hope."

"You were dreadfully handsome, and knew it."

"Not the most admirable quality."

"I was just as bad. Worse."

"No, just prettier."

"I was afraid to cable you the other day. Isn't that funny? I didn't know if you'd even want to see me."

"Why wouldn't I?"

"Because I was selfish and unkind."

"You were young," he said, and if, as grounds for absolution, it was slippery, he didn't need her to explain or apologize further. It was enough that she'd acknowledged not what she'd done but, simply, him. Strangely, after torturing himself for so long, he didn't want her to feel badly.

"How was your sole?" he asked.

"Very good, how was yours?"

"Delicious. Good choice."

"You can't go wrong so close to the ocean."

When he'd agreed to see her, he feared they'd have nothing to say. Now, having broached the unspeakable past, their memories came naturally. She hadn't forgotten their days and nights on the lake. Just the mention of the boathouse made her smile.

"I was wicked, wasn't I?"

"You were wonderful," he said.

She was meeting people at one, so they skipped dessert and waited for them in the bar. She had a second glass of wine, and to celebrate their friendship he ordered a Tom Collins. He'd forgotten how mesmerizing her eyes were, that unnerving sky blue. The drink and his new mood made him ebullient.

"Your husband's a fool."

"Please, you don't know the first thing about him."

"I don't have to. How could any man not adore you?"

"You mean, how could any man put up with me for that long?"

"You're not so awful."

She laughed. "You forget."

"I didn't forget. What do you think I've been writing about this whole time?"

"I wasn't going to mention it. I recognized myself in some of your books."

"Which bitch did you think you were?"

The word made her smirk.

"All of them," she said.

"Not all," he said. "Just the irresistible ones."

"I suppose I should be flattered."

"You should."

He wanted to ask which books of his she'd read, and what she thought of them, but couldn't, and let her grill him about the writer's life, and living in New York, and on the Riviera. He wondered if she regretted never leaving Chicago, and imagined what would have happened if, after Scottie was born, they'd stayed in St. Paul.

Too soon her friends arrived, a trio of stout society wives in fashionable hats with netted veils which on Ginevra might lend a bridal air of mystery but in their case made them look like frumpy beekeepers. She introduced him as an old and dear friend. They appraised him as if he were her new beau.

"Sorry, girls," she said, "he's taken," getting an easy laugh.

They parted as they'd met, with smiles and happy platitudes. It was so good to see you. We really shouldn't wait twenty years next time. He squeezed her hand as he kissed her cheek, then let her go.

"Gorgeous," he marveled when he was alone, and stood at the bar, unfocused, lost in contemplation. He'd hoped seeing her might finally lay her ghost to rest, and here she was, alive and real. He wanted another drink, but thought of Sheilah. Despite her pretense of not caring, she'd ask how their lunch went, and for that he needed to be sober. Grudgingly, with the indignation of a slave, he retraced his route to the studio and spent the afternoon restoring a scene Paramore had gutted, and then, punching out at six, felt exceedingly virtuous.

All evening he waited for her to call, the clock on the stove and the news on the radio counting off the hours. At eleven fifteen he called her, letting it ring in case she was just walking in the door, then gently set the receiver in the cradle and went around turning off the lights.

When he tried her in the morning she didn't answer, though that wasn't uncommon. On the lot, before he punched in, he stopped by the newsstand and scanned her column. Among the casting rumors and studio press releases was a tidbit about Dick Powell and June Allyson getting cozy in a booth at the Victor Hugo. He told himself he had no right to be jealous, no cause. While it stung just as much, it was possible she'd been working rather than purposely ignoring him.

Neither guess proved to be true. That night, when he finally called, she apologized. She'd been with Donegall.

He was standing at the mantel, and buckled as if punched. Looking back, he should have expected it.

"I broke it off."

Anything he might say would implicate him, so he said he was sorry.

"I felt sick after I told him. He's a decent man. The awful thing is, I think he'd still have me."

"What did you tell him?"

"I told him I couldn't marry him because I'm in love with you."

There was silence, as if he'd lost her.

She choked, releasing a low keening that broke in a wild sob, and then she was crying. "I hurt him, Scott. I hurt him—all because you couldn't bear to be alone. I never wanted to love you. I tried everything I could not to care about you, but you made me, coming around, sending me flowers. Why did you have to do that?"

The force of her despair simultaneously frightened and moved him more than any desire he felt for her. He hadn't realized she was that abject. Her helplessness left him at once giddy and terrified. He accepted that it was his fault, being the original pursuer. As if she were his responsibility, he pledged he would try to be worthy of her sacrifice.

"You were right to tell him. He had to know anyway."

"He didn't."

"Then it's better he found out now. You did the honorable thing."

"I was not *honorable*. He trusted me and I cheated on him. We're not honorable people, we're liars! What are we doing? You don't love me, you just wanted me. Now you don't even want me. You'd rather drink and chase after some old girlfriend who threw you over."

"I do want you. And I'm not chasing after anyone." He might have said that she was the one who'd been avoiding him, but chose diplomacy. He told her he loved her, and promised he'd try to stop drinking. He said everything he could short of saying he'd marry her, but even as he reassured her that she'd done the right thing, he feared that—especially after seeing Ginevra—he didn't love her as much as he should.

When she asked about their lunch, his account was factual, brief and incomplete, and accepted with skepticism.

"You don't still love her?"

"I haven't seen her in twenty years."

"That's not what I asked."

"No," he said, "I don't love her. I don't even know her anymore."

"Is that what's going to happen to us?"

Beyond the daunting assumption of oneness, it was an impossible question, bordering on the rhetorical.

"Whatever happens," he said, "I know I'm happier when I'm with you. I didn't like not having you around this week."

"I wasn't happy either. I was so sick I couldn't eat."

"You made it to the Victor Hugo."

"That's where we went. Oh Scott, it was awful. He thought we were just having a nice evening out. The whole time I wanted to throw up."

That she was strong enough to tell the story was a good sign. After listening to her confession, he asked if she wanted him to come over.

"No, I need to sleep. I've got an early call at Republic, out in the valley."

He offered again, to show he was in earnest, but she was sure. They'd have dinner tomorrow, somewhere nice—not in Hollywood. She seemed calm, back to the brassy, practical Sheilah he admired, and after saying good night, alone again in the quiet bungalow, he was embarrassed and a little ashamed that he'd panicked. By any measure, he did love her. As his past was with Zelda, realistically his future was with her.

Which was why he was puzzled, a few nights later, after several gimlets poolside, to find himself leaning against the mantel, phone in hand, speaking with Ginevra.

For a few weeks he chatted with her regularly, never telling Sheilah, but though they always said they should get together

again, they never did, and when she returned to Chicago to final-
ize her divorce, they fell out of touch. He wasn't entirely surprised
when, just before Armistice Day, he received in the mail an invitation to her wedding at her parents' home in Lake Forest. He still
had the invitation to her first, baled with her letters, and like that
painful reminder, this less ostentatious version he couldn't throw
away either, stowing it in an old hatbox of his mother's beneath his
royalty statements and cancelled checks and Zelda's and Scottie's
letters, a hiding place from which, occasionally, to distract himself
while he was writing, he would take it out and reread the gilt embossed script and remember how he'd felt the first time she kissed
him in the shadows of the boathouse, holding his face in her
hands, pulling back and looking at him with those lucent eyes,
and how, like the silly children they were, with the greatest se-
riousness and most honest hearts, they vowed to love each other
forever.

LILY

All fall he missed the East, the melancholy turning of the leaves and the smell of woodsmoke as the days grew shorter. He missed the gloomy rains and darkening afternoons, the squirrels busy burying acorns for winter. Here the sun burned down clear and unchanging on the palms and cars and boulevards. Hot winds blew in from the desert, and the hillsides caught fire, a mockery of his favorite season.

This time of year Princeton was at its neo-Gothic best. At dusk the lancet windows of Old Nassau glowed like a monastery, and walking across the quad as the carillon struck the quarter-hour and swallows darted round the bell tower, one could believe it was England a hundred, two hundred years ago. Perhaps it was a matter of sensibility, or maybe just fatigue, but he saw nothing romantic in brilliant, half-built California.

UCLA was a bricklayer's idea of a campus, the halls stark boxes. Even the football stadium was new, a concrete copy of the Coliseum left over from the Olympics, far too large. Every Saturday he and Sheilah joined the student body in the bleachers to watch Kenny Washington run the single wing. In prep school

Scott had been a second-string quarterback, small but shifty, with a popgun arm. One of his fondest memories was the muddy November afternoon at Groton he'd relieved their injured starter and led Newman to a late victory. He'd taken a beating, plunging through the line time and again on the winning drive, defenders gouging him while he was at the bottom of the pile. What he thought was a cramp turned out, in the training room, to be a broken rib. It had sealed his reputation on campus, after an inauspicious beginning, and though at Princeton he was cut after the very first tryout for being too small, he had a reverence for the heroic nature of the game and anyone who played it with grit and grace.

As the lone negro in a collegiate arena, Kenny Washington was subject to hits after the whistle and all kinds of punk stuff, yet never complained to the officials. He took his revenge directly, doling out straight-arms like left hooks and trampling defenders, and then, on the other side of the ball, knifing in from linebacker and riding their quarterback down. Scott tried to impress upon Sheilah how singular a player they were witnessing, but she had no appreciation of the game. She was only there to be with him.

Since she'd thrown over Donegall, they both made an effort to spend more time together. He wasn't used to dating a working woman, forever waiting for her to be done. Her schedule was exhausting—she always seemed to be in her car. Part of her job was being out on the town, and they savored their rare free weekends like a married couple, waking late and eating breakfast on her balcony. He was at her place more than he was at the Garden, yet, despite the extra toothbrush and dresser drawer ceded him, he was still a visitor. The newspaper's idea of propriety was the same as the studio's. He could accompany her to premieres and awards ceremonies, but couldn't move in with her.

She didn't want him to, or so she said, as if this munificence were to her credit. She liked living alone and just assumed he did too. He didn't, but over the last few years had grown used to it, an accidental recluse. Having his own place made it easier to keep his old and new lives separate. He was also secretly relieved he wouldn't have to actively hide his drinking from her. And yet, like her wearing her brassiere while they made love, her assuming he didn't want to live with her bothered him, as if she were keeping something from him.

For someone whose job was gossip, she rarely talked about herself. He'd told her about his father's failures, and the family's wanderings from St. Paul to Syracuse and Buffalo and back again, the townhouse on Summit Avenue and his grandparents intervening to send him to Newman. All he knew about her was that she had a younger sister Alicia who lived in London and at sixteen she'd been presented at the Court of St. James. Conveniently, she had pictures illuminating both of these facts, framed and facing each other on her mantel. Of her parents she said little. They were dead—her father, who was older, shortly after her birth, her mother in a car accident when Sheilah was seventeen—leaving only an Aunt Mary to look after her. For a society girl her education was spotty. She claimed to have been on the stage yet didn't know Ibsen from Strindberg, and occasionally, when tired, dropped her aitches, stopping herself before she could break into full-blown Cockney. Though they'd been intimate for months in some novel ways he and Zelda never were, he still didn't know Sheilah.

"That's good," Bogart said. "A woman should have a little mystery. Take Sluggy—I never know what's in her head. The other day I'm reading the paper and she hauls off and socks me in the arm. 'What was that for?' I say, and she says, 'Because I love you.' It keeps things interesting."

"I've had interesting. It's not interesting after a while."

He didn't tell him about the bra. He thought it must cover a secret from her past—a scar or tattoo. His imagination flashed on childhood accidents, mutilation, white slavery. Though he himself had been naked with her only in the dark, under the covers, he suspected her reticence was more than simple modesty.

Like a lecher, he peeked at her in the shower and when she was dressing behind her japanned bamboo screen, using the mirror on her dresser to get another angle. She pulled the curtain to, turned her back on him. All he caught were illicit, thrilling glimpses of her sugar-white skin, soap bubbles foaming over her curves, nothing definitive, until one lazy Saturday morning before the California game.

They'd made love so heartily that his chest ached and his blood beat in his ears. She went to take her shower, leaving him to recover. He lounged a minute, letting his breathing settle, listening to the toilet flush, the creak of the knobs and then the pattering in the tub before he swung his legs out of bed and crept to the door. She liked it scalding. Steam roiled, wetting the ceiling. By chance she'd left the curtain open an inch. He craned forward, an eye to the slit, as if at a peep show. She was shampooing her hair, leaning back into the stream, her face tipped up, water rilling off her chin. She wasn't deformed or marked or bristling with dark hairs, but beautifully made—a mystery in itself.

As he gazed on her, slaking his curiosity, she opened her eyes.

She crossed an arm over her chest and with the other drew the curtain. "Go away."

"I'm just admiring you."

"I don't appreciate people staring at me, thank you."

"You look positively classical."

"Thank you, now go away."

He didn't have to ask. He'd been so obvious—so obnoxious— that after she'd gotten dressed she explained she wore a bra all the time because when she didn't, her back hurt. It had nothing to do with him or with sex, it was just more comfortable. She said she wasn't angry with him, but the next morning she locked the door. From then on she guarded her privacy so tightly that he kept his one vision of her like treasure, giving it to his producer to revisit whenever disillusion threatened.

The weekends were theirs, mostly. The week meant punching the clock, eight a.m. to six p.m., plus the twenty-minute drive, a schedule he wasn't accustomed to. Some nights she had to make staged appearances at clubs or restaurants, arriving on a rising star's arm, and as well as missing her, he was jealous, brooding by the pool, trying to fill the evening with gin and charades.

At the studio, when she interviewed one of Metro's own, he ate lunch with her, sharing a table at the commissary or, when there was time, taking a box lunch and roaming the false-fronted metropolises and midwestern towns and medieval villages of the back lot till they found a quiet spot. The courtyard set from *Romeo and Juliet* was a favorite. One of his conceits was that he could have been an actor—Lois Moran once offered to get him a screen test—and there, on the same balcony where Leslie Howard entreated Norma Shearer, Scott recreated the famous scene, feeding Sheilah her lines, his accent making her laugh.

The back lot was a playground free of the real world. Even the sporadic gunfire in the distance came from the Western set. It was an endless adventure finding new places, because there was one around every corner. New York, Paris, Rome—everywhere they went was elemental and enchanted. They ate chicken salad sandwiches in the train station from *Anna Karenina*, BLTs on the Shanghai docks, Reubens in the Casbah, then walked back through the fogless streets of Whitechapel, holding hands.

He kissed her a last time before they crossed Overland to the main lot, then let go. Though by now their affair was an open secret throughout the Iron Lung, during work hours they pretended to be no more than good friends, a role he resented and at which he was certain he was unconvincing.

He felt equally false telling Zelda he was hoping to come East for Christmas, depending on the shooting schedule for *Three Comrades*. While it was true, and beyond his control, in the face of her helplessness the greater omission shamed him, and his usual rationalizations seemed cold-blooded and convenient. He didn't believe in divorce—not as a Catholic, which by now he was only nominally, but as a romantic—yet he understood that while a bond remained, that aspect of their love was over, ruined by anger and sickness and grief, by too many others and too many nights apart. If he'd fooled himself these last few years, thinking she might recover and be his again, he also never expected to find anyone else. Drunk, he might take confused comfort in a fellow lost soul, but the old hurt would immediately return, reinforcing the fact that there was no one like Zelda, and the Zelda he knew was gone. He was never unhappier than when he woke, not quite sober, and realized he'd done what he promised he'd never do again. With Sheilah he didn't have that excuse, which made this betrayal worse, and worrisome.

The arrangement didn't seem to bother Sheilah. She didn't demand, as most women would, that he marry her. She was happy with her job and her place and her car, and while he admired her independence, on those nights he wasn't invited over, he sulked. Occasionally, unable to stop himself, he headed down Sunset and up into the hills, only to find her driveway empty and her windows dark—expected, yet less than reassuring.

Like everyone in the Iron Lung, he made it through the days by thinking of the weekend. He was sick of fixing *Three Comrades*, which should have been done a month ago. Paramore had a terrible ear yet kept making changes to the dialogue Scott then had to restore. Heeding Ernest's advice, he'd fortified the original ending, knowing the studio would want to soften it. In the final scene at the cemetery, after the local brownshirts have killed their friend, and the girl they both love has died, the two survivors hear gunfire coming from the town and head toward it, ready to fight for their country again. While he felt nothing for the script at this point— the freshest part had been ruined by a thousand compromises—he was prepared to defend his work. At the end of December his contract was up for renewal, and after *A Yank at Oxford* he needed to show at least one screen credit for his six months there. If Metro didn't pick him up, he'd catch on somewhere else. He'd already decided he wasn't going back to Tryon.

"Not on my account," Sheilah said.

"Entirely on your account," he joked, because, though he'd never told her how much he owed, she knew he needed the money.

With no family to host, they spent Thanksgiving together, taking the day boat to Catalina. The white villas and dusty olive trees reminded him of Greece, and the time the goat stole Scottie's straw hat.

"I've never been," she said.

"Oh," he said, "we should go."

Instead of turkey they had lobster, with a view of the harbor.

Returning on the last ferry, they stood at the rail and watched the searchlights crisscross the sky.

"Someone's opening," he said.

"And I don't care."

"It's still pretty."

"It is."

She was free for the whole weekend. He packed a bag, sneaking out the side entrance of the Garden, and stayed at her place. As if to appease him, that night she took off her bra. She stopped kissing him, rolled away to unhook the catch, then turned back to him, resplendent. Afterwards, she retrieved it from the floor and refastened it in the bathroom.

The next morning while she was in the shower, he made an inventory of the top of her bureau—perfumes, a modest jewelry box, a monogrammed silver comb-and-brush set. She was neat, everything square, her hairpins entombed in a glass sarcophagus, all facing the same way. He ranged the room, inspecting the alarm clock on her nightstand and the unlit candles on the mantel. Except for the mussed sheets, it might have been a film set. There were no silly knickknacks or pictures of her as a girl, no clues to her as a person. He suspected the closet held a deeper knowledge of her, one's wardrobe being a kind of self-portrait. He was reaching for the knob when the water stopped.

He had time for just a quick peek. What struck him was how bright and bold her clothes were, compared to the decor. She loved color—greens and pinks and crimsons. It was like opening a door on a garden. With a stir of pleasure, he recognized some of her dresses from their evenings out, and her gold sandals. A high shelf was piled with hatboxes, and he wondered if she'd kept Donegall's letters, or her other lovers'. Would he find his own among them, alternately flirting and begging forgiveness, or were his kept closer, being current?

He shut the door before she finished in the bathroom, but the thought of her past lingered, needling. While he liked to think of her as young and innocent, in this city a woman of her charms would be besieged. It had made her strong, but because his own history was rife with misadventures, he feared hers was too. To share her with anyone was unbearable, yet at some time, irrefutably, she had been another's. He knew he shouldn't care, that he was being a fool. For all his modern thinking, in personal matters he had a midwesterner's insistence on virtue, making him eternally prey to shame, and prone, in his weaker moments, to ascribing it blindly to others.

She came out in a towel, routing his thoughts, and dressed behind her screen. "Hurry up and take yours. I'm famished."

"Where are we going?"

"I was thinking Tom Breneman's. I have a craving for ham and eggs."

"Doesn't it have to be four in the morning for Breneman's?"

"Bogie?" she guessed.

"It was Mayo's idea."

"I didn't know she had ideas."

"She has about Bogie."

"I wouldn't call that an idea, really."

The day was theirs. The city was sleeping off the feast. After breakfast they drove up to Malibu and walked barefoot on the beach, deserted now that the weather had cooled. She wore a baggy oatmeal sweater and had her hair pulled back in a black elastic band, her face rosy without makeup. As the casting directors said, she could play younger. Every so often she knelt to inspect a shell or stone, holding out her palm like Scottie to show him her treasure. The strand and sky made him think of Long Island, those years when the world was full of promise. Was that still true? It was only Friday. He was tired, despite taking his wake-up pills, and thought of Prufrock.

Ahead curved the arm of the movie colony, the cottages of the stars ranked side-by-side like miners' shacks boarded up for the season, the patio furniture shrouded. In its exquisite emptiness, it might have been a ghost town.

"I'm surprised," he said.

"It's always like this. I know someone who owns one. He only comes out for the Fourth of July."

"Producer?"

"Don't. He's a proper gentleman, and old enough to be my father."

"I didn't say anything." But thought: like Donegall. Like me.

She ignored him, walking on, then stopped, making him turn to her. "Isn't it enough that I gave him up?"

"I'm sorry."

"I haven't asked a thing of you."

"And you have every right to."

"I shouldn't have to ask. Anyway, it wouldn't do anything but make us unhappy."

"I wish I could promise you more."

"You can't, so why ruin a perfectly beautiful day?"

It was too late. Nothing was resolved, and even after she took his hand and they kissed and walked on, he was afraid of saying the wrong thing. The breaking waves filled the silence. The shingle was flat and wide here, the surf foaming cold over their toes. There were supposed to be seals and dolphins, but all they saw were gulls.

"That's the one," she said, pointing to a clapboard cottage topped with a tarnished weathervane shaped like a whale. It was closed like the others, the windows shuttered, but they left the sea and trudged up the beach for it as if they lived there. A low wall fronted a brick patio drifted with sand. She sat and patted the wall for him to join her. The stone was cold. Far out, a great motor yacht inched along, probably headed for Catalina, its engines rumbling like an airplane's.

They shared a cigarette, the wind taking the smoke away.

"Do you know who Frank Case is?" she asked.

"Of course." He owned Dottie's old haunt, the Algonquin, among other holdings.

"When I first came out here, it was like starting over. I had nothing. No family, no friends. My editor arranged with Frank Case for me to stay here till I could find a place of my own. I'd never even met him, and he let me stay here—alone. For that I'll always be grateful to him."

"He sounds very generous."

"He is."

"I was once thrown out of the Gonk, though I suppose that's not exactly a singular distinction."

"You needn't be jealous of everyone I've ever met, is what I'm saying."

"I am. I can't help it, I'm selfish that way. I want to go back and get to know you as a schoolgirl."

"You wouldn't like me as a schoolgirl. I was tubby—and mean."

"I can't picture you as either."

"Oh, I was vicious." She seemed to take pleasure in confessing this. "I treated people horridly because I was unhappy. I'm much nicer now."

"Why were you unhappy?"

"Why is anyone unhappy?" She squinted out at the dwindling motor yacht, a blip on the horizon, and he thought she would let the question stand. "I suppose I felt cheated. When I was little we hadn't any money. I was too young to understand, and any time I wanted something we couldn't afford, my mother would call me ungrateful."

" 'How much sharper than a serpent's tongue . . .' "

"She did worse than her tongue. She was a believer in not sparing the rod. I was lucky. She was harder on my stepbrothers."

"That's awful. I didn't know you had stepbrothers."

"I didn't have them for long. They left with my stepfather and I never saw them again."

"So it was just you and Alicia."

"This was before Alicia."

"Hadn't your father already passed then?"

"She was my stepfather's, actually."

"I didn't know."

"Does it matter?"

"No. You just never told me before."

"Probably because of what you'd think. It's all very compli-cated and sad, and all a long time ago. That's why I don't like to talk about it. I don't have a family in the sense that other people have family."

"You have your Aunt Mary."

"Please can we talk about something else? I don't know why you brought it up in the first place."

"Because I wanted to know you then."

"You know me now. Trust me, you're getting the better part of the bargain. Here, finish it." She handed him the cigarette and stood, took a few steps back the way they came. He could tell he'd offended her by prying. To apologize again would only prolong the awkwardness, so he rose and followed her, rueing yet another lost opportunity.

He was being greedy, wanting all of her, when she'd given him so much. He knew how she took her tea and where she had her hair done. He could confidently order for her at a hot dog stand or a French restaurant. Her favorite star was Janet Gaynor, who'd granted her her very first interview. She hated Constance Bennett and couldn't bear Charles Boyer, who'd made a lazy pass at her on the set. She walked briskly, as if she were late, and drove like a maniac. She was organized and clean, meaning he had to pick up his place when he knew she was coming over. She was vigilant about brushing her teeth, and loved going to the dentist. She was a better speller than he was, but knew fewer words. When she was typing a column, she scratched the side of her head with the eraser end of her pencil and stuck out her bottom lip like a bulldog. She liked it when he kissed her neck but not her ears. She thought her nose was crooked and that her eyes were too far apart, neither of which was true. More than anything, she loved to sleep. Wasn't that enough?

After opening boldly, he'd become tentative. If, like his producer, he was replacing his long-lost love with this newfound one, he needed to be sure of her—impossible, and yet, indisputably, she was perfect. Perhaps that was what frightened him most.

Saturday they piled into the Coliseum with a hundred thousand other Angelenos for the traditional city game. For three quarters they waited for Kenny Washington to break loose. When he finally did, Sheilah jumped up and cheered with everyone else. Typically, Scott thought of Zelda, missing it, and afterward, filing down the long concrete ramps with the drained and giddy Bruins fans, he felt strangely dislocated. The feeling only deepened when they walked the few blocks up Vermont to where they'd parked and discovered his car was gone.

Sheilah comforted him, knowing he'd grown fond of the old jalopy.

"Probably just college kids," he said, feigning equanimity, and held to that bland assumption even after, a week later, the police found it in Tijuana, missing its tires.

He'd gotten the call just before lunch, and because it was Friday and the impound lot closed at five, he had to either leave now or wait till Monday. He had to grab his passport, and money to pay the Tijuana PD for storing it—*la mordida*. On the phone Sheilah dithered, asking if Bogie couldn't drive him, but Bogie was away on location.

If she was busy, he could just take the bus down. It might take a little longer with all the stops.

"It will," she said vaguely, as if she were still debating, then relented.

She picked him up at the front gate, waited in the car while he ran into the Garden and the bank. She'd had to cancel an interview. To make up for inconveniencing her, he treated their race for the border as a mad adventure rather than the unhappy errand it was.

"I haven't been down Meh-hee-co way in ten years, I bet." He flipped through his passport. He'd forgotten their last trip to Bermuda, mercifully. Otherwise the stamps ended six years ago, when he'd given up on the clinic in Zurich and brought Zelda and Scottie back on the *Aquitania*. The pages before that testified to the restlessness of a generation, cataloging their jaunts to Nice and Capri and Biskra. It seemed impossible that he hadn't been abroad since then, yet here was proof. Ernest was right: he'd wasted so much time.

"Well?"

"It doesn't go back that far."

In his picture he was thinner, light-haired and high-cheeked with a wolfish smile, radiating the confidence of the lucky. He didn't recall for which trip it had been taken, but from the watery shine in his eyes he appeared to be tight. He was torn between feeling embarrassed but also sorry for this vain, unserious man, ill-prepared for what awaited him.

"It's true what the natives say. Every time someone takes your picture, the camera steals a little bit of your soul."

"That explains Bette Davis."

"What's yours look like?" he asked, wondering what story the stamps on hers told.

"My soul?"

"I'm sure you look stunning."

"It doesn't even look like me."

"Let me see."

"No."

"Come on, don't be shy now."

"Stop, I'm trying to drive."

It took him a minute to understand why she was so adamant. She was afraid he'd see her real age. There was no way to tell her he already suspected, or that it wasn't uncommon, so he let it go, tuning in a Mexican station and swaying to a swoony accordion.

At the border he wasn't surprised when she received her passport back from the clerk and, covering half of it with a hand, held it out to show him her picture. He didn't try to take it, just complimented the younger, unsmiling version of her and let her slip it into her purse.

After a frustrating half-hour circling the dusty town, they found the lot, paid the clerk a storage fee and bought a used set of tires the yard mechanic offered to mount for another five dollars while they ate dinner at a cantina across the street.

"Think they do this to all the gringos?"

"It *was* rather convenient, having them right there."

"They're probably mine. It's the perfect set-up. Who are you going to complain to?"

It was dark by the time they finally got going. He gassed up and followed her back through the neon carnival of Tijuana, the sidewalks alive with zoot-suited touts trying to entice sailors into the clip joints. The mechanic had mounted the tires but not balanced them, and the car fought him like a stubborn horse, pulling to the right. After they made the border she drove fast, as if trying to lose him, her disembodied taillights floating out ahead of him, smaller and smaller, the black void of the ocean dropping off to the left. The carne asada had been too spicy; a hot bubble lodged in his chest, threatening, any minute, to burst. He pictured the highway patrol finding the car off the road, overturned, his body flopped out one window in the glare of a spotlight.

He tuned the radio to San Diego and, as if summoned, it appeared, its wide streets bright as a stage. His stomach settled, and his thoughts. He was turning melodramatic in middle age, like his mother, seeing death and disaster everywhere, when he should have been grateful. Even more important than getting his car back was the fact that Sheilah had begged off an assignment and spent half the day helping him without the slightest complaint. It had been so long since he'd had someone he could rely on that her generosity—her friendship—seemed a lavish gift, one he'd done little to deserve, and which, in the dark warmth of the Ford burrowing through the night, banished any lingering hesitancy. He wanted to catch her and declare himself right there by the roadside, to thank her, in the soberest way possible, for saving him.

This was the glowing coal he tended as they rolled up the coast and through the low beach towns and working suburbs and into the city itself, and by the time they reached Sunset and climbed the snaking road to her place, he'd convinced himself that the trip had brought them together in a way no evening of dinner and dancing could. So he was surprised to find, when he stepped inside, that her eyes were swollen from crying.

"What's wrong?" he asked, baffled, the eternal male.

"I can't do this anymore."

His first thought, as always, was Zelda. He was ready to plead for time and understanding, but Sheilah spun away from him and dug through her purse.

"Whatever it is . . ."

He didn't finish because she was holding out her passport to him as if it were a gun.

"You wanted to look at it, so look."

"It doesn't matter."

"It does," she said, pushing it at him. He fended her off but she was grimly insistent, and rather than let it drop to the floor, he took it.

The cover was bible black, with the rampant lion and unicorn in gilt.

"Whatever it is, it doesn't matter."

"Open it."

"Sheilah—"

"Please, Scott," she stopped him. "Just open it. After that, if you still want to speak to me, we can talk."

"If I still want to speak to you."

"I won't blame you if you don't."

"This is nonsense."

"You'll see, it's not."

The answer came to him, glaringly obvious: Donegall. They'd been secretly married this whole time.

She took a seat at the dining room table, turning her back as if to give him privacy. He sat on the couch where he normally read and opened the cover.

There she was, younger, with duller, flatter hair, facing the camera with the humorless rigidity of the accused.

Beneath her picture was her name—or no, there must have been a mistake, one of those clerical errors that changes a family's destiny. Instead of Sheilah Graham, it read: Lily Sheil.

He looked to her for an explanation.

"What is this?"

"That's my name," she said.

ROBINSON CRUSOE
IN MALIBU

Like everyone in Hollywood, she wasn't who she claimed to be. Sheilah Graham was a stage name she'd assumed at sixteen, when she made her West End debut—not in O'Casey or Shaw but the Brompton Follies. She was a dancer, meaning a chorine, decorating variety shows and musicals in scanty costumes. She had the ingenue's usual ambitions, but when she tried out for speaking roles, she was told her accent was suited only for chambermaids and ladies of the evening.

She hadn't come from money, as he'd so hopefully thought. She'd grown up in the East End, the youngest of six children. Her father died when she was just a baby—that was true. Her mother was from Kiev, a washerwoman who couldn't read or write. She took ill when Lily was six and sent her to live at the Jewish orphanage where they shaved her head the first of the month and paddled her with a hairbrush when she stole moldy biscuits from the kitchen. She stayed there till she was fourteen, old enough to go out and earn money to support the family.

They lived in Stepney Green then, in an alley behind a brewery. There was no Alicia, no Aunt Mary, no stepfather. Her stepbrothers were her brothers, only one of whom remained, Henry, an army deserter who slept on the sofa and suffered from night terrors. She had to share the one bedroom with her mother, in the early stages of the stomach cancer that would kill her, and guiltily missed the dorm at the orphanage.

She'd been presented at court—that photograph was real—but later, after her transformation. Before taking to the stage, she'd been a seamstress, a waitress, an assembly line worker in an Addressograph factory, a maid at a seaside hotel in Brighton, and, lastly, a salesgirl at a milliner's, where she'd been discovered by another dancer who, for a finder's fee, introduced her to the man who would become her manager. To make the leap from dancer to player, she paid for elocution lessons as if she were training to be a governess.

It worked. She started getting bit parts—secretaries and party guests. Her looks had always garnered attention, often the wrong kind. Now they made casting directors envision possibilities. She already knew how to move.

Her big break came in a manor-house farce called *Upson Downs*, playing the innocent young piano teacher aroused by the power of music to seduce her pupil. The role was supposed to be risqué, involving a brief striptease to Liszt's Hungarian Rhapsody no. 3. Each night when she took her bows she was surprised at the catcalls and bouquets. She'd shown more as a chorus girl.

She was singled out in reviews, her name in boldface. The papers ran flattering photos of her, attracting London's high-profile bachelors and not a few married men, among them a judge. Backstage, department store heirs and shipping magnates lined up to take her to the best restaurants, bearing roses and diamonds. Donegall wasn't the first nobleman she'd spurned. Every week brought a new proposal. Having scraped by her whole life, she enjoyed arriving in a Rolls-Royce and ordering the pheasant under glass. It was comical, her good fortune, unreal. She treated it like a dream that was bound to end, leaving her unchanged.

Despite their elevated stations, her suitors were not all gentlemen. Having matured early in a rough neighborhood, she had practice at discouraging advances, but several of her dates were shockingly ardent and then furious when she defended her honor. Once she was put out by the side of the road like a common tart. Another time she had to bite a lord who refused to let go of her breast.

Most, though, only wanted to be seen with her, her beauty an accessory to their vanity, and after *Upson Downs* closed and the papers chose the next fresh face, the rush subsided. She signed to do another racy part for more money, but at the last minute the backers pulled out and the show folded. Her next show was a flop. She'd been right about her fame being short-lived. She kept working, but instead of a queue of millionaires waiting backstage, some nights there was no one. It was then, after a poorly attended matinee, that she met Major John Gillam.

He was decades older than her, a dashing war hero injured at Gallipoli, tall and dark with a pencil mustache and a slight limp. Unlike her other suitors, he didn't insist that she quit. She skipped their courtship, mentioning only that he was funny and gentle, arriving too soon, as Scott dreaded, at their marriage.

Gillam came from military royalty, a line of generals going back to the first graduating class at Sandhurst. His injuries ended his career, leaving him dependent on morphine and the family fortune, both of which warped and unmanned him. In the world of business he was defenseless, always chasing the bold stroke. His few conjugal ventures with her failed as well, their marriage a union in name only. At the same time he was presenting her at court as the model of English womanhood, he was encouraging her to see other men, an edict she resisted on principle, but she was eighteen and life in the theater was ripe. Looking back, she could see they had used each other badly.

She related all this in bed, in the dark, her head on his chest, alternately repentant and incredulous, as if she couldn't believe this Dickensian past was hers. She'd never told anyone her story before. It was one reason she'd called things off with Donegall, the fear she'd be found out. Scott lay pinioned beneath her, absorbing the onslaught of new information, weighing it for truth. He felt at once betrayed and vindicated. He knew she'd been hiding something. Now he knew the reason. It made sense, keeping her secrets from the rest of the world, but why did she have to protect them from him?

"You must think I'm an awful person."

"Not at all."

He said he understood. As a child he'd learned the need to conceal the family's true situation. Her striving reminded him of his Saturday mornings at Miss Van Arnum's and the sting of his classmates at Newman knowing he was on scholarship. She might have been describing his life. He remembered that first heady success, when the whole world wanted him, except, dreamy egotist he'd been, he'd thought it would last forever. He told her he didn't care that she'd been married, which was only partially true. The past was the past, there was nothing to be done about it. She was teary, relieved. All weekend they clung to each other as if they'd survived a sudden wrenching tragedy, staying in and making confused, desperate love, confiding smaller, less damning deceptions they could laugh at. It was only when he left her for work on Monday that he felt bereft, as if this were the end of them.

It was cloudy, and his office, like the entire building, was cold. Again, for no good reason, he reworked Paramore's dialogue, getting up from his desk and pacing, standing at the window and rubbing the back of his neck, searching the yards and porches for Mr. Ito. The streetlamps were hung with silver bells and gold stars made of wire and tinsel, and as he tried to picture the boulevard and red-car tracks smoothed over by snow as they would be in St. Paul, what came to him instead was the image of the teenaged Sheilah onstage, bare-shouldered and spotlit, the audience watching from the dark all men. He banished it, scowling, and shoved the armchair against the vent.

A blind woman with a long white cane was navigating the entrance of the drugstore when, behind him, the doorknob rattled. Wisely he'd locked it.

"Open up."

It was Mank. He'd never descended from the fourth floor to visit him before, and Scott figured it was bad news.

Mank shut the door, frowning as if unhappy to be kept waiting. He had Ernest's thick build, and the same bluff certainty, only more animated. With his chomped-on stogie and scuffed brogans, he resembled the owner of a traveling circus.

"Tracy's out—busted his appendix. He's fine, just laid up for a while. I got Mayer to give us Franchot Tone. I know, he's not perfect, but he's as close as we're going to get. We've got two weeks to rewrite it for him."

Two weeks meant four, meaning Scott wouldn't be going East for Christmas—another promise broken. And Tracy was the draw. Without him they had no box office, a fact *Variety* would trumpet from their front page.

"We're lucky," Mank said. "It could have happened in the middle of shooting."

"That's true."

"The good news is we like your work. I already told Eddie, but I wanted to tell you in person, we're picking you up for next year."

"That is good news. Thank you." Scott shook hands with him to seal the deal and saw him out.

He was surprised they'd decided to keep him, and grateful, after how little he'd accomplished these last six months. He'd have to write Zelda and Scottie and tell them he wasn't coming, but that would have to wait. First he needed to call Sheilah. If not an outright sign, the renewal was something to celebrate, reassuring, he hoped, for both of them.

She wasn't home, which meant nothing. She wasn't at her office either, and he set the phone down and slouched in his chair, the good news cooling, draining away. How easily she'd fooled him, and how long. He wasn't so different from Donegall. She'd never intended to tell him the truth. She was only with him because he was married and there was no chance of him asking her to change her life, when all along he'd felt terrible for not being able to make that exact promise.

All day he was prey to venomous thoughts, calling and calling until he was afraid something had happened. On his way home he drove by her place. Her car was gone, the drapes pulled. He thought, with the wild illogic of romantic comedies, that maybe she was waiting for him at his place, and raced home to an empty villa.

Obviously she was off doing her job, but the knowledge didn't appease him. She would be on some fledging Lothario's arm, posing for the shutterbugs like they were a couple while he sat home alone. Monday was a quiet night at the Garden, everyone recovering from the weekend. Bogie and Mayo were on location, so he ordered in from Schwab's and tried to distract himself with yesterday's paper, willing the phone at his elbow to ring, ready to pretend he was glad to hear her voice.

When it did, at half-past ten, it startled him. He waited three more rings to pick up, as if he were busy.

She apologized. She'd wanted to call him earlier, but at the last minute she'd been offered the chance to do the interview she'd had to cancel, and naturally she'd taken it, except she had to drive all the way up to San Simeon.

It took a second to register, and then didn't seem real. She'd stood up Marion Davies for him.

"Why didn't you tell me that on Friday? I would have understood."

"I wasn't allowed. It's all hush-hush until it runs. Anyway, it went long, and then they invited me to stay for dinner, and I couldn't honestly say no, could I? Marion's lovely but she does go on. It was very strange being there, with the servants hovering about. I felt like I was in Dracula's castle. You know she calls him the Chief—he thinks it's funny—but they were very nice, and the piece is going to be very good."

"I'll bet." He'd wanted to be hard and distant, but couldn't resist her excitement. He could picture it: little Lily Shiel sitting down to dinner with William Randolph Hearst. "Congratulations."

"Thank you. How was your day?"

"Metro renewed my contract, so you're stuck with me."

"That's wonderful. We'll have to go out and celebrate. I can't tomorrow, but Wednesday, definitely."

"What's tomorrow?"

"There's a big museum benefit at the Egyptian."

"I like the museum."

"I'm sorry, I wish I could take you."

"Who's your date?"

"Leslie Howard."

"I guess that's all right."

He told her about Tracy.

"I heard."

"It really is a small town."

"A small town full of busybodies."

"And you're the busiest."

"I try. Wednesday then."

"Wednesday," he said, and let her go.

After the weekend's hysterics, it nagged at him that they'd spoken so casually, as if nothing had changed. She was a completely different person, one she'd trusted him to meet only after he'd fallen for her outward image. Perhaps that was always true. It had been with Zelda, though in her case he'd fooled himself. Why was he drawn to complicated women, or were all women—all people, finally—complicated? He didn't think he was, particularly. He'd done everything he could to simplify his life, winnowing the confusion down to a room, a desk, a lamp. Pencil and paper.

After fretting for months over whether or not I will earn a blessed credit, he wrote, *Metro has decided I'm good enough to keep even without one. I'm glad for the vote of confidence and the opportunity to continue digging us out of debt, but it means I have to postpone our Christmas plans till mid-January at the earliest. We just replaced Spencer Tracy, whose appendix didn't like the script. I'm most sorry for Scottie, who I'd wanted to take to see the windows at Gimbel's and Macy's for old times' sake, and maybe stop in at the Plaza and see the tree. The Obers will be happy to have her, but I remember staying over in the dorms at Newman one Thanksgiving, and it's not a proper holiday. We'll have to do something special for her at Easter. If your mother isn't able to take you home for Christmas, maybe we can make a side trip to Montgomery next month. Dr. Carroll agrees that you should be visiting there regularly if that's where you ultimately want to be.*

When he was finished it was nearly midnight. He took his keys and walked by the quiet pool and down the drive of the main house and across Sunset to the mailbox outside of Schwab's, opening the weighted lid, then letting it clang shut. While everything he'd said was true, he felt duplicitous and cowardly, and coming back he searched the darkened windows for the accusing specter of Alla. There was nothing, just the stars, the palms, the black hedges flanking the paths. His footsteps echoed as if someone were following him, and when he reached his villa he locked the door.

The next night, as if to reassure him, Sheilah called him after her benefit. Leslie Howard had been a perfect gentleman.

"That's what I've heard."

"Stop."

"Was he a good dancer?"

"Not quite as good as Hemingway."

"What did you wear?"

They stayed on the phone, unable to say good night. Again, there was no mention of her revelations, and out of delicacy he didn't bring them up.

Wednesday they ditched Hollywood altogether and dined downtown, in the Palm Court of the Biltmore, a salon of mahogany, brass and marble favored by bankers and oilmen. He asked for a table next to the fountain in the center of the room. There, beside the plashing waters, they batted around plans for Christmas like newlyweds choosing a honeymoon.

Catalina would be too crowded, Santa Barbara too far. She was leaning toward Malibu, if she could arrange for the cottage. He wanted to go somewhere with no history, like the mountains. Wouldn't she rather have snow? They could rent a cabin on Lake Arrowhead or Big Bear and lounge by the fire.

"They're so damp, and there's nowhere to eat."

"Frank Case doesn't have a place up there too?"

Deliberately she set down her butter knife and fixed on him. "If you must know, I was there for a friend's wedding. I have witnesses if you need them. And if I *was* with someone, why should that matter?"

"It doesn't."

"Obviously it does."

He didn't want to argue in front of the other guests, and softly apologized. This was supposed to be a happy occasion.

He was used to scenes—screaming, glasses smashing—but she wasn't Zelda. She'd begun her newspaper career as a stringer, and had that scavenger's obdurate patience. She tacitly agreed with him not to ruin dinner, and was pleasant all the way through dessert, in the cloakroom letting him drape her fox stole over her shoulders. She waited until they were in the car, safely out of earshot.

"You cannot speak to me like that," she said before he could turn the key. "I will not stand for it."

He apologized again, hoping it was over.

"I knew I shouldn't have told you. I knew it would be too much."

"I'm glad you told me. You have to admit, it is a lot."

"You have no reason to be jealous."

"I'm not jealous because of that. I'm jealous because I'm a man and you're a beautiful woman. If I weren't jealous, there'd be something wrong with me."

"I meant what I said before. You need to think before you say things."

While he contritely agreed, privately he thought the fault lay somewhere between them, both being overly sensitive on the topic.

The evening was supposed to be a celebration, but as they wound into the hills above Sunset, she announced that she had an early call tomorrow. He escorted her to her door and kissed her goodnight, waited for the outside light to go off, then walked back to the car, poring over what had gone wrong. He should have said that in a way he liked her better now. As a midwesterner, and one himself, he had a deep-seated reverence for the self-made.

If, as he thought, she was punishing him for his lack of faith, then what was she rewarding him for Saturday morning, when she came to him pink and warm from the shower? Apology or reconciliation, it didn't approach the sad abandon of the previous weekend. There was a languorous playfulness to her, laughing when the pillow half eclipsed her face, and again he wondered what had changed, if anything, or was this her way of saying they'd passed through the worst unscathed?

He wasn't a strong man. He could never deny a woman anything. Against his better instincts, he agreed to Christmas in Malibu.

He'd spent Christmas far from home most of his life. Part of celebrating the holidays in Paris or Rome or the North Shore of Long Island was the melancholy casting back to his wide-eyed boyhood, the snowbanks piled high along Summit Avenue, the chilly cathedral redolent with freshly cut pine boughs and smoking tapers, or later, coming home from Newman with his fellow boarders, taking the night train up from Chicago, the snow streaking through the blackness outside like comets. Christmas was candles on the mantel, and his father carving the goose his Grandmother McQuillan had bought, and his mother asking him to say grace—the same simple rituals performed the world over and all the sweeter now that they were gone, except here in the thin desert air with the bougainvillea blooming, that quaint candlelit past seemed impossibly far away, as if it had never happened.

He was getting old, yes, but it wasn't sheer nostalgia. Like its motley architecture, the city's traditions were borrowed, and in many cases the transplants hadn't taken. Winding strings of lights around the trunks of palm trees and trimming every roadside orange juice and hot dog stand with shimmering tinsel icicles didn't make them any more festive. On the shadowless street corners of Beverly Hills, holy-roller bell ringers and dime-store Santas and scarf-wearing carolers sweltered, pestering tourists in shirtsleeves for a holiday that felt months off. His distrust was natural, ingrained. His skin told him it wasn't the right season—the sun was too close.

I was sorry to hear about your car, Zelda wrote, *and glad you have*

it back from those enterprising Mexicans. Congratulations on being re-
newed, though it is a shame you and Scottina can't be here for Christmas.
The great hall is done up in Venetian red and gold and there are flocks of
cotton ball angels made by the schoolchildren who visited and put on a
lovely concert. I have a chance to go to the Ringling Museum in Sarasota
next week and take a life study class if you think we can afford it. I hope
we can, because I really do need to improve my musculature. That could
be my present, if you like. Mama says she'd love to have me home for the
holidays as long as Sara is there to help. I said I can help, to which she
replied, Sara makes things easier. I wish I made things easier for her and
for you but I suppose we all have our lot in life, n'est-ce pas, Do-Do?
Mine right now is to keep busy and organize myself for the future rather
than despair of it ever arriving. I promise, all of this will be forgotten by
the time you arrive next month. Till then, I am yours, as always, grate-
fully.

Her writing was neat and even, and as he had since Mank told
him, he protested that it wasn't his fault he couldn't be with her. It
wasn't a lie, and yet it stung him, just as, later, he was ashamed of
shopping for her and Scottie's and Sheilah's presents all at the
same time.

Though technically she was Jewish, as Mrs. Gillam, Sheilah
had embraced the Nativity with the fervor of a convert, and insisted on a tree. In St. Paul he would have hopped in the car and
struck out for the country where a farmer sipping hot chocolate by
a bonfire would hand him a saw and point him toward a field of
blue spruce and Norwegian firs loaded with snow. Here they
drove to a used-car lot on Pico and chose from a few drooping
specimens lined up against a fence like prisoners while a loud-
speaker hectored them with tinny carols. The salesman charged
him an extra fifty cents to wrap the tree in burlap and lash it to the
roof of the Ford, and then, on Ocean Boulevard, as Scott braked for
a light, it slipped its bonds, sailed free like a torpedo or a body
prepared for burial at sea, banged off the hood and continued into
the intersection where it finally came to a stop. They saved it with
the help of an amused Okie who happened to have a length of
clothesline among the water bags hanging off his Model A, but not

before a brief panic seized Scott, hardening to a bitter resentment of the tree and the reason they needed one in the first place. When they finally got it to the cottage, she wanted it not inside by the fireplace but out on the patio, centered in the picture window overlooking the ocean, as if she'd done this before.

They combed the wrack for a suitable starfish. He stretched to fix it on top.

"Is that it?" he asked.

"For now. Isn't it perfection?"

Metro's Christmas party further confounded him, a daylong, lotwide bacchanal sponsored by his Jewish bosses from which they were conspicuously absent.

"No one loves Main Street more than L.B.," Dottie explained.

"Therefore," Alan said, "L.B. loves Christmas."

"I love Christmas," Dottie said. "It's Main Street I hate."

"And L.B."

"And L.B." She and Alan clinked glasses.

Even though his contract had been extended, Scott abstained, making the day that much stranger. The studio was an open house, stars and carpenters and secretaries mingling freely, the commissary turned into a dancehall. The projection rooms, normally reserved for the producers' more serious deliberations, played stag films from someone's private collection to hooting standing-room crowds bombed on eggnog. Couples necked in stairwells, and from locked offices came tender and profane urgings. The elevator in the Iron Lung stank of reefer. When he left, Oppy was perched like a jockey astride the lion that guarded the front steps.

Scott offered him a ride, but he declined. "The night is young. Listen, can you spare a pal a fiver? I'm a little short."

Though he knew better, Scott did.

Driving away, instead of relief he felt adrift, and wished he'd stayed. Through all of their problems, he'd managed to be with Zelda and Scottie for the holidays, even if it meant eating Christmas dinner in the hospital cafeteria, and as he tooled up the coast highway into the blinding sun, leaving the city behind, he was certain he was making a mistake.

Sheilah was waiting for him in an apron, her hair tucked under a scarf. She was baking a pumpkin pie, and the cottage was warm with its scent. She'd cleaned, and set out cut flowers, and he thought he should have gotten her roses. When he offered to take her to the Inn tomorrow, she showed him the stocked icebox. They had everything they needed right here.

Before she started dinner, they pulled on their sweaters and took in the sunset, strolling hand in hand past the shuttered fishing shacks and battened-down compounds. The sky was the color of sherry, gulls straggling home. She seemed pleased the beach was all theirs, as if she'd planned it.

"We'll see how long that lasts," she said, since tomorrow was Christmas Eve.

Dinner was lamb chops, potatoes Lyonnaise and green beans with slivered almonds. From this one meal, he conceded she was a more accomplished chef than Zelda, though that wasn't hard. What touched him was the amount of preparation. She must have been working all afternoon. Afterward, like a dutiful husband, he did the dishes. Once the sun was down, a chill set in, and he laid a fire, the two of them snuggling on the loveseat, each reading a book, the picture of domesticity. The logs hissed and snapped, sending up sparks. He marked the quiet, broken only by the crash of the occasional wave, the approach of a car on the highway.

The pie was too much. By nine he couldn't keep his eyes open. She showed him where they were sleeping, and after the insult of the freezing bathroom, they leapt into bed, clutching each other for warmth under the covers.

In the morning he was surprised he'd slept the night. The sea was flat, the light so precise he could make out the Greek flag on a freighter headed for port. The beach was empty in both directions. They wandered along, filling a pail with crabs and sand dollars and garlands of seaweed for the tree. She'd borrowed his sweater, far too large for her, and flitted around him like a child, batting at him with the empty sleeves and laughing, making him chase her. He caught her, kissed her, took her hand again and walked on. The same quiet reigned during the day, and for a moment, strolling barefoot beside her with the water glittering and the sun on his face, he thought how fateful it was that they'd washed up on this gilded shore, two refugees fleeing their beginnings. He could picture them living here, shipwrecked on their own private desert island. It was an idle wish, and a selfish one, to be rid of the world, and yet, as with any daydream, there was some truth to it. Whoever she was, he wanted her, as he wanted these peaceful days to last, and this new life, impossibly, to be his.

EASTER, 1928

She understood that he had to go back East once the script was turned in. It was harder after spending Christmas together. They shared a strained fatalism, never discussing the situation at length, or his itinerary there, only when he would be leaving. She seemed to accept the trip in the same spirit he presented it, as an unhappy yet necessary task, knowing he'd be back in two weeks, and then when Mank finally gave him the okay, she sulked, as was her right. He could only sympathize, he had no basis for complaint. The night before he left, they said good-bye gravely, as if he were going to war. He went back to the Garden and slept alone and in the morning drove himself to the airport.

He didn't like to fly—the noise and vibration gave him a headache—but, as with anything new, he was excited by the strangeness of it. The disjuncture intrigued him: stepping through a door in one place, sitting still for a few hours, then stepping out a thousand miles away. It seemed to him a very American mode of travel, even more so than the car, not simply going farther faster, but eliminating any temporal experience of the journey, skipping over whole sections of the country, the sole focus on arriving, with

the help of expensive and arcane technologies, at one's destin-
ation, except, of course, when one didn't—a thought brought on by
his own instinctive disbelief and the bumpiness of the flight. He
liked the idea of a plane crash, being indicative of the times, for a
third act climax. Like Icarus, his producer would dare the sun
and, like all men, fall. The forces joined against him were medi-
ocre but legion—that was the tragedy of Hollywood. His man, like
Thalberg, would be the last lion, feared, fawned upon and ultimately run to ground by dogs.

They stopped to refuel in Memphis, where it was dingy and
drizzling. The airport was a low brick garage with plate glass windows facing the tarmac. The time change almost fooled him.
Though it was dark as night outside, it was only three. He was
tempted by the bar but held off, smoking and sipping a Coke,
watching the drops dimple the puddles. As he searched his memory for that line of Byron about the world set shivering on a leaf,
beyond the trees a fissure of white light split the sky, illuminating
the clouds. A bolt exploded close by, making the lights blink and
the whole place go *oooo* like a roomful of schoolchildren. A gust
pushed at the window, followed by waves of rain. The front they'd
leapfrogged had caught up with them. An announcement confirmed his suspicions: they were stuck there till it passed.

The boredom of provincial airports, the same as train stations.
The delay made him late getting into Asheville, and by the time
he'd hired a car and driven out to Tryon it was past visiting hours.
He'd called Dr. Carroll to let him know, but worried that Zelda
might be upset. The smallest disappointment could trigger her.

Already there'd been a misunderstanding over the moccasins
she wanted to replace her old pair. They were light as toe shoes and
fur-lined, perfect for the open ward, which could be chilly this
time of year. She wanted real ones, hand-crafted by the Navajo,
decorated with beadwork. In her letter she'd asked him to get off
the train in Tucson and buy her some, though he'd specifically told
her he was flying. To placate her he'd sought out a suitable pair in
the souvenir shops along Hollywood Boulevard, probably made in
Japan. With her, any gift was precarious; this one, being a patent

fraud on two counts, seemed even more fraught. The trouble, as always, was divining her state of mind.

His rooms at the old hotel were available at winter rates, but he only needed a single. The clerk wasn't surprised he was staying just the night, and he wondered if, like a flagellant, he carried a visible mark of his suffering. Brushing his teeth, he thought he was different from the man who'd lived here, or was that vanity? Nights on the verandah, nights at the Garden, nights on the Cote d'Azur. At least he was consistent in his dissipation.

The next morning, before they could be reunited, Dr. Carroll ushered him into his office for a progress report. Though across her stay at Highland Zelda's behavior had fluctuated wildly— from catatonic to attacking her nurses—the doctor spoke as if, thanks to her new regimen, she was steadily getting better. She'd had only the one episode all fall, after coming back from Charleston, and she'd enjoyed their trip to Sarasota.

"It will be interesting to see how she does in Montgomery," the doctor said. "That's going to be the test."

First they had to make it through Miami, Scott thought, but didn't contradict him.

"I know you and Mrs. Sayre have had your differences."

Mrs. Sayre was an indulgent old busybody whose children tended to kill themselves.

"In the end I think we want the same thing," Scott said. "We just disagree on the timing. After the last time I want to be certain she's ready. If you think she is, I trust your judgment."

"I wouldn't say we're anywhere close to that. This is more of a dry run. I'm hoping she'll feel comfortable there, so we want as little tension as possible."

What gall, to admonish him on that woman's word.

"I'll do my part," Scott promised, leaving the rest unsaid.

In the lobby, yet another version of Zelda stood beside her bags, hat in hand, as if waiting for a bus. She was thinner, in someone else's drab hand-me-downs, her bangs razor-straight. When she smiled he saw her front tooth had been fixed. It had been five months, and he wanted to apologize, again, for leaving her here.

As they embraced, he was seized by the irrational fear that he smelled of Sheilah's perfume.

"Merry Christmas, darling," she said, confusing him for an instant.

"And a Happy New Year."

"Look at you, you're brown as a bear. Your hair's so light." She reached up and touched it as if it might not be real.

"It's the sun. Your new tooth looks good."

"You like it?" She bared her gums, turning her head so he could inspect the dentist's work. Close-up, the crown stood out, a whiter white.

"It's very nice."

"I wanted to look beautiful for you."

"You do."

"I'm so glad you could come."

"I'm sorry I couldn't be here for Christmas."

Was everything he said a lie? Because he could see himself on the beach with Sheilah, their seashell tree. There was a ring of Hell for the deceitful. Maybe this was it, eternally returning to find her waiting for him, still hopeful.

Walking them to the car, the doctor went over her medications like a referee explaining the rules to two fighters. He had an extra copy of her prescriptions for Scott. After all the talk of clean living, he was shocked at the number. Besides the Seconal, which he recognized from his own medicine cabinet, the rest were new to him, most likely tranquilizers. He wondered if she was doped up right now.

"Have fun," the doctor instructed, waving them away.

"We will," she said.

In another time they would have, flying down to Miami and staying at the Biltmore with the hoi polloi. In their flaming years they'd played a drunken round of golf with Babe Ruth there, and skinny-dipped in the huge pool modeled after the Roman baths, dressing the terrace statuary in their underwear. Now the grandeur of the place only reminded him how much he was paying a night. They swam and played golf and woke up early one morning to go deep-sea fishing, and dined each evening in the grand salon, but he could not imagine a less restful vacation.

The doctor was right, she was agreeable, even sweet, but spending every minute with her was grueling. For their belated Christmas she gave him a self-portrait, cat-eyed and high-cheeked in the flowing gold raiment of a high priestess, portentously holding up three fingers. He summoned a surprised delight even as he mulled where he would hide it in his villa. She gushed over the moccasins, but she gushed over the room-service eggs, and the parakeets in the lobby, and the croquet pitch, like someone slightly tight. The world was "perfect," and "lovely," and "divine." He thought she was just happy to be free, to be with him again. She'd always had a theatrical personality, and naturally wanted to put the best face on their time together, as if that might win him back, but such saccharine enthusiasm was too much. He viewed her effusiveness as an unsubtle act, expecting at some point she would break character, reverting to her true, troubled self. Her cheeriness was relentless, inhuman. As his patience waned, he began to think it might be a trick of his imagination, fueled by guilt. No matter how well she behaved, he would find fault with her.

They were playing tennis one morning when he realized she wasn't acting. She was better than he was, and viciously competitive. As a girl, one of her favorite pastimes was beating the boys in front of the whole country club. She regularly trounced him, but today he was beating her easily, calling out encouragement as she shambled after his volleys. As she ranged to her right to return an easy forehand, her feet got tangled up as she swung, and she fell, rolling on her shoulder as the ball dropped into the net.

"Are you okay?"

"Nice one," she called, brushing herself off. Her right side was a giant grass stain.

"Are you sure?"

"I'm fine. Thirty-love."

It wasn't until they switched sides that he saw her chin was brushburned, a raspberry patch beaded with blood.

"You're hurt."

She touched a finger to it and laughed as if it were a joke.

"It looks like it stings."

"It does a little."

She seemed more amused than concerned, and as the week wore on, he noticed that was her reaction to everything. A dolphin leaping free of the water, a pat of butter falling on the tablecloth—she regarded both with the same dazed appreciation. The drugs she was taking made her imperturbable, and he wondered if this wasn't Dr. Carroll's way of inoculating her against the world. He couldn't imagine anything that would make her mother happier.

They swam, they ate, they danced. It was all a pantomime at three-quarter speed. At bedtime they took their pills and lay down separately. She didn't bother him like she used to, and lying awake listening to her sleep, he thought he should be grateful. She was thoroughly pleasant, asking nothing of him but his company. Any other visit he would have been relieved, so why did he picture himself creeping to the bathroom and flushing her pills? Why not his too?

In the morning she dabbed cover-up on her chin so it wouldn't look as if he'd hit her, only to break the scab with her napkin at breakfast. She smiled at him, the blood oozing through like yolk. He called the waiter and paid.

The whole thing was grim, and yet as their time there narrowed, he wished they could stay. Mrs. Sayre would have her way in the end, he had no doubt. Eventually Zelda would go home. It was his wish too, for lack of a happier solution. Long ago they'd both abdicated their deepest responsibilities to each other, leaving this empty vestige. His hope now was that she could live a quiet life surrounded by the people she loved. That could only happen in Montgomery, and still, helping her onto the plane, he felt he was delivering her to her fate.

Her cousin Sara was waiting for them at the airport with their driver Freeman in threadbare livery. While two of Zelda's three sisters lived here, they had their own families, and she, having no one, had been appointed Mrs. Sayre's lieutenant. She was a religious woman with a concave body and long face that betrayed an exhausted disappointment in the world. She embraced Zelda and inspected her chin, flicking him a critical look, then took her hand as if she might run away. Scott helped the driver with their bags, though the man implored him, "Please, sir, let me." Outside, watched over by a cop, sat Judge Sayre's magnificent old LaSalle, the nickel hood ornament and grille glinting, the work, most certainly, of the chauffeur. As a legacy, the car went unloved by the Sayre women. He'd been dead seven years and none of them drove.

Sara sat Zelda in the middle—again, as if she might break loose—and the driver pointed the LaSalle for town. The land was flat out here and worked hard, the fields for cotton, the piney woods lumber and turpentine. Scott remembered the red dust that blew into their tents at Camp Sheridan, giving their bedrolls a rusty tint. It had been some sharecropper's farm, sold from beneath him to the war department for a fortune, the barracks and mess hastily improvised. The spring rains turned the earth into a chili-colored muck, and in the summer there wasn't a single shade tree to escape the heat, but they were young and beguiled by a violent glamour. At the same time they groused about camp life, they lorded themselves over the locals. Friday nights, hair carefully watered, they took the bus along this very road at dusk, invading the movie houses and soda fountains in search of girls, plundering the town as it emptied their pockets. It was then he found her, that heroic summer when they were all going to march onto ships. Instead the war ended, broke off like a failed romance, leaving them unblooded and ashamed of their thwarted desires. Years later, when she was recovering from her first bad spell, they retreated here, taking a house near her parents, and one warm spring day he drove out and tramped the muddy fields, trying to find any remnant of the company streets and rolled square of the parade ground, but the earth had been turned too many times and he couldn't be sure this was the right place anyway, and he conceded it was fitting that his near-glorious past had been plowed under, as lost to history as the tents of the Spartans or Napoleon's armies.

"I do love that old barn," Zelda said of a bleached, leaning relic.

Sara tutted. "Mr. Connor would never let things go like that."

"Is Tad still at the mill?"

"He's run off to Mobile again. It's a shame. No one knows what's going on with him."

"And he can be such a dear."

They nattered on, Zelda mimicking Sara's sleepy lilt, drawing out her vowels into diphthongs, becoming, as they neared town, more and more the belle. She delighted in gossip, though by tomorrow—perhaps tonight—her arrival would be the hot item, traded across dinner tables and in the better restaurants. Locally she was held up as a cautionary example, her fall the price of her earlier notoriety. He'd seen children ride by the house, pointing and making cross-eyed faces. Once, outside the Grand Theatre, a gang tricked a slow boy of ten or so to shout "Bryce" at her, that being the name of the state hospital in Tuscaloosa. Scott had chased the boy down to teach him a lesson, dragging him back by the collar, only to have Zelda comfort the crying child.

Ahead, the dome of the Capitol rose over the city like a medieval cathedral, the seat of power and privilege. A faithful servant of the law, the judge and his family lived in its shadow, along the elm-lined, aptly named Pleasant Avenue. The houses on her block weren't antebellum mansions boasting porticoes and slave quarters but the same stolid turn of the century brick piles he knew from St. Paul, with four chimneys, wraparound porches and maids' rooms tucked under the eaves, as if the designers of that era had signed a convention. The Sayres', when he'd first seen it, recalled his Grandmother McQuillan's, down to the stained-glass window on the stair landing, which he associated with old money and the antique majesty of the church. They shared an air of permanence at once easeful and suffocating. In a house like that nothing ever changed, and while the judge was patient with her, if vague, and her mother doting, Scott understood why Zelda was wild to get out. Leaving her there would be sentencing her to the dead past.

The house, now, as the LaSalle slowed for the drive, looked the same, the barbered lawn and box hedges, the white-pillared porch.

She leaned across him, dipping her head to check the upstairs windows. The last time she was home was over a year ago, the summer before last, for her birthday. By the end of the visit she'd stopped talking, spending all of her time in the garden, wearing her father's old straw boater and filling her present of a sketchpad with messy studies of flowers her mother cooed over, saying she'd love a framed one for her birthday.

The car stopped. She'd gone quiet, after all the chatter, and when he offered his hand, she took it. Sara was already out. Still, she didn't move.

"Ready?" he asked.

"I am," she said, nodding as if to convince herself.

Flanking the steps were leftover poinsettias, and a pinecone wreath adorned the front door, which opened before the driver could get it for them.

Leaning on her cane, Mrs. Sayre tottered out, a knit shawl draped over her shapeless housedress. She'd had Zelda late in life, and by the time Scott met her, her face bore only the slightest resemblance around the mouth. Since the judge had died, she'd become frowzy and heavyset, her cheeks gray with liver spots, eyelids sprigged with moles, a state his own mother didn't live long enough to attain. With her bifocals and rat's nest of ashen hair she would have seemed a pitiable opponent if he didn't know how expert she was at wielding her helplessness.

"There's my baby," she said.

"Mama," Zelda said.

Mrs. Sayre closed her arms around her, pulling her to her bosom, rocking side to side. "I was afraid I'd never see the day." She said it for everyone to hear, a bad actress, and he wished he could get back in the car. "What in the world happened to your face?"

"It was my fault. We were playing tennis and I tripped over myself."

"I don't know why they have you playing such a dangerous game in the first place. I think they need to look after you better, that's what I think." She fixed on Scott as if she'd just noticed him standing there. "Thank you for going out of your way. You don't know how much we appreciate it."

It had been the plan all along, and the "we" was calculated, but he was a diplomat. "My pleasure."

"I wish Scottie could have come."

"Me too."

"How is the darling?"

"Very well. She sends her love."

The judge would have shaken his hand and ushered him inside, regaling him with the political intricacies of his latest case, but Mrs. Sayre held on to Zelda as if she were her nurse. He and Sara trailed them to the parlor, where a Christmas tree shimmering with tinsel stood by the fireplace. Hanging from the mantel were stockings embroidered with the names of the Sayre children. Even in death her brother Anthony was represented. Not Scott. Later, when they went upstairs to get settled, he discovered Freeman had installed him in Anthony's old room in the back hall, as if he were a lodger.

For Zelda's sake as well as his own, he resolved to absorb these slights with Christian largesse. When Mrs. Sayre held forth on how Zelda's old beaux were prospering, or brought up the debacle of her last trip to Baltimore, or told, as a joke, the story of Zelda running naked around the country club pool as a child, he reminded himself that in five days he would be in New York, lunching with Max and Ober.

The centerpiece of the visit was Christmas dinner with her sisters Rosalind and Marjorie and their families. As if he might redeem himself through good works, he volunteered for every chore and errand, riding around town in the front seat with Freeman, drawing stares until the man asked him, plaintively, if he wouldn't mind sitting in back. In chastised silence he watched the signs and storefronts scroll by. The city was hers, its soul inscrutable to a northerner. More than any place they'd lived, the streets were overlaid with memories, one past folded atop another. A trolley stop, a park bandstand, a Confederate field gun guarding a square—everywhere he went he was met with the empty stage sets of their courtship.

Though she was encouraged to revisit her favorite places, Zelda didn't go out. She scuffed around the house in her moccasins like a prisoner, playing casino with her mother and listening to the phonograph while Sara polished the silver. Her only job was to make the place cards, which her mother fawned over as if she were Picasso. She napped in the afternoon, on her narrow bed in her old room, decorated with the painted fans and paper roses of the war years. Her bookshelves were filled with nursery rhymes, her closet with frilly organdy dresses. Curled up with her face turned toward the wall, she might have been a girl again.

Anthony's room, too, belonged to another time, with his crusty baseball glove and tarnished diving trophies and stale cigar box of marbles. At night, alone in the cold bed, Scott fended off visions of his final minutes—the window and the long drop. In Saint-Raphael he'd had a nightmare in which he'd fallen off a cliff, or been pushed, going over backwards, flailing as if he might right himself. He and Zelda had been fighting, and their hotel balcony perched above the rocks, so it made sense. Still, every night he dreaded the sensation. He couldn't imagine it being a relief.

Not quite arbitrarily, Mrs. Sayre had chosen the twenty-fifth for Christmas. In the morning a fire blazed on the hearth and they watched Zelda spill her stocking out on the carpet. He made sure she'd taken her pills so there wouldn't be any problems, and felt like an accomplice. Along with the walnuts and oranges and candy canes, Santa had left her an expensive set of charcoal sticks. She held them up for all to see, smiling for the camera, and Scott, who hadn't been asked to contribute, was jealous. Sara gave her a sheer lilac scarf she knotted about her throat and wore for the rest of the day. From her mother she received a set of tea-rose silk pajamas and a chenille bedspread with matching hand-appliquéd pillowcases, and a gold charm bracelet, and a box of chocolate-covered cherries, and, lastly, carried in by Sara from its hiding place in the library, sporting only a red bow, a full-sized easel—none of which she would be allowed at Highland.

"That's for your studio when you come home," her mother explained. "I was thinking we might do something with the solarium."

"Thank you, Mama."

"Merry Christmas, Baby."

"Yes, thank you," Scott said. "That's overly generous."

"Don't think we've forgotten you." Her mother handed him a present the size of a book but lighter, rigid as glass beneath the silver wrapping paper.

"You haven't opened any of yours yet," he protested, but tore away the foil to reveal a framed picture of the judge and Mrs. Sayre, Zelda, Scottie and himself dressed for church with the LaSalle in the background. It might have been Easter: Zelda and her mother held lilies. Scottie, in a blinding white pinafore, barely came to his waist. It had to have been ten years ago, before the Crash, and struck him as a non sequitur. He had no idea why she was giving it to him now. "Thank you. It's very nice."

"Look on the back."

As if captioning the picture for posterity, she'd listed their names and *Easter, 1928.*

"That was the last time we were all together for a holiday."

Was the implication that this was his fault, or was it a general lament? There was nothing he could say to rebut her, so he showed it to Zelda.

"Look how darling Scottie was," she said.

"She's still darling."

"You know what I mean."

"I know." He was being oversensitive, reflexively. He would always defend Scottie from her, as he did his best to protect her from her mother.

"Thank you again," he said, and when they were done, put it upstairs with Zelda's self-portrait.

The day was given over to the production of dinner, which consisted of Mrs. Sayre sending Sara in to check on Melinda the cook every fifteen minutes. Following a longstanding tradition, they were having goose. By midafternoon, when Zelda went up for her nap, the fat was crackling in the pan and the whole house smelled richly, recalling the holidays at his grandmother's. Mrs. Sayre worried that they'd put the bird in too early, but, as with most of her fears, it was a way of making people obey her, and nothing came of it.

The sisters and the branches of their respective families arrived all at once, as if they'd caravanned together. The judge and Mrs. Sayre had had Zelda so late in life that most of her nieces and nephews were older than her. While Mrs. Sayre presided from her rocker, their children gathered in a ring around the tree while Zelda played Santa's elf, doling out presents. Scott stood back between his brothers-in-law, with whom, over the years, he'd been summarily paired at garden parties and golf outings. As the two nursed their bourbons, Scott sipped his ginger ale. Usually they talked football, but the season was over. They were both lawyers who worked at the Capitol, sound, calculating men more interested in what was happening down the corridor than in Europe, but the menace had grown impossible to ignore. Country by country, strike by strike, the Communists were undermining the system. He thought of Dottie and Ernest, conjuring their arguments, but there was no point here, and soon enough the talk turned to Hollywood, which, having never been, they saw as a charmed and glamorous fairyland. They asked him the same questions everyone did, as if, between briefs, they read the scandal sheets: Was Gable shorter in person? Did Garbo really not speak to anyone off the set?

"Garbo's actually very smart," he told them, and spun a yarn about her knowing six languages and walking in on her talking with an Armenian tailor in Metro's wardrobe department in his native tongue. It was a naked fabrication, for their sake. While he'd never met her, he knew, as Photoplay did, that they wanted him not to dispel but to deepen the mystique.

The children weren't interested in the adults' gifts, and Mrs. Sayre sent them off to the library with Sara. Zelda started to follow, till her mother called her back. He was afraid they'd have a repeat of the morning, but her sisters' presents were practical—a

camel sweater, wool socks, a pack of linen handkerchiefs. Scott
had gotten them French perfume and golf balls and, on Freeman's
recommendation, their favorite pralines, accepting in return a
leather-bound journal and monogrammed pen and pencil set he
coveted on sight.

Dinner went equally well. To Mrs. Sayre's surprise, the goose
was perfectly juicy. Along with the teetotaling Sara, he and Zelda
refrained from the champagne punch, while the rest of the adult
table gradually dissolved into a sloppy jollity. He hadn't wanted to
come, but as Zelda laughed along with everyone and the candles
cast their wavering shadows across the walls, he was glad he could
give her a real Christmas.

A grateful guest, he made the mistake, the next day, of seeking
out her mother and thanking her for inviting them. The whole
time he'd pointedly avoided being alone with her, knowing she'd
use the opportunity to plead her case, but it was their last day, and
while part of him wanted to make a clean escape, he needed to
offer her that courtesy. They sat on opposite sides of the fireplace,
she ensconced in her rocker, he on a low ottoman, a peasant attending a dowager queen.

"I have to say there's a world of difference," she said. "I can't
remember her ever doing so well."

"That's the effect of the medication."

"It's working."

"She doesn't seem subdued to you?"

"She seems happy. It's been an absolute treat having her."

"I'd like to see how she does with a lower dosage."

"I thought you'd be thrilled, after the last time."

"I want her to be well but also to be herself."

"She's more herself than she's been in ages. She's been wonderful company, that's what I'm going to tell Dr. Carroll."

"That's fair."

"I think this is progress."

Rather than quarrel with her, he strategically retreated. In
their own ways they both wanted the best for Zelda, and yet discussing her fate with her mother seemed a betrayal, partly because

she seemed less interested in Zelda's well-being than in possessing her again. His position was just as entrenched, based as it was on resentment, if not outright dislike. As long as she was sick, he was convinced that if he let her go home she would never get better. But, as her mother in her Pollyanna optimism couldn't bring herself to argue, if she was never going to get better, wouldn't she be happier at home?

That night he helped Zelda pack her bags, and the next morning lugged them down the stairs and outside over Freeman's protests. He expected a teary parting scene, but after her pills she was bemused, leaving her mother wet-eyed and sniffling on the porch, waving her cane as they backed away. In the LaSalle, she watched the fields roll by without comment, slouched against him as if she were tired. The bumpy flight over the Smokies didn't faze her, or the winding drive up the mountain. They might have been going anywhere.

"Oh, too bad," she said, looking out at the rhododendron. "The snow's all gone."

"I thought you didn't like snow."

"I like it here. It reminds me of Switzerland."

The old places, she meant, Gstaad and St. Moritz, not the clinic with its caged staircase and white-tiled baths. Why was the past so keenly double-edged, or was it the present, being middling and empty? He tried not to think of Sheilah, of his life waiting in L.A.

"If I can get the time off, I'd like us to spend Easter together—you, me and Scottie. We could try Virginia Beach again."

"That would be nice."

"I'll ask Dr. Carroll."

Whether it was possible or not, he'd wanted to promise her something, as if that might make up for him leaving. He signed her in at the front desk, held her a moment, then stood beside her until a nurse arrived to escort her back to the ward.

"Good-bye, Dodo. Merry Christmas."

"Merry Christmas," he said, and, watching her go, wished he were taking her pills.

Mrs. Sayre had already talked with the doctor, calling, apparently, while they were in the air. "It sounds like the visit was a great success."

"Not exactly," Scott said, and described how, as the trip went on, Zelda grew more and more inward.

The doctor nodded as if this was normal. They could step down the dosage and see how she responded, though, as with any inhibitor, that would limit its effectiveness.

"But overall," the doctor said, "it went well?"

He agreed, grudgingly. It was only the next day, in freezing New York, after seeing Max and Ober and stopping in at several of his old haunts on Third Avenue to warm up, that he realized what he should have said. "Fuck you," he told the bar at large, repeating it with amused and grandiose satisfaction, and then he was out in the street, swinging and being hit in the face, tasting blood. It felt good to fight—it felt true, as if he'd made the right choice, though now it seemed he had several opponents and they were laughing, pushing him around a closed circle, taking turns. Even as he fell, he stuck to his answer.

INFIDELITY

He hated coming home to an empty place, the still silence a reproof. The only mail was an overdue bill from the cleaners. He'd left the stove light on, and the milk in the fridge smelled. At least Bogie was back.

"I'm guessing your mother-in-law's a southpaw," he said, turning Scott's chin to examine the damage.

Mayo said she could put some concealer on his eye, and though there was no hiding his fat lip, he sat for her like an actor in makeup.

Sheilah was disappointed in him, as he knew she'd be, wincing in sympathy as she touched his face. Was it going to be like this every time he went East? She spoke as if there must be an end to it, a hope he'd long ago dismissed, and which, coming from her, seemed unearned and unfair, leading to a brittle stalemate. He didn't understand. In Alabama he'd daydreamed of seeing her; now his head ached. She had good news—her agent had arranged an audition for a syndicated radio show, a five minute spot each week—but the mood was ruined. He didn't tell her his plans for Easter, and she didn't invite him to stay the night. In a way he was glad.

To regain himself, he wrote. A storm front had blown ashore, blanketing the city, and the weather was perfect for it. Mornings he woke early and put in his hours at the kitchen table, the rain tapping the roof. For years they'd lived on his stories, but sometime during Zelda's troubles he'd lost the knack for those tales of young love the *Post* favored. His last few had appeared in *Collier's*, who paid half what the *Post* did, and *Esquire*, who paid even less. Ober might have set his sights lower, but Scott hadn't. He still believed he was as good as anyone out there, and when he turned a paragraph he'd been struggling with, he nodded with the satisfaction of a craftsman, lit another Raleigh and forged on.

At the studio he hid from Eddie till his lip healed, having lunch sent in and working late, trading last-ditch revisions with Paramore, who'd taken the opportunity while Scott was gone to rewrite the entire script. Every couple of hours new memos came down from upstairs. Couldn't Margaret Sullavan be in a wheelchair rather than a bed so the scene would have more action? Did the car have to be a Daimler? Why not a Ford? Next week they started shooting on Stage 11. The sets were already waiting.

"I don't know why you're wasting your time," Dottie said. "Mank's just going to change it anyway."

"I'd rather have him change my lines than that bastard's."

Alan tossed her a goggle-eyed double take. "You can't argue with that kind of logic."

"The Nazis are still the bad guys," she checked, and Scott remembered Ernest's warning.

"That's the one thing we agree on."

"Then you've done everything you can. Time to push it out of the nest."

"And lay another egg," Scott said.

"You've done this before," Alan said.

Turning in the script was anticlimactic. He gave his messy final draft pages to his secretary, who gave the typed pages to Paramore's secretary, who gave the script to Eddie, who gave it to Mank, who, several long days later, sent Scott a copy with an official Metro stamp declaring it APPROVED. His name still came first, but Paramore had completely changed the big hospital scene.

To protect his work, he needed to be on the set. He made his case to Eddie, but Mank didn't want either of them in his hair. There was no point complaining. He was getting a credit, his first in three visits, and on a prestige picture. It qualified as a triumph, except now he had nothing to do.

My Dearest Pie, he wrote. *I want to apologize for not making it up your way while I was in New York. I'd hoped to steal an afternoon and rescue you and Peaches from the horrors of the dining hall but got caught up in some nonsense in the city. Suffice to say I was overdrawn both physically and emotionally by then, and poor company. Your mother and I survived Miami and she was happy to be home. The doctor has her on a new medication meant to render her less excitable but which goes too far, I think. She was entirely pleasant yet entirely lacking the high spirits that make her the exceptional woman she is. My hope is that she will be more herself at Easter, and that you can join us then. Details to follow.*

As for your Latin, please stick it out. While it may seem a burden now, you'll discover it is indispensable, and the better schools will expect it. You have three months left. For all of our sakes, please apply yourself. You'll have the whole summer to loaf around. Think of June as a finish line. I wasn't joking about Europe. The way things are going this may be the last chance to visit there freely, and while we're not completely out of debt yet, I could happily see it as an investment. Everything, of course, depends on what you want.

Let me know your thoughts when you have a chance. Sometimes I feel I'm talking to the air out here.

He thought it was natural: after spending every minute with Zelda, he was lonely. Sheilah avoiding him as punishment only made it worse. The rainy season was upon them, mudslides cutting off the canyons. He had a story to work on, but woke up late, then wasted his days at the office dipping into Conrad and watching the wet hedges for Mr. Ito.

Bogie understood. Those empty stretches between jobs were the most dangerous.

"Idle hands," he said, toasting him and pinching Mayo.

It was true. As a boy, he'd always had some elaborate project that had nothing to do with school. On Summit Avenue, alone in his aerie, he drew the stately homes across the street and numbered the many windows and doors, compiling a detailed log of his neighbors' activities. In sixth grade, simultaneously, he kept a diary concerning the girls he liked and a ledger chronicling every penny he made and spent. These secret fascinations led nowhere in the end, were left mysteriously incomplete like the detective novel he patterned after Sherlock Holmes, to be replaced by his next obsession. At Princeton, when he was supposed to be cramming for exams, he wrote a musical. In the army it was a novel. Nothing had changed. He was still that boy, happiest pursuing some goose chase of his own making, and lost without one.

The temptation was to start his Hollywood book. He knew his producer; it was the business he needed to learn. All along, in his own disorganized fashion, he'd been taking notes. He had a good enough grasp of that world to begin, but he'd only be pulled off it anyway.

Joan Crawford saved him. She was nearing the end of her contract, and after flopping with *The Gorgeous Hussy*, she needed a hit. While she was the studio's top female star, over the years her range had narrowed. No longer the wide-eyed flapper or plucky shopgirl, she lacked the youth and softness to be a romantic lead. Now she specialized in playing the scorned woman in her own brand of weepies, enduring mortifications in the second act to reap a bittersweet revenge in the third. Eddie came down to give him the good news in person. Hunt Stromberg wanted Scott to adapt a *Cosmopolitan* story for her, a love triangle teasingly titled *Infidelity*.

"Sounds like typecasting to me," Dottie said, and for a shocked second he thought she meant him.

"She's the wife."

"So it's a fantasy," Alan said.

"She's slept with everyone at Metro except Lassie," Dottie said.

"You'll like Hunt," Alan said. "He's not like Mank. He doesn't think he's Shakespeare."

The story itself wasn't much. A rich businessman invites his beautiful secretary to dinner at his mansion while his wife is away in Europe. The next morning the wife returns early and surprises them at breakfast, and as the three of them calmly sit there, served by the faithful butler, the man knows his marriage is over and imagines the great mansion empty and echoing. From these two scenes Scott was supposed to come up with a whole picture.

He met with Stromberg that afternoon, not in an overpopulated conference room but privately, man-to-man, in Stromberg's office, a mahogany den lined with bookshelves. He was young, of a different generation than Mank and the others, gangly in tweed, the new junior professor. As Scott suspected, he'd read *Gatsby*. He pitched the picture to him as if Scott might say no.

"We want modern and adult but still warm. We need to feel sympathy for all three of them, that's the only way it works."

Scott wanted to say it was impossible with Joan Crawford, but nodded, jotting notes.

"The location's open, what line the husband's in, all that business. She doesn't have to be his secretary, she can be a scientist or a concert pianist, we just have to like her, or at least understand why she does what she does."

"Love," Scott offered.

"Kick it around. I've got Myrna Loy for the girl."

He couldn't think of a tougher combination. Somehow she had to be innocent—they all did, otherwise the audience would turn on them. In his experience, people in love were helpless, except, rather than pure of heart, it made them selfish, walled-off, so focused on their own happiness they'd let the rest of the world burn—a mistake he'd almost made with Lois Moran. He felt the same murderous indifference from Zelda that awful summer in Juan-les-Pins and recognized it in himself with Sheilah. How could he show that coldness overtaking the husband without making him despicable?

He was free to invent any solution, which in the beginning made the challenge harder, but also meant the script was all his. Working for Stromberg was a step up, everyone said, and Scott could see why. Where Mank pitted his writers against each other to get his way, Stromberg sat back and let him figure out how to tell the story.

The first thing he needed to figure out was how to use Joan Crawford. He studied her like a test subject, skipping lunch to sit in the flickering dark of Thalberg's old projection room with a Coke and a chipped ashtray, watching her arch her eyebrows and smirk her way through *Possessed* and *Chained* and *Forsaking All Others*, trying to discern her strengths. She had good cheekbones and her clothes showed off her figure, but she wasn't a natural actress. In her wronged women there was no depth, no shading. When she was supposed to be happy, she smiled too brightly; when betrayed, she raged like a harpy, coming off not just false but ridiculous. She was consistently mawkish and overwrought, with one interesting exception.

In every picture, for the bulk of the second act, she was asked to bear her heartbreak and carry on. Family and social standing lost, she was reduced to menial jobs to support herself. She clenched her jaw and wrung out laundry, did dishes, scrubbed floors, at first resentfully, but then, as she recovered herself, with an avidity and pride that struck him as genuine. This was why she was a star, not the maudlin hysterics. Beneath the sweeping, cantilevered gowns by Adrian, she was steely and practical. Her character would have to be strong, maybe stronger than her husband. Yes, and obviously stronger from the very beginning, a Lady Macbeth who drives him into the secretary's arms—but with nobler ambitions, a reformer or humanitarian.

"When they break up, she doesn't crumble," he told Stromberg. "He does. Then when he realizes what he's done, it's her decision to take him back or not—which works, since it's her picture. Her audience will understand either way."

"What about the secretary?"

"The secretary really does love him, she's just a kid. We have her play her a little wide-eyed, the small town girl with a big heart. It's tougher on her than anybody."

Stromberg mulled it, drawing on his pipe.

"How soon can you have a draft together?"

"Six weeks."

"You've got eight. Give me something good."

He would need them. By the end of the first week, all he had was his opening, a long shot of a wedding reception in the Waldorf's rooftop gardens, where he and Ginevra once danced under the stars. Through matching opera glasses, two older women in a neighboring building spy on the various couples, divining the state of their love lives. To distant music, panning, we get the candy figures atop the wedding cake, the newlyweds stepping out for their first dance, the proud parents clapping, a bridesmaid and her date strolling hand in hand among the rose beds, cherubs kissing atop a fountain, till we come to Crawford and her husband, off in the farthest part of the garden, the corner parapet, facing away from each other, looking down the dark canyons of Manhattan, lost in their separate thoughts. "Oh dear," one of the grannies says. "What happened to them?"

He liked the question, the way it set the stage, but then bogged down in false starts. The source material was so skimpy, it was like writing an original script. After wrestling with her profession for several days, he settled on her being a fashion designer, except he knew nothing of that world, and had to walk over to wardrobe and get filled in by one of the dressers.

He already had the wife and the husband, they were easy. The secretary was trickier, stuck in the middle, and as he had with Vivien Leigh in *A Yank at Oxford*, he based her on Sheilah.

They were back together after another campaign of poems and roses, another promise to stop, or at least try. He didn't dare say that on average he hadn't been this sober in years. Valentine's was coming up, an opportunity to redeem himself. He made reservations at the Cocoanut Grove and hit Bullock's for a new tux, taking a detour through the Women's section with his notebook open.

Bullock's, Schwab's, the Troc—everywhere he went he pictured Joan Crawford, imagined her character parsing the other women on the street. He began to pay attention to fabrics and hemlines, and to be dismayed at the epidemic of slacks.

One noontime, walking over to the commissary after working all morning, he ran into her—unmistakable, with that great, haughty face. Up close she seemed smaller, her waist tiny from dieting. She didn't recognize him, and he had to introduce himself.

"I'm writing your new picture."

"Ah," she said, smiling as if he'd cleared up a mystery, and wagged a finger at him like a teacher. "Two things. I never die in my pictures, and I never, ever lose my man. Write hard, Mr. Fitzgerald."

"I am," he said, though he was already well behind schedule.

He expected Stromberg to check on his progress, but the only memo he received had to do with the censors. Ever since the announcement in *Variety*, the Legion of Decency had been petitioning the Hays Office to do something. To placate them, Stromberg was changing the title to *Fidelity*.

"Smart," Oppy said.

"He'll have to do more than that to get it by them," Dottie said.

"There's a tasteful kiss," Scott said. "That's it."

"Tasteful's worse, actually," she said. "The guy's cheating on his wife. If you make him a heel, maybe, but then he's got to come to a bad end. So does she."

"It woulda passed in the good old days," Oppy said, meaning five years ago, before the Code.

"I'll be surprised if L.B. goes for it," Alan said. "It sounds more like something Warner's would do."

Stromberg told him not to worry. Scott saw it as a challenge—irresistible, really—but as he blocked out the first act, he kept in mind Mayer's puritanical streak, and second-guessed his effects, doubling back, working slower and slower till he was nibbling at the stage directions when he needed to be bashing out scenes.

Late one afternoon as he was fixing a playful exchange between Myrna Loy and the husband, Dottie burst in without knocking, Alan at her heels. They gathered close about his desk, whispered as if someone might hear them through the vents. They'd just seen the Nazi in the elevator.

The car was going up, and stopped to let a messenger off. The Nazi stayed on, headed for the fourth floor.

"I'll bet he's come to watch your dailies," Dottie said.

"Already," Scott said, since they'd only begun shooting.

"He knows what he's looking for," Alan said. "He's had the script since you turned it in."

"What are we supposed to do?"

"Just hope it's Mank that's showing him," she said. "He may be a dumb son of a bitch, but he's still a Jew."

"Unlike L.B.," Alan said, "who's a Jeunuch."

"You know his secretary," she said, pointing to the phone. "See if he's in."

Scott hesitated, wondering why she couldn't call, and then felt cowardly. He thought of Ernest during the air raid, bumping his head.

Mank's secretary verified it. They were headed over to the projection room.

"Come on," Dottie said, and raced down the hall to their office, which faced Main Street. There, below, crossing the broad, palm-lined plaza toward the commissary, Mank and the man called Reinecke were engaged in conversation, Mank gesticulating with both hands. Scott's first thought was that the German was older, and slight—hardly a threat. He wore a bowler and a black suit like a Charing Cross banker, and carried a briefcase, the contents of which Scott ridiculously imagined included top secret documents and a gun.

As they neared the newsstand, Mank stopped Reinecke to make a point. The German tossed his head back and laughed, and Mank patted his shoulder like an old friend.

"First rule of business," Dottie said. "Start 'em off with a joke."

They turned the corner of the payroll office and disappeared. Scott thought she might want him to shadow them like a detective, sneaking into the booth to eavesdrop, but she had a simpler solution: call Harry the projectionist and have him hold on to the cans.

"I take it you've been doing this a while."

"We like to know what's going on."

"Not that it does any good," Alan said.

"Don't be naive, darling. The most important thing in the world is knowing who's on your side. Isn't that right, Scott?"

She turned a feline smile on him, and what could he do but agree?

They broke up, going back to work, though now he couldn't concentrate.

They reconvened after Mank's secretary tipped them. It was a quarter to six. In the shady alleys between soundstages, grips and day players loitered, waiting for the siren. Dottie cut through the production office and out the back, as if they were being followed.

Harry had propped open the side door for them. He was grandfatherly, gaunt and bald as a light bulb, and wore a vest like a Wild West barkeep. Scott knew him from watching Joan Crawford's catalog, though they'd barely spoken. He was one of those studio functionaries who resented any attempt at chit-chat. Alan gave him five bucks for staying late, and like moguls, they took the front row.

The lights died, the projector whirred, and the screen glowed white. A numbered header snaked past, replaced by a chalk-marked slate, the lens racking, pulling focus. Though he'd worked on it for months, seeing the title made the film suddenly real, and for an instant he was inordinately proud. The clapper boy snapped down the gate and stepped out of frame, revealing the interior of Alfonso's Café.

The scene was an early one between Robert Taylor and Margaret Sullavan. He and his two mechanic friends had raced her rich boyfriend's Buick on the way to town and beaten it with their jalopy, and now, while the others were carousing in the background, Taylor was making a play for her. The tone was light, Sullavan breezily parrying each advance, which only made him want her more. Scott had brought his script to see if they'd changed anything. There was only one line that might be objectionable. Of the three veterans, Erich was the rugged, apolitical one, but she purposefully confused him with Franchot Tone's crusading Communist. The dig was: "You're the one who was so upset about the state of the country."

"You're the one who was so upset about the state of the country," she said.

It was all there exactly as Scott had written it.

"For now," Dottie said. "Make a note. The bastard wasn't here for his health."

The next scene also took place in the café, though it came much later in the script. They'd probably shot them all at once, using the same set-up. Franchot Tone was telling Sullavan that Erich needed her more than he did. It was a speech Scott and Paramore had battled over, and as it played out before him on the screen, with a creeping sense of disbelief he realized the whole thing had been rewritten. They hadn't kept a single line of his.

"Son of a bitch."

"That's Mank," Dottie said, as if he should have expected it.

"He's still the good guy though," Alan said. "Comrade Franchot."

"That's exactly what they'll want changed," she said. "The Communist can't be the hero."

"Then they'll have to change a lot," Scott said. "Especially the ending."

The next scene had been gutted as well, and the next, just stray scraps of dialogue left.

"Christ, why does he even need a script?"

"Welcome to Hollywood," Dottie said.

"And this is the raw stuff," Alan said. "Wait till they cut it."

The prospect made him wish he'd never seen the footage. Now he felt truly powerless, and the next day struggled to make headway on *Fidelity*. To catch up he took it home, working at the kitchen table until the rest of the Garden had gone to bed. He brought it to Sheilah's for the weekend, stealing a few hours Sunday afternoon. He was going to make himself sick, she predicted, and as if she'd jinxed him, he did.

It started as a cough, a dry catch at the back of his throat and then a hollow racking that left him gasping and teary, his lungs tight. He blamed the dampness, fashioning an ascot from a hand towel to wear around the house, as he had that wet summer in Baltimore when he was trying to finish his novel and Zelda, out of her mind, set the place on fire. He was certain it was a recurrence of his TB, the beginning of the inevitable weakening, his only recourse, like Stevenson or Lawrence before him, a desert sanitarium, and then one morning after not sleeping all night he spat in the sink and it was green. Just a chest cold.

He recovered enough by Valentine's Day to take Sheilah to the Cocoanut Grove. It didn't matter that it rained. Inside, the palms swayed, the waterfall cascaded softly behind the orchestra. They danced every dance, and between sets, at the same table where they'd first flirted, he gave her a pair of earrings with her birthstone, sapphire, which made her cry. He didn't tell her that Zelda had sent him a card, or how strange he felt, spending the day with someone else.

By the end of the night he was tired, and though it was late and he had to go to work the next day, he knew she expected him to stay over. It had become a pattern with them, the long droughts and tender reconciliations, and as they climbed the hill to her place they were silent in anticipation. He walked her to the door, and she held it open for him.

He was grateful, after blundering once again, that she wanted him back, and did everything, short of promising the impossible, to be worthy of another chance. They talked best in bed, as if making love was just a preface. She compared her weakness for him to a sickness, or a sin. She didn't care. In some way she didn't understand, she needed him. When they were apart, she confessed, sprawled across him, she starved herself.

"Feel my ribs. Here."

He didn't know whether to be frightened or flattered. He was sorry for her, and resolved to do better. He'd had a talent for happiness once, though he was young then, and lucky. But wasn't he lucky now, again? When he was with her like this, he could forget the past. No one else had that power, and yet in the end he feared he would disappoint her.

They were making love a second time, well after midnight, meeting each other sweetly, when, at the edge of release, straining to his limit, he felt dizzy. He was on his knees behind her, arching, his whole body clenched, and the room, dark save moonlight, dimmed briefly as if the power had flickered. A curtain of purple spangles swam before his eyes like the afterimage of a flashbulb. An exalted, floating sensation buoyed him, as if he were drifting up out of himself. He thought he might faint. To keep from toppling off the bed, he held on to her waist.

"Don't stop," she said.

He kept going. The feeling was momentary, as in boxing, shaking off the shock of being hit in the face. He was back inside his skin again. As he breathed, the world returned in all its fullness, warm and soft and dark, and he gave himself to it without regret.

"Are you all right?" she asked, lying beside him afterwards, because he was still panting.

"You're going to wear me out."

In the morning, pondering that rapture as he stood at his window, watching the door of the drugstore, he supposed it was a kind of ecstasy, an overload of the nervous system. Part of it was working too hard, and a lack of sleep. He couldn't help but think of Zelda. They'd been dedicated to pleasure, yet even at their wildest, raging on Pernod and cocaine, reproducing the *Kama Sutra* page by page, he'd never been transported like that.

He waited for it to happen again, those nights he stayed over, waking her for athletic seconds, trying to recreate the same conditions until she protested. Did he know what time it was?

Fidelity eluded him as well. He wasn't going to make eight weeks. Easter was coming, and he feared that Stromberg, like Mank, would assign it to someone else while he was gone. He had no choice. He'd promised Scottie.

His solution, as always, was to put in longer hours. He came home from the studio, started a pot of coffee and kept going.

"You'd think you owned stock in it," Bogie said, dropping off some of Mayo's chicken soup. He knew not to linger, just set the bowl in the fridge and tiptoed away again.

It was easier late at night, with the Garden asleep, but then, stuck on a line of dialogue, he looked up and the clock on the stove said it was a quarter to three. He'd wasted too much time on the beginning. Now all he could do was block out the remaining scenes and fill them in after he got back.

In the midst of this, as anyone could have predicted, Hitler invaded Austria, making *Fidelity* not merely tiresome but pointless as well. Dottie, in solidarity, quit work on her picture and dedicated herself to fundraising for the displaced. Scott envied her the luxury. Like Oppy, he wasn't allowed to stop.

Two weeks before Easter, he finished a big scene and stood up from the table, dazed and achy. He wasn't done, but he needed a break, and he was running low on cigarettes. The clock said he could make it to Schwab's before midnight, so he grabbed his keys and jacket and set off down the steps and across the patio. A wet mist hung in the air, the lamps along the walkway haloed. Though it was too cold to swim, the pool was lit, and the ringed trunks of the palms, their fronds rattling in the breeze. On the top floor of the main house, like a beacon through the murk, a single window glowed yellow. In it, featureless, centered as in a formal portrait, stood the silhouette of a figure.

He stopped, the only sound a fountain splashing.

The figure didn't move. He thought it might be a joke—a clothestree or dressmaker's dummy placed there by Benchley to scare him.

Why should he be frightened? He wasn't a child. He had his own ghosts, one he would never outrun, no matter how far he fled.

If it was Alla, though. He waited to see if, as before, she might give him a sign.

The figure looked down at him—in judgment or with mutual curiosity, he couldn't say.

He waved in acknowledgment, then felt silly. He checked his watch: five minutes.

When he looked again, the window—the whole house—was dark.

"Okay," he said, "you got me," and walked on, frowning and peering up as if, from the dark, the figure were still watching him. It was no specter, probably just an overnight guest staying at the main house, tired like him but unable to sleep.

Crossing Sunset in the middle of the block, he had to wait for a car. As it approached, the racket of the engine growing, its headlights threw shadows across the palms. As if he'd conjured it from his imagination, it was the Daimler from *Three Comrades*—a black phaeton gleaming under the streetlamps. He wouldn't have been surprised to find Reinecke behind the wheel, a Luger in his gloved fist. That was the problem with Hollywood: everything turned into a plot. He could picture the car swerving, and a flash of his own last-minute reaction. Dottie and Alan and Ernest would band together to avenge him.

The car roared past, racing to make the light at the corner, sped through the wash of red neon that marked Schwab's and down the long straightway to LaBrea, growing fainter and fainter in the mist till there was only the buzzing of the sign. Empty, the road was wide as a river. He crossed at an angle, trying to save time. Before he reached the far curb, the neon blinked off.

His instinct was to run, but after sitting all day the best he could muster was a hobbling trot. Once again, the world had conspired to remind him of his age. He was almost angrier at his own debility than the store closing early.

Inside, the lights were still on. A counterman he knew from too many chili dinners and late night forays was emptying the register. The clock behind the soda fountain said he had three minutes left.

He tried the door, expecting it to be locked. It swung open, but only halfway. He had to give it an extra tug, grunting with the effort, and felt a twinge in the shoulder he'd broken a few years ago showing off his diving skills. He gritted his teeth, afraid he'd torn something, when the lights around him dimmed. He recognized the feeling as the one he'd desired, only he was alone. Even now, as the aisles of Schwab's turned purple, part of him thought he must be wrong, his body confused. How was it possible, all this time, that he'd mistaken oblivion for joy? He opened his mouth to call for help, but his breath left him, and before he could grab the magazine rack along the wall, he was gone.

THE CURE

The doctor wouldn't call it a heart attack. His diagnosis was angina, for which he prescribed Scott injections of calcium and iron and a vial of tiny nitroglycerin pills he was supposed to carry everywhere. He needed to rest and cut back on the cigarettes. No running, no stairs, and for the next few weeks at least, no sex, rules Sheilah enforced with a nun's humorless efficiency.

She installed herself at the Garden, limiting his visitors, not letting him out of bed. Stromberg was fine with him turning in the script late, which gave Scott the opportunity to catch up. He fashioned a lapdesk out of a tea tray and wrote like Flaubert, propped on his pillows. At five she stopped him, taking away his yellow pad, gathering the draft pages strewn about the floor to type up later. He could read or listen to the news from Europe while she made dinner, when all he wanted was to go join Bogie and Mayo for a stiff gin. As much as he enjoyed being pampered, he resented being treated like an invalid, and by the third day he was planning his escape.

They were skirmishing over his trip East. She was afraid it

would be too strenuous, despite the doctor giving Scott his express permission. She petitioned him daily, saying Scottie would understand. She was coming out later this summer anyway. Bedridden, he couldn't evade the question, and fielding each new argument wearied him. He could only hold to what he'd told her in the first place: he'd promised Scottie, plus he'd already made the arrangements.

"It's only a week."

"And then a month to recover. It's not good for you, especially now."

"I have to go. You know that."

"I wish you didn't."

"I wish I didn't either." He could give her that, though it wasn't nearly enough. Nothing would be, short of renunciation, a complete break. He could see why lovers sometimes turned to murder.

Their last night, she changed the sheets and they slept together in his narrow bed, overly conscious of the doctor's orders. She hadn't relented. She needed to remind him of all that he was leaving behind. Even in his baggy pajamas, with her bra on, she incited him. She rolled over and he pressed against her soft bottom.

"Sorry," she said. "You have to wait."

"It's not going to kill me."

"You're right, it's not."

"I'm willing to chance it."

"That's very generous, but you're not the one who'd have to tell the doctor what happened."

"What would you tell him?"

"I'd tell him I tried to help you but you wouldn't listen to me."

"That's a bit cold, isn't it, considering I just died."

"It's true," she said. "You don't listen. You do what you want to do and then expect me to take care of you when you fall apart."

He wanted to deny it for the gross oversimplification it was, but couldn't.

"It's my fault," she said.

"It's not."

"Listen, I'm trying to tell you. I used to do for my mum the same way. She'd get on a kick and I'd have to make supper and put the boys to bed. I was ten or eleven then. Nothing's changed."

He wanted to say he'd been better lately, but knew not to contradict her.

"I understand," she said. "People are the way they are. Will you do me a favor this time and try not to hurt yourself? I can't bear to see you like that."

Why should he feel cornered by the one person who cared for him? To anyone else he could have lied.

"I'll try," he said, and then regretted it.

In the morning her request had the weight of prophecy, lingering as he kissed her good-bye and boarded the plane, though gradually as they cleared the mountains and cruised over the trackless stretches of desert, it lifted, and he fixed on what lay ahead, as if in these long hours aloft he might come up with some ingenious plan—impossible, not knowing how Zelda was. Scottie would be cool to her regardless, setting herself apart, leaving him, as always, to draw them together. He'd brought along his script, hoping, before Easter, to cable Stromberg that it was finished, but instead canvassed the cabin, taking notes on his fellow passengers. Salt Lake City, Denver, Omaha. They tacked across the continent, the stewardess loading on sandwiches and fresh newspapers at each stop, helping them make up their sleeping berths. Rather than risk spilling it, he drank his two tablespoons of chloral straight from the bottle and was under in minutes. When she woke him, they were almost to Baltimore, dawn streaming in the windows. He sipped his coffee and thought of Sheilah, still asleep in the hills, and wished the trip were over.

Scottie was waiting for him at the train station in a smart navy outfit he'd never seen before, doubtless the work of Anne Ober. Jesus, what he owed them.

"Don't you look swellegant," he said, holding her by the shoulders. "Remind me to thank her. How's the Latin?"

"*Bonum.*"

"Ah, *bene factum.* I'm telling you, it'll come in handy this summer."

"In case I meet a nice cardinal."

"By the way, not a word to your mother. I haven't told her. Did you write her like I asked you?"

"Yes, Daddy," she said glumly.

"Don't act like it's such a burden. One letter a month isn't asking too much."

"I don't mind writing, it's what she writes back. Did she tell you she's bicycling through Provence?"

"No." He looked at her as if it might be a joke.

"According to her, she's going there this fall with some woman from the hospital. They're going to stay at a chateau."

"She's confused."

"I figured."

"What it actually is is the doctor doesn't want her to take any more vacations without supervision. I guess they've had problems."

"I can imagine," she said. "So she's not going to Provence."

"No, but she is going to have a nurse with her."

"Goody."

"I think it might help." He understood her worry. A stranger was one more complication, one more witness to their embarrassment. He didn't tell her how much he was paying for it.

When the train came, though he knew he shouldn't, he took her bag and lugged it up the steps with his. The line ran along the shore, and he found two seats on the left side of the car so they could watch the inlets and marshes scroll by. The tide was out, gulls stalking the mudflats. A fishing shack he remembered from the last time had burned down. She was quiet, copying a list of verb declensions while he leafed through Collier's. As father and daughter they'd reached the stage where the only time they saw each other was on holiday, their real lives rarely intersecting. She was a dependable traveling companion, sharp-eyed and quick-witted, but often he felt a distance engendered by the time they'd spent apart, as if she wasn't interested in him. It would only get worse. In the fall she was off to college.

"Want to read something?" he asked, pulling out his script. "You have to promise to be merciless."

"I promise. Has anyone else read it?"

"You're the first."

She stashed her Latin and dug in with a pencil, bent over the pages like a copy editor, occasionally releasing a chuckle or thoughtful murmur. When she sat up straight, the pencil scratched. Like any child, she couldn't resist correcting a parent. He was content to hide behind his magazine, skimming yet another dissection of the crisis in Europe, peeking from time to time to see how far she'd gotten. If only she concentrated as hard on her studies, though at that age he'd been the same way—worse, to be honest. At Princeton he'd lost the better part of his sophomore year to the late-night ecstasies of theater life. Impossibly, he wanted to save her from his mistakes.

When she turned the last page, he pretended not to notice.

She slapped at his leg, a playful backhand. "So, what happens?"

"What do you think should happen?"

"There are only two things that can happen in a love story," she began, quoting his own advice.

"Only two?"

"Happiness or heartbreak."

"So which is it?"

If he'd instilled anything in her, it was a love of storytelling. They were batting around the possibilities when the conductor passed through the car. "Norfolk, Norfolk is next."

He thought: if they could just stay on, keep rolling down the coast till they hit Florida.

He expected the nurse to be in uniform like at the hospital, a matron ushering her charge through the chaos of the waiting room, but the blonde with Zelda was stooped and wore a brown sweater and skirt ensemble like a schoolteacher. With their matching bobs and skimpy figures they might have been spinster twins, except up close the woman was rucked and crepey beneath her makeup and had a tragically upturned nub of a nose that made her appear perpetually stunned, as if she'd just run into a glass door.

Zelda looked the same as she had at Christmas till she smiled. Somehow she'd chipped her new tooth and the canine beside it, a jagged break. As always, seeing her, he realized how little he knew of her life at Highland. He held her a moment before giving way to Scottie.

"This is my friend Miss Phillips. By coincidence she's from Philadelphia, which is an easy way to remember her name."

"Actually I'm from Pottstown," the woman said, shaking hands with them.

"Miss Phillips is here to make sure I don't tear my clothes off and run wild through the streets."

"Have you been up to that again?" he asked.

"It's been too cold. How about you?"

"Too busy."

"Be careful what you say in front of her. She likes writing people up even more than you do."

"I thought you said she was your friend."

"She is, but she's very scrupulous."

"That's good," he said. "We all need someone like that. Welcome."

"Thank you," Miss Phillips said.

The trolley out to the beach was a screechy old interurban that stank of graphite dust and ozone. There was nowhere to pull her aside and ask what Dr. Carroll expected of them. The whole undertaking had the feel of an experiment without parameters. As they rode along in silence, he sensed her observing, noting how he sat like a buffer between Zelda and Scottie. In his family's defense, he wanted to say their problems, like Zelda's, were no more solvable for being obvious.

The Cavalier Hotel, like the Beachcomber, was a relic, tiered like a wedding cake, a swaybacked casino and dance pavilion jutting out over the breakers on weedy pilings, just waiting for the next hurricane. Before he was born, his Grandfather Fitzgerald's store had furnished its three hundred rooms with white wicker chairs and sofas and headboards, and as a child—until his father lost the business—he spent one week a summer here, exploring the labyrinthine stairwells and lounges and galleries, so that returning was a kind of bittersweet homecoming. The last time he'd visited, two years ago, Zelda and Scottie had fought, and though their positions were entrenched and he was weaker now, he was hoping Miss Phillips would act as a neutral second, helping defuse the tension.

Her inclusion also changed the sleeping arrangements. Instead of the close quarters of a suite, the three of them each had their own room, a grave expense but essential, and which for himself and Zelda conveniently eliminated the most treacherous aspect of being together. He expected her to protest, but she followed Miss Phillips to their door like the ward she was and went in to get settled.

Dinner was at six in the Neptune Room, the carpet and drapes and walls all varying shades of aqua, even the crystal chandeliers, as if they were guests of an undersea kingdom ruled by middle-aged waiters. There, wearing the same brown outfit, Miss Phillips shared Dr. Carroll's schedule with them. Breakfast at eight, a stroll on the boardwalk, tennis, a light lunch and a half-hour for digestion, then golf—the idea being the days would take on the same rhythm as the hospital.

"Eight's a little early for vacation," Scottie said.

"I'm up at six every day," Zelda said. "Rain or shine."

"If it rains do we still play tennis?"

"If it rains we stay in and play mah-jongg," Scott said. "What if we all meet on the boardwalk around nine, how's that?"

Scottie also wanted to appeal the prescribed bedtime of nine o'clock till he gave her a single shake of his head to show it wasn't for their benefit, a fact he made plain after Zelda and Miss Phillips turned in. He appreciated that it was her spring break. They needed to be patient. It was just a week.

"I hate playing games with her," she said. "She always ends up pitching a fit."

He looked around as if Zelda might hear, though there was a whole room separating them. "She can't help it."

"She shouldn't play them then."

"It's supposed to be good for her."

"How?"

"Pie," he said. "Be sweet."

"I'll try."

"Thank you."

In the past his strategy had been to keep them apart, which sometimes meant stepping between them and taking blows from both sides. He could show up for breakfast and be pleasant and stroll the boardwalk, but his own doctor's orders forbid him from playing tennis. He was hoping to use that time to write, but when it came to it he couldn't leave Scottie on her own, and sat courtside with Miss Phillips, watching them volley with the club pro.

Of the two, Zelda was by far the stronger player, aggressive to a fault, chasing shots she had no hope of returning, while Scottie held her ground behind the baseline, content to hit the ball on the second bounce, an offense Zelda pointed out as if she didn't know the rules. Her backhand was weak, and as the pro tried to correct her swing, Scott could see her losing patience.

"There you go!" he called when she sent one over the net, and she gave him a face.

After they'd warmed up, they played Canadian doubles, Zelda and Scottie against the pro, who fed their forehands effortlessly, letting their better shots drop in for winners.

On a ball down the middle, Zelda stopped and called "Yours," but Scottie wasn't ready. They stood there looking at each other as it split them and hit the fence.

"Rule of thumb," the pro coached. "Don't say, 'Yours.' Say, 'Mine.'"

"Not if it's on her side," Zelda said.

Scottie didn't argue.

"You have to talk to each other. If it's close enough to call and you don't hear your partner, it's fair game."

"Even if it's on her side."

"Even if it's on her side."

From then on, as if to prove her point, Zelda called everything down the middle, stepping in front of Scottie until the pro had to ask her to let Scottie handle a few, the first of which she foul-tipped over the fence, making Scott walk around and search for the ball in a tangle of beach plum.

"Thank you," he told her afterward.

"Why can't she just play by herself?"

"That's not what she wants. She wants to play with you."

"I wish you were coming golfing with us."

"Miss Phillips will be there."

The idea provided little comfort, and though he wrote well that afternoon, the image of them adrift like three white dots on the great greensward of the course intruded. As if gifted with foresight, he anticipated Scottie's report, the blunt criticisms and the inevitable run-in with the instructor, a repeat of the morning. In her latent phase Zelda was predictable. Miss Phillips helped, taking her aside and apologizing to the man, but the whole episode was unpleasant, and tomorrow they had the same tee time.

"I told you," Scottie said.

"I know," he said. "I know."

At dinner, when he asked Zelda how the golf went, she said she'd driven the ball well but her short game was a mess. "It's hard when you don't play regularly. How'd you write?"

"What you said."

"At least you didn't have someone standing behind you the whole time telling you how to hold your pencil."

"He thought he was being helpful," Miss Phillips said.

"He wasn't," Zelda said, smiling, and stabbed her salad.

With their various dietary restrictions, only Scottie was permitted dessert. Over the years her figure had been a flashpoint between her and Zelda, and rather than rekindle the subject, she declined, settling for coffee. They retired to a salon to play euchre, another torture for her. When the chimes struck eight, he asked how her Latin was coming, giving her an out she happily seized, pecking his cheek.

"What, no kiss for your mother?" Zelda asked, and dutifully Scottie bent to her.

"Have you noticed," Zelda said when she was gone, "she's hardly said a word to me."

"She probably doesn't know what to say."

"I'd love to hear about her classes and her friends and her writing. You get to hear all of that. I don't."

He relayed the complaint to Scottie, as if giving her notes. "It doesn't have to be anything important, just small talk."

"That's the problem with her. You say something and she gets stuck on it, then all of a sudden she's biking through France. She only hears what she wants to hear."

"I understand. Just try to be nice to her."

"I *am* nice to her. She's the one who says awful things and then pretends she's innocent."

He held up a hand. "I know how she can be. Try. Please."

"I wish I'd stayed at school."

"No you don't."

"Yes I do."

"Pie."

"Don't 'Pie' me."

"Pie, Pie, Pie," he said.

"That's not fair."

"Nothing's fair," he said. "We just have to do our best."

Later, in his room, by the hot light of the desk lamp, he picked at the script, aware of them sleeping on either side of him, and the shuttling of the elevators. He was smoking too much and needed a Coke to cool his throat, but room service was expensive and he didn't want to disturb them. After midnight, when he'd finished the scene and gotten a start on the next one, he grabbed his jacket and rode up to the Crow's Nest for a nightcap, watching the fishing boats twinkling offshore, letting the cold gin settle his nerves. One was just enough to ease him into sleep without the knocked-out grogginess of the chloral.

It became his reward for making it through the days. With them every vacation was the same. He was a fool thinking it might be different. Zelda cursed the golf instructor and was banned from the course, meaning their afternoons were free. Instead of writing, Scott joined her and Miss Phillips for long, therapeutic rambles down the beach, while Scottie chose to sunbathe and read in peace, a decision he considered politic but which Zelda saw as an insult, privately calling her lazy and spiteful. He lobbied them separately, a feckless appeasement that left them equally aggrieved and gave him a headache. They stopped short of fighting outright, but meals were dicey, and by the time he'd gotten them to bed and finally sat down to write, he was already looking forward to that chilled first sip.

Maundy Thursday he wrote poorly. He wasn't going to finish by Easter and consoled himself with a second double, and then a third, imbuing the full moon and its silver slick on the water with a doleful sympathy. Gazing through his own dark reflection, he thought of the good places—Annecy and Lake Como, their first summer at White Bear Lake, their first visit to Bermuda. So many hotel balconies, so many warm nights, the doors flung open to the stars. In Monte Carlo for carnival, she wore nothing to dinner but her jade kimono, undoing the sash in the palace gardens and taking him like a geisha while in the narrow streets below the masquers danced. He was young and trusted they would always be that way.

Though there was no one else in the Crow's Nest, the barman rang a ship's bell for last call. "Something else for you, sir?"

"I'm fine, thanks," Scott said, and, feeling virtuous, signed the bill to the room.

The hallway rolled beneath him as if he were belowdecks on some great, oceangoing liner, making him grin and shake his head. In the elevator he stabbed at the button but missed, hitting the rigid panel. He got it on a second try with his thumb, and still the doors didn't close.

"I did," he argued, jabbing it harder.

As he descended, he rested against the wall as if he might sleep there. The car slowed, stopped; the doors rolled open. Their rooms were to the left, but he checked the signs to be sure, his mind fumbling with the numbers. He turned, following the arrow, looping wide on the busily patterned carpet and then correcting, aiming for the middle, and, looking up, realized he wasn't alone.

Far down the long hall, like a wraith in the dim halo of a sconce, stood a woman, facing him. She was small and blonde, in what appeared to be a nightgown. For a panicked instant he imagined it was Miss Phillips, come to check on him, and then, as if she were lost or had forgotten something, she wheeled and started back the other way. He was relieved, and let his face go slack, plodding after the white smudge of her retreating figure. She floated out ahead of him like an apparition. Around them the vast hotel slept, and with the muddled logic of the drunk he imagined she was a spirit come to show him some unpleasant vision of himself.

Ahead the hall jogged left, passing through an airy solarium before entering their wing. He wouldn't have been surprised if she continued through the wall. She flitted around the corner, drawing him on. When he reached the end, she was running away, racing down the moon-drenched gallery with a familiar, girlish stride, the soles of her feet flashing white, and he understood, dully, that it was no ghost fleeing him but Zelda.

His instinct, like a dog's, was to chase after her. He had no idea what she was doing roaming the halls, he only knew she was supposed to be in her room and that Miss Phillips was useless.

He shambled on, unsteady, his feet wandering. She was faster than he was, and he'd been drinking, except it wasn't a race, it was a game of hide and seek. She'd already lost.

He knew exactly where she was going, and let up, expecting she'd duck back into the room and pretend she was sleeping—or, as someone who wanted to resolve this quietly, that was his hope.

He lumbered around the last corner, panting, and pulled up short. She was stopped in the middle of the hall, waiting for him. She held a heavy glass vase full of lilies before her like a shield.

"Get away from me!"

"Shhh," he said, holding up both hands. "It's all right."

"Get away!"

"It's okay. We're just going to go to the room now."

"Help!" she yelled, "Help!" and raised the vase over her head, spilling water on herself, wetting the front of her gown. For a moment it distracted her, and he crept closer. She backed away, brandishing the vase as if she might throw it at him. Instead she spun and flung it against a door.

The glass smashed, loud as a gunshot, spraying shards, the flowers falling to the carpet.

"Help!" she shouted, banging the door with her fists, "Somebody help me!" and before he could close the distance, she whirled and ran screaming down the hall.

He bolted after her, forgetting everything his doctor had told him.

"Help! He's trying to kill me!"

Though it made no sense now, she was trying to get to her room. She ran like a child, tireless, easily pulling away. At Shepherd, once, a slow freight approached as they were strolling the far edge of the grounds, and she shed his hand and dashed for the tracks. He was younger, his lungs clear, but even then she'd nearly made it up the right-of-way before he tackled her.

The hall stretched on and on, an endless succession of doors and mirrors and tables with vases. He trailed her, fading badly, keeping her in sight. He wished she would stop screaming. He barely had the air to breathe.

She was fighting with the knob when he finally caught her. She'd probably forgotten the key. He closed on her slowly, trying not to spook her. "Okay," he said, "enough," because she was tugging at the door as if he were a murderer. He took her arm and she twisted away and struck him across the face. He grabbed at her wrists, catching one, but she kept slapping at him with her free hand, making him bob and weave, and as they grappled, he was yanked backwards and thrown against the wall.

He fell at the feet of her rescuers, two hairy-legged men in matching hotel bathrobes. He'd hit his head; there was a heat that might be blood. He touched his skull to assess the damage, and they jerked him upright and slammed him against the wall, shaking him when he tried to break free.

"Let me go!"

Up and down the hall, other guests had come out to investigate. They stood by their doors, staring at him as if he were a criminal while Zelda cowered. In her nightgown, with her broken teeth and her hair in her eyes, she was the picture of a madwoman.

"He's crazy," she told them. "He escaped from a mental hospital."

"I did not."

"Shut up," one of the men said, pinning an arm across his windpipe.

"He's tried to kill me before, that's why they put him away."

"That's not true."

"He's crazy when he drinks. He beats me."

"That's a lie."

The man pressed harder on his throat. "I told you to be quiet."

"I called the police," an older woman said.

Scottie came out. "That's my father," she told the man holding him. "What's happening?"

"He's drunk," the man said.

"I am not. She was out running around in the middle of the night."

Miss Phillips opened the door, squinting in the light. Zelda ducked behind her as if she might save her.

"Ask her," Scott said.

"He tried to kill me," Zelda said.

"I found her roaming around like that." He pointed over the crowd, back toward the elevators.

"Zelda, is that true?"

Like a scolded dog, she shied away.

"You were supposed to be watching her," Scott said.

"Sorry to disturb you all," Miss Phillips said, one hand raised like a teacher. "I don't know what happened. This woman is my patient. I take full responsibility for her. It won't happen again." With that, she guided Zelda inside and shut the door.

"I told you," Scott said, shrugging off his captors.

Neither offered an apology. When he insisted, one of the men said he was lucky they'd gone easy on him. Without Zelda to gawk at, the crowd focused on this new drama.

"Daddy, stop," Scottie begged, and before anything developed, pulled him into her room.

"Thank you," he said, penitent. He sat at the desk, testing the tender egg already rising on the back of his head. Now that the excitement was over, he was tired, as if he'd lost a fight. He sighed at how easily preventable the whole thing was, the stupidity of it. "Sorry for all that."

"I guess by now I shouldn't be surprised."

"She wasn't like this at Christmas. We're lucky I was the one that found her. Who knows what she thought she was doing."

"What were *you* doing?" she asked.

The question wounded him. When he hesitated, she crossed her arms like a prosecutor.

"I had a little nightcap at the bar upstairs. I didn't think it would turn into a big production."

She nodded at his admission as if he'd broken a promise. Guilty or innocent, he had no defense against her disappointment.

"I should see how they're doing." He stood and put his ear to the door, hoping by now the rubberneckers had dispersed. Through a susurrus like the ocean trapped in a shell, he could make out the cushioned footfalls of someone approaching, and then, next door, three brisk knocks.

"Hello?" a man asked officiously. "Mr. Fitzgerald?"

"Stay here," he told her, straightening his jacket and smoothing his hair.

It wasn't the police but the house detective, a plump Brit with a pencil mustache and cheap dentures. There'd been a complaint, several actually.

Scott apologized. His wife suffered from a nervous condition. It wouldn't happen again. It *shan't*.

There was also the matter of some property damage. He'd have to speak with the manager about that.

"Of course," Scott said, "I'll take care of everything. Thank you."

He thought it had gone well—the man seemed decent enough— but in the morning the manager called Scott down after breakfast and presented him with a finalized bill, including twenty-five dollars for the vase. The Cavalier was a family hotel, the manager lectured, pious as a banker. He was afraid he couldn't tolerate that kind of behavior. They gave him no choice. Politely yet firmly he explained that they were being asked to leave.

Instead of spending Easter supper with Zelda's cousins in Norfolk, they became their houseguests for the weekend, doubling up in the children's old bedrooms, an arrangement which mortified Scottie. Zelda was back on her tranquilizers, sleepwalking through the days. He wrote nothing, and didn't touch a drop till he'd gotten Zelda and Miss Phillips off and put Scottie on the train to New York. He flew back on the sleeper, tippling from a pint, imagining what Miss Phillips would put in her report. He bought a second at breakfast in Kansas City, and by the time they landed in Albuquerque he decided he would marry Sheilah. He called from a payphone to inform her.

"Did you ask her for a divorce?"

"Yes," he said, but when she came to pick him up, she saw he was drunk and he admitted he hadn't. She dropped him at the Garden, telling him not to call her.

"To our next ex-wives," Bogie said, toasting Mayo, and Scott raised his glass.

Alone again, housebound in his robe and slippers, he was determined to finish the script. He abstained during the day, but the weather was perfect for stargazing, and some mornings he slept through his alarm and then couldn't concentrate. Joan Crawford wanted her freedom more than revenge, the difficulty was showing that dramatically. After a dozen false starts he came up with a scene in which the husband returned to the mansion to plead his case, only to find her leaving for Europe, this time for good. The servants were busy covering the furniture, the Rolls laden and waiting.

"Why don't you write me a letter," she said, brushing past him.

"Where shall I send it?"

"London, Paris," she said, with a wave of her hand. "I don't care."

He was still trying to get the scene right when Stromberg called. The studio had killed the picture. Mayer didn't like it on principle, and they were never going to sneak it by the censors anyway. Scott would continue to be paid, Stromberg would find him another project to work on, but for now he should take the week off and rest.

"You haven't seen the new pages yet."

"I'm sure they're wonderful. I'm disappointed too. It happens. For what it's worth, Miss Crawford likes you. Right now the thing is to clear your head. Go to Palm Springs for a couple of days and come back fresh."

Scott didn't say he'd just been on vacation, or that he had no one to go with. He hung up and sat down at the kitchen table again, and as if he hadn't heard Stromberg—as if the news were mere rumor—kept kneading the scene, questioning the logic behind every phrase until, little by little, it yielded.

Over the next few days, knowing he'd never get another chance to fix the script, he bent to the final corrections as if he were racing a deadline. After he submitted his finished pages to Stromberg's confused secretary, his mind was still plucking at loose threads, and to quiet whatever professional conscience he had left, he tried reading Keats. When that failed, he knocked on Bogie and Mayo's door. It was three in the afternoon on a Thursday, and they were out, as were Dottie and Alan, and Don Stewart, and Benchley—all working, while he was being paid to do nothing.

He began with the gin in the Quaker Oats tin in the depths of the kitchen cupboard, savoring it cold and breathtaking over ice. He turned the radio up so he could hear the music outside and sat on his steps, closing his eyes and tipping his face to the sun. *Fascinatin' rhythm, got me on the go. Fascinatin' rhythm, the neighbors want to know.* Stromberg had told him to clear his head. It couldn't get much emptier, he thought, and then remembered Zelda yelling in the hall and Scottie wanting to protect him, Sheilah telling him not to call unless he was willing to quit. He tipped his glass and the mass of ice sloshed against his upper lip.

Bogie and Mayo were the first to come home, followed by Don Stewart and his Japanese girlfriend, Sid and Laura Perelman, Pep West and his wife, Dottie and Alan, Ogden Nash, the party growing incrementally until Benchley arrived with a flock of starlets, one of whom sat on Scott's lap, poking him in the face with her stiff brassiere and making fun of the way people danced. The torches were lit, the Capehart blaring from the balcony. He danced several fast numbers with the starlet and lost his glass. The gin was gone—they'd switched to whiskey and soda, Mayo blasting the unsuspecting with a seltzer bottle. He remembered going inside at some point and playing darts blindfolded, one of Alan's throws sticking in a painting before Dottie took the rest away, and later, tearing at a charred steak he held in his hand like a sandwich.

He woke alone on his kitchen floor, sunlight flooding the window above the sink, spangling the dirty dishes. His bad shoulder hurt, the muscles throbbing and weak, and he feared that while he was asleep he'd had an attack of angina. His pills were in his pants. He took two, but as he undressed to shower he could barely lift his arm to get his shirt off, and he realized he'd done something to himself.

Bogie and Mayo weren't home, or weren't answering. He could drive one-handed, except he didn't know where to go. Sheilah might think he was looking for sympathy, and maybe he was, but she was the only person he knew in the city and he was too tired and in too much pain to care, and rather than play the stoic hero, he gave in and called her.

"Are you sober?" she asked.

It was all she wanted to know.

"Yes," he said, and buried the empty bottle deeper in the garbage.

Seeing her again, he understood he was a fool. She knew everything, and still she'd come.

She drove him to the emergency room where they took x-rays and a nurse bound his arm in a sling. It was just a sprain. They gave him painkillers and released him to Sheilah.

In the car, in a swoon of gratitude, he apologized. He didn't know why he did these things. Maybe he should stop going East. One thing was clear—he needed her.

Like any victor, she had conditions. It was simple. He would take the cure and move out of the Garden, as if his friends were a bad influence. While he knew that wasn't the case, he wanted a fresh start as much as she did, and the next Monday, after Bogie and Mayo threw him a raucous going-away party, a private nurse arrived with a black bag full of syringes and sat by his bedside, swabbing his brow with cold compresses and catching his vomit in an enamel basin until he was empty. As he slept, cleansed and wretched, Sheilah folded his clothes and boxed his books and moved them to Malibu. Thursday, when she drove him out to the cottage, his room was made up and waiting for him.

MARIE ANTOINETTE

Here at the end of the continent the days were the same, the sea and sky elemental, endless, interrupted only by a ship, a plane, a wayward blimp. To pay his bills he was restaging the French Revolution as a tragic love story for Garbo. He sat at a child's desk tucked into a drafty dormer, wandering the gardens of Versailles. The waves broke and foamed, slid back and gathered again. The neighbors' flagpole was a sundial, its shadow angling across the patio, ticking off the afternoon. On his dresser stood a picture of himself in a sombrero and Sheilah astride a donkey in Tijuana, a birthday present. It was May, a month for picnics in the Bois. He thought they would see more of each other, like at Christmas, the two of them hiding from the world, but she was busy with her column and her radio show, her opening night galas. What was love compared to the ruthless ambition of youth? From the widow's walk he could see the peak of Catalina, and in his weaker moments, squinting out over the water at the last of sunset, breasting a westerly breeze, he felt the chill of exile.

He wasn't entirely alone. She'd hired a cook named Flora who took the bus from San Pedro five days a week, arriving on foot, waving to the guard at the gatehouse and tramping the sandy lane normally reserved for Barbara Stanwyck's or Dolores Del Rio's Rolls, singing and talking to herself out loud as if she were in a musical. She was from Louisiana and called him Mister Scott, prodding him to eat with the teasing familiarity of a nurse or nanny. "I never met a grown man so scared of a little okra." She reminded him of Ettie, their housekeeper at Ellerslie, who poured any booze she found down the sink and hid his guns when he was drunk. Like Ettie, Flora treated him like a willful child, a role, in his brittle state, he was comfortable playing. They ate lunch together, listening to the news from Europe on Frank Case's Philco before he headed back to his desk. At six she served him dinner and waddled off to the bus bench in front of the Malibu Inn, a walk he might take later for a Hershey bar or a pack of cigarettes.

The grocery there sold liquor, the bottles ranked with military precision, including his Gordon's. No doubt he would break down eventually, but so far he'd resisted, buying only a few harmless beers he quaffed like water.

At night the isolation was complete. Most of his neighbors' places were still closed for the season. Besides the light at the gatehouse, the Colony was dark, and on foot it was hard to see. The drive was littered with fallen fronds dried like husks. Ahead, with every step, lizards fled, rustling the leaves. On his left, running unbroken to the highway, stretched an open wedge of field—alfalfa and wild mustard. Deer came down from the hills to feed on the new shoots, coyotes trailing them, baying at all hours. Once, one loped across the road with a rabbit in its jaws, still kicking, stopped, golden-eyed, to fix on him as if he were a threat, then slipped under the split-rail fence. He was too used to the city, the comfort of other pedestrians, illusory as it might be. He welcomed the watchman with his wobbling flashlight and the lone fisherman surfcasting by the glow of a railroad lantern as if they were old friends.

Despite the shuttling of the waves, he didn't sleep. There was no heat upstairs and the bed was cold without her. He banked the fire and lay down on the couch beneath a heap of musty blankets, wondering how she'd convinced him to leave the Garden. Some nights, under the chloral's spell, he swore he could make out voices in the breakers, tootled bars of music, the call of a party right out-side his door—a siren song that fooled him each time. In the morning he blew on the embers, set a fresh log on the grate and lugged the blankets upstairs again so Flora wouldn't know.

Sheilah visited weekends and evenings when she could get away. They strolled the beach at sunset, roasted wienies and played ping pong under the stars, but her schedule was unsettled, subject to last-minute changes, and when she had to cancel, he sulked, roaming window to window, the empty hours spread be-fore him gray and featureless as the sea—how Zelda must have felt when he reneged on his promises.

Dearest Heart, he wrote. *I'm sorry it all went so badly. I should have known you were struggling, only I was struggling myself. I hadn't felt well for some time and was hoping to use the week to recover, a plan which in retrospect sounds wildly hopeful. I suppose I assumed your nurse would look after you, since she had no other reason to be there. Obviously she doesn't know you well enough to see trouble coming. I take part of the blame for asking Dr. Carroll to change your medication after how dulled you were at Christmas. There must be a middle course that lets you be the bright, lively person you are.*

As for my own role in that opera buffa, I can honestly say that since I've been out here I've had only two brief bats, both of which I paid for dearly with my health. Having recently taken the cure, I remain vigilant, afraid this old heart won't bear the strain again. The reprobate carries an unfair burden of expectation, as you know. I go so far as to steer clear of office parties and bars lest the studio get wind of rumors.

You don't give Scottie nearly enough credit. She's thrilled that you and Rosalind are coming up for graduation. I expect pictures of her with all of her firsts.

To Scottie he wrote: *You know I'd be there if I could, but this isn't your real graduation anyway. That would be Vassar (God and Louie Mayer willing). Be patient with your mother. This is her first trip to Simsbury, and she's anxious to make a good impression on the horsey set. I expect she'll do well, since in essence those are her people. It's more a*

matter of confidence, which was once her long suit. If there are any prob-
lems, Aunt Rosalind has all the information.

He'd never planned on going. After spending both Christmas and Easter back East he didn't have any vacation left, but as the day neared, he resented the situation more and more, the idea of not being there after slaving to pay for it, as if he were being deprived of his one reward.

He detested Marie Antoinette. To make her sympathetic he had to cheat, showing her as a newcomer trying to navigate the warring factions of the court—as if Garbo could still play the ingenue. Saturday was payday, and after driving over to the studio to turn in his pages, he and Sheilah were having dinner at the Vine Street Derby when the maitre d' came to their booth with a phone. Scott thought it must be for her, but the man stopped beside him and proffered it like a gift.

"We need to talk," Stromberg said. "You know my place?"

He didn't, nor did he know why they had to talk now, or how Stromberg had found him. Typically he hadn't seen him since being assigned the script, though a rumor circulating the Iron Lung blamed his absence not on his normal indifference but the resurgence of a nagging opium habit. Having often been the subject of gossip, if not, like Thalberg, outright legend, Scott tended to discount it.

"I suppose that means no dessert," Sheilah said.

"I'm sorry."

"Please, of all people, I understand. You've been summoned."

"You can stay."

"Don't be silly."

The directions Stromberg gave him took them up Beverly Glen through Holmby Hills into the older part of Bel Air where the roads meandered and mansions bulked darkly behind wrought-iron fences. It was dusk, the trees like cutouts against the deepening sky. Somewhere around here, years ago, before Gable got ahold of her, he'd danced with Carole Lombard at a party, her hand warm in his, her smile inviting. Now, in his rattletrap Ford, he poked from driveway to driveway, reading the street numbers like a tourist.

Sheilah's eyes were better than his. She found it first, a rambling Spanish Revival with Moorish arches and neatly spaced poplars. "This used to be Warner Baxter's place."

"Yes," he said, because this was it. "I've been here."

"Of course you have."

Before he could pull up to the buzzer, the gates yawned open and he eased the car through. Sheilah twisted in her seat to watch them close behind them again. "Trapped like rats."

"You could have stayed and had your grapefruit cake."

"And sit there all by myself? No thank you."

A valet was waiting for them in the portico, and came to her side of the car first, a small, balding man in white gloves and tails. She waved him away.

"I'm sure you'd be welcome," Scott said.

"I'm sure I wouldn't."

"I'll try to be quick."

"Mester Fetzgerald," the valet said in a rich Scottish burr. "Mester Stromberg's expecting you." He had a few greased strings of auburn hair combed across his dome and his pants were as baggy as Chaplin's. Silently he led Scott up the stairs, through a paneled and parquet-floored anteroom and down a long, ceremonial hallway ranked with niches housing grim marble busts, giving the place the air of a museum or a gallery of severed heads.

He'd been summoned before, to the dean's office at Newman and then Princeton. Whatever news Stromberg had to break to him in person couldn't be good, yet at the same time he had the feeling of being chosen, admitted to an inner sanctum. He didn't know the man at all beyond his reputation, his youthful success, already fading. He imagined the valet taking him upstairs to a tower room where Stromberg, dope-ravaged and half out of his mind, would pontificate on the temptations of Hollywood from his four-poster sickbed. Instead the valet turned left at the end of the hall, knocked on an open door, announced him, and with a nod, stepped aside.

Like a miser hunched over his ledger, Stromberg was working in a small circle of lamplight, the corners of the room dark. As in the Iron Lung, he captained a desk piled with scripts, the walls a library, only here rather than tweeds he wore a sport shirt and his jaw betrayed a faint smudge of stubble. He rose to shake Scott's hand and apologized for interrupting his dinner. There was no other chair, so Scott stood, a sophomore called on the carpet. He was prepared to hear that his pages were uninspired and he was being replaced.

"We lost Garbo," Stromberg said. "L.B.'s letting us have Norma."

Meaning they were screwed. As Thalberg's widow, Norma Shearer was a reminder of his genius. Since his death, Mayer had actively miscast her, trying to drive her from the studio. He wondered if Stromberg was in L.B.'s doghouse.

"What happened?"

"That's just how it is. I've got something else if you're interested. The last thing I want to do is waste your time." He held out a script.

Like a volunteer, Scott stepped forward to accept it: *The Women*, by Claire Booth Luce. It was a gossipy farce enjoying a long run on Broadway, utter fluff. He smiled to hide a grimace. "I've heard of it."

"Take a look and get back to me. Miss Crawford asked for you specifically."

"That was kind of her."

"I'm pretty sure we can get Greer Garson and Claire Trevor. It's not Garbo, but I think it'll make a nice picture. We shelled out enough for it."

Scott played along, trying to be gracious. Only in the hall, on the way out, following the little Scotsman, did he let his face drop. There was no reason he should feel insulted. It was just the business. As a professional, he needed to be grateful for another chance.

"That was fast," Sheilah said.

He tossed the script in her lap. "I've got a new job."

"What happened to *Marie Antoinette*?"

He gave her a double take. "You didn't hear?"

It became a favorite saying, referenced when anyone asked an obvious question, but also shorthand for the vicissitudes of life at the studio, where so many hopes met abrupt, unhappy ends. He'd been there almost a year now, working steadily, and all he had to show for his efforts were a couple dozen pay stubs. Of the scripts he'd written, only *Three Comrades* had made it into production, after the most savage battles. Its fate was still in doubt. Though Dottie and Ernest had warned him, he couldn't stop it from being sabotaged. Between Paramore, Mank and Reinecke, he feared there was nothing left of his script, and as the premiere neared, he steeled himself.

By chance the picture was opening the same weekend as Scottie's graduation, casting his bifurcated life in even greater relief. As he was fixing his cuff links and zipping Sheilah's dress, Zelda and Rosalind were taking the night train up the coast to New York. The route ran through Baltimore, hard by their old house, La Paix, their very last home, the three of them together, before she set fire to it—accidentally, or so he'd told the police, when honestly he couldn't be certain. Would she recognize the old place in the dark? And what would she think? At Pratt she begged him to take her home. He would when she was better, he said, a promise which, while true, proved empty. He didn't expect they would ever live under the same roof again. He wasn't sure why the idea surprised him, but caught himself making a sour face in the mirror as he tied his tie, and clenched his jaw to erase it before Sheilah walked in on him.

The premiere was at Grauman's Egyptian Theatre, a grand, pillared temple among the luncheonettes and pawnshops of Hollywood Boulevard. Crossing Wilshire, they could see searchlights sweeping the sky, as if anticipating an air raid. The mob was already there, the uninvited penned behind police barricades, shaking 8 x 10 glossies and autograph books at the chosen. He'd insisted on taking his car as a joke, and inched along as limousines dropped off the stars, each new arrival sparking a volley of flashbulbs.

When it was their turn, he gave the car to the valet and hurried around to offer Sheilah his arm. Her dress drew wolf whistles and catcalls she acknowledged with a wave, sending up a roar.

"They love you."

"They think I'm somebody," she said, and he wondered if that was what she wanted. He was aware that the last time she was here she'd been with Leslie Howard.

With its flickering torches and stone obelisks and staring Sphinx, the Egyptian's courtyard had been designed for the open-air pageantry of premieres. Once they reached the red carpet they had to stand in the glare of the klieg lights, bunched with other couples waiting to process. It was like being on a set, every movement orchestrated. Among the pairs he recognized several lesser Metro stars not involved with the picture, there to add color and be seen. On both sides, packs of photographers cordoned off behind velvet ropes jostled for shots. As each party approached the gauntlet, a studio flack announced them like a butler. The man knew Sheilah, but had to ask Scott his name.

"I wrote the picture," he explained, knowing that in a few hours he might disown it.

"Miss Sheilah Graham and Mr. F. Scott Fitzgerald, writer."

They posed, holding their smiles, blinded by a galaxy of flashes. In her heels she was almost his height, and he lifted his chin and stood straighter.

"Now if we can have some of just Miss Graham," the flack directed, and Scott stood aside, at once jealous and admiring. She was every bit as fetching as the stars, and fresher.

Farther on, a radio host waylaying guests for comments let them pass without a second glance, restoring their anonymity, and by the pillared entrance, as if to reinforce their unimportance, Margaret Sullavan, Robert Taylor, Robert Young and Franchot Tone were having their picture taken with the film's poster, the ceremony documented for posterity by a Pathé News crew. Like everyone else, he and Sheilah stopped to watch.

Franchot Tone was unhappily married to Joan Crawford. Last month Mayer had sent them off to New York on the Super Chief to squash a rumor they were breaking up. Looking around, Scott was surprised she wasn't there.

"I'm not," Sheilah said.

His first thought was craven: Would it make selling *The Women* easier or harder? The problems of the stars were part of their appeal. As Sheilah's readers knew, the failures of the famous made them human in a way their successes never could. Some were forgiven, others forever condemned, depending. Between Chaplin and Fatty Arbuckle stretched an unbridgeable gulf. Knowing Joan Crawford's fans, he expected they'd blame Franchot Tone.

Inside, the lobby was jammed and boisterous with small talk. Following custom, concessions were free, and the lines were long. He spotted the novel's author, Erich Maria Remarque, in the midst of the crowd, laughing with Thomas Mann, Lion Feuchtwanger and several others from the German émigré contingent, while Sheilah, whispering, picked out the Mexican Spitfire, Lupe Velez, in a plunging neckline, and her husband and sparring partner Tarzan, Johnny Weissmuller, and Cesar Romero squiring the thyroidal Mary Astor, who was rumored to be insatiable, and brandnew item Merle Oberon and George Brent, and red-faced Wallace Beery with ghostly pale Joan Blondell, and Elvira Eichleay, the architecht's daughter, and Tingle Barnes, the Welsh soprano—all waiting, patient as cattle, for their popcorn and candy.

He scanned the sea of people, expecting, any second, Ernest to appear with Dietrich on his arm. Dottie and Alan were probably here somewhere, and Reinecke, checking on his handiwork. He thought if he saw Mank or Paramore he'd cut them dead, at the same time recognizing the impulse as childish and self-defeating. It was Hollywood. Just being there was a compromise.

"Would you like something?" he asked.

"You can get something if you want."

He wanted chocolate but passed, citing the line, and immediately rued the missed opportunity.

"Is it always like this?"

"Always," she said. "But I'm excited for you."

Their seats were a fair barometer of where he stood at Metro. The center of the orchestra was reserved for the producers and stars and their guests, while the wings on both sides were packed solid with early birds, leaving them to fend for leftovers in the loge. They had to climb to find two together, high up in a corner.

One of their neighbors was the dresser from wardrobe who'd helped him with *Infidelity*, which he thought fitting, except her job was steady, where he was being paid piece rate.

Down front, the stars were filing in, posing for last-minute shots before taking their seats. He thought he saw Mank in a tux, shaking hands like the father of the bride. The dumpy uncle beside him might have been Mayer; so far up it was hard to make out faces. In vain he searched the rows for the pinned-up sleeve of Eddie Knopf, the only honorable one among them. On principle Thalberg never attended premieres, another reason to admire him.

The house lights dimmed, a signal for the stragglers.

"Are you nervous?" Sheilah asked.

It seemed an unfair question just then. "I'm anxious to see how badly they mangled it."

The lights went down, quieting the crowd. Finally the curtain parted. Before the show could start, a spotlight followed Mank across the stage to a microphone where he thanked everyone for coming and everyone involved in this important international production, fawning, calling on each of his great stars to stand and take a bow, and his incredibly talented director, Frank Borzage, and the brilliant author of the bestselling novel, Erich Maria Remarque, a gush of self-congratulation repeated minutes later during the opening credits. Leo the Lion roared—ARS GRATIA ARTIS, an outright lie—and as their names flashed, thirty feet high, the crowd applauded wildly for their favorites and politely for the rest, as at a graduation. Scott thought of Zelda and Rosalind pulling into Grand Central, the vast marble hall teeming with people at midnight.

Beside him, Sheilah squeezed his hand. It was his turn. For a few seconds, to a lukewarm ovation, he and Paramore shared the screen. Even if the billing was strictly alphabetical, he was relieved to see he was on top.

She kissed his cheek. "Congratulations."

"Thank you."

It was what he'd come here to do, and while the picture itself wasn't his vision, was likely a mockery and a flop, he was still proud to have earned his first credit.

After all the back-and-forth with Paramore, all the niggling memos and tone-deaf corrections, he was prepared to find only the faintest traces of his script left, so he was surprised to see they'd kept his opening, a squadron of German aviators celebrating the Armistice in the airfield mess. The introduction of the three friends was right, but Mank had gummed up the toasts with a speech about Peace and Home.

"He couldn't just leave it alone," Scott said, and Sheilah patted his knee.

The dialogue was all wrong—too slick and punchy, as if it was a comedy.

The scene where Franchot Tone tossed a grenade into his plane and walked away was still there, and the road race was largely intact, the comrades and Margaret Sullavan meeting cute. It all played, but they'd changed the café debate between Robert Young and Franchot Tone to avoid any mention of the Nazis, and the Jewish shopkeeper's plea after the riot was gone altogether.

Also missing was the rally where the brownshirts burned *All Quiet on the Western Front.*

"Gutless," he said, and a man in the row ahead turned and glared at him.

Margaret Sullavan was supposed to be dying of TB, but in her close-ups she was rosy, her eyelashes spidery with mascara.

Franchot Tone couldn't turn off the radio in the garage when Hitler was making a speech because apparently in this Germany there was no Hitler.

In the dailies he and Dottie had seen, he would have sworn the bass drums the marchers played had swastikas on them. Here they were solid black. He shook his head. It looked like some scenes had actually been reshot.

"It's possible," Sheilah admitted.

He wasn't mistaken. In the background at the train station there were no flags, no heroic pictures of Hitler. It was a total whitewash. Reinecke would be pleased.

He couldn't watch any longer. "Excuse me," he told Sheilah,

sidled past their neighbors and strode up the aisle, the picture nattering at his back.

The lobby was bright and surprisingly busy. There were still lines at the concession stands, and the doors were open to the courtyard, where people had gathered in circles, smoking in the glow of the torches. He didn't recognize any of them, which he considered a mercy. The Cecil B. DeMille pillars made him think of the ruined Samson, pulling the temple down on the Philistines with the last of his strength. It was just a silly movie. How much of his self-righteousness, like Samson's, was injured vanity? Above, the night was cool and clear, a lone searchlight sweeping the sky. He lit a cigarette, inhaled deeply and blew out a cloud like a sigh, just as Sheilah appeared in the doorway.

She took the cigarette from him, took a puff and handed it back. "She's very good."

"It's hard to tell with all that makeup."

"You knew you weren't going to like it."

"I don't know why I thought they'd play fair."

"The Nazis."

"What Nazis?" he said. "I don't see any Nazis."

"We don't have to stay."

It was tempting. All he had to do was give the valet his claim check.

"There's not much more," he said.

"You want to see how it turns out."

"Happily ever after. Just like Germany."

"I'm sorry they ruined it."

"I can't say nobody warned me."

"No, you can't," she agreed.

On the way back to their seats they stopped for some Hershey bars, only to be told the concession had sold out.

"This is not my night," he said.

The usher pulled back the curtain and led them in. Their neighbors seemed annoyed at being interrupted again. Instead of the picture he watched the beam of light from the projector, gray as smoke, flickering above their heads. Franchot Tone was stalking Robert Young's killer outside a snowy church, gunning him down as the Hallelujah chorus reached its bombastic climax. The camera lingered on Franchot Tone's shadow, centered in a rosette window like a bull's-eye.

"It wasn't me," Scott said.

All that was left of the love story was Margaret Sullavan's operation and then her death scene, shot in gauzy close-up, her face radiant. Dottie was right. In the end, it was all about the girl.

The final scene showed Robert Taylor and Franchot Tone leaving the cemetery, flanked by the spirits of the departed. The image was his, but Mank had added a flimsy exchange so that instead of heading back into town to rejoin the fight, they were off to South America to seek adventure. Not knowing any better, the audience applauded.

"I wouldn't call that happily ever after, exactly," Sheilah said.

"It's just a mess. Too many cooks. Two, specifically."

They were close enough to the exit to beat most of the crowd outside, and hand in hand made a beeline for the valet stand. Again, his obscurity protected him. No one stopped him to offer congratulations or ask what picture he was working on now. He thought he should wait and find the author so he could apologize, but feared what he might do if he ran into Mank or Paramore. Discretion, in this case, was the better part of valor, or cowardice, depending on where one stood. The valet brought his car, now an unfunny joke, and they escaped, tooling down Hollywood Boulevard, chased by the searchlights.

They were safe in Malibu, staying in all weekend. Saturday it rained and they slept late, wasted the gray afternoon reading by the fire and listening to Schubert's last sonatas. She made tea and waited on him as if he were sick. Normally he would have protested, saying he was perfectly capable of serving himself, but after last night he felt depleted, and for the sake of peace let her nurse him.

Sunday Scottie graduated. Fog sat on the water, mirroring his mood. He'd arranged for a bouquet and a card, a poor substitute for being there. As the hour neared, he distracted himself with chores, sweeping the patio and gathering driftwood for kindling. To cheer him, Sheilah baked cookies and packed a picnic basket with Flora's leftover fried chicken and deviled eggs. They trekked all the way to the lagoon, where the creek emptied into the sea and greedy seals surfed the breakers. She brought a blanket, and after eating, they lazed, reading Keats to each other.

Introducing her to the classics had become a project ever since she confessed she'd never read them. He was dumbstruck. He just assumed that as a British subject poetry was her birthright. She was so polished it was easy to forget she was a child of the slums. She'd never read Milton before, or Keats, or Joyce, and was sick of feeling lost every time Scott and his friends mentioned Proust. Her eagerness to learn appealed to the professor in him, and he took pleasure in lending her books and then quizzing her like Scottie with her Latin. It was partly a joke—that she was Fitzgerald University's sole student—but she knew there was no surer way to lift his spirits.

Much have I travell'd in the realms of gold
And many goodly states and kingdoms seen;
Round many western isles have I been
Which bards in fealty to Apollo hold.

They lay there, trading stanzas, declaiming to the seals and the fishermen lining the pier. The fog burned off to reveal a blue day, Catalina rising like Ithaca in the distance. They explored the reedy shore where the ducks nested and dared the muddy sandbar to hunt for clams, and by the time they shook out the blanket and hiked back to the cottage, he trusted the ceremony was safely over, the proud families grouped outside the chapel, snapping photos.

He wondered how Zelda had done, and hoped Scottie was happy. *Farewell, dear Newman, farewell,* he'd sung at his. *We'll return to you al-ways!* Somewhere he still had his cap and gown. He wished he'd been there, and then felt guilty toward Sheilah.

She left the next morning before Flora arrived, sending him

back to his desk to wrestle Joan Crawford. He was scattered and couldn't make any headway, and was grateful, just before lunch, for the rare distraction of a car turning into the drive. The bell rang. He waited, an ear cocked toward the stairs, as Flora answered the door.

"Western Union."

He thought it would be from Ernest, a dressing-down from the barricades of Madrid for letting the picture get away from him.

"Mister Scott," Flora called up. "Telegram."

KUDOS ON BOFFO REVIEWS, it read. SCOTTYS DAY PERFECT. ZELDA GOING SOUTH TOMORROW. REGARDS OBER

He wanted to argue with the first part, but a call to Eddie Knopf confirmed it. *Variety*, the *Hollywood Reporter*, the *Times*—everyone loved Margaret Sullavan.

"Because they're idiots," Dottie said.

"Oh," Alan said, "I liked her."

She'd heard it was Mayer who capitulated to the Germans. "Mank told them to blow, so they went over his head."

"It's not Metro-Goldwyn-Mankiewicz," Alan said.

"L.B. made him go back and reshoot whole scenes."

"I thought so," Scott said.

"It's still obvious," she said. "Anyone with half a brain can tell who the bad guys are."

It was this hope he clung to, rather than his first impression, when he thought of *Three Comrades*. The picture quickly became a hit, and Margaret Sullavan a star, earning an Oscar nomination. Its success only confused him further, having so little to do with the original script. He worried that Ernest might think he hadn't tried, or hadn't fought hard enough for his vision. It seemed fitting that Ernest should have the last word, having admonished him in the beginning. Since they'd met he'd served as Scott's political if not his artistic conscience. Whether Ernest was disappointed or sympathetic or both, his opinion meant something to him. Every day, for weeks, Scott expected him to write or call or cable, willing, like a guilty sinner, to abide by his verdict, but he never did.

BELLY ACRES

With summer and its Mediterranean days came the neighbors, en masse, their fantastic cars lining the drive. From Metro and Fox and Universal and Warner's and Paramount and lowly RKO they came, the big names seeking respite from shooting schedules and interviews, bringing their cooks and housekeepers and nannies. "Hoity-toity," Flora said. For all its rustic charm the Colony was an extension of the studios, another gated enclave reserved for the stars. Out of costume, glimpsed against the vast backdrop of the sea, they seemed diminished, merely human, unworthy of either adoration or gossip. They swam and sunned and frolicked with their children while he watched from his dormer, scratching away at *The Women*. He'd forgotten how much little dogs barked. This was the real season here, families wiling away the blue afternoons building sandcastles and flying kites. After the long months alone, he welcomed the influx of life, if not the disruption.

Everyone wanted to be at the beach. He had guests himself. In August he hosted Ober, out to check on the Hollywood office, taking him to the Cocoanut Grove and the Clover Club, as if trying to impress a date. So far Metro hadn't said anything about renewing his contract, which Ober thought a bad sign. He'd spent too much time off the lot. They didn't care that he was sick, or that Stromberg said he could. They needed to see his face.

As hoped, Scottie had gotten into Vassar. After her sojourn in Europe, she and Peaches Finney trained west and stayed a week, lolling on the beach and palling around with Sheilah before heading off to college. She'd grown taller, and seemed older to him, more thoughtful.

"You were right," she said. "In Paris they expect war any day now."

She'd taken pictures of their old place in the Rue Tilsit, of Saint-Sulpice and the Boul Mich and La Coupole, where the maître d' remembered them.

"How is Louis?"

"He asked after mother."

"What did you say?"

"I said you were both well."

"Thank you."

"I think he was a little in love with her."

"Everyone was back then. She was fascinating."

He wanted her to stay longer. Each night after dinner they talked by the fire until Peaches was yawning, and still it wasn't enough. He wanted to follow Scottie east, take a flat in Poughkeepsie and feed her on weekends. The next time he saw her she would be a know-it-all coed, enthralled with Harvard men. In a sense, his dream for her was coming true, except now he had no role in it. Saying good-bye at the station, he gave her his copy of Ovid. *Non scholae, sed vitae discimus,* he wrote. *Love, Daddy.*

Like any shore resort, after Labor Day the place emptied out, leaving the pelicans and sandpipers as his sole entertainment. The weather was too good. It hadn't rained in weeks, and the hills were brown and dry, the chaparral like tinder. Heeding Ober's advice, he commuted to the studio, driving into the sunrise every morning, expecting to come home and find the Colony burned to the ground. He was in his office, fixing *The Women,* when Max called to tell him Tom Wolfe had died.

He'd known Tom was laid up in Seattle with pneumonia, but blamed it on overwork. For months he'd been traveling the Northwest on foot, doing research. He was obsessive in his enthusiasms, immersing himself in material. He'd rest and get well, as he always did, and bash out a generous, messy book. Instead he'd left the hospital and taken a train east and his heart had given out. At Scribners he'd been a brother to Scott, along with Ernest, and the idea that a man of his gargantuan ambition and vitality could suddenly be gone shocked him. Sheilah had never met Tom. Trying to describe him, Scott raised his arms wide, outlining a giant. In that sense it wasn't entirely a surprise. He had to have weighed three hundred pounds, and ate and drank like a Khan. Scott didn't mention that Tom was three years younger than him.

I envied his powers, he wrote Max, *as I envy Ernest's, knowing they're not mine. I like to think the three of us—and in a different fashion, Ring—were after what might be called the American soul. Being surer of himself, Tom was more open about it, where Ernest and I hide behind the cover of art and irony. At heart Tom possessed a religious feeling for the country and his best work has an ecstasy that can't be manufactured. While it may be too much to wish for, I hope he found his way again in this last book.*

He didn't brood as he had after Ring's death, but sometimes, standing at his window overlooking the boulevard, he thought of his mother's last days in St. Paul. He'd been holed up in Asheville, Tom's old hometown, frittering away the summer, and couldn't be reached in time. She'd doted on him, her golden son, and he'd repaid her stingily. How much of the past—how much of life—was unrequited?

His funk deepened when Stromberg pulled him off *The Women* and handed it to Anita Loos, removing any chance of him getting a credit. From the beginning he'd despised the play. Being relieved of command was just a further indignity.

His new assignment was *Madame Curie,* from a treatment by

Huxley. Once again he was supposed to be writing for Garbo, though by now he'd come to understand that every producer at Metro invoked her name when they were pitching a project. He tried to picture her, smoldering and aloof in a white lab coat. The whole idea was ludicrous, as was Huxley's treatment, a May-December romance framing the discovery of radium, capped by the dogged scientist's inevitable tragic death. He dutifully went back and read her autobiography, only to find it equally pat.

The truth, as every Frenchman knew, was that she was sleeping with the young lab assistant. It had been a great scandal, complete with photos in the papers of the love nest, a bedroom naked save, curiously, a picture of her elderly husband nailed like an icon above the headboard, but, as with *Infidelity*, he couldn't tell that story.

Though both Scottie and Zelda seemed to be doing well, the run of bad news left him scattered and worried for the future. Late one day he was driving home when the radio said Hitler had annexed the Sudetenland. He was poking along the Coast Highway with the sun glittering off the water, the tawny mountains rising in the distance, while from the dash the voice of the dictator raged, urging the German people to take back their rightful living space.

He'd missed the last war, and imagined what part he might have in this one. If Metro wasn't going to renew him anyway, he could beg an assignment from *Esquire* as their Paris correspondent, rent their old pied-à-terre in the crooked streets of Montparnasse and report on the French High Command. He could hire a driver and wire stories from the front. Unlike Ernest, he was a trained soldier. Live fire didn't faze him; he'd faced it a dozen times in camp and had always done well. He was still a decent shot. Last fall when he'd hunted pheasant with Sid and Pep, he'd bagged his share. If he wasn't the cocksure lieutenant he'd been twenty years ago, he liked to think he was wiser. While he no longer saw death in battle as glorious, after his angina scare he wasn't afraid to die.

"You have got to be joking," Sheilah said.

"Why?"

"You can barely climb the stairs."

"I climb them ten times a day. Ask Flora."

"Well you shouldn't. What if they use gas?"

"It's illegal."

"You're not even supposed to be smoking. I'm sorry, I think it's foolish and irresponsible."

As if to prove her point, later that week he came down with a barking cough.

Fall was upon them, the nights growing colder, dampness stealing in, lingering through morning. His lease was up at the end of October. As much as he loved the sea, his lungs weren't suited to it, and Sheilah began looking for a new place for him.

He would have been happy to go back to the Garden. Bogie and Mayo had gotten married, and his old villa was available. The simplest solution would be to move in with Sheilah, but she wouldn't discuss it. Everything close to the studios was too expensive, and after several weekends nosing around Hollywood, viewing ghastly furnished flats, she canvassed her friends in the English colony and by chance found a cottage even cheaper than the one in Malibu.

The reason it was so affordable was the location. It was out in the valley, beyond the matchstick tract developments and the great dam and basin built to sustain them, a guesthouse on an estate surrounded by ranchlands. Hemmed in between the mountains, the climate was warm and dry, a point Sheilah made repeatedly. Technically it was Encino, though there was no town, only a crossroads general store and filling station. It was horse country, white board fences running for miles. The dusty hills reminded him of Montana the summer he'd worked on the Donahoes' ranch, playing poker with the cowboys in the bunkhouse and writing slavish letters to Ginevra.

BELLY ACRES, the wrought-iron arch above the gate read. The manor house perched atop a knoll that commanded an expansive view of the San Gabriels, while the cottage sat at the base, a plain raised ranch with a white picket fence and empty pool. The owner was Edward Everett Horton, a dandyish Anglophile character actor known for his flowing mane and prissy dithering. He spent most of his time in London and New York, directing for the stage, leaving his diction coach Magda as a caretaker. A ginger spinster in a coolie hat, sunglasses and culottes, she showed them about the grounds, treating them like guests rather than prospective tenants, introducing her titled rosebushes with a grandmother's pride. She and Sheilah bantered in the same chirpy, flitting English, talking too fast for him to make sense of each exchange, and as they toured the gardens he trailed behind, feeling left out, as if they were speaking another language.

The cottage was bright and airy, furnished like a Nantucket saltbox with Wallace Nutting reproductions: rag rugs, dropleaf tables and ladderback chairs. The kitchen and downstairs bath were modern and freshly scrubbed, smelling tartly of ammonia. There was a girl who came once a week, Magda said, very dependable. Sheilah nodded, pleased. Upstairs, a picture window in the master bedroom framed the distant peaks to the east. A verandah that could be used as a sleeping porch overlooked the pool, which Magda called an absolute godsend in the summer.

It was his for two hundred a month, a savings of a full hundred over Malibu. Besides its remoteness and ridiculous name, there was nothing to which he could reasonably object, yet even after signing the lease, he resisted Sheilah's enthusiasm. He wasn't ungrateful, but as providential as the new arrangement was, it was temporary, another step down, and the fact that she'd found the place through well-connected friends added an unpleasant dash of public charity.

He'd miss Malibu. Though he'd been lonely there, the blue days were ample recompense, and the fortunate sense of living in a private Eden. No one would ever colonize Encino.

At the office he slogged away on *Madame Curie.* At night he packed. His wanderings after leaving Baltimore had made him an expert at traveling light, but since coming West, somehow without realizing it he'd gradually added to his wardrobe so it no longer fit his bags. He'd also accumulated a distressing number of books. Likewise, as he cleaned out the closets and dresser drawers, he discovered empties he couldn't remember hiding. He would have said he'd been good about drinking, but he'd only been here six months and just upstairs there were a dozen bottles. He gathered them in a burlap sack, waited till the night watchman had passed and stuffed them deep in Bing Crosby's trash.

That weekend Sheilah helped him move, the two of them caravanning over Laurel Canyon in their loaded Fords like homesteaders, leaving the city and the sea behind. Encino was actually closer to the studios than Malibu, a fact not lost on the developers of Edendale, yet topping the pass and winding down the far side of the mountains felt like crossing a border, as if the valley were a different country. After the mobbed commercial blocks of Wilshire and Sunset, the wide-open fields seemed empty, strangely depopulated. A farmer hauling a hay wagon with his tractor waved them on. A mile later, a raven tore at something smashed flat in the road. Except for the mountains, they might have been in Nebraska.

He wasn't opposed to the rural life. Its slowness was better for getting work done. They'd rented the same kind of out-of-the-way estate in Delaware when he was beginning *Tender*, and though Zelda hadn't been well at Ellerslie, and they had too many weekend guests, he'd written the first and best section there. If Metro wasn't going to extend him, maybe he could finally start his novel. He thought he understood enough about Hollywood, and he'd never find a cheaper set-up.

The gate was unlocked. Magda had left fresh-cut roses by the sink, and an extra key which he presented to Sheilah. It didn't take long to get settled. The closet in the master bedroom was meant for a couple, and his things looked meager, as if he were just visiting. The place was spotless, but Sheilah insisted on scrubbing the kitchen before they made a run to the store at the crossroads to stock the larder. Like the Malibu Inn, it had his Gordon's. They noticed the bottles at the same time, and she gave him a look like a warning. He didn't joke that the price was lower here.

To celebrate—or was it a bribe?—she made him his favorite, steak and mashed potatoes and gravy. They read Shelley and Donne and Byron, and later, by candlelight, christened the lumpy bed.

"I hope you like it here."

"I hear the girl's very dependable."

"Be serious."

"I like being here with you."

"That's not what I mean."

It was the same impasse they always reached, the inevitable yet impossible next step that kept them apart. In everything else they agreed, but here her sympathy ended and they both turned hard, fighting with silence. He was to blame, yet felt helpless, bound. The only worthy sacrifice was the one he couldn't make.

"I'm sure I will," he said, and thanked her.

He would get used to it, he knew. Asheville or Santa Monica, a flophouse or a palace—after the last few years he'd become adaptable as a hermit crab. Soon enough, as he set to work, this estrangement would fade and blur into a new routine. He was a poor boy from a rich neighborhood, a scholarship kid at boarding school, a midwesterner in the East, an easterner out West. If he'd ever belonged anywhere, those places were gone, the happiness he recalled there as fleeting as the seasons. Tom was right, and yet his fear was that he would die like him, a wanderer far from home— the fate of all men. Why should he be an exception?

Encino wasn't that much different from Malibu. The nearest neighbors were miles away and passed him on the highway without a hint of recognition. Besides Magda and the man at the store, he knew no one. His first week, Sheilah found reasons to make the drive out, as if looking in on an elderly relative, bringing him a fuzzy bathmat and new pillows, but that Friday she had a premiere. He ended up working late and eating dinner in the commissary with Oppy, whom he suspected had taken up residence in the Iron Lung. He and Sheilah rendezvoused for some dancing at the Zebra Room, and by then he was tired. Tomorrow UCLA was playing Carnegie Tech, a big game. It was more convenient—and nicer—to stay at her place. They spent the weekend together, which made returning to Belly Acres that much harder.

The girl Magda bragged of he never saw. Wednesdays when

he came home the dishes in the drainer were put away, the waste-baskets emptied, the toilet spotless.

He missed Flora, as he knew he would. He hated cooking for himself almost as much as he hated wasting money on restaurants. He was capable of making hamburgers and grilled cheese sandwiches and heating cans of soup, but the results, while perfectly edible, were depressing, plus he was never home, so half of what he bought went bad. In Tryon he'd lived on potted meat, soda crackers and apples, and he laid in a supply of these for emergencies, along with his Hershey bars, the worst thing for his insomnia. Left alone, he ate like a child and felt dull and unhealthy. Because the commissary was lively and cheap, he began to eat all of his meals there, sharing a table with Oppy three times a day.

At night they were the only writers, surrounded by extras and technicians working swing shift. *The Wizard of Oz* was shooting, and the booths were full of munchkins and flying monkeys forking up chicken croquettes and spaghetti, napkins tucked into their collars to protect their costumes. In his desk Oppy kept a bottle of rye he broke out before the siren died, and by dinnertime he was loose-lipped. His mood depended on how his afternoon picks had done at Santa Anita—usually poorly, though once in a while he was ebullient. Like Scott, he was afraid he wouldn't be renewed, which at his age would be disastrous. He had five children by three wives he was still paying alimony. He'd been in pictures from the beginning, churning out two-reelers for Griffith and Biograph, and Scott attended his stories of the early days as if they were sacred lore. Unlike Anita Loos, he'd never graduated to the big money. He'd worked for everyone from Goldwyn to Hal Roach, bouncing around town, latching on to any assignment he could find.

"They don't have a clue. Know how many credits I got? A hundred forty-six. Know how many Huxley's got? One. They're paying him three grand a week, and they want to give *me* the ax."

Scott, who was making only twelve-fifty, didn't say that *Pride and Prejudice* had won the Oscar. "You ever get one for *The Louis Pasteur Story*?"

"Lousy bastards stole it from me. I handed them the set-up on a platter and they gave it to Goldwyn's brother-in-law. Everyone talks about the unions. When it comes down to it, it's a family business."

"What are you on now?"

"Some godawful pug pic for Wally Beery. I got a beaut of a title for it though." His hands framed an invisible marquee. "The Roar of the Crowd."

"Not bad. I'll trade you *Madame Curie.*"

"That piece of crap? No dice."

"So what do you do if they don't extend you?"

"Call my agent and wait for the merry-go-round to come around. It will, it just takes a while sometimes. Don't worry about me, I got some rainy day money I can fall back on."

While they talked, Oppy kept peeking over Scott's shoulder as if he was spying on someone. When they'd finished and were leaving, he stopped beside the table directly behind them. It hadn't been cleared, and with no attempt to disguise his actions, as if he were a customer at a bakery, he plucked two hard rolls from a basket, wrapped them in napkins and shoved one in each pocket.

Here, Scott thought, was his future.

After dinner he left Oppy to his office and pecked away at *Madame Curie*, but there was no one to impress. He could only postpone going home so long. Eventually he had to pack up his briefcase, get in the car and drive over the mountains again, the city glowing in the rearview mirror as he climbed the pass, then absolute blackness. The store at the crossroads was closed, a pink neon clock guarding the darkened filling station. For miles the road was a straight shot. Beyond the sign for the dam the only landmarks were telephone poles. Twice he slowed for the gate before he finally turned in. He never remembered to leave a light on, and rubbed his thumb over the doorknob to find the keyhole.

"Here I am," he said to the living room. "Did you miss me?"

Part of his disaffection was the holidays. For Christmas he'd arranged for Scottie to see Zelda in Montgomery, but he and Sheilah had no special plans. He had trouble summoning the mood when every day he expected Eddie Knopf to walk into his office and tell him he was finished. Ober said he didn't know anything, and Scott armored himself against the inevitable. Instead of putting his last check against his debts, he told Ober to go ahead and pay Scottie's spring tuition.

The morning of the Christmas party he was deep in his easy chair, lost in Conrad, when there was a knock at the door. He thought that out of decency they would wait till next week, but closed the book and stood, ready to accept his fate.

Before he could get it, Dottie burst in with the paper, Alan shutting the door behind him.

"Did you see this?" she asked, shoving the front page at him.

"We thought maybe you knew something," Alan said.

FOREIGN ENVOY LEAPS TO DEATH, the headline read, with a picture of the Arroyo Seco Bridge in Pasadena. It was a famous jumping-off spot, taller than the Hollywoodland sign. The city had erected fences. Scott skimmed the article, stopping on the name: Gerhardt Reinecke.

"Not very original," Alan said. "But effective."

"When did it happen?"

"Last night," Dottie said.

"Merry Christmas." Alan made a heave-ho gesture.

"Jesus." His first thought was Ernest. He refused to believe he would execute someone in cold blood. He could see Mank walking with the German, patting his shoulder like a mob boss coddling a nervous accountant. Producers were men who knew how to solve problems. All the studios had underworld ties, not just Metro. It wasn't politics, it was business. This is what happens when you cross Hollywood. After the riots in Berlin, there was no need to pretend anymore.

"No more European market," he said.

"No more European censor," Dottie said.

"So they just picked him up and chucked him over," Alan said.

"I imagine he was dead by then."

"I wouldn't bet on it," Dottie said.

They hadn't heard anything more from their sources, and told him to keep an ear out, as if the three of them might somehow be implicated. He'd never met the man, the connection between them tenuous at best, and yet he felt vaguely guilty.

The news made the Christmas party stranger than usual, a ghoulish celebration. He wandered through the bacchanal in shock, stopping at the commissary to watch the grips and secretaries dancing, aware that in a safe in some producer's office—if not here at Metro, then on another lot—there was likely a coded ledger akin to a bookie's cryptic dib sheets that could testify to the industry's collective and murderous intent.

As he was fleeing, crossing the plaza in front of the Iron Lung, Oppy intercepted him, plowed and wearing an artfully crushed stovepipe hat. "You there, my fine fellow. Do you know if they've sold the prize turkey that was hanging at the poulterer's?"

"Why, Mr. Scrooge," Scott played along. "I thought Christmas was a humbug."

"The hell it is. They picked me up for six months. Took 'em long enough, the dopes."

"Congratulations."

"How 'bout you?"

"Not a word."

"That's tough. Listen, if there's anything I can do."

"Thanks," Scott said.

He saved his consternation for the drive home, frowning as the radio burbled on. He didn't blame Oppy, the old rummy was just trying to survive, and still Scott couldn't believe it. He'd worked hard on all of the projects they'd given him and hadn't touched a drop on the lot. It must have been something he'd said, an unintentional slight. Like Reinecke, he'd crossed the wrong person.

Sheilah had heard the murder rumors, but not even the *Hollywood Reporter* would touch them. Every so often Dottie checked in with him, bringing news from Pasadena. Officially Reinecke was a suicide. There was no investigation, no formal inquest. Benchley never mentioned him, and as Christmas came and went, Scott understood the whole town was content to let his death remain, like Jean Harlow's or Thelma Todd's, an open secret.

In Encino, so far out in the hills, the nights were quiet. The rainy season was underway, and when he couldn't sleep, he took his chloral and waited, listening to the downspouts run and the cottage settle, conjuring from a single creak a dark figure on the stairs.

He dreamed he'd killed a woman. Barefoot, wearing a white gown, she lay in the high, haylike grass of a field just beyond his headlights, her eyes open. He didn't know how he'd killed her, or why, only that he had. He'd brought her here in his car. Her death was an accident, but he was afraid it would look suspicious. To save himself he needed to bury the body, which he did, digging her grave deep, sweating with the effort, terrified that eventually she'd be found, his life ruined. Within the dream, he had a creeping dread that it wasn't a nightmare but a memory, his sin, like the woman's identity, willfully forgotten. His fear was so strong that on waking—as if he were mad or an amnesiac—he couldn't be sure it hadn't happened.

He asked Magda to lock the gate, and in the mornings remembered to leave a light on. In the store he watched the other customers, letting them check out first. Once, driving home, he turned early to see if he was being followed, but the other car went straight.

He didn't have to be a detective to know what was coming. Friday after lunch, Eddie called. Could he please come upstairs and see him? Scott was tempted to take his briefcase and leave. Sunday was New Year's Day, and half the offices in his wing were dark. Oppy was tapping away, likely filling pages with gibberish, but Dottie and Alan were in New York, Huxley on a beach in Mexico. Childish as it was, as Scott made the long walk to the elevator, he thought that now he'd never get his name on his door.

Eddie was apologetic, shaking his hand, telling him how great he was, how much everyone loved *Three Comrades*. As of today, he was off *Madame Curie*. Whatever pages he had he should turn in to his secretary.

"All I need is another week."

It wasn't Eddie's decision. For the last month of his contract, Scott was being loaned out to Mayer's son-in-law, David O. Selznick. He needed all hands on *Gone with the Wind*.

Only in Hollywood could you be simultaneously fired and put on the hottest property in town.

"That piece of crap?" Scott said. "No dice."

But Monday he showed up on time.

HANGOVER, NEW HAMPSHIRE

S elznick was of the new generation. Unlike Mayer and Goldwyn and Laemmle, he hadn't sold buttons in Minsk or shirtwaists in Krakow on the narrowest of margins to leave the bosom of his family and endure weeks in steerage dreaming of streets paved with gold only to wash up in the shtetl-like tenements of the Lower East Side where daily he fought his neighbors, those same margins and the Italian rackets, earning a second fortune he used to bankroll a third and, as mere by-product, creating from the dusty foothills of West L.A. a gilded fiefdom called Hollywood. He was American, therefore soft, without Thalberg's genius. To compensate he paid more, buying the talent he lacked, and put in longer hours than any of the old guard, aided by prescribed doses of amphetamines.

Scott's job for him on *Gone with the Wind* was to polish the previous polish of Sidney Howard's script, a task that changed from moment to moment as Selznick, distracted by every fleeting notion and under pressure to start shooting, produced a gusher of memos.

Scene 71: Wouldn't Scarlett be mad when Rhett laughs at her? Would she really let him get away with it without saying something? One good kicker here.

Scene 75: We should feel badly for Charles but also understand it's not Scarlett's fault her trap has caught the wrong man. She can't laugh at him for falling for her and neither can we. It's a comic misunderstanding but he has to keep his dignity.

Scott was further hamstrung by Selznick's dictum that he use only Margaret Mitchell's dialogue. It was like trying to finish a vast, intricate puzzle with the wrong pieces.

The novel wasn't awful, as he'd feared. When it had first come out he'd dismissed it as a bloated costume drama, all hoopskirts and magnolia blossoms. Now, having to read it closely, he found it shallow yet compelling, staying up late and closing the fat book with satisfaction. In Scarlett he saw Zelda's wildness and pride, in Rhett his own rage and dissipation. They weren't innocents like Romeo and Juliet. Their love was undeniable for the same reasons it couldn't survive. It would end in ruin, which, thematically, fit with the backdrop of the Lost Cause, doomed from the start. Selznick was right, it would make a great movie, if he'd ever let go of it.

Gone with the Wind was his. He'd personally acquired the rights while the novel was still in manuscript, staking fifty thousand dollars on a first-time author. The casting of Scarlett had taken over two years, becoming a public sweepstakes, with stars like Lana Turner and Joan Bennett openly campaigning for the role, which, in Cinderella fashion, finally went to a Brit, Scott's leading lady from *A Yank at Oxford*, Vivien Leigh, scandalizing the book's fans.

Like Mank, what Selznick really wanted was to write the script himself. Scott was the ninth writer he'd hired, and he was still sending out dozens of notes on each scene. Like Ahab, he thought of nothing else, but he was trying to turn over drafts too fast and his mind wasn't organized. Often Scott was asked to restore lines Selznick had ordered cut that same day.

The process was made harder by the fact that he didn't sleep and expected his writers to keep the same hours, pulling all-nighters with him on the top floor of the production office while in the soundstages graveyard shift was finishing the sets. Afraid of taking pills, Scott relied on his insomnia and his Cokes to keep him going, fixing lines with a broken-backed copy of the novel open beside him like a dictionary while his secretary catnapped, shoeless, on the couch. Every couple of hours Selznick called them in for a story conference, going over the last set of changes scene by scene, reading the dialogue out loud in his Yiddish-tinged Pittsburgh accent while chomping on a cigar so that Suellen and Melanie and Prissy all sounded like two-bit fight promoters.

"Whaddya think?" he asked the room, making the secretaries look up from their dictation. "I know it's right outta the book, but something's off. I want her to say something stronger, like, 'I could never love a man like that'—not that exactly, but close. Scott? Carolyn? Anyone?"

Thalberg, when Scott had worked with him, said almost nothing, instructing by his silences. At the end of a story conference, after listening to everyone's pitches, he would simply nod to anoint the winner or shake his head and make a single oblique suggestion reframing the main difficulty. He didn't worry about dialogue or costumes or music. He had people to do that. Selznick lacked his trust and bogged down in the small stuff, going round and round.

Technically they were already in production. Back in December Selznick had shot his climactic scene, the burning of Atlanta, torching RKO's old exteriors from *King Kong*. Instead of Gable and Vivien Leigh, their stand-ins drove a buckboard through the flames, doubled over to hide their expendable faces. Since then Selznick had been paying his contract players—most, like Scott, on loan—to wait around while he fiddled with the script. Unlike Metro, the studio was too small to absorb so much overhead, and the trades knew it, speculating on his downfall and questioning Mayer's judgment. "The Son-in-Law Also Sets," *Variety* taunted.

For Scott it was like watching a mad king hold court as the castle was laid siege. Night after night they leapfrogged along, finishing one draft and starting another, addressing questions Selznick had forgotten he'd asked the last time. Scott's contract was up in two weeks. Though he had no shot at a credit, the longer he hung on the better chance he had of being hired by another studio, and he matched Selznick's maniacal singlemindedness with his own, sleeping in his spare time and dreaming of the characters, carrying the novel around like a bible. He knew better than anyone how to live in an imaginary world.

He was tired. Once he'd been a night owl, a prowler of back alleys, brimming with cash and passwords. Now the late hours made him dull. Like Selznick, the studio never rested. While the stars slept safely behind the monogrammed gates of their Bel Air mansions, the elves of third shift mended their costumes and pieced together their scenes, added music and sound effects and titles. To revive himself, Scott took the elevator down and walked outside past the cutting rooms and scoring stages to the commissary for a piece of cherry pie à la mode or a square of fudge, wondering at the odd carpenters and painters playing cards where during the day the famous kibitzed, as if they might be actors as well. At three in the morning the lot took on a fantastic aspect, the moonlight imbuing the false fronts with a pregnant solidity, and as he walked back to the office he imagined his producer unable to sleep and haunting the empty streets. He would meet his girl here as if she were a figment born of his separateness. The question was how.

He had a week left on his contract when Selznick summoned him for their first conference of the night and there at his place at the table sat another writer with another secretary.

"John Van Druten," Selznick said, as if Scott should know who he was.

While he understood it was inevitable, he was still jealous. He shook the man's hand and took the chair opposite him, recalling Paramore.

They weren't collaborating. He was off the project. As with *Madame Curie*, he was to hand over everything to his successor. He'd be paid for his remaining days. He'd done good work. Selznick would be happy to give him a recommendation. All he had to do was call Carolyn and she'd arrange it.

For this, Scott thanked him.

At midnight he found himself outside the gate, suddenly unemployed, his briefcase weighted with unopened Cokes. In the oil fields beyond the lot, plumes of fire spouted geyserlike above the derricks, burning off impurities. He called Sheilah from a chop suey parlor on Crenshaw and she told him to come over. He still had to drive across town. After she'd done her best to comfort him, she slept, soughing, while he lay there wide awake, leafing through scenes like Selznick, second-guessing himself.

His pass was good for another week. Rather than waste this last opportunity, each morning he reported to the Iron Lung, sending Eddie pitch memos with ideas for Joan Crawford and Garbo. His entire time at Metro he'd been assigned to women's pictures, but with war imminent, spy thrillers were big. Why not combine the two? With the shamelessness of a carpetbagger he cobbled together a scenario in which a happily married wife discovers her husband is secretly a Bund member. In another he made it a mother and son, a mother and daughter, two best friends, a next-door neighbor, the parish priest. He worked out his plots in detail, each of them taking place around a submarine base, or sometimes a shipyard. The secretary's eyes went dead when she saw him coming, and the memos were full of typos. Treachery was everywhere.

Will consider, Eddie replied.

Though Scott hadn't told anyone he was leaving, Friday Dottie and Alan and Benchley and Oppy took him out to Stern's Barbecue for a proper send-off. They joked about him raiding the supply closet.

"What are you going to do with all of your free time?" Dottie asked.

"What I came here to do," he said. "Write."

They raised their glasses as if he were the lucky one.

In his office he watched for Mr. Ito, and was gratified to see him a final time, stalking through the weeds beneath the billboard, tail twitching. He would miss the boulevard with its trolleys, and the drugstore, even the dusty parking lots, each car, including his own, carrying its mystery. He left *Nostromo* for the next resident, and his marked copy of *Gone with the Wind*. When the siren blew, he packed up his briefcase as if it were any other Friday, took the elevator down and wished the guard a pleasant weekend.

He spent it with Sheilah, putting off going home until Monday, and then was stuck there when his car died, completely and finally, a mile short of the gate, forcing him to pay a tow truck and take out a bank note at extortionate interest to buy Sid Perelman's old Ford. He called Ober, who called Swanie Swanson in the Hollywood office to scare him up another job.

Compounding his bad luck, he came down with a rattling chest cold. As Sheilah predicted, he'd worked himself sick, and took to bed again, sketching a short story on his lapboard—a fired screenwriter trying to sneak back on the lot.

By design he'd avoided spending time at Belly Acres. Now he knew why. For whole days he spoke to no one, padding to the bathroom and the kitchen in his house slippers. The quiet was unearthly, dispelled by only the trains calling across the valley, the occasional plane headed for Glendale. He wished he were at Sheilah's but didn't dare presume.

Wednesday he met Magda's housekeeper Luz, not a girl at all but a tiny, graying Filipina who muttered to herself in her mother tongue as she cleaned. He apologized for his whiskers and his robe and the wastebasket full of balled tissues.

"Is okay," she said, nodding, and kept dusting.

According to Swanie, Scott was on Selznick's short list for *Rebecca*. Sheilah brought him a copy from the library, and he started blocking out a treatment. The novel felt like a gloss on *Jane Eyre*—a humble heroine marrying into a landed family. He saw echoes of Thornfield Hall and Tara in Manderley, and there was some genius in having the first Mrs. DeWinter hover over the proceedings like a ghost, though how he would suggest that on-screen he had no idea. Selznick would line up a dozen hacks behind him anyway. As with *Three Comrades*, he'd have to build his draft to withstand their chisels if he wanted a credit.

He calculated his wages on paper. At the least he'd get six weeks at twelve-fifty, enough to stake him for the summer and part of the fall. If Selznick paid him what he was worth, he'd be able to start his novel, though if *Rebecca* was a success, he could choose his next two or three jobs and put away a serious nest egg. He was aware—as he was aware of his dwindling savings—that he was counting on the man who'd just let him go to hire him back again, but ascribed the irony to the madness of the business. Like a starlet, he waited for Swanie to call.

I wish you could go to Havana with the group too, he wrote Zelda. *If I had the means, you know I would happily pay your way, but currently I'm between engagements, which is a polite way of saying Metro has decided they can survive without me. I'm again that sorriest of species, the freelancer. I have prospects but must stand ready to snatch whatever chance is offered me. The good news is that Scottie is planning to come down there for Easter, so you at least have that to look forward to.*

Out of obligation more than any real desire, he wanted to say he'd try to visit her soon, but knew she'd take it as a promise and dun him with it later. Better to be honest than feed a false hope.

As the days passed, his own fluctuated between the grandiose and the desperate. He was deciding which of his old friends he could appeal to for a loan when Swanie called with a job—not *Rebecca* but a college picture for United Artists starring Ann Sheridan. Six weeks at fifteen hundred.

"What happened to *Rebecca*?" Scott asked. What happened to *Marie Antoinette*?

"Hitchcock wanted his own guy."

"Did you show him the treatment?"

"You'll like UA," Swanie said. "It's cake compared to Selznick."

Winter Carnival. There was no point arguing. It was only after he said yes that Swanie told him he had a cowriter, a kid named Budd Schulberg. It was his treatment. The picture was set at Dartmouth; he'd graduated just a few years earlier.

"Schulberg as in B. P. Schulberg?" The head of Paramount.

"Nice kid."

Not surprisingly, he was. When Scott met him the next day at the studio he was polite and earnest, telling Scott how much he admired *Gatsby*. Like a fledgling prince, from birth he'd been raised to rule with equanimity. Though his profile belonged to the ghettos of the Old World, like Scottie's dance partners from Choate and Andover he possessed a courtliness that spoke of money. He was tweedy, affecting a pipe, but stubby as a bulldog, a shorter version of Stromberg. He'd majored in English and wanted to know Scott's opinion of Malraux, and was pleased to hear he was a fan of *The Trial*. Europe was falling, the war was just a matter of time. And what about the Screenwriters' Guild? Could the unions work with the studios? Though they'd just met, he was forthright to the point of being unguarded. Scott thought his confidence came from being born into royalty. No one had ever told him to shut up.

Their producer, Walter Wanger, was a Dartmouth man as well, making the picture feel like a vanity project. They had nothing besides a muddled ten-page treatment. Passing through Hanover, Ann Sheridan gets caught up in Winter Carnival. Scott's first job was to figure out how, and to what end.

As at Metro, the most imposing structure on the UA lot was the front gate, a triumphal arch of plaster meant to resemble white marble. Despite its blatant fakery, every time he pulled in and flashed his pass at the guard he was comforted by the fact that he had a job. The commissary was cheap and filling, and all day, in return for Scott's recollections of Ernest and Gertrude Stein in Paris, Budd regaled him with tales of growing up the son of a mogul. His godmother was Clara Bow. Gloria Swanson had been his babysitter. As Scott concocted a reason for Ann Sheridan to enter the Queen of the Snows pageant, he stockpiled notes toward his novel. He was almost ready to start when Wanger announced they were all going to Dartmouth for the carnival.

While a camera crew scouted backgrounds, he and Budd would roam the campus soaking up local color, as if that might inspire them. It was a fool's errand, an excuse for the producer to return to his alma mater the conquering hero, but Scott couldn't refuse.

Sheilah's syndicate was based in New York. Taking advantage of her growing celebrity, she arranged a visit to the home office to interview the stars on Broadway and be seen around town. Once he was done in New Hampshire, they'd rendezvous in the city. The prospect struck him as complicated and maybe unwise. Wanger had made it clear the trip was strictly business—spouses weren't welcome—and while she'd already met Ober, and Scott wanted to take her to 21 and the Dizzy Club and the Montmartre, the thought of showing her his old haunts seemed a betrayal of Zelda. At the same time he couldn't discourage her without hurting her feelings, and played along, feigning anticipation.

There were only so many flights a day, and by chance the syndicate's travel agent booked her a ticket for the same one he and Budd were on. The usual subterfuge obtained. She sat in the back of the plane as if they were traveling separately, incognito behind her sunglasses.

It was Budd's first assignment, and his father had brought two iced magnums of Mumm's to see him off. The zaftig bottles reminded Scott of La Coupole, the wide-shouldered jeroboams and balthazars and nebuchadnezzars ranked by height between the booths, representing endless plenty. Once they were airborne, Budd popped the corks and helped the stewardess serve the cabin. In his blue blazer and white turtleneck, he presided over the festivities like the junior commodore of a yacht club. Tomorrow morning they were meeting Wanger at the Waldorf for a story conference, and they still hadn't nailed down the third act. The plan had been to brainstorm as they crossed the country. A glass or two of champagne seemed the perfect stimulant, though a glance back at Sheilah earned him a pursed-lipped warning. He gave her a shrug as if it would be rude to refuse.

"She needs to win the money for her train fare to Canada," Budd said.

"If she wins, her picture will be in the paper, and they'll find out where she is."

"So how does she get the money?"

"She needs to be in the pageant. That's our whole set-up."

"How does she get the money?" Budd asked, stumped.

Scott finished his paper cup and motioned for a refill. "Okay. She wins. They see her picture in the paper and come after her, but she's already on the train. It's a race to the border. Scratch that. She's got to lose, I don't know how exactly. The topper is that the kids save her out of the goodness of their hearts."

"I can see you've never been to Dartmouth."

"At the end they all sing the school song on the quad by torchlight. The snow's falling. We go close on her as she joins in, her eyes are filled with tears of gratitude. And curtain."

"How does she know the words?"

"You get the idea."

"What about the daughter?"

"Haven't figured that one out yet."

Rather than let it go to waste, they split the second magnum between them. Somewhere over New Mexico they stopped working and took up Lawrence and Dos Passos and raised a toast to poor Tom Wolfe. The champagne was still cold but the first giddy lift had worn off, and he was having trouble following Budd, who was telling a rambling story about Valentino showing up at a childhood friend's birthday party, the point of which had something to do with *Gatsby* and decadence and the Decline of the West. Budd stuttered, tripping on his consonants, and Scott was relieved to see there were only a couple of inches left.

At the stopover in Kansas City, Sheilah waylaid him while Budd was in the john. In her headscarf and dark glasses and pea coat she might have been a spy. She leaned close so no one could hear.

"Please be careful."

"We're just having a good time."

"That's what I'm worried about."

"He's in worse shape than I am."

"I don't care about him."

"We're all done anyway."

"Are you ready for tomorrow?"

"Yes." He tried to steal a kiss, but she shied away, glancing around.

"Get some rest," she said. "You look tired."

Aloft again, the stewardess prepared their berths like a nurse. Budd gave him the choice. Scott took the lower, drawing the curtains as if they might keep out the noise. He didn't expect to sleep, despite the champagne. His mouth was sour and the pillow was thin, so he was shocked, hours later, to wake in the fusty, buzzing darkness with a stiff neck.

He didn't get to say good-bye to Sheilah in Newark. A company car was waiting for her, a limo for them. It was Thursday and raining; the Lincoln Tunnel crawled. They had an hour before their meeting at the Waldorf. Last night they'd almost solved the third act, but now Budd couldn't make sense of his notes. His stutter had returned, and his face was puffy, his eyes slits, as if he'd lost a fight. Like soldiers, they'd slept in their clothes and gave off a vinegary musk. Scott feared that Wanger might blame him for corrupting the lad, when it was the opposite.

They checked in, showered and met back in the lobby, clean-shaven but still bleary.

"Let me do the talking," Scott said in the elevator.

The producer greeted them wearing a forest-green Dartmouth tie, and Scott knew he had the right ending, with the firelight playing over the ice sculptures and the whole student body and their dates singing the school song. What he didn't have was the motivation for the other girls to give their kissing booth money to Jill, beyond her need and innate nobility. In his pitch he made the case that as a mother and a woman of the world she'd helped each of them in some way backstage, dispensing wisdom as well as beauty secrets. She wasn't a professor with a fancy degree, she taught from humble experience, and as he followed his conceit to its logical conclusion, he convinced himself. When her rival won, it made sense that the others crowded around Ann Sheridan in sympathy, leaving the winner to storm off, leading to the big finale, fire and ice, the crane pulling away to show the whole quad as the song finished. Roll credits.

"It's nothing like the treatment," Wanger said, addressing Budd. "I like the mother angle. But do me a favor, both of you."

"Yes, sir."

"Lay off the sauce. I'm serious. I'm not paying you to go to Carnival, I'm paying you to write. I'm only going to say it once."

"Yes, sir."

In the elevator, Budd shook his head in wonder. "Where'd you come up with the mother stuff?"

Scott tapped his temple. "Old Metro trick. L.B. loves his mother."

To celebrate they repaired to the Oak Room for brunch and Bloody Marys, and then a brief interlude at McNulty's on Third Avenue to show Budd the booth where Ring used to hold court, and then a quick one at the Algonquin for Dottie and Benchley. By late afternoon when they met the train at Grand Central they were fully resuscitated.

The Winter Carnival Special was a rolling sorority party rocking along the Hudson in the dusk, stopping at forlorn stations to pick up the red-cheeked daughters of Barnard and Vassar loaded down with skis and skates and snowshoes. Besides a few lucky frat brothers from Columbia and New Haven, they were the only men onboard. Wanger had reserved them a first-class stateroom between his own and the camera crew's, who'd gotten their shots and, now that the light outside was dying, had packed away their lenses and settled into an endless poker game, openly handing around a pint of bourbon.

It was Budd's idea that they should go mingle and take notes, a valid if transparent excuse to ditch Wanger. Scott went along with it, though as they made their way through the cars, he was intimidated by the profusion of youth and beauty. The girls were Scottie's age, fresh from Ethel Walker and Miss Porter's, abounding with health and raucous as an infantry company on leave, taunting Budd for being short and making fun of Scott's jacket. As the only men, they were objects of curiosity. When they stopped, a circle gathered around them like a mob.

"Does Daddy go everywhere with you, or do they let you out by yourself?"

"He's actually a very famous writer," Budd said.

"Is that right?"

"I'm not," Scott said.

"What's your name?"

"F. Scott Fitzgerald."

"You're right, you're not."

Someone pressed a flask on him, and they laughed as if he might be offended. He raised it to the car.

"'O for a draught of vintage that hath been cool'd a long age in the deep-delved earth.'"

"'Tasting of Flora and the country green,'" a jet-haired girl in a red sweater answered, "'dance, and Provencal song and mirth.'"

"Now that's a famous writer." Scott took a pull—cherry brandy, sweet as cough syrup—reached across the seats and handed her the flask.

"Give us another one."

"No, no."

"Yes, yes."

"'She walks in beauty, like the night,'" the girl began.

"'Of cloudless climes and starry skies.'"

They tried to pass the flask back to him. He held up both hands as if it were a grenade, tipping his chin at Budd. "You must know something by heart."

"'The boy stood on the burning deck,'" Budd declaimed, and took a slug.

"There's your first note," Scott said when they'd moved on to the next car. "Cherry brandy. Bleh."

Like the children they were, the girls of the Winter Carnival Special were partial to sweets and campfire songs. As Scott and Budd ventured deeper into the coaches, they ran across isolated bands swilling blackberry and peach brandies and peppermint schnapps, the sugar coating their teeth like lollipops. What he'd give for a simple fifth of gin.

Budd was proving to be the perfect accomplice. Like Ring, he had a genius for finding a drink. Long after midnight, when they stopped in Springfield, he led Scott to an all-night drugstore across from the station to buy a pint. The rain had changed to a blowing snow, and Scott had left his overcoat in their compartment. As they trudged back through the slush, bareheaded, flakes swirled beneath the streetlamps and landed on his cheeks, making him blink. The train seemed to be moving, though with the wind it could have been an illusion.

"Is it?" he asked.

"I don't think so."

The yellow windows kept sliding along the platform, and now he could hear the engine, and the clanking of the trucks, picking up speed. The red lights of the caboose slipped behind the station-house.

"We missed it," he said.

"It's not supposed to leave till a quarter to."

It was too dark for him to read his watch.

"Hell," said Budd, and looked around.

Scott laughed. It was exactly what happened in the script.

"What's so funny?"

"This is how she misses her train. We should be taking notes."

"Let me get my pen out."

There were no cabs, but the stationmaster called a wrecker that would take them to the next stop. The driver wore a fur hood like an Eskimo and apologized for the heater being broken. In the dash he had a bottle of applejack, and as they plowed through the darkness, racing the train, the snow buffeting the windshield like a process shot, Scott shivered, keenly aware they were having an adventure.

"You ever done this before?" he asked the driver.

"Two, three times a week. People always think they have more time than they do."

Scott made sure Budd was writing it down. If Wanger caught them, they could say they were doing research.

In Northampton the platform swarmed with the Smith and Mount Holyoke contingents. Scott tipped the driver for getting them there on time and followed Budd through the slush. He'd thought to bring gloves but not galoshes, and his socks were soaked. While there was a men's room in the station where he might dry them, he couldn't risk missing the train. Once they were onboard, he stopped at a lavatory and wrung them into the sink. His toenails were blue as those of a corpse.

The camera crew was still playing cards, but Wanger's compartment was dark. Budd gently closed their door and pulled the shade, and they turned in, Scott once again taking the lower berth. He knew he should be tired, yet instead of sleeping he kept replaying their escapade in the wrecker. Without writing a line they'd nailed down a dozen scenes. Deepening this feeling of bounty was the knowledge that in his briefcase his pint of gin waited, safe as a bank deposit. Warm under the covers, swaying with the rhythm of the train, he thought it had been a good night.

As they sped north the snow fell steadily, hour upon hour, so that the next morning, when they reached Hanover, the world was drifted, blinding white, reminding him of St. Paul. The entire student body greeted them at the station, along with the marching band, as if the train were carrying their mail-order brides. The scene was staged; Wanger had arranged everything. Before the porters would let anyone off, the camera crew scrambled into position, high-stepping through the knee-deep snow for the ideal vantage. Only when the one named Robinson chopped his arm like a clapper were the girls allowed out. Scott and Budd hung back, not wanting to ruin the shot.

A bus dropped them at the Hanover Inn, where their reservation had been lost. Wanger and the camera crew all had rooms. Theirs alone was missing. Since the Inn was sold out for the weekend, the best the manager could do was offer them the lumber room in the attic and a pair of cots.

The room was beneath the eaves, and unheated. Their breath hung in the air.

"This is a joke," Scott said.

"More like an initiation," Budd said, and he got it. A king's son, he had to constantly prove himself to his future subjects. Scott's shoes were still damp, and he felt a cough coming on, but if Budd was game, so was he.

After a meeting with Wanger and the camera crew, they tramped the campus, the blocky, red brick Federal halls nowhere near as interesting as Princeton's. Scott really should have thought to bring boots. The paths that crisscrossed the quad had been plowed but were still slippery in spots, and twice Budd had to catch his arm. The sun was out, dazzling, and from the glistening snow, like totems, rose a giant penguin and rampant polar bear and pie-eyed owl, the Thinker and the Sphinx and the fierce, bearded head of Old Man Winter, a hipped pagoda worthy of Grauman's Chinese, a castle complete with a working drawbridge, a sleigh the size of a locomotive, and a half-dozen other whimsical marvels of engineering Budd dutifully logged in his notebook. At the very center, jacketless and ruddy in the cold, a brigade of students was building the bonfire, heaping the logs up in a huge pyre, and again Scott envied their animal vigor. A proud alum, Budd showed him the skating pond and the ski jump and the toboggan chute, all of which figured in key scenes and none of which was inspiring. He didn't want to sound like a slacker, but hadn't they walked enough? His shoulder hurt from the berth, and he wanted to go back to the Inn and warm himself by the fire. With the overnights he'd lost hold of what day it was and had to remind himself: Friday, it's only Friday.

If the ride up was a party, the carnival was a debauch. Once the sun went down and the torches were lit, the quad filled with dark mobs of revelers, the sculptures casting quavering shadows across the halls. On all sides the classroom windows gave back flames, as if the campus were under attack. A swing band commanded the steps of the library, and above the tribal drumming and the wailing of a sax came cries of aggression and ecstasy. To fortify himself against the cold, Scott nipped at his pint, lending the clear night air and firelight an inscrutable beauty. Years ago, right after they were married, he'd taken Zelda to Winter Carnival in St. Paul. She'd hated it, her Southern blood too thin. He hadn't been back since. Now he felt an atavistic kinship with the tradition, as if he were meant to be here. Atop Old Man Winter, riding his stormy forehead like an elephant, sat two dateless girls, drinking and watching the fray. He raised his bottle and they returned the salute.

At eleven, when the band finished, the dancers headed for fraternity row. Budd had been treasurer of Pi Lambda Phi, and they walked straight past the waiting line and inside. The brothers drew them tankards of grog, a brew whose ingredients Scott didn't recognize. The president offered a long, ceremonial toast. Budd thanked him and allowed that, being a Princeton man, Scott didn't have to chug his.

"Like fun," he said, and beat them all to the bottom. "Who won? Prince-ton!" he cheered, his chin dripping, and was shouted down.

In the backyard they had their own fire going, singing bawdy songs to shock the girls, sparks corkscrewing up to the stars. The brothers waited on Budd like the emeritus he was, making sure their tankards were never empty. Some of the girls were roasting marshmallows, and Scott burned his tongue on one, and then was taken with a sneezing fit. Though his nose was running, he no longer felt the cold. The grog was filling. In the bathroom he braced a hand on the wall, impressed with the island of bubbles he was making. Outside again, he discovered his pint was killed. Frowning, he tossed it in the fire. The crowd had thinned to just a few brothers; the girls were gone. After the last two nights, he was ready for bed.

"One more," Budd said, holding up a finger.

"Just one."

It became their watchword, both a joke and a goad. They stayed out too late, stumbling up the maid's staircase, afraid Wanger would be laying for them in the lobby.

The next morning they tried to placate him, giving the camera crew a new list of master shots they wanted, which seemed to displease him.

"That's why I've got a director. What I need from you is scenes—action, words. What have you been doing all this time?"

The rest of the day they hibernated in the library, pacing and smoking as they hashed out the second act, which further worsened Scott's cough. They were sober to meet the dean and some of the English faculty for dinner, including Budd's old professor who assigned his classes *Gatsby*. Once it broke up, they bolted for the carnival like children let out for recess.

Tomorrow was the pageant, and the torchlight procession of skiers down the mountain. Tonight was just a warm-up, and accordingly they treated it like an evening off, hitting the frat for some grog and then the skating party, not bothering to take notes. They passed from fire to fire like beggars, trading industry gossip for whatever the students would share with them, becoming connoisseurs of mulled wine and hot toddies and schnapps. It never failed. Everyone wanted to know what Hollywood was like.

By now Scott's throat was raw. His breathing was raspy and with every swallow his tonsils stung, yet he kept drinking, fueled by the camaraderie and the promise of adventure. There was a sleigh ride, and a party in a barn decorated with crepe paper streamers, and a snowball fight during which he caught one flush in the face, bloodying his nose. He was sitting on a log with his head tipped back, trying to stanch the flow, when in town a bell rang the hour: one, two. He waited for three, and was disappointed.

Later, somehow, they ended up at the toboggan chute. There were no lights, and as they were climbing the stairs, he slipped and fell, banging his hip, and stayed down.

"You alive?" Budd asked.

"Go ahead."

"I'm not going without you."

"I'm gonna rest here."

"It's not that far."

"Go."

"Come on," Budd said, hauling him to his feet and taking his weight as if he were an injured comrade. "One more."

"One more."

There were several dozen more steps, and then at the top, through the trees, a view of the moon and the whole campus below that made him clutch the railing with both hands. The chute fell away into darkness. On Summit Avenue the sledding hill was in the cemetery. At the bottom a stone bridge crossed a stream, and when he was a toddler a neighbor girl had been killed there, prompting the caretaker to erect a wall of hay bales every winter.

"Sit here," Budd said, guiding him down behind a husky boy and then fitting himself against his back. "All right, on three. One. Two."

The others joined in and the toboggan slid forward, hung, stuck on the edge a second, before it tipped into the chute. They plunged, shuddering down the rutted ice, the snow rushing up his cuffs. The wind siphoned tears from his eyes. He couldn't see a thing and huddled against the boy's broad back, using him as a shield. As they gathered speed, hurtling headlong for the trees, the toboggan caught a bump and they were airborne, floating weightless and unmoored, at the mercy of gravity. He didn't know what he was doing here, away from everyone he loved. If he should die of a broken neck, he'd have no explanation. He could hear Budd and the others screaming with glee, and then the toboggan yawed and bit as it landed, tipping sideways, spilling them like a handful of dice across the hill before continuing down backwards, trailing its rope.

They were young, and laughed at disaster. Except for Scott, they all wanted to go again.

"One more," Budd said.

"I'll see you at the Inn."

"You know where it is from here?"

Scott waved toward campus.

"Okay, pal," Budd said. "Let's go."

They didn't take the road Scott would have followed. As they crossed the quad, the sculptures loomed like the ruins of forgotten idols. It was colder now, the walks were glazed. Budd supported him by a forearm to keep him upright, and still Scott lost his footing, dropping to one knee again and again like a skater with weak ankles. "Here we go," Budd said. "Upsy-daisy." It would have been comic if it weren't so exhausting. He fell a last time, spectacularly, on his back, in the middle of the street before the Inn. As Budd picked him up beneath the arms, a car turned the corner and blinded them with its headlights. Though it was impossible, Scott thought of Reinecke returned from the grave to take his revenge.

"I'm sorry," Scott mumbled as Budd dragged him to the curb. The porch light was on, and as they stumbled up the stairs, closing on their goal, the door opened, and there, glaring like a worried father, was Wanger.

"Hey, boss," Scott said before Budd could shush him.

"What in the hell do you two think you're doing?"

"We were j-j-just heading to b-bed."

"You can pack your bags, both of you. I meant what I said. I don't care who you are, I'll be damned if I'll let a pair of drunks ruin my picture. I don't know when the next train is, but you boys are going to be on it."

"Drunks?" Scott started.

"Yes, sir," Budd said, cutting him off.

"I'll show you who's drunk," Scott said, fumbling with his gloves, as if challenging him to a duel. One fell to the porch floor.

Wanger didn't wait for him to retrieve it. He slammed the door and stalked across the lobby, leaving them standing in the cold.

"What kind of name is *Wang*er anyway?" Scott asked.

Upstairs, on his cot, he bet Wanger would change his mind in the morning.

"No," Budd said, "he's not like L.B. We should have gone in the back. I'm sorry, I should have thought."

"The hell with him then."

"At least we don't have to spend another night in this god-damned icebox."

"Amen," Scott said.

It was too late, the damage was done. In the morning his lungs were tight and he was running a high fever. On the train he came down with the sweats, shivering in his overcoat. Outside, the Hudson swam by, gray and dizzying. It wasn't just the booze, it was everything together. From Grand Central, Budd phoned Sheilah at her hotel.

She met them at the hospital. When she saw Scott propped on a gurney in the emergency room, she shook her head as if she should have known better, and still she came to his side.

"What have you done to yourself now?"

LA VIA BLANCA

Like a weakness for underage flesh or declaring oneself a Bolshevik, drinking was a pardonable offense in Hollywood, but not indefinitely. Owing to his youth and bloodline, Budd was immediately hired back on returning, while Scott, the old reprobate, was blackballed. He'd betrayed Wanger's faith, and Selznick's word, and by extension Mayer, who had no use for him anyway. His sentence was house arrest while Swanie beat the bushes, though as the weeks passed and Scott regained his strength, the prospect seemed hopeless. He woke early and wrote stories in his robe and slippers, sipping coffee, the house deathly still around him, and found he enjoyed it. The simplicity of pencil and paper was refreshing. Somewhere in this latest humiliation there was a lesson in self-reliance. He'd failed so completely that he'd become his own man again.

Sheilah was cool to him, breaking dates and using the drive as an excuse not to visit. She was justified, he supposed, yet the longer she held on to her anger, the less it felt directed at his lapse than at him. He knew her frustration from years of trying to help Zelda. In Sheilah's eyes he was old and weak and unreliable. She was tired of playing nursemaid, and he couldn't blame her. In his lower moments he thought she would be better off rid of him, and then when she told him she had to go to the Clover Club with Young Doug, he accused her of planning exactly that.

He understood why she didn't want to be seen with him; he was a disgrace. He barely rated a mention in the *Reporter* anymore.

Why, she asked, did he have to be such a damned ass?

They fought with a despair that came from having waived all expectations. He was sure she hated him for wasting her time. He did.

UA had paid him for only the one week, and most of that had gone to the hospital. The remainder had to last the month, unless he could sell a story. He put off Magda and made his car payment. The rest of the bills he collected in a drawer as if he might forget them.

He went door to door, calling everyone at Metro and his friends at the Garden, bugging Bogie to put in a word at Warner's, asking Sid if Pep could get him in at Republic. He wasn't above a B picture or even a short subject. Don Stewart took him at his word and recruited him for a dog at Paramount called *Air Raid*. Six weeks at three-fifty. He wondered if Budd had a hand in it. He really was a decent kid, even if the money was rotten.

It seems unfair that my stock has fallen so precipitously, he wrote Ober. *The Dartmouth trip was a folly from the start. There was nothing whatsoever to be gained by my going East. I was in no shape to undertake a goose chase on a producer's whim, but felt I had no choice. I'm entirely recovered save my pride and my pocketbook, and have managed to get back to my desk, where I belonged all along. Here's "Strange Sanctuary," as discussed. I'm happy with how it turned out after much tinkering with the ending. You might try Collier's if it's too short for the Post, though I do think it's right up their alley.*

He was careful at Paramount. *Air Raid* was dreck, but like Oppy, he'd come to appreciate his lot privileges, and vowed to stick there. Chastened, as always, by his last disaster, he was determined to stay sober and show them he could outwork anyone. Every morning he rose before the sun and drove over the pass, his briefcase clinking with Cokes. The credit was his and Don's to split. There was no jockeying or backstabbing in meetings, no other team waiting in the wings. When the producer—aptly named Lazarus—wanted a bigger scene or a beauty shot of the star, they went back to their shared office and churned one out. It was like cooking eggs to order. He deposited his paycheck and admired the growing balance in his bankbook as if it were proof of his virtue. He could pay his bills. Soon he could start his novel. It was all he wanted.

For her Easter break Scottie visited Zelda, taking the train down by herself. After missing Christmas once again, he wished he were there, inimical to his own health as it might be. He hadn't seen Zelda since the debacle in Virginia Beach, and Saturday as he ran his errands he was tempted to cable Dr. Carroll and see how they were faring. If she was able, maybe this summer they could take that trip to Cuba she'd missed, just the two of them. He had some money now but no time. He held off making any promises, pending Scottie's report.

Later that week, as he was working on a story, he got stuck and stood up to pace the floor. He was dressed for the studio, including his good shoes, the same slick-soled Oxfords that had failed him in the snow, now shined to ebon perfection, as if he were back at Newman or in the army again, subject to the morning line-up. His usual route, as he roamed his mind, was through the living room, skirting the coffee table, into the kitchen for an unseeing look out the window at the blond hills, then back behind the sofa to the dining room table, where his pad waited. He stood, lips pinched, still mulling his last sentence, and stepped clear of his chair. He had a habit, like Pierrot, of tipping his head back as he walked and questioning the blank page of the ceiling, as if the answer might be written there. Nothing—just a water stain, a few loose flakes of paint held in place by spiderwebs Luz was too short to reach. He turned for the living room, bridging with one stride the perilous canal of bare wood between the two ugly rag rugs, and as his right foot lighted, the boards beneath it gave like the spongy floor of a funhouse, then recoiled, knocking him off balance. To avoid falling over the coffee table, he dove for the sofa as if it were the goal line, just as, in the kitchen, a pewter plate commemorating the Golden Spike leapt from its nail, struck the counter on the way down and clattered to the linoleum.

He held his breath, expecting the room to move, but it was finished. He'd survived his first earthquake. There was probably no surer sign that he was an easterner, but it seemed an accomplishment. For weeks he would recall the spastic, wavering sensation, as if to prove it had actually happened.

At the studio no one was impressed. A water main had broken in the back lot, sending an impromptu river through the Chinatown set, and the commissary was closed. After his drugstore lunch he surveyed the damage. Capsized in a muddy pond, nested in the lath-and-canvas wrack of a dozen scrims like a cottage swept from its foundation, lay a serene Buddha. Rips in the idol's jade skin disclosed it was made of foam rubber. A trio of grips conferred by a crane, debating its fate. They were technicians, practical men. The plates of the continental shelf—the world itself—had shifted, and their first concern was putting things back in place. He could have told them it was no use, though his whole life he'd done the same.

Scottie wasn't good about writing, too busy with school and boys and other extracurricular exploits, and finally he lost patience and prodded her. Inevitably, their letters crossed in the mail, and he regretted not holding off.

I'm so glad your visit went well, he wrote. *It's easy to forget that your mother when fully herself can be the pleasantest of companions. Despite all of her tribulations she's managed to retain a playful charm I find touching. Some part of her will always be young and devil-may-care, for better or worse. I know she worries that you've seen her in more of her worse than her better moments lately, so maybe this will even the scales a bit.*

My own plans here are unsettled, but once I have the time I intend to take her on a long-overdue vacation. I have three more weeks on the bomb-shelter picture, which is the best I can say for it. I'm giving it my strongest effort nonetheless, as you should with Philosophy. You must know by now that life presents us with only so many opportunities, and

the greatest regrets attach to those we squander, whether through sloth or
weakness or pride. What I am asking is that you stick with it, whatever it
is, so that when you get to be my age you can look back and say you did
everything you could. Thus endeth the lesson. (And no, I will not apolo-
gize for the headmasterly tone. You know I think you're a lovely person
and brag about you to everyone who will listen, but Pie, you are not and
never will be a C student. I know this because I have been a C student and
a D student and an F student and wish I had never been. Do as I say, etc.)

He took his own advice. Without Sheilah his evenings were
free, and as *Air Raid* neared its explosive climax, he wrote morning and night, shipping off two more stories to Ober. At the least,
he figured, they were worth two-fifty apiece. With the extra money
he could hire a secretary to transcribe his piles of notes for the
novel. He'd start this summer, once he was done at Paramount.

He was hoping to catch on there for one more project. He
didn't want a six-month contract like Don's, just another picture to
pad his bank account, another credit for his resumé. His next-to-last
week he asked Swanie to talk to Lazarus. Before Swanie could call
him, word came down: *Air Raid* was being shelved.

Scott wanted an explanation, as if a valid reason might cush-
ion the shock. Don, Swanie, Sheilah—they all shrugged. That was
Hollywood.

He'd be paid, but he was off the lot, and Swanie couldn't get
him back on. He had all day to write now, wandering the house
like a ghost in his robe and slippers. He'd grown so used to his
routine that being let go broke his rhythm. He wasn't ready to start
the novel, and every story idea seemed trite.

Ober had more bad news. The *Post* and *Collier's* had both
passed on "Strange Sanctuary," as had *Esquire*. He didn't want to
submit it elsewhere without talking with Scott.

"Where is 'elsewhere'?"

"*Liberty.*"

Had it come to that? They'd gone there only once before, when
he was at his lowest.

"What about the *Century*?"

"They're not reading right now."

"*Redbook.*"

"Not their thing."

"*The American.*"

"Folded a year ago."

"What if we go out with the other two instead?"

"We can do that," Ober said, his lack of enthusiasm plain.

"How much is *Liberty* paying nowadays?"

"Same as before—a hundred."

"Fine," Scott said, "let's try them."

But they didn't want it either.

Of the three stories, Ober thought the first one the best. He didn't think it would be useful showing the other two to the *Post* or *Collier's*.

"What about *Esquire*?"

"We can try *Esquire*."

Scott couldn't decide if it was his tone he resented or the empty concession. Both. Wasn't Ober supposed to believe in him?

The next week he received an envelope in the mail from Ober's accountants, his full name printed in the cellophane window. It was a check, though for what he didn't have a guess. Perhaps this was Ober's way of apologizing. He saved it till last, setting the bills aside and composing himself before ripping open the flap. It was a royalty check from Scribners, along with a detailed statement. Combined, for the period ending in January, his books had earned a total of $1.43.

"That is cute," he said, then turned the check over and endorsed it.

Alone, with no prospects and nothing to work on, he was wasting his time, and decided, while he had the means, to take Zelda to Cuba for their anniversary. He prepared by drinking beer and fighting with Sheilah. She surprised him, driving out to Encino unannounced. After weeks of ignoring him, she didn't want him to go.

"You know what's going to happen. Look at yourself—it's already starting."

"It's been over a year."

"You can see her in the hospital."

"I promised."

"Didn't Scottie just visit her?"

"She says she's doing well. Even if she wasn't, she's my wife."

"I just don't want you to hurt yourself again."

He had nothing to rebut her, and thought of his producer and his English girl. They would never fight like this.

"Go," she said. "I can't stop you."

"You can't."

"At least promise me you won't drink on the plane."

"I promise."

"Or in the airport."

"Or in the airport."

"Not even a beer."

He raised his bottle. "Not even a beer."

But then, two nights before he was supposed to go, he ran out of beer and opened a bottle of gin. In his stupor he called her to come rescue him. By the time she arrived he'd forgotten calling and told her to leave him alone. For reasons unknown, his gun sat on top of his bureau. When she tried to sneak it into her purse he grabbed her wrist. She slapped him hard across the face, knocking him to the floor.

When she discovered the gun was loaded, she railed at him.

All he could say was that he was sorry. He wasn't going to do anything.

"I didn't pull myself out of the gutter to waste my life on you," she said, and left, taking it with her.

There wasn't enough time to make up. There was barely time for him to get sober. Maybe the trip would be good, a break for both of them.

As if to prove her wrong, he abstained the whole way across the country, sleeping the last leg, and arrived fresh and rested. Tryon never changed—the train station, the library, his old hotel. He might have been gone for the weekend. Along the winding drive to the hospital, the rhododendron were in bloom.

Before he could see Zelda, Dr. Carroll took him into his office
and filled him in on her progress. She'd been stable almost five
months now. There was still a touch of religious mania—no more
than your average Baptist, he joked. Overall she was responding
to treatment. How had he been? Last time there'd been some
trouble. They didn't want to upset her, especially now.

Ober, Sheilah, now the doctor. Why did everyone speak to him
as if he were a child?

"Of course not," Scott said, and signed the papers.

The Zelda the nurse delivered from the women's wing was
new to him, another imposter. Her hair was dark as chocolate, a
bad dye job, her bangs cut straight as a monk's. For the first time in
her life she wore glasses, gold wire rims, which, combined with
the hair, seemed a clumsy disguise. In his absence she'd grown
moon-faced and jowly like her sister Rosalind, fine lines like cracks
around her mouth. After Sheilah she seemed dowdy and middle-
aged, an effect only exacerbated by her lost-and-found clothes.

"Dodo," she said, claiming him, but stood apart, as if out of
modesty or following orders.

After an awkward second he moved to embrace her. "Happy
anniversary."

"Yes, happy anniversary."

"How many is it now?" the doctor prodded.

Nineteen. She'd been nineteen when he married her, his wild
belle, and if that girl was gone, so was the dashing lieutenant he'd
been, with his pocket Keats and his overseas cap and his dreams
of immortality. The years may have shown more outwardly on
her, but the two of them were a pair in a way he and Sheilah, with
her indomitable health, would never be.

"You look well."

"Thank you."

"Scottie said you had a good visit."

"We had a nice time. She was very sweet."

In front of the doctor they spoke with a saccharine courtesy as
if at the last second he might change his mind. Zelda was bringing

her box of watercolors to do a few seascapes. It would be nice to have something new to paint for a change. He told them to have fun, an injunction Scott thought misbegotten.

She didn't take his hand as they crossed the lobby, and he saw he'd been wrong. Her earlier reserve wasn't abstract but purposeful, directed at him, as if, without his prior knowledge, they were fighting. He wondered if somehow—not necessarily through Scottie—she'd found out about Sheilah.

She was subdued in the car, waiting till they were outside the gates and into the shade of the woods to make her opening statement.

"I think I'm ready to go home."

"Right now, you mean."

"I'm serious. When we come back I'd like you to talk to the doctor."

"I will," he said.

"You'll see, I'm really so much better."

"You'll excuse me if I've heard that before."

"That's why I want you to see for yourself."

He'd observed her enough to know when she was off. She might seem fine now, reasonable and alert, but that was typical of the first day. Inevitably would come the slippage—the blank spots and delusions and outbursts. She wouldn't be able to hide it for a week at close quarters.

"Fair enough," he said. "I hope you are."

She would be sane. He would be sober. Even before they boarded the plane, their time together was an experiment, one they'd attempted for more than a decade, in all the best places. He had no reason to believe the results would be any different here, yet out of a stubborn loyalty or inborn urge to punish himself, he was willing to try again. In the airport, when she returned from the ladies room, about her neck she wore a tiny silver cross she touched from time to time, as if for luck. As they fought the trade winds across the Straits of Florida, the Keys below white as salt in the glimmering turquoise, the fatalist in him thought it would be easier if they just got it over with now instead of spending the week dreading the inevitable.

Ernest had a place near Havana, but held everything that had happened against Zelda. Scott would have to visit him some other trip.

Varadero was an hour outside the city on the north shore, at the end of the Via Blanca, a highway bordered by cane fields and whitewashed churches. Donkey carts shared the road with blaring diesel trucks hauling sea salt from the Bay of Cardenas. The Playa Azul ran the length of the peninsula, the grand hotels set down like temples among the fishing villages.

They were at the Club Kawama, in the main house, a lichened granite villa with balconies overlooking the pool. With its royal palms and Moorish fountains and stucco bungalows, it might have been the Garden of Allah; all that was missing was the ghost of its owner. The season had ended and one wing was closed, its windows shuttered. In the dining room their first night, he heard another couple speaking German and wondered if they were spies or exiles or both. The woman was younger, a dark blonde dressed for the casino, her bare shoulders caramel colored. He and Zelda had a suite with separate beds, and with a wistful envy he watched the couple finish and head out for the evening.

"You should introduce yourself," she said. "I'm sure they're more fun than I am."

"Fun's the last thing I need. I have too much fun, I get in trouble."

"That's not fun, that's everything. We were never good at moderation, either of us."

"I never wanted to be," he said.

"And now you do."

"Now I don't have a choice, if I ever did."

"You did," she said. "You just didn't care."

"You were like that too."

"I'm not saying I wasn't. I know I was awful."

"You were wonderful," he said.

"Wonderfully awful."

"I thought so."

"You didn't always."

"Mostly I did."

"Mostly," she said, because the exceptions were great and un-forgivable on both sides. All they had was the past, but they couldn't go back.

It was night out and bats fluttered above the lighted pool as they walked across the courtyard to their room. The air was humid and still, waves falling softly in the darkness. He thought of Sheilah in Malibu, the two of them lying on the cool sand, watching the planes glide blinking through the maplike backdrop of stars. *I didn't pull myself out of the gutter to waste my life on you.* Later, in his narrow bed, after Zelda had said her prayers and turned in, he heard splashing and padded to the balcony. It was the Germans, frolicking like otters. For a long moment he watched them from the shadows, then quietly closed the doors.

In the morning they were open and a pink dawn washed the sky to the east. Zelda was gone. Her bed was made, on the nightstand a Gideon Bible, her place in the middle of Ecclesiastes kept by a black ribbon. Outside, a rooster crowed and crowed. It was only five thirty. He pictured her at the bottom of the pool or face-down in the breakers and tugged on yesterday's clothes, raced down the stairs and through the blinding courtyard and across the shuffleboard courts, only to find her on the beach with her easel, trying to match the color of the sunrise. With her coolie hat and sunglasses and pale limbs, she looked like any tourist.

"What are you doing up?" she asked.

"Looking for you."

"Go back to bed. I don't need a keeper."

That's the whole question, isn't it, he might have said. Or, better: I have no desire to be one.

"How about breakfast when you're done?"

"Can you wait an hour?"

He'd waited ten years. What was another hour?

"You know where to find me," he said, and then couldn't get back to sleep.

They ate on a patio off the main dining room, watching the

high-piled clouds and a red-funneled liner making for Havana. He had tarlike coffee while she attacked her English breakfast with the gusto of a parolee. She offered him a sausage; he wasn't hungry. He didn't remember her ever having an appetite like this and wondered if it was the drugs.

The rumpled *New York Herald* the waiter retrieved for him was a week old. Again, imitating Hitler, Mussolini sent his troops into Albania unopposed.

Already the day was hot, the waves glinting as they rose and broke.

"I love the beach," she said. "The light's so clear here. Are you going to write today?"

"I'm going to try," he said, though in truth he had no plans. All his life he'd believed in the primacy of work, yet he'd written nothing since he'd talked to Ober. Did it really take so little to discourage him? For years her dabbling had struck him as slapdash and glib, lacking the discipline of the professional. Now he envied her simple love of creation. He'd written too much for money.

The light and heat reminded him of Saint-Raphael. Their days there shared the same tropical languor. He sequestered himself in his room while she made studies of the sea and sky, the fishing boats, the village with its busy *mercado*—baskets of purple squid and whiskery rockfish, pullets sticking their heads through the bars of wooden cages. They rendezvoused at noon and ate lunch at a cantina facing the zocalo, arroz con pollo for thirty centavos. Beer was just three, and probably safer than the water, but he was good. She asked him for a cigarette as if it weren't forbidden, blew out a cloud and murmured with pleasure.

"It's nice to be able to do what you want," she said.

"Even when it's bad for you."

"Especially then. 'Sin in haste, repent at leisure.' "

"The other way around makes no sense," he agreed.

Later he wondered if she was referring to herself or to him, to the ancient past or the immediate present. He was used to divining her riddles when she was sick. In this case she'd left room for interpretation, the comment intentionally barbed. He was pleased she was better—he wanted her to be strong—but it was also unsettling, as if he'd lost some advantage.

After lunch, while the sun hung directly overhead, the Germans emerged, lanky and dark as natives, spread their towels on the sand and lay down to bake. The woman looked nothing like Sheilah, yet recalled her, by nubile youth alone. When he was stuck he wandered out to the balcony to spy on them, and toward the end of the day was horrified to find Zelda in her coolie hat stopped beside them, her easel folded away, engaged in conversation with the woman.

"They're Danish," she reported. "From Copenhagen. They come here every year. I invited them to dinner but they're going to Havana to see the opera."

"They don't get enough opera in Copenhagen."

"I guess not. They're very nice. Bengt and Anna. He's a professor of archaeology. She does some sort of social work with children."

While he was curious about them as well, he imagined what they made of this stout older woman in her pageboy haircut and paint-smeared blouse asking them to dinner. Could they tell she wasn't quite right, or did she come across as your typical off-season busybody? Either way, short of an enforced luau on the beach, he didn't expect to be dining with the Danes.

It was a blow, he supposed, to admit they were no longer an amusing couple. They ate in the main room, undisturbed, one of three far-flung tables attended by a single waiter. The menu was the same as last night's; from the stains he assumed it never changed. He'd had better carne asada on the streets of Tijuana. Zelda was telling him her plans for tomorrow, which involved painting the different faces of the village church all day. "Like Monet," she said. From across the room the bar called to him, promising release. He ordered the tres leches cake with rum sauce and a coffee and left feeling slightly high.

As loudly as Zelda touted her new freedom, she stuck to her hospital schedule, turning her light out at nine, leaving him to read. He thought of sneaking down to the bar for a nightcap but resisted. In the morning she was up with the sun, not wanting to waste a minute of light.

There was something obsessive in her painting. Like his writing, it was an escape, a way of making time pass. What would happen if they had to spend the whole day together? But they hadn't in years. Even in Saint-Raphael their lives were separate, given to solitary pursuits. Why should that change now, with Scottie gone?

She seemed fine at lunch, not at all tired, relating what the sexton had told her about the church being the only building to survive the great hurricane as if it were proof of divine intervention.

"What about the fort?"

"They all drowned."

"All."

"That's what he said."

He wasn't used to her being so sure of herself, and expected, any minute, the bowed head and slumped shoulders, the mumbled liturgy. Instead she was direct and pleasant, making him impatient. He'd waited so long for her to be well again that he was skeptical, as if she were playing a trick on him.

That afternoon while she was occupied with the church he went through her room like a guard tossing a prisoner's cell. On her bureau rested a five-and-dime comb and brush set and a single vermillion lipstick, in the drawers several new pairs of underwear and hose. Her closet was a mélange of shifts without personality. She hadn't brought a swimsuit or sandals, which was unlike her. The nightstand held the Gideon Bible, a vial of her medication and a glass of water. The drawer was empty. He wasn't sure what he was looking for—an incriminating diary, maybe— but most of what she owned didn't reflect her, coming, as it did, from the hospital. The only real clue he could find was left in plain sight on the desk: a cardboard portfolio of her watercolors.

As she would admit, they were studies, quickly done. Technically, while the palms and fishing skiffs were somewhat clumsy, in the best of them she'd managed to capture the wide open feel of the sea and sky. They were pastoral—cool and blue, a touch bland.

There were no burgeoning orgies of flowers, no molten whirl of demonic faces, no lapping flames. They were the work of an earnest amateur, and if they were less interesting, they reassured him as nothing else could. He closed the portfolio, set it back on the desk and shut the door.

At dinner she went on at length about her afternoon. She had to go back tomorrow. She'd spent hours on the bell tower alone—she needed to buy some more white. The pictures of the hurricane the sexton showed her were fascinating. She thought she might do a whole series on them. He'd written badly at his story and was immune to her enthusiasm. He knew he was being uncharitable, in a mood, and forced himself to concentrate on what she was saying, but it was a struggle. Was it a side effect of the medication or his being sober that made her so dull?

After coffee she wanted to go for a stroll on the beach—an innocent request, yet inwardly he balked. They left their shoes by the lifeguard stand. The sand was cool and soft as flour. There was no moon, only the lamps of the fishermen spreading their nets, laughter floating across the water. Far down the strand a tiny kaleidoscope of a Ferris wheel beckoned. As they walked toward the colored lights, he was afraid she would take his hand.

"What is she like?" she asked.

At first he thought he'd misheard.

"Who?"

"Please, it's obvious." She didn't stop, didn't glance at him. "Let me guess. She's an actress. Blond and petite and very young. She thinks you're a genius."

He scoffed as if it were impossible. She might have been describing Lois Moran, fifteen years ago.

"I know you, Dodo. You're no good on your own."

"There isn't anyone."

"Really, I don't mind. I'll give you a divorce if you want."

Was she bargaining with him—a divorce for her freedom? The one had nothing to do with the other. And why, after all this time, would he want one now?

"I don't want a divorce," he said. "I want you to get better."

"And once I'm better, then what?"

"Then you can go home."

"What about you?"

They'd been so miserable together that he'd never invented a happy ending for them. He assumed they would go on like this indefinitely.

"I'll go wherever I have to go."

"Will you still come see me?"

"Of course I will."

He believed it when he said it, though later, wide awake in bed, he wondered if it was true. The whole conversation was strange. Until she'd brought up the possibility, he never dared imagine a life without her. Now the idea teased him, exposed him as weak and unprincipled. He was tempted to go down to the bar but held off, and then, the next night, when he finally gave in, he found it dark, the doors locked.

He ended up at the cantina, nursing a beer and admiring the local rituals of courtship as the young slowly processed around the zocalo beneath the eyes of the entire village. The waiter, as if it were a standard courtesy, asked if he wanted a woman.

"No, *gracias*," he said, waving him off. "I have too many already."

"You like the marijuana?"

"I'm happy with my *cerveza*."

"*Uno mas?*"

"No *mas*," he said, shaking his head, because he'd promised Sheilah.

Beyond the main square, the side streets were shadowed and rife with vice. On his way back to the hotel he passed a nightclub exuding a slinky rhumba, and a barker for a cooch show dabbing his forehead with a handkerchief, and, down a sinister alley, a crowd gathered in a garage lit by a bare bulb to bet on a cockfight, and thought of Ernest. When had he lost his sense of adventure?

The Danes were in the pool, naked, the water turning their

bodies cubist. He detoured around the shuffleboard courts so as not to intrude. Upstairs, he closed their balcony doors, brushed his teeth and went straight to bed, knowing Zelda would be up early.

The next morning, to avoid writing, he went fishing, taking a charter out into the straits with a couple other guests. Hopeful pelicans rode their wake. From the water the peninsula was a green strip of jungle dotted with white and pink and yellow boxes. Columbus had been here, and the conquistadors. Though it wasn't yet lunchtime, the other men drank beer and smoked cigars as if at a stag party. He concentrated on his casting and caught a sizable tarpon and an impressive hammerhead shark. Did *senor* want the kitchen to prepare them for dinner?

"Oh, you should have," Zelda said.

"That's what tourists do."

"We're tourists."

"We don't have to act like them."

"Didn't you want to take a tour of the fort?"

That night, as if to refute her, he lingered at the cantina, switching from beer to a local cane liquor, tipping the waiter outrageously. On the bandstand in the middle of the zocalo, a guitarist picked limpid tunes. Scott watched the young couples promenade beneath the strings of lights and remembered his first cotillion with Ginevra, the soft white gloves and boxed orchid he saved all month to buy, giving up cigarettes, and, later, on the balcony of the club, the darkness of the golf course and the lights on the dock, the sleek yachts at anchor. That summer the world was all promise and sweet fumbling, driving her father's Pierce-Arrow along the north shore to their lake house. She kissed him in the garden and at the rail of the ferry and in the boathouse with the rain tapping in the rafters. Everything unattainable was his, bestowed like a gift. By winter all of it was gone as if it never happened.

He sneered at his own sentimentality. His glass was empty again.

"*Uno mas?*" the waiter asked.

"*Uno mas,*" Scott said, holding up one finger.

Later, after the indestructible church had tolled midnight and the paths of the zocalo were empty, a fat gray moth lit on the rim of his glass. It sat there a long time, it seemed to him, flexing its wings as if testing them before fluttering away over the other tables. He thought the moment remarkable, charged, but the waiter had vanished and there was no one to bear witness. He decided he needed to leave, otherwise he might not make it home, and then was amused when, attempting to don his suit jacket, he kept missing the armhole.

The waiter appeared, bottle in hand.

"No *mas*," Scott said, swaying with the palms, and gave him two more pesos. "*Muchas gracias, amigo. Buenos noches.*"

Did *senor* want a taxi?

"No, *gracias*. I can walk."

He could, miraculously, from years of practice, leaning forward and keeping his feet moving, using an occasional pole or wall to correct course. An insistent music thumped from the nightclub, all congas and maracas. He vamped, waggling a hand and shaking his hips as he passed the open door. He was sweltering and his mouth was dry. He could use a cold beer, but he needed to get to bed. Zelda would be up early, ready to paint the whole damned island.

He thought he was going the right way, but must have made a wrong turn, because he never reached the cooch parlor. The street he was following dead-ended at the churchyard, giving him a chance to pay his respects and relieve himself against a tree. Zipped up again, he reversed field, heading back toward the zocalo, tracing a maze of unfamiliar streets, led on by a riot of mingled voices like bidders at an auction till he found himself at the mouth of the alley with the brightly lighted garage he'd seen last night.

There were no tourists here. The garage was airless and stank of men's sweat, old motor oil and cheap cigars. Under a bare bulb hanging by a wire and haloed with smoke thick as opium, a circle of field-workers pressed against a knee-high ring of rough boards, waving pesos and calling out bets. *Cinco, el negro! El rojo, dos!* In the middle of the arena, to show their champion's fighting spirit, the two handlers danced toward each other, mimicking the sexual combat of the tango, the birds flaring, trying to strike. He'd seen this type of fight before, in a gypsy camp outside Nice, with Ernest, who'd propounded upon the savage nobility of the sport, imparting lore from the age of Charlemagne before two half-starved chickens cut each other to pieces.

The birds squawked and slashed the air. The ceremony was designed to excite the bettors as much as the combatants. As the only white man there, in his linen suit, Scott drew stares. To deflect suspicion, he unfurled a peso note and declared himself for the smaller El Negro, siding, as always, with the underdog. As if he possessed some occult knowledge, the betting shifted to the black one. The mob had all the logic of the stock exchange.

If they had simply let the cocks fight to the death, satisfying their atavistic drive for dominance, that would be cruelty enough. To improve on nature, the handlers fitted their claws with spurlike razors. Then, as now, Scott thought it a perversion. Ernest liked to believe the war had made him pitiless, but, having boxed with him, Scott suspected he enjoyed the superior feeling that came from watching another suffer. He'd never liked Zelda. When she was going through her first bad time, he told Scott directly that he was better off without her. True or not, they'd broken over it, though Scott still wished to be friends. Since then, Ernest hadn't missed an opportunity to kick him.

The handlers were ready, bent over their birds, whispering last-minute instructions. The ringmaster collected the final bets, locked them away in a tin strongbox and high-stepped over the boards and out of the arena, leaving behind an expectant silence. The handlers met in the center of the ring with all the solemnity of duelists. They went to one knee, setting the birds on the stained concrete, still restraining them. Around him the crowd was reverent, ready for a sacrifice. The ringmaster raised a hand like a starter, nodded to each handler in turn, and then, without a word, chopped his arm down.

The handlers stepped back and the crowd shouted. The birds flew, spurs flashing, colliding in a flurry of feathers under the bright light. They squabbled in midair, locked together, flapping and clawing, then dropped to the ground, stalking each other. They reared and tangled, scratching and jabbing. Three, four times they clashed and rested before one did any damage. Scott didn't see the blow, but after a skirmish the black was dragging a wing. The fellow beside him, a backer of El Rojo, laughed and clapped him on the shoulder.

The birds faced off and launched themselves again. With only one wing, the black barely left the ground, the red sailing high, stabbing it below the eye, landing near the far wall, where it strutted about as if the fight were over. The crowd jeered, and the handlers prowled the ring, urging the birds on. The red charged and the black squared, game. It tried to fight, but the red flew and struck it in the breast, the spur sinking in to the hilt. The black staggered back and fell on its side directly in front of Scott, its inky eye blinking up at him, a fresh drop of blood on its beak. The spur must have punctured a lung because its breast was wet and bubbled with every breath. Again, the red strutted in the center of the ring, declaring victory.

Still the crowd demanded the kill. The black's handler cursed and flung up a hand in disgust, disowning it, while the red's enjoined his bird, clapping. The black flapped and blinked up at Scott, its beak opening and closing mutely, and as the red homed in and the crowd howled, Scott stepped over the boards and scooped up the dying bird like a loose fumble.

He hadn't known beforehand he was going to do this, and had no plan. He made for the far wall, thinking he'd vault it, stiff-arm the ringmaster and keep going. There had to be a back door. Once he reached the street he could outrun the mob like Groton's heavy-footed secondary. He had surprise on his side, God and the right, like a knight errant, but he was drunk and old and caught his toe on the wall going over, and before he could get up they were on him.

CHER FRANÇOISE

He could not remember a hotter summer, or a lower time in his life. For weeks there wasn't a cloud, the arroyos drying up, the fields withering, sparking a water war between the valley farmers and the city. He couldn't stop drinking and fought with Sheilah and the platoon of nurses who invaded Belly Acres to give him the cure. Overtaxed, he collapsed and his TB flared, stealing his breath, drenching him in night sweats. The doctor prescribed strict bed rest and IV fluids. He was confined to his room, the blinds drawn against the heat, and as the stifling days eked by and he slowly regained himself, Sheilah visited less and less.

While he was incapacitated, rather than tend to him herself, she brought in a full-time housekeeper, a blue-black churchwoman from Fort Smith, Arkansas, who might have been Flora's cousin. Erleen wore a lavender turban and listened to the afternoon soap operas turned up loud while she cleaned the downstairs, talking back to the characters as if she had a role in the show. Though he didn't use any of the rooms, she ran the vacuum daily. Every morning while he was in the shower, she made his bed with clean sheets, laying out a fresh pair of pajamas and taking away the soaked ones; later they would be drying on the line like the dissected halves of a scarecrow. She catered to his sweet tooth, whipping up angel food cake and egg custard and generally making herself indispensable, and though Scott enjoyed her company, her presence only served to remind him of what she was—a paid stand-in for Sheilah.

He understood her reservations. He shared them, knowing too well his own faults and weaknesses. He'd apologized many times for the scene with the gun, for his constant lapses. In the beginning his shame had moved her, as if it were her responsibility to save him. Now she saw him as he saw Zelda, a helpless purveyor of chaos.

With rent money in the bank and no job prospects, he was free to start his novel, and resolved to win her back via sober industry.

Before he could write a sentence, he needed to get organized. The first step was registering at an employment agency for a secretary. After interviewing her to make sure she had no ties to the studios and swearing her to secrecy, he hired a bookish young woman named Frances Kroll. Lithe and pale and slightly knock-kneed, she was a transplanted New Yorker like Dottie, unimpressed with L.A. She said she'd read some of his stories in high school, which pleased him, though she couldn't recall which ones. Her father was a furrier in Hollywood, a connection he thought might prove useful. She was also Jewish, which would help him with his hero, Stahr, a far-flung son of the Old World.

They set up shop in the spare bedroom downstairs. Propped on pillows, he pawed through his boxes of notes, dictating character sketches and background details and ideas for scenes. She was a touch typist, holding her perfect posture as she rattled off staccato bursts, sometimes finishing before he did.

"Read that back to me," he asked, and she would have it.

She brought her own dictionary from home, and quickly he learned to defer to her on matters of spelling and grammar. She really belonged in college, but maintained that she was more interested in life. She was punctual and unstintingly chipper, helping Erleen in the kitchen and doting on him like a daughter, snipping a rose for the bud vase on his bureau and reminding him to take his pills. Even with the windows open and a fan going, the room was muggy, yet she never complained. After a particularly oppressive afternoon, when they were finished for the day, she came to him formally, as if petitioning for a special dispensation, and asked if she could wear shorts.

Early on, the work was bookkeeping. When he'd gone through all the boxes, he jotted a number by each entry, assigning them to categories she then collated on new pages. He went over these closely, making changes and passing them back, gradually, draft by draft, building a notebook while the fan paddled the sluggish air. Occasionally she couldn't read his handwriting and had to ask what a certain word was, but for long stretches they could go without talking, their shared effort, like the book's potential, filling him with contentment. Like him, she was a whistler, the two of them unconsciously picking up each other's tunes as they worked, twining, falling silent, beginning again. "The Bear Went Over the Mountain." "Tea for Two." He wondered if her boyfriend knew how funny she was.

The coincidence of their names tickled him. Franny, he called her, but more often, recalling Proust, Françoise.

"Françoise, take a letter, s'il vous plait."

"Oui, monsieur."

I hope the doctor takes into consideration what a peach you were to me through the whole ordeal, he dictated. *I'm still in bed but practically recovered, no thanks to the hellish weather. Water has become such a precious commodity that the dam here is guarded by armed constables and ice cubes have become a form of currency. Please don't fret about my health. It will not be four months. That quack in New York doesn't know my recuperative powers. The real shame is that it ruined what should have been—and still was, I submit—a triumph for you. I've written and told the doctor this. You were heroic and tender and lovely in every way, and I won't forget it.*

Frances didn't ask what had happened, though he could see she was intrigued. The hospital's address was an irresistible clue, and once again he struggled with how best to explain Zelda. Rest home and sanitarium were evasions, asylum frightening. He was afraid Frances might see him as tragic, and tried to be matter-of-fact.

"She's in a mental hygiene clinic."

"I'm sorry."

"Thank you. She hasn't been well for some time now. Lately she seems better, so we're hopeful."

"That's good."

"It is," he said.

He was honest, she was sympathetic. So why did he feel he'd betrayed their dearest secrets?

"Is this her?" Frances asked, pointing to a picture of Sheilah and himself at the Cocoanut Grove.

"No, that's just a friend."

"She's very pretty."

"She is," he said, noting the innate female prejudice against the better-looking.

He didn't have to explain Sheilah to Frances, and yet he courted her approval. He was still sending Sheilah roses with breast-beating notes. As he dictated his entreaties to Frances, she must have thought she'd walked into a Restoration farce, though she gave no sign. Friday, when he introduced the two of them, he felt the same trepidation he had that first dinner at the Troc with Sheilah and Scottie, and was relieved when they seemed to get along.

"She's very young," Sheilah said later.

"You make it sound like a bad thing."

"What I'm saying is that she's at a very impressionable age. She obviously thinks you're wonderful."

"I'm not?"

"You can be, when you're not being an ass."

"I believe it's pronounced 'arse.' "

"Case in point."

Terrible as it was to confess, during the week, with Frances there, he didn't miss Sheilah as much. The days were full as Stahr's Hollywood opened to him, another world. He woke early and worked so she would have fresh pages to type. At lunch Erleen made iced tea with sprigs of mint and served them on the shaded verandah overlooking the pool, taking a chair and fanning herself with her apron in lieu of a breeze. The hills were baked brown. In the distance rose the snow-covered peaks, promising a false relief. He had his one illicit cigarette for the day and they sat listening to the shrilling cicadas, invisible in the trees.

"Well," Erleen said when he was done, "time's a-wasting," and collected their plates on a tray.

His life was quiet, focused solely on the novel. With the heat wave he stayed inside, free to dream, never leaving his keep. If he needed a book from the library or a prescription filled, Frances had her father's Pontiac. He called her at all hours, rousting her from sleep with lists of things he wanted for tomorrow. He prevailed on her to deliver roses to Sheilah and choose Zelda's birthday card. No errand was too intimate. A confederate, she disposed of his empties and bought him extra cigarettes. She became his envoy, representing him at the bank and the post office and Western Union. If she were a conman, she could have taken him for everything he was worth—a toothless risk, since he had nothing.

With no job, he was vigilant with expenses, but as the weeks passed and the bills rolled in, his savings dwindled to an alarming figure. In a month Scottie was visiting him, and her fall tuition was due. There was no way he could pay it. He pressed Ober to send the stories to more places and met with the same indifferent resistance. Swanie said it was a bad time of year to approach the studios. Town cleared out in the summer. Everyone was in Malibu or up at Big Bear.

In the midst of his panic, Scottie wrote to say she'd sold an essay on the differences between her generation and his to *Mademoiselle*. It was scheduled for next month. Could he look it over for her?

KUDOS PIE, he cabled. MLLE FINE DEBUT JE TAIME DADDY

He was proud, yet the news left him feeling sour. He was aware that he was being small, and yet part of him suspected the magazine was taking advantage of her name—a hunch which proved true when he read the piece. Its thesis was that his views were as old-fashioned and outmoded now as the Charleston and bathtub gin, as if that generation didn't run the country. He told her he admired the wit in it and gently suggested she revise the piece to reflect a deeper continuity between the eras. *Without a real cataclysm like war,* he wrote, *very little changes. It's impossible for you to know, but 1920 and 1939 have more in common than 1913 and 1919, just as after the coming war 1939 will seem entirely a lost world. The luck I had was being old enough to see the new world clearly and so put in perspective both the admirable and the absurd.*

He expected she would ignore him, as usual. A father, his duty was to offer advice in excess and hope some stuck.

While he awaited her reply, he received Pep's novel about Hollywood, *The Day of the Locust.* After hearing Sid talk it up, he was afraid Pep might bird-dog his best material, but like Pep's other stuff it was wildly morbid and overwrought, including a truly marvelous riot at a premiere. There was almost no overlap with what he had planned. In his relief he wrote Pep a glowing note.

A few days later he got a call from Scottie—rare, given the cost of long distance. He thought she might be sore at him.

"What? No. I wouldn't call you for something like that. This is serious. Right before exams I started having stomach pains. I thought it was just nerves. I tried buttermilk and Bromo-Seltzer but nothing helped. Finally I went to the doctor. He says I have to have my appendix out."

"That's not so bad. Your mother had hers out." He tried to remember how much he'd paid for the operation, but it was fifteen years ago, and in francs.

"He said it's not urgent, but I should definitely have it done this summer."

"You're not in pain, are you?"

"It comes and goes. I'm sorry, Daddy."

She spoke as if she'd failed him, when, if anything, the opposite was true. Again he wondered what he was doing here. Seeking his fortune.

"It's all right, Pie. We'll figure something out."

"How are you doing?"

"I'm working," he said.

He had been, until then. Now he dropped everything to schedule her surgery. She was already going to visit Zelda in Asheville before heading west, the two of them staying in a Saluda boarding house like two matron ladies taking the waters. A few years ago when he'd broken his shoulder, the doctor in the hospital there had done a good job setting it. Was he available then? Perhaps she could come down a week earlier. Could Dr. Carroll give Zelda another week of leave? What time did the train arrive? He called back and forth with a calendar in his lap, and once he'd gotten it all in place, had Frances make the arrangements.

To pay for it, he had no choice but to appeal to Ober. In Scott's two years in Hollywood he'd completely paid off his debt, more than thirteen thousand. While he hated to go back to their old credit system, an advance of fifteen hundred was nothing against his future earnings. The novel was underway and he had two new stories for him.

Ober wired and told him to try Swanie.

He didn't want to swear in front of Frances. *"Merci,"* he said, and set the telegram aside.

Over the decades, how many tens of thousands in commissions had Ober skimmed from his labors? Scott had stood by him when he left to form his own agency. Now that he'd built a stable of moneymakers like Agatha Christie he didn't need Scott and his problems. Ober had always considered him irresponsible, especially with money. The last few times he'd seen him in New York had been at the end of binges—unrepresentative, he might argue. If this was about his drinking, Ober could have thrown him over ten, fifteen years ago. Why abandon him now when he was sober and doing good work?

DONT UNDERSTAND SUDDEN CHANGE IN POLICY, he cabled. WOULDNT ASK EXCEPT THREE FITZGERALDS UNDER DOCTORS CARE. PLEASE RECONSIDER.

After hearing nothing for a week, he wired Max: CAN YOU LEND ME 600 ONE MONTH. AM BROKE AND SCOTTIE NEEDS OPERATION. OBER REFUSES TO HELP. HAVE STARTED NOVEL.

GLAD TO, Max wired that afternoon. LOOKING FORWARD TO
PAGES WHEN READY.

Ober's response, when it finally arrived, was long and closely
reasoned, betraying, in spots, like an editorial, a moralistic tone.
Its theme was that darling of the prosperous, self-reliance. By becoming Scott's banker, Ober had done them both a disservice.
He'd hoped that finally squaring their accounts would put an end
to the loans and prod Scott to live within his means—which, given
how much he'd made last year, were comparatively generous. If he
needed more to cover his expenses, he could take on more assign-
ments there, or they could ask Max for an advance on the novel,
once he had a sizable chunk of it done.

Though he could argue that he'd never worked harder, or in
worse circumstances, there was nothing he could fully refute, and
no point. The sentiment was clear. Ober had carried him for years,
like the corner grocer in Buffalo extending credit to his mother
when they were short. No more. When he was flush Ober would
be there to collect his share, but in the lean times Scott would have
to fend for himself.

What galled him most was how slowly Ober had gotten back
to him after he'd wired the second time. Once again he'd made the
mistake of thinking publishing was a gentlemen's game. Before he
wrote to break formally with him, saying how sorry he was and
how much he appreciated him and Anne giving Scottie a home, he
sent the two new stories to *Esquire* and offered *Collier's* first serial
rights to the novel.

Max, who was a gentleman, asked him to reconsider, as if he
were being rash, until Scott explained it wasn't a case of him losing faith in Ober but vice-versa. *I'm sure it's a result of those wintry
afternoons memorizing the Baltimore Catechism—apostasy being the ul-
timate sin. All shall be saved who believe in me.*

He had a harder time explaining the break to Scottie, who,
with the egotism of the young, thought she was the cause of the
problem. She and Zelda were in Saluda, awaiting her operation.
He'd made a deal to pay the doctor on the installment plan, as if he

were buying furniture, and lied when she asked how much it was. He still had to pay the hospital and the day nurse.

"Put your mother on," he said. "I love you, Pie."

"I love you, Daddy."

Zelda sounded mousy and abstracted, like her own mother. She spoke haltingly in her impassive drawl, the dreamy belle. "You'd like it. It's cool at night. We're having a lovely time, just the two of us."

He wondered if she was drugged. After he'd hung up he realized he hadn't talked to her on the phone since she was at Pratt.

The day of the operation, he had Frances send Scottie her favorite, gladiolas. She was fine, already bragging about her battle scar. He was at Universal, where Swanie had gotten him on a dog of an academic comedy called *Open That Door*. A milquetoast geology professor leaves his ivory tower to climb a mountain and finds gold—and romance. Six weeks at three-fifty. It folded after one.

Esquire accepted a story, a reprieve, but he'd lost momentum on the novel, and with Scottie coming, he'd only have to set it aside again. He hadn't heard back from *Collier's*, which worried him. Having broken with Ober and already put the touch on Max, the list of old friends he might implore was short. Just contemplating borrowing money from Sheilah paralyzed him. Out of pride he wouldn't bother Ernest or Dottie, though, good comrades, they had it to burn. Bogie and O'Hara he didn't know well enough, or Pep or Sid. Ring would have given him fifty thousand without blinking. Sara and Gerald were a possibility, though Sara hadn't been happy with him after *Tender*.

In the end, heeding Ober's call of self-reliance, he took to bed with his lap desk and ashtray and churned out two more stories for *Esquire*. Frances sent them airmail, following up with a wire.

He wasn't new to ruin. He'd ducked creditors before, in Westport and New York, Montreux and Rome. After paying Zelda's monthly bill at Highland he couldn't make rent, and so, the day before Scottie arrived, against doctor's orders, dressed in his rube's suit, he drove the Ford to a hock shop on Wilshire. Frances followed in her Pontiac, waiting in the lot while he signed over the title and pocketed a hundred and fifty dollars. It would have to last until something else came through. He had nothing left worth pawning.

"*Merci, Françoise,*" he said as they rode through Hollywood.

"*Mais bien sur,*" she said.

Scottie was to understand the car was in the shop. He'd promised her driving lessons this trip and used the excuse to have Frances take her out in the Pontiac, the two of them cruising around Encino like best friends home for the summer. Along with her appendix she'd lost the last of her baby fat and her hair was light from the sun. In the afternoons the pool was full of boys from back East. At night they barbecued and sang campfire songs under the stars. Ober, maybe in conciliation, forwarded a check for radio royalties, and the car was fixed. To help celebrate, Sheilah made a rare appearance, meeting them at the Troc for an anniversary of sorts, though, wary of his lungs, they barely danced.

"She seemed different," Scottie said when they were alone at the end of the evening, sitting in Erleen's kitchen, eating blackberry pie.

"How so?"

"I don't think she was having much fun."

"She's worried about me."

"I worry about you too. I don't know, she felt different to me."

"You're not turning mystic on me."

"Stop," she said, and regrouped, looking at her hands in her lap, then seriously at him, as if she had grave news. "I told mother, and I wanted to tell you in person. I'm writing a novel."

"God help you. Is it about us?"

"That's what she asked. No."

"That's wonderful, Pie. And very brave of you, I must say. How far along are you?"

"Not quite a hundred pages. I was hoping, maybe later, if you have time—"

"I'd love to see them," he said, thinking with alarm that she was ahead of him.

"They're not ready yet."

"When they are, just let me know. I'd be honored. Will you be showing them to your mother as well?"

She wasn't sure of the right answer.

"She'd like that," he said.

"I will."

"Oh God, we've failed. Our baby's a writer."

Her visit raced by like a week at the beach. It seemed she was always leaving. Her last day, she passed her test, acing the course in the Pontiac. At the train station she hugged Frances like a sister, and he felt rich.

Friday the Germans invaded Poland. England and France declared war. It was the first of the month, and he couldn't pay his rent, let alone her tuition. While the world burned, he closed his door and carefully wrote Gerald and Sara. *As Keats said, illness and want are poor companions.*

He didn't wait for them to save him. Monday morning he bothered Swanie, who called in a favor at Fox and got him on the lot. He did a story conference for *Everything Happens at Night*, a thriller starring Sonja Henie and the Gestapo that Ernest would have loved. He thought it had gone well, but they never called him back.

In his desperation he resurrected a treatment he'd done for the silents, *The Feather Fan*, from one of his early stories, punching it up on spec. It was the kind of romance he'd excelled at when he was beginning, a boy and a girl and the shifting mores of the times. What passed for honesty, for honor? He had to admit, on this count Scottie was right. The story seemed so old-fashioned he thought it might play as a period piece. He asked Swanie to show it to Metro. With the war there was a market for nostalgia, and no one was more nostalgic than L.B.

He paid Frances and Erleen and the pharmacy bill, letting the rest hang. The morning mail arrived just before eleven. He stood at his window, peeking through the blinds as the truck pulled up to the gate. A hand yanked down the lid, shoved in a bundle and slapped it shut again.

"Françoise, if you would do the honors."

He watched her on the way back, weaving as she leafed through the envelopes.

"And what does the great wide world have for us today?" he asked, though he could tell by her face.

Bills and overdue notices from collection agencies. His *Princeton Alumni Weekly*, previewing the football season and asking the faithful sons of Nassau for donations. If nothing came through soon, he supposed he could go back to Max.

He'd given up on Metro when Swanie called. They'd passed on *The Feather Fan*, but he'd had lunch with Goldwyn and persuaded him to give Scott another chance. Next week he was starting on a remake of *Raffles*, with David Niven as the dashing jewel thief and Olivia de Havilland as his highborn ideal. They were reusing Sidney Howard's old script, God rest his soul.

"What happened to Sidney?"

"His tractor ran him over."

"Jesus."

"He's a shoo-in for the Oscar."

"That's rude."

"It's true."

Sidney had been a Harvard man, a Pulitzer winner who just wanted to be a farmer. Scott would doctor his dialogue on the set. Four weeks at five-fifty. The schedule was tight because Niven was going off to fly Spitfires for the RAF, a fate Scott thought noble and doomed.

He was glad to be on the lot again—Frances was thrilled, gawking at the stars—but after *Open That Door* and so many other crack-ups, he didn't count his chickens. He loaded his briefcase with Cokes and showed up on time, dictating to Frances between set-ups and jotting down details on the shoot the two of them would have to decipher later. True to their characters, Niven was a gentleman, de Havilland a pill, keeping to her dressing room. The stage was insulated from the light of day but also from any suggestion of a breeze. The air smelled, like an old attic, of baking dust. By lunch the swing gang and cameramen were soaking, and makeup had to redo the players' faces.

Occasionally Goldwyn stopped in and sat with the director, leaning over as if giving him notes. His real name was Goldfish, the -wyn was his own invention. He was of the generation before Thalberg, the money men, ruthless as gangsters. Scott wanted to thank him for the opportunity, but never got the chance. The fourth day of the shoot, while Scott watched, Goldwyn and the director engaged in a shouting match that ended with the director stalking off the set. The next morning, without explanation, Scott was let go.

"I should have told you," Swanie said. "He's one of my guys."

"I see," Scott said. "A package deal."

Payday wasn't until Saturday. The mail held nothing of value. There were no last-minute telegrams. He'd put off Magda long enough, and drove the Ford over the pass, through Hollywood and down Wilshire again. Frances followed in the Pontiac.

The man knew the car but not his name, for which he was grateful.

She was waiting for him with the engine running.

"Merci beaucoup," he said.

"Mais bien sur, monsieur."

THIS THING
CALLED LOVE

Gerald and Sara rescued him, temporarily. He arranged with Vassar to pay Scottie's tuition in installments like her hospital bill, and still he had to beg Dr. Carroll for a month's credit, and then another and another while Zelda's mother pestered him to let her come home. He sent a synopsis of the novel to *Collier's*. They were going to pay him fifteen thousand if they liked the first sixty pages. It was too early—he was just beginning to know Stahr.

By November he was close. The voice wasn't quite calibrated, but he could fix that later. He was braced for an editorial letter he'd do his best to ignore. He never expected they'd decline it outright.

He tried the *Post*.

They said no.

All along he'd seen the serial rights as his deliverance. *Esquire* was buying stories but paid so little he couldn't get ahead of his bills. Without Ober he didn't know where to turn. He wouldn't let the uncertainty undermine his work, but at the end of the day, when Frances and Erleen left, he was alone and, frustrated, began to drink.

He caught himself, calling the doctor and bringing in a nurse before he did too much damage, and then, just after Thanksgiving, when he was almost better, he got into a bottle, argued with her and went on a rampage, smashing a lamp and chasing her from the house. She called Sheilah, who tried to calm him with Mozart and tomato soup. Like an infant, he threw the bowl against the wall.

The nurse stood there with her useless needle.

"Lily Shiel's her real name. She didn't tell you she's a Jew, did she? No. Lily Shiel. 'er royal 'ighness from the East End, shaking 'er tits all over London."

He shimmied, laughing, then ran. When the nurse blocked the door to his room, he kicked her in the shin and ransacked his bureau for his gun. Sheilah called the police, but, being in the country, they were miles away. While the prowl car wailed down the valley, he locked the bathroom door and swallowed a bottle of sleeping pills.

Later, sedated and penitent, he remembered none of it, which only magnified his shame. The nurse returned. Sheilah didn't.

He thought she would forgive him once he was recovered, but she wouldn't answer her phone. He had Frances leave roses on her doorstep, and sent ones he couldn't afford from the florist with their favorite poems. Every day he expected her to call or show up at the gate and say she'd been out of town. She stayed away, and he was afraid he'd ruined things.

Erleen took her side.

"The way you were cutting up, I don't blame her. What you need to do is go over her place and set on her stoop till she comes home."

"I don't think she wants to see me."

"You let *her* tell you that. Whatever she says, you listen and don't say a word. When she's all done, you say you're sorry and you'll never do it again, and you mean it. If that doesn't work, nothing will."

He wasn't brave enough to risk her gambit. She didn't know

Sheilah the way he did. Waste my life, she'd said. He could argue, but at heart, in his misery, he agreed.

There's no excuse for what I've put you through, he wrote in his most painstaking hand. *Clearly after this last time it's not a matter of me being drunk or sick but a pathology in which I take advantage of your kind and generous nature. You've been overly patient with me, Sheilo, far beyond what I deserve. I promise I won't bother you anymore.*

After work he drove to her place so he could deliver it in person. Her car was gone, her grass shaggy. He still had the key she'd given him and thought of dropping it in her mail slot with the letter, but didn't, as if holding back a last chip. He remembered their first date with Eddie Mayer playing chaperone, dancing close with her at the Clover Club. He didn't know her at all, this fascinating stranger. Everything he'd learned about her since then only made him like her more, yet he'd chased her away.

Though he was tempted, he wouldn't embarrass her by sitting on her stoop all night. He got in his car and wound down the hill to Sunset, poking his nose out like she'd taught him, waiting for someone to let him in.

As a test, for Christmas Zelda was going home without a chaperone. Scottie was in Baltimore with the Finneys. He had nowhere to go, no money and no one to share the day with, but enlisted Frances to help find presents for everyone, including, for Sheilah, a jewelry box that played the Moonlight Sonata. Christmas Eve he left it on her doorstep. The next morning, Frances reported, it was gone.

Dear Miss Graham, he dictated, *Mr. Fitzgerald has often warned me not to involve myself too closely in his personal affairs. At the risk of overstepping my position I feel I should let you know he feels awful about treating you and Miss Steffen so badly. With the help of Miss Steffen he is now fully recovered and regrets everything that happened and dearly wishes to make amends. I believe he is sincere and can personally vouch for his recent behavior.*

I would be careful, Sheilah wrote back. *Mr. Fitzgerald has a tendency to hurt the people closest to him. He's a selfish, angry little man who thinks he's superior because he reads poetry and was famous once twenty years ago. If he ever treats you the way he's treated me, I hope you have the courage to leave and never speak to him again, because that is what he deserves.*

He nodded, shrugged. "It's progress."

She'd left things behind. For weeks, around the house, he confronted her in a cigarette case, an address book, a nightgown. Now he bundled these up with a handwritten apology, saying he'd leave Hollywood altogether if that would make her happy—a fake ultimatum, really an appeal for mercy.

He heard nothing for several days, as if she were weighing the offer. The rainy season was upon them again, Southern California's poor excuse for winter refilling the great basin, giving the farmers hope. In the airless spare bedroom he and Frances toiled on the novel, cobbling together episodes. It had been pouring all morning when, just before lunch, the drumming slowed and stopped and the sun appeared, glinting in the trees. He went to open the window beside her desk but it was stuck, swollen shut. He'd grown so weak resting in bed. When it resisted him, out of habit he gripped the top like a weightlifter, planting the heels of his hands under the sash, and pushed, and from the twinge in his chest, knew he'd made a terrible mistake.

This time the world didn't turn purple but black, the light fading like a dissolve, the trees outside melting into a dark mass. He reached for the wall and found it, solid, but he was blind now, as if hooded, and before he could reach for his pills, he tipped sideways, his leg caught on the desk, and he toppled against Frances like a corpse, making her scream, though he would know this last part only later, a comic bit to leaven the telling.

The first person Frances called was her father. The second was Sheilah, who met them at the hospital, in tears.

"If you died I'd never forgive myself," she said, her fear taking the place of logic.

From then on they were together, Frances their boon companion. For now he stayed in Encino. At the end of the day Frances handed him off to Erleen, who handed him off to Sheilah, like guards changing shifts. He didn't have a moment alone to break his promises.

When Sheilah moved to her new apartment a block from the Garden of Allah, he thought she might ask him to live with her, but she never offered. She was still inscrutable, the beauty who turned down the marquis. He was always forgetting how young she was, how tough. She thought Swanie was doing a bad job and found Scott a new agent who helped sell *Babylon Revisited* to an independent producer. A thousand for the rights and ten weeks at five hundred, guaranteed, plus a bonus if a studio picked it up. The story was set in Paris and based on Zelda's sister Rosalind trying to take Scottie from him after Zelda was first committed. He would write the script with an eye toward Shirley Temple, which he thought hilarious. He would be Cary Grant.

"At least they got the chin right," Sheilah said.

"I'd rather be Bogie. Plus, he'd be cheaper."

The weeks evaporated as his savings grew. In April, at the Oscars, *Gone with the Wind* won big, and he thought, happily, that some small part of Sidney Howard's award belonged to him. It wasn't just vanity. In less than three years Margaret Sullavan and now Vivien Leigh had taken Best Actress with his dialogue. Whatever else he did in Hollywood, he could be proud of that. Funny how much easier it was to be magnanimous with money in the bank.

Now that he could pay for Zelda's treatment, Dr. Carroll sided with her mother and recommended she be released. Scott was afraid she'd relapse without professional care and exacted a promise from the doctor that he'd readmit her if that happened, and then, on leave, a week before she was supposed to go home, she was seen at an Asheville soda fountain drinking a chocolate malted.

The doctor cabled him as if she'd stabbed a matron. Her parole was on hold pending a board meeting.

Scott would have understood if Highland were a fat farm, but it seemed vainglorious to keep her in a mental ward for enjoying a milkshake when the Germans were marching into Denmark. He cabled, pleading her case, and that Saturday she was free.

I'm sorry the world you're returning to is so unsettled, he wrote. *At least there you can count on your mother and Sara and the comforts of home. Do let me know if thirty dollars is enough of a clothes allowance these first months, as I imagine you'll need all new things. My hope is that Scottie will be able to visit you in June before heading off to summer school. Now your mother can tell her friends we have a daughter at Harvard.*

It is restful, Zelda wrote, *to think of Scottie among the Puritan repositories of knowledge when all and sundry are declaring war. Here the morning garden twitters with impatient rondelets of birdsong and Melinda clattering in the kitchen and the pure solemn bells of St. John's defining the hour. The town is green and welcoming to my prodigal heart which overflows with succulent nostalgias. I might be six, taking the streetcar to the library with Mama where they give me a new card. Do-Do, please don't fret about me. If I have a place in the world this is it. I am grateful and will strive with every ounce of health to achieve that regular life that brings happiness.*

He could have said he was trying to do the same. As she acclimated in Montgomery, to escape another valley summer Sheilah helped him move to an apartment in Hollywood around the corner from her. The building had once been a fleabag, with a brass cage protecting the front desk, and the furniture seemed to be holdovers. His couch was a dark broccoli green, lesioned with cigarette burns. His neighbors were starlets and grips hoping to do better. Across the hall lived an obese woman who sold her screams to the movies and treated them to free samples, rehearsing at all hours. Next door was a leggy redhead improbably named Lucille Ball whose Cuban boyfriend played the Bamboo Room and didn't get off till two in the morning. After the tomblike quiet of Encino the sounds of life were inspiring, if detrimental to sleep.

He could have afforded a more chichi address but the location was ideal, close to the studios and old haunts like the Victor Hugo and the Troc. He and Sheilah stayed in, eating dinner together, one night at her place, the next at his. They shared her cook, Mildred, who, like Erleen and Flora before her, was a champion baker of pies, but sometimes when they'd been cooped up all day they dismissed her and walked down Sunset to Schwab's and sat at the counter, leafing through magazines and eating French dips and cottage fries and hot-fudge sundaes, strolling back hand in hand at twilight as swallows skimmed the treetops and cars flared past.

They were careful sleeping together, proceeding gently. Like any muscle, given enough rest, the heart would heal itself. Every visit the doctor brought last week's cardiogram to show Scott his progress. Like Zelda, he had restrictions. No more coffee, and absolutely no more Benzedrine. He still snuck a cigarette here and there, but not enough to matter. He'd smoked his whole life. It wasn't like he'd get his wind back. Since he'd quit, he'd developed a potbelly he was keenly aware of in bed. He'd always been slender, a natural bantamweight. Now even a sit-up could kill him.

"Are you all right?" she asked, because he'd gone silent beneath her. Sometimes he was so focused he forgot to breathe.

"Yes."

"How's that?" she said.

"That's lovely."

He wished she wouldn't talk. Zelda had, and in the dark he saw her face, her wanton smile. He reached up to touch Sheilah, the taut hollows of her ribs.

"Be careful."

"I will," he said, and he was. He wanted to stay right here and never leave.

Deep in the night there were sirens, shouts, bottles smashing. He'd missed the city, and lay awake with a hand on her soft bottom, imagining the streets running down to the sea, the lone cars roving the coast highway out past Malibu. Where was Stahr at this hour? Where was his girl? He wanted to offer them this boundless feeling of luck while it was still ripe, as if it might save them. They must know it won't, he thought, and yet it's everything.

In the morning the notes he'd scribbled in the dark were cryptic, useless. He had an *Esquire* story to finish before Frances arrived, and all day on the script, which was taking too long. He showered and started coffee for Sheilah before kissing her goodbye and was let down to find the world outside unchanged.

"Bonjour, Françoise."

"Bonjour, monsieur."

She liked the new place, despite the clientele. She could sleep later now that she didn't have to make the drive. With Sheilah right around the corner, there were no more late-night calls, no Cyrano-like errands, though she was too polite to say so. She tucked her skirt under and hitched her chair closer to the desk, straightened her pages. The *Esquire* stories were broad comedies set on the lot, and as she typed he attended her laugh like a lover's sigh.

"Comme toujours, Françoise, parfait."

"Bien sur, monsieur."

The week was for work. Weekends he and Sheilah packed a bag and drove up the coast to Santa Barbara or Monterey, taking a room with an ocean view, skirting scandal. The scene at the front desk was a cliché, the cheating husband paying cash while the femme fatale waited in the car. The clerk turned the register for him. *Mr. and Mrs. F.S. Monroe*, he wrote. *Mr. and Mrs. L.B. Mayer.* He could dance, and as the hotel orchestra serenaded the brandied glow left by the setting sun, they swayed under the palms, her neck fragrant with Chanel and suntan lotion. He was forbidden to dip her but couldn't resist, earning him a stern look. Later, in bed, they took breathless risks they would apologize for in the morning, exonerating each other, guiltily pleased. They were fugitives, they had to steal everything.

The war dwarfed their problems. What was a broken molar when the Germans were pushing through the Ardennes? He went to the dentist and Belgium fell. Luxembourg, the Netherlands. He thought of Gerald and Sara's villa, and Sheilah's brother in London. Ernest was probably there somewhere, filing hot copy.

They were on their way to the World's Fair in San Francisco when the radio broadcast the evacuation of Dunkirk. It was a victory, saving the British army to fight again, but there was nothing to stop the Germans from taking Paris. He was there every day, on the Quai du Louvre with Scottie, as Cary Grant in the Ritz bar. Selfishly, he felt it was his city, his past they were taking from him—the gray, rainy streets and scabby sycamores and hennaed doyennes walking their little dogs in the Jardin des Plantes. He wondered if he would feel the same if the Japanese bombed Los Angeles.

At the fair, by chance, they ran into Bogie and Mayo, both sozzled and ready to fight the Germans there in the Frigidaire Hall of Progress.

"Fitzy!" Bogie said. "You make me feel young again, brother. You look like hell."

"I had a little heart trouble," Scott said, declining a pint.

"Sorry to hear it."

"Sorry to hear what?" Mayo asked, because the pavilion echoed with ballyhoo.

"He's got a bum ticker," Bogie said.

"You don't have to yell. I can hear just fine."

"You don't *listen*, that's your problem."

"That's cause I have to listen to you all the time. Bah-bah-bah-bah-bah."

"Is that what we sound like?" Scott asked Sheilah at the hotel.

"Yes," she said. "That's exactly what we sound like."

He didn't tell anyone for fear of being labeled a hypocrite, but he liked being back in Hollywood. Mornings with Françoise, whistling "La Marseillaise," evenings with Sheilah, making love with the windows open. He knew this idyll was an illusion. Nightly the radio brought worse news. Convoys sank, cathedrals burned. The front page of the *Times* showed disastrous maps.

The day Paris fell he received a letter from Mrs. Sayre. *Sara and I are deeply concerned about Zelda's current frame of mind. Last night at supper she suffered some sort of toxic attack, possibly triggered by something she ate. She began talking gibberish and when I tried to help she was openly abusive to me and Melinda and broke several pieces of tableware as well as our large mantel clock, which you may remember. She has since calmed down and is making sense again, but for most of the evening she refused to leave her room and threatened to hurt Sara if she attempted to open the door. We have followed the doctor's instructions religiously so I am at a loss as to what else we can do. Perhaps because she visited us for only short periods of time I didn't realize how ill she really is.*

Scottie was supposed to arrive there Friday. That morning Zelda cabled: CANT STAY HERE ANY LONGER. PLEASE WIRE BUS FARE ASAP. WILL SEE SCOTTIE IN ASHEVILLE. I TRIED.

And then, two hours later: DISREGARD LAST. FEEL FINE NOW. ANXIOUS TO SEE PIE.

Knowing her, none of it surprised him. He shook his head and went back to work.

She seems the same to me, Scottie wrote. *Most of the time she's fine, just a little vague around the edges. When she gets excited and starts going on about God and the cosmos, it's obvious, but that's not often. It's when she runs out of gas and just sits there that you notice, and that happens regularly. I think Grandma's afraid of her since she broke the door. She's still walking five miles a day and rides a bike all over town. Everybody knows her, which is good. She has the church and the library. I don't think she's lonely. Is she better? No, but I think she's happier.*

Wise Pie, voting for compromise. She'd been too young to know the real Zelda and so didn't hold out for the impossible. Part of him understood she was lost from the beginning. Another part would never accept it, just as he both admitted and denied that he was at least partly to blame. The truth was in the middle, hidden from him, too close to his own failings. He had loved her above all others, but not enough—not as much, his conscience insisted, as he loved himself.

Between the tragedy in Europe and Zelda's struggles, he had the debilitating sense that his life was governed by forces beyond his control. As if to confirm the notion, his car was stolen again. He used it so rarely he didn't know it was missing. The police found it in the middle of Hollywood Boulevard, out of gas. With Frances's help he retrieved it, parking in the same numbered spot behind his building, checking the locks as if that would protect it.

"That's why we got out," Dottie said. "The neighborhood's gone to hell." She and Alan had moved to a chateau in Bel Air. They threw a dinner party for some Garden alumni, with Benchley and Don Stewart, Sid and Laura, Pep and his wife Eileen. They were overly solicitous, telling him how good he looked. Bogie must have told them. They could see he was on the wagon. "I feel a million percent better," he said like a press agent, knowing they'd spread the news. They danced and played charades, and at the end of the night, by the wavering light of tiki torches, Dottie led them in "The Last Time I Saw Paris." As they sang he realized it was the piece he needed, and in the morning wrote it into the script.

His producer sent a copy to Shirley Temple. "She'll love it," he assured Scott, without force.

To their astonishment she did, and in pursuit of his bonus he had the novel pleasure of eating lunch with the star and her mother on their patio. While the child's trademark curls and cheeks were the same that graced a thousand magazine covers, she was much older than he'd thought, taller, around twelve, with a pudgy suggestion of breasts. The mansion was tucked in a cul-de-sac behind Pickfair and backed up on Chaplin's tennis courts, where Paulette Goddard was playing the man himself in a white bicycling cap. From time to time a ball came sailing over to land in the pampered grass, and Shirley jumped up and heaved it back like DiMaggio. While they pushed their tuna salad around, the mother did all the talking, saying how moving the story was, how beautifully written, to the point where he wondered if Shirley had even read the script, and then when they were finished eating, she turned her alert eyes on him and asked, "What kind of name is Honoria? It sounds English."

"It's the name of the daughter of some dear friends of mine."

"Are they English?"

"They're American."

"We were talking before," the mother said, "and we agreed. If the father is American, we think she should have an American name. I hope that's all right."

"Of course."

"The opening scene," Shirley prompted.

"Right. The first time we see her playing in the gardens, we think she should be by herself, not with other children."

He should have known—it wasn't lunch, it was a story conference. They were giving him notes. He left with three pages of changes he dutifully inflicted on his script, only to receive, a month later, a second set, and though the producer claimed they were still interested, by then Cary Grant had passed, and Joseph Cotten, and Scott promised his agent never to write anything on spec again.

His next project was for Darryl Zanuck at Fox, *The Light of Heart*, a holiday weepie starring John Barrymore as a drunken department store Santa with a crippled daughter. Ten weeks at seven hundred. If all went well he'd have enough to finish *Stahr*. Mornings he got up early to work on his *Esquire* story, then drove to the studio. As a late heat wave settled over the city and the hills caught fire, he conjured his father in snowy St. Paul and came down with a fever. He couldn't sleep, and woke Sheilah at odd hours, obsessively taking his temperature. Bogie was right: in the mirror he looked gray and drawn. Every week a nurse came to shoot him full of vitamin B, and still he was tired. A month in, he thought he wouldn't mind if they killed the picture, but he'd never quit, and then was angry when Zanuck brought in Nunnally Johnson.

They bought him out, an insult, giving him a free month. It was October, the weather finally cooling. He had no excuses.

Here were the days he'd paid for, too precious to waste. After so long away from the novel, and everything he'd learned in between, he was impatient with his old pages, and despaired of fixing them. The girl was wrong, the plane crash hackneyed. He'd have to tear it apart, start again. In the depths of the night, like a needy ghost, Stahr woke him. He put on his robe and sharpened his pencils while the kettle warmed. He opened his notebook and wrote: *Stahr knows he's going to die. That isn't the tragedy. Hollywood is.*

He tacked up maps and charts and timelines on the walls, signs of commitment. It would be like *Gatsby*, the action proceeding from mood and situation. All he needed to do was be true to the characters and their world. He knew them well enough. He wished he were stronger, but didn't doubt himself. He already believed in Stahr.

He was best first thing in the morning. At lunch he had a Coke to keep going, and around three a Hershey bar. By five he was done, punchy with keeping it all in his head. It was then he wanted a drink to soothe his nerves. Some days he gave in, sneaking a sip from a half-pint hidden in the hatbox with Ginevra's wedding invitation, savoring the taste before disguising it with Lavoris. Just one, as Budd might have said, never a second, and never after dark. He wanted to be fresh for tomorrow.

Frances ran to the library and Stanley Rose's for books on Griffith and Ince and the early flicker parlors, and to the airport for schedules. He liked her to read Cecelia's parts out loud, since she was of the same generation. Every day he asked for the first page to reacquaint himself.

"Repetez, s'il vous plait."

" 'Though I've never been on the screen, I was brought up around pictures. Valentino came to my fifth birthday party, or so I'm told.' "

"In pictures. *Repetez, s'il vous plait."*

A born bookkeeper, she wasn't bored. Having typed up his notes, she knew the story almost as well as he did, recalling lost details with the pedantry of the young. She was good with dialogue, all right with plot, and happy as teacher's pet when he took one of her suggestions. He could tell how well he was doing by how eager she was to reach a scene, and when he skimped or made a wrong turn he could hear the disappointment in her voice. Stahr meeting Kathleen at the screenwriters' ball had to be perfect, all the rest depended on it. He watched her face as she read, knitted with worry, softening toward the end, her lips parting to release a held breath. She looked up at him, plaintive, like a girl waiting to be kissed.

"It's beautiful."

"You think so?"

"It's like Cinderella."

"Too much?"

"No." Then a shrug. "Maybe a little."

Honest Françoise, the tailor's sharp-eyed daughter.

In the midst of this delicate construction, Ernest sent him his new one, *For Whom the Bell Tolls,* with an affectionate inscription. The tale of a lone, heroic American vainly trying to save Spain, it was the Book of the Month for November, and had sold to Paramount for a hundred thousand. To Scott it seemed adolescent and thin, probably because Stahr was with him all the time now. He carried him inside him to the Troc and Ciro's and the Hollywood Bowl like a third eye, transforming the city. At the Coliseum and Malibu Pier he gathered ornaments for his story, attuned to Stahr's thoughts, stealing from the real world to furnish his universe. Lying beside Sheilah, he walked Kathleen to her door and chastely kissed her goodnight. In his Rolls, its lights dimmed, his faithful chauffeur waited.

Congratulations on the grand success of your big book, he wrote Ernest. *No one could have written it but you.*

HARD ON IT, he wired Max. MAKING EXC PROGRESS. EXPECT DRAFT BY JAN 15. PLS DONT DISCUSS WITH OBER.

He felt better when he wrote well, as if he were fulfilling his duty. To help him think, he smoked more than he should have, and every day drank three or four Cokes, but his lungs were clear and the doctor was happy with his cardiograms. Now that the weather was cooler he was walking for exercise. He took his digitalis, and he and Sheilah were careful, mostly. After months of looking washed-out he'd gotten back some of his color. From all evidence he was nearly recovered, so he was unprepared when, one night after Thanksgiving, he hopped down to Schwab's for a pack of Raleighs and was standing at the register when he felt a familiar twinge in his chest.

He'd done nothing strenuous, yet his arm throbbed. He rubbed it as if that might get rid of the ache, opened and closed one hand experimentally. A dull pang like heartburn made him wince and grit his teeth.

"Blast it," he said, and groped his way to a stool.

The darkness held off. In minutes he was fine, just clammy, blotting his brow with his handkerchief. He could stand, walk.

"Mister," the clerk stopped him. "Your cigarettes."

The doctor called it a spasm, not an actual attack. He upped his dosage to the limit and told him he needed to quit smoking.

No sex, no stairs. The most important thing was rest. He shouldn't work more than a few hours a day.

Sheilah didn't think he should be alone and moved him into her spare bedroom.

"All it took was a heart attack," he joked.

He didn't feel weak but, like Stahr, distrusted his heart, knowing it was faulty. He stuck the unopened pack in a drawer, stopped drinking his Cokes. He couldn't send Frances to rescue the half-pint and for the first time in his life became a bona fide teetotaler. His only vices now were Mildred's pies and poring over yesterday's pages when he couldn't sleep.

The voice was right. The novel was solid. He should have worried yet he was madly happy. He wasn't mistaken. Three hours a day wasn't enough. The room was too small. There was no desk, there was barely room for a chair. Frances sat by his head like a nurse, taking dictation in shorthand. At noon she ran the new pages around the corner to his place and came back with fresh typescript. His schedule slipped to February, March at the latest. Max didn't care. He'd already missed his deadline by three years.

It was just a mild episode, not an attack, and I'm feeling much better, he wrote Scottie. *I want your mother to have a good Christmas, so while you're down there please don't mention it. Be especially patient with her and with your grandmother. They've had a trying year.*

For several weeks he didn't leave the apartment, and then, Friday the thirteenth, he and Sheilah trekked over the pass to Pep and Eileen's in North Hollywood for a dinner party. The weather was warm, and they sat in the backyard around a trestle table while on a great stone barbecue Pep roasted woodcock he'd shot, telling them it was pigeon from Pershing Square. The talk was of London, three months into the Blitz. Sections of the East End had been leveled. To give them a sense of the destruction, Sheilah used Los Angeles as a stand-in.

"Imagine all of Hollywood and half of Beverly Hills gone."

"With pleasure," Dottie said.

Scott couldn't dance, and after dinner sat out with her, watching

Alan and Sheilah and Bogie and Mayo swaying beneath the night sky. Dottie had been drinking scotch since they'd arrived and had reached a scowling, foul-mouthed state. He wasn't used to being the sober one and was ready to go home. On his lap desk today's pages waited.

"What a cunt," she said.

"Stop."

"Alan, I mean. Did I tell you, they cut my insides out. Snip snip."

"I'm sorry."

"They were all rotted anyway. Now he doesn't have to worry about having kids, the bugger. What about you?"

"What?"

"Kids." She waggled a hand at Sheilah. "She's got all the right parts."

"Oh, I don't know."

"You should. Everyone should have kids."

"I don't know if she wants them."

"She's crazy. They'd be beautiful. You were beautiful."

"Thank you," he said. "You were too."

"We should've had kids. To our beautiful children." *Byooful.*

She crashed her tumbler into his, spilling whiskey on the table-cloth. She dabbed her fingers in the wet spot and flicked droplets over her shoulder for luck.

"Look at him," she said. "If I ever kill him, you'll know why."

On the ride home he told Sheilah a bowdlerized version.

"I think I knew about the surgery."

"I didn't," he said.

"It's also going around that he's seeing another woman."

"A woman."

"Believe it or not."

"No wonder she's angry." He watched the shadows from the streetlights slide across her face. "She asked if we're going to have children."

"Did she?"

"She did."

"What did you say?"

"I said I didn't know if you wanted them."

"I do," she said, glancing at him, her smile a dare.

"She'll be happy to hear it."

"I wouldn't go that far," she said.

It was the last week before Christmas, and she needed her tree. He was still forbidden to lift anything, so Frances helped her get it in the stand. It stood a little crooked, topped with a gold star made in Japan. With a pair of pinking shears she pruned away the ragged branches until she was pleased with its shape. She'd listened to his boyhood tales and set bayberry candles on the mantel, nestled in the fresh-smelling boughs. At dusk she lit the wicks and the apartment might have been his Grandmother McQuillan's parlor, a dry snow falling outside.

For Scottie's big present, as a surprise he hired Frances's father to alter one of Sheilah's old furs, a silver fox she no longer wore. He'd spent his life in the business, a true professional. When she saw it on Frances, she wanted it back.

Friday they ventured out again, to a special press premiere at the Pantages: *This Thing Called Love*, starring Melvyn Douglas and Rosalind Russell as newlyweds. The premise was at once quaint and risqué and utterly moronic. To make sure they were compatible, for the first three months the wife insisted they remain celibate. Scott savored his free chocolate bar and watched the audience as Stahr would have, concerned about the low turnout. Publicity should have known, it was too close to Christmas. With each cut the light from the screen jumped, revealing the pendulous chandeliers and gilded bas-relief on the ceiling. It might have been the season, but in their scale and splendor there was something religious about movie houses. Every day the faithful came by the millions to witness new parables. If the actors were their saints, what were the producers?

Melvyn Douglas tried every angle and in the end was on the verge of sweet success when he contracted a bad case of poison oak. He and the audience both had to settle for a rain check, a cheat

Stahr would have caught in a story conference. With the logy indifference of the newly awoken, the crowd stretched and gathered its belongings. He stood and edged his way to the end of the row, and as he turned and started up the aisle behind Sheilah, the house lights flickered and an electric jolt sizzled up his arm into his neck and lodged there, tingling.

He lurched and grasped an armrest to stay upright, managed a breath. Ahead, Sheilah kept going.

"Sheilo. Wait."

She glanced back, puzzled, unsure what he was doing, then seemed to understand and came to save him. She took his elbow, steadying him as the crowd filed past.

"It's all right, I feel better now."

"Do you want to sit?"

"They'll think I'm drunk."

"They won't think anything."

"I can walk."

"Can you?"

He could, with her help, propping him on one side as if he had a bad leg. In the lobby there was a water fountain where he could take his pills. She watched him like a mother, her lips pursed in worry.

Outside on Hollywood Boulevard the night air revived him. He was fine. He could drive—"If no one's stolen the car," he joked. There was no need to call the doctor. He was coming tomorrow anyway. What would he do for him, tell him to get some rest?

"When we get home you're going straight to bed," she said.

"Yes ma'am."

He took an extra spoonful of chloral and slept till noon.

He felt fine, just tired, his back kinked from sleep. He could have used a cup of coffee or a Coke. It was a brilliant day, the sun sharp on the carpet, twinkling off the ornaments on the lower branches. In London it was nighttime and bombs were falling around Edward R. Murrow, sirens keening. The docks were on fire. All of Hollywood, Sheilah had said, and half of Beverly Hills. They listened till the end, unable to turn away.

Around one Frances popped by with the mail from his place and Sheilah told her what had happened.

"*Comment allez-vous, monsieur?*"

"*Bien. Ce n'est pas grave. Merci, Françoise. Au revoir.*"

"*Au revoir, monsieur.*"

Sheilah made deviled ham sandwiches for them, and when she finished with the dishes, put on the last movement of Beethoven's *Eroica* Symphony. She was reading a big biography of him, and stretched out on the settee while Scott took the wing chair by the fireplace, leafing through the *Alumni Weekly*. The doctor was coming at two to take a new cardiogram. He expected another setback, and stewed, skimming an article on who was the greatest Tiger gridder of all time. While he was still at Newman he'd seen Hobey Baker run back a punt late in the Yale game and would never forget it. That year's team was legendary, undefeated. Three would die in the trenches, Baker in a plane crash. He'd thought of them as men but of course they were just boys.

To test his memory he took a pencil and in the margin tried to name the starting eleven. Prescott at center, Holloway and Stanton at guard, Dietz and someone at tackle. Chewing his lip, he filled in the roster as the *Eroica* built to its finish, Sheilah nodding to the ponderous chords, a symphonic bombardment inspired by another war. Why did Beethoven idolize Napoleon? He'd have to ask her.

The needle lifted, the arm retracting, clicking in place, leaving silence. Sheilah looked over and smiled. He smiled back to reassure her.

"Do we have anything sweet?" he asked.

"I have a Hershey bar if you want it. I'll get it, you stay there."

She traded it for a kiss and retreated to the settee.

He opened it, broke off a pane, then snapped that into three pieces. The chocolate dissolved on his tongue.

"Sure you don't want some?"

"I'm sure."

"It's delicious."

"Shh."

The backfield was easy, and the ends. Dietz and who else at tackle? Carroll, Coffin. Something with a hard C. He could see the team picture in the trophy case in Old Nassau, the unit insignias of the dead. Baker had died in his Spad, nosing it in. Collins. Carrington.

That quickly the bar was gone, the empty wrapper a shed skin. He stood to throw it away, the distraction just enough to dislodge the name—Carpenter!—when a tremor shocked his heart.

It was more than a twinge. A bolt shot up his arm, and his teeth clenched. A bubble burst in his shoulder, then a prickly fizzing in his neck, the tide of blood rising inside him, cutting off breath. He staggered, reaching for the mantel, caught it and hung on, seizing, trying to signal Sheilah in the mirror, the scent of pine and bayberry dizzying, calling him back to St. Paul, to the view from the attic window and his mother combing his hair with her fingers, his father's whiskery jaw. The room flickered, dimmed. Stahr was with him, standing to one side like a kindly spirit, his plane doomed to crash, his girl out there somewhere in the sprawling, limitless city. He tried to breathe but his throat closed and he gagged. He lost his grip and felt himself falling, flailing blindly, and with his last helpless thought before the darkness swallowed him, protested: *But I'm not done.*

From all accounts, Sheilah wrote, *your father would have been very pleased with your words at his service. I wish I could have been there but Frances and I have been busy taking care of arrangements on this end. I'm hoping we can get together in New York late next week. I'm flying in on Tuesday and will be bringing some personal things of his I know he would have wanted you to have, including several notebooks and photo albums as well as the presents you sent. I'm not sure he had a chance to tell you how proud he was of your story in the New Yorker. He had poor Frances running all over town trying to find copies for his friends. She sends her condolences. We're still in shock, as I'm sure you are, and will be for some time. This last year he was taking better care of himself and was genuinely happy, working on his book. I miss the sound of him whistling away in the other room. The place is too quiet without him.*

It hardly seems possible, Zelda wrote, *that Daddy will no longer be coming East bearing gifts and stimulating news and audacious plans for the future. I am necessarily here for the time being after some difficulties owing to real rather than imaginary sadness. I would rather be at home but am decidedly poor company, I've been told, and must agree. The days are haunted with vagrant memories this holiest of seasons and not even the prospect of a new year affords pleasure.*

The soul aspires to be known. Mine will never be again so deeply now that he is gone. As creatures we are here so precariously. Death reminds us of Time's exigencies and the transience of this corporeal world. At times like these we are grateful for the inalienable bonds of family and the blessings of faith, without which life would be a succession of inevitable tragedies. Christ the King knows—only in love are we redeemed. Rejoice. God answers all prayers.